whe

young

Mary Fitzgerald was born and brought up in Chester. At eighteen she left home to start nursing training. She ended up as an operating theatre sister in a large London hospital and there met her husband. Ten years and four children later the family settled for a while in Canada and later the USA. For several years they lived in West Wales, northern Scotland and finally southern Ireland until they settled again near Chester. Mary had long given up nursing and gone into business, first a children's clothes shop, then a book shop and finally an internet clothes enterprise.

Mary now lives in a small village in north Shropshire close to the Montgomery canal and with a view of both the Welsh and the Shropshire hills.

Also available by Mary Fitzgerald

The Love of a Lifetime (previously titled Richard Wilde)

Available in Ebook
Mist
Knight on the Potomac
Traitor's Gate
The Fishing Pool

Mary Fitzgerald

When I Was Young

arrow books

Originally published as an ebook titled *The Imperfect Tense*, 2011

First published by Arrow Books, 2014

2 4 6 8 10 9 7 5 3 1

First published by Cornerstone Digital, 2013
Arrow Books
The Random House Group Limited
20 Vauxhall Bridge Road, London, SW1V 2SA

www.randomhousebooks.co.uk

Addresses for companies within The Random House Group Limited can be found at:
www.randomhouse.co.uk/offices.htm

The Random House Group Limited Reg. No. 954009

A CIP catalogue record for this book
is available from the British Library

ISBN 978-0-099-58538-1

The Random House Group Limited supports the Forest Stewardship Council® (FSC®), the leading international forest-certification organisation. Our books carrying the FSC label are printed on FSC®-certified paper. FSC is the only forest-certification scheme supported by the leading environmental organisations, including Greenpeace. Our paper procurement policy can be found at www.randomhouse.co.uk/environment

FSC www.fsc.org MIX Paper from responsible sources FSC® C016897

Typeset in Palatino by Palimpsest Book Production Limited,
Falkirk, Stirlingshire

Printed and bound in Great Britain by Clays Ltd, St Ives plc

Chapter One

'Quand j'étais jeune . . .'

'When I was young,' Miss Baxter would say. '*Quand j'étais jeune*. An example of the imperfect tense, girls. Now, in the next few minutes make five sentences starting with that phrase, if you please.'

When I was young the war started. When I was young my father was a soldier. When I was young I lived in town. When I was young my grandparents died; when I was young I moved to the country. These five sentences, full of utilitarian experiences, could be done in a flash and looking back they tell all the important things that happened to me before I was seventeen. At least to a stranger.

Suzy would lean towards me begging the French word for theatre, or for rocking horse. 'Tell me how to say "my great-aunt gave me a beautiful gold and pearl necklace",' she whispered.

'No,' I breathed back. 'Miss Baxter is looking.' In the end, though, I always gave in. And Miss Baxter always knew.

My ability to speak French was a strange talent which came from nowhere. Certainly not from Mother and neither, as far as I knew, from Dada. It was like a person being immediately able to pick out a tune on a piano and then go on, with tuition, to play a concerto. I was like that natural pianist. I quickly absorbed French vocabulary and with tuition became almost bilingual. And then, when I went to France, nothing sounded strange. Listening to Étienne and Grandmère seemed more normal than listening to Mother shouting in the yard or Dada's rare muttered words.

These nights I dream about those first weeks in France more and more. They're strange, lucid dreams. Events pass at breakneck speed like an uncontrolled slide show where each picture flashes by, all slightly out of focus, until, shockingly, the machine is switched off.

I awake shaking, half of me still in the dream and my head full of vivid green trees and the dusty yellow of the hay in the barn. Sometimes I can even smell the hot sludgy stench of the river and hear Étienne calling a greeting from the bridge.

And no matter how long I lie in bed, eyes squeezed shut, hoping for the dream to continue, it never does. The images disperse like early mist on the hills, evaporating in the crystal sharp glitter of morning sunlight. That life I dream about happened more than fifty years ago and even then was only lived for one summer. One glorious summer when I was young.

The odd thing is that in this dream, like those other dreams where you find yourself entering rooms full of unrecognised but useful furniture, new aspects of that life are revealed to me. I see it estranged by the experience of age and catch nuances and inferences that in reality passed me by. In my dream, I'm a watcher, not a participant. Someone there but not there.

Perhaps that reflects something I want to feel about the time I really was there. A girl, naive, untried, unsure of what was said and, more important, what was meant. I know now that I was used. A pawn in a larger game.

It is a comforting thought that it wasn't my fault but it's not entirely true, of course. I *was* a participant. A reluctant one at first perhaps, nervous like someone suddenly transported to an alien planet where life is different. The plain, the ordinary existence of my childhood, vanished overnight and was replaced by an enticing world which grabbed me and held me a willing prisoner. And, as the days and weeks went by, the replacement existence became so absorbing, so precious, that I was prepared to do anything to have it continue.

A sixth example for Miss Baxter. When I was young I fell in love. And love at seventeen is a dangerous thing.

I went to France three days after my seventeenth birthday in July 1950. I was on a school exchange programme, one of the first to be organised after the war.

'Remember, you represent your country!' shouted Miss Baxter, straining to be heard above the noise and bustle of the railway station platform. She was our form teacher and head of French at the grammar school to which I had won a scholarship.

'You represent your country!' Those were her words as we lined up at the station in our northern town, fifteen girls dressed in school uniform, chattering and excited. I stood with my best friend Suzy Franklin, who, surprisingly, admired my pigskin suitcase but only after demanding admiration for her own new luggage. The set, which all the other girls had exclaimed over enviously, consisted of two black crocodile-skin cases and a matching vanity case. It stood out, looking altogether too

Hollywood, amongst the grime and post-war austerity which surrounded us.

'D'you like it?' asked Suzy, snapping open the catch on the vanity case and displaying the interior where she had put illicit make-up inside a bundle of lace-edged handkerchiefs. She moved the hankies aside and I could see little glass jars held in broad elastic bands snug against the pink sateen lining.

'Yes.' I nodded, very impressed. 'What's in the jars?'

'Nothing yet. I'm going to buy scent. It's very cheap over there and if I put it in these bottles I won't have trouble getting through customs. It was Mummy's idea.'

I nodded again. 'Your cases are very stylish.'

'Aren't they.' Suzy smiled proudly, showing her perfect white teeth. 'Daddy got them for me as a surprise. He said good luggage lasts a lifetime.'

Mr Franklin was a solicitor and on the few occasions I'd met him seemed to me a nice person. Suzy's mother, Phyllis, was different. Less friendly and always on her way out of their house to go shopping or play bridge or do anything away from the family home. She wasn't exactly beautiful, but she was glamorous in a film star sort of way with styled blonde hair and bright red lipstick and a wardrobe of clothes that patently didn't depend on the availability of coupons. I saw her picture often in the local paper because she was on committees, the sort that organised balls and charity dinners.

'You have to do something,' she said once when I mentioned that I'd seen her photograph in the newspaper. 'Life has been unutterably boring since the war ended.' And she'd taken a quick elegant puff on her cigarette before waggling her fingers in a brief farewell. She had come to the station with Mr Franklin, though, to see Suzy off and even now was standing by the kiosk chatting to some of the other parents, although not mine. Mother had dropped me off at the station entrance and gone straight home.

'Your suitcase is smart too,' Suzy said, kindly. She barely concealed her surprise. 'Pigskin, isn't it?'

'I think so.' I was unsure. I knew it was leather and heavy before I'd put anything into it. Fortunately I didn't have much to pack. Clothes were at a premium in those days, unless you were Suzy and her mother, so my couple of dresses and two pairs of shorts and Aertex tops and one pair of sandals didn't take up much room. I had put three books in as well, hidden under my underwear so that my mother, coming into my room the night before the journey, couldn't make her usual sarcastic remarks and throw them out.

'Where did you get it from? It must have cost a fortune.' Suzy was still intrigued with the pigskin case.

'Mother found it in the loft. It belongs to my father, I think.'

'Oh.'

That put an end to the conversation, as anything to do with my father invariably did.

'Be careful, girls. Step away from the edge.' Miss Baxter's screeching voice was nearly lost in the roar and steam as the London train pulled in. I got a smut in my eye then that stayed with me all the way to the Gard du Nord. Even the wind and rain on the cross Channel ferry couldn't dislodge it but suddenly, as I stepped down on to the platform in Paris, it melted away and I could see clearly. Was it an omen? I think so.

The French exchange had been first talked about in the middle of the spring term. I remember going home on the bus reading and re-reading all the details about it from the information leaflet Miss Baxter had handed round.

Each girl who applied and paid the thirty pounds fee would be assigned to a family in France. She would stay with the family for three weeks and at the end of that time the child of the French family would return with her and enjoy a three-week stay with the English host. It was essentially a language improvement course with a taste of Entente Cordiale thrown in.

'I think you, Eleanor, particularly, would get a lot out of this.' Miss Baxter handed me the paper.

'I want to go,' said Suzy, straight away. 'What about you?'

'I don't know.' I pretended to be doubtful. Of course I did know really. I couldn't think of anything I wanted more, but the thirty pounds would be impossible to raise. Besides, how could I possibly bring a French girl back to my house?

'Remember, I need an answer within a week and a deposit of five pounds,' called Miss Baxter as we trooped out of our form room.

On the bus home I looked again at the leaflet. A deposit of five pounds was to be paid within a week and the rest when the exchange family had been found. Added to that was a suggestion that one would need spending money and buy a small gift for the host family. My heart sank. Mother couldn't find that sort of money, even if she wanted to. And she wouldn't want to. She would think that the whole idea was 'silly nonsense' and certainly not for the likes of us. Any spare cash in our house went to improve the stock on our farm. Apart from food and soap we never bought anything and my mother must have had the biggest collection of clothing coupons in the county. The only time they were used was for my school uniform and shoes. And even then I had to demonstrate that my blouse buttons wouldn't close over my burgeoning breasts or that my skirts were halfway up my thigh and not the regulation knee length before she'd bother to go to the shops. Getting clothes for the weekend was another and constant battle.

I had four pounds and ten shillings saved in Post Office stamps but that wasn't enough. It would do for the spending money and probably for the small gift, but the rest . . . ? I stuffed the leaflet into my satchel. It was simply another experience I wasn't going to have.

'Nearly there, Eleanor.' Fred Gates, the bus driver, looked at me in the driving mirror. I was the last passenger on the bus as I was every afternoon. Our home was a bleak farm on the Pennines and almost the highest place on the bus route before it wound down again to the villages that bordered the town.

I looked out of the bus window. It was February and cold. Horizontal rain swept across the hillside, flattening the few wild daffodils which had bravely flowered early. I could see groups of sheep huddling against the stone walls which bordered our land, the pregnant ewes heavy and patient with vacant eyes and slowly moving jaws. Beyond them, on a flattened patch of hillside, our house stood out, the largest of a collection of grey stone buildings. It was built of the same stone as the outcrops in the fields and looked as ancient as the land that surrounded it, like a thing placed by nature not built by man. I hated it.

The bus stopped and I slung my satchel over my shoulder and went to the exit.

'Ta-ra,' mumbled Fred Gates. He was relighting his Woodbine as he did at every stop. 'See you in the morning.'

'Bye.'

The driveway up to our house was rutted and potholed. It must have been better once but in my memory had never been anything but a mud- and puddle-ridden mess. On her one visit to our house, Suzy had examined it for a moment and then looked down at her light shoes.

'Sorry,' I muttered, embarrassed. 'I'm afraid it's the only way in.'

'Oh well. Here goes.' She set out carefully stepping from one dry spot to another, her pretty mouth turned down in distaste but all the time proclaiming loudly that this was an 'adventure'. Afterwards she told me that she couldn't live how I did and that I was a heroine. I laughed, but I was grateful to her for saying that. Whatever faults Suzy had, snobbery and easy judgement weren't among them.

She lived close to town. In an avenue with neighbours and parked cars. Her house was brick with white-painted woodwork and surrounded by lawns and flower beds. They had a garage which housed Mr Franklin's Wolseley and the lawn mower. The only stones in their garden were the ones surrounding the pond in the middle of their lawn. And every time I went there I wanted to stay for ever.

Now I did the hopscotch down the drive, easier for

me because I did it every day and knew the higher patches amongst the mud, where the ground was firmer. Even so, I could feel the puddle water seeping into my shoes and knew that they would have to spend the evening stuffed with newspaper in front of the range.

The rain was coming down harder and I couldn't wait to get inside. I was cold and hungry and wanted tea and a jam sandwich or something to keep me going until supper time.

My plans were destined to be curtailed, however, because I could see Mother in the field above the big barn. She was cutting the twine which bound a large hay bale, and as I watched she hefted the loosened hay into her arms and started spreading it in a line across the field.

I knew I would have to help her move the sheep into that field as soon as I'd changed out of my uniform. Belle, the dog, would help us but it would still take ages and leave me no time before supper to do my homework. The book I'd got out of the library and was so looking forward to would have to wait.

'Oh hell,' I muttered as I walked into the yard. Why couldn't my life be easier?

Dada was sheltering by the open door of the big barn, leaning his long shambling body against the wooden frame. I called hello to him as I walked past. He didn't reply and quickly ducked his head away but I knew that as soon as I'd gone he would lift his eyes and follow me. I'd seen him do that with other people. When I looked back he was watching me and I smiled, but, as I'd expected, got no answer.

Suzy had tried her bright conversation on him when she came to visit but he'd bolted into the farm buildings and stayed there until she'd left.

'Goodness!' she'd said. 'What's up with him?'

My face must have been scarlet. It was the first time I realised I should be ashamed of my family. Mother, angry and contemptuous about everything, and Dada . . . well, Dada being himself. They let me down.

Later, at supper, I showed Mother the leaflet about the French exchange. We were eating mince and potatoes, which was our evening meal three times a week. The mince was pale brown and tasted of fat and Bisto and I loathed it. We served ourselves from the saucepans on the stove and I always put as little as possible on my plate, covering the tiny amount with a helping of potatoes and watery cabbage. If she noticed, Mother said nothing. Food was of no interest to her.

'What's this?' She held the leaflet up to the weak overhead light. We had electricity but Mother always bought low voltage bulbs as an economy measure.

'It's from school. About a French exchange visit. Miss Baxter said it would be good for me to go, but . . .' I left it there. Once Mother read it, the leaflet would go on the back of the fire.

I got up and took my plate to the sink. Any moment there would an explosion of scorn and I steadied myself by washing up my plate and then going to the dresser and picking up the cheese plate. Mother only made a pudding on Sunday, an apple pie which we ate until it was finished, usually Tuesday. After that it was cheese or stewed apple and custard.

Behind me I could hear Mother slapping the sheet of

paper on to the oiled cloth which covered the kitchen table and I turned round slowly.

'Good God!' She was looking down at the paper. 'I've never heard of such nonsense!' Her voice was sharp with derision. 'Have you taken leave of your senses? What makes you think for one moment that I would waste good money on a . . .' she struggled for a moment, 'a jaunt like this.'

She jabbed her forefinger at the paper and I noticed again, with a shudder of distaste, the dirt ingrained into the skin over her joints and beneath her nail. Mother never looked entirely clean although she did make an effort with carbolic soap every day. Even her weather-beaten face seemed to be covered with a film of grey mud and a faint sheep smell of lanolin always emanated from her. Only her hair was bright. It was red and so curly that it seemed to spark off her head in wild spirals. I think she hated her hair and had it cut short every month at the hairdresser's by the market. It was the only indulgence she allowed herself. I didn't like it either and thanked God always that my hair was dark like my father's, curling a bit at the ends but nothing like hers.

When I was at Suzy's, I often found myself staring at Phyllis Franklin's hair and skin and particularly at her hands. They were white and smooth and her nails were painted the same colour as her lipstick. They looked as if they'd never done any work, which was probably true. It wasn't fair, of course. Mother ran a hill farm and worked the land and sheep like a man and had no time for manicures or even hand cream. But when those hands slapped tea and batch cakes on the table only minutes after dragging sheep through a chemical bath, it was no wonder that Suzy picked at her meal when she came on her only visit.

'I knew that sending you to St Elizabeth's was a bad idea,' Mother raged, jabbing at the leaflet again. 'You should have gone to the high school like all the other girls. You're getting above your station, like that friend of yours.'

'It's all right, Mother. I knew I couldn't go.' I said it evenly. It was always better to agree with her. She had a vile temper. 'I just thought I'd show it to you, that's all.'

She stood up and gathered her and Dada's plates and crashed them into the sink. Fortunately we ate off thick china.

Dada sat silently in his place at the head of the table and unseen by Mother, who was pouring water from the kettle on to the plates to give them her usual cursory wash, I saw him put out a thin hand and draw the leaflet towards him.

The French exchange holiday wasn't mentioned at home again that day or during the days that followed. Not so in school. Everyone was excited, discussing where in France they could go and whom they might meet. Suzy gave Miss Baxter the filled-in form and the five pounds deposit the very next morning, as did several other girls.

'I can't,' I said, when Suzy begged me to join them. 'We haven't got the money.'

'Poor you,' she said, sympathetically, and I think she meant it.

'Is there no way you can arrange it?' asked Miss Baxter.

'You of all girls, Eleanor, would get so much from this trip. Would you like me to talk to your parents?'

I was horrified. 'No.' I swallowed. 'No, thank you, Miss Baxter. It simply isn't possible.'

'Oh well.' She nodded. I think she knew something of my circumstances at home. She turned back to the class. 'Quieten down now, girls. We have our work to do.'

The rest of the week was very hard. My friends talked of nothing else, particularly Suzy. 'Mummy is taking me into Manchester after Easter to buy clothes for the trip and we're thinking about a present to take. It'll have to be something very special. I so hope I'll go to a smart sort of place. Daddy said he'd have a word with the organisers.'

As far as I knew the French exchange programme was an international organisation and Mr Franklin 'having a word' seemed an impossible concept, but then the Franklins seemed to be able to do anything. Suzy and her family took advantage of every situation.

'Maybe you'll meet a boy in France,' I said. We talked about boys all the time.

'I jolly well hope so.' She giggled and dug me in the ribs. 'French men are terribly handsome, you know. Mummy said she wished she'd known one when she was young. She said Englishmen are so dull.'

We were sitting on a bench in the school garden. It was lunch time and after our cheese pie and blancmange we'd wandered out, huddled in our coats, to spend the remaining twenty minutes before classes started again. Our friendship had started on the first day at St Elizabeth's when I felt horribly out of place. Many of the girls were classmates from the junior department and a few of the others had the confidence imbued by private education and seemed totally at ease in their new surroundings. Not me. I was a scholarship girl from a village school and hovered, yearning for invisibility, in the corner of the hall where we had to wait for the headmistress. I didn't know what to say or even how to approach anyone. It was Suzy who rescued me.

'Hello,' she said, smiling, leaving her group of chattering friends and coming over to me. 'I'm Suzy Franklin.'

She had that downy blonde look then that many young English children have, her cheeks rosy with good health and her hair shining in the September sunlight which pierced the diamond-paned windows of the old school building.

'I'm Eleanor Gill.' I swallowed the nervous lump in my throat. 'Hello.'

'Well, Eleanor Gill,' she ordered, matter-of-factly, 'come and join us.' And that was that. She made me part of the group and subsequently, when I could have killed her for the stupid things she did and said, I never forgot that initial kindness. We were best friends.

Five years later, sitting on that cold bench on a raw February afternoon, she'd changed very little. Still blonde, still glowing with good health and entirely confident of her future success in life.

I hadn't changed either, much. My hair had darkened, which, as Susie generously said, did make my eyes look bluer, but I was as naive as ever. The world outside school, home and the books I read remained a mystery.

'Come to our house on Saturday,' Suzy said as we huddled on the bench. 'We can talk about things.'

I shook my head. 'I can't. I have to help Mother with the sheep . . . they may have started lambing.'

That was a lie. They weren't due to lamb for at least another ten days and we didn't do much to help them in those days. They generally got on with it themselves and if we lost a few, it was too bad.

I didn't want to go because she would talk about the French exchange. Either that or about boys. Both subjects made my heart sink. I wasn't going to France and the possibility of my having a boyfriend was beyond a joke.

'Sorry,' I said, as we went back into school, 'but thanks for asking.'

'It's all right. I'll go shopping with Mummy instead.'

As it turned out I was quite busy on that Saturday. We had a storm on Friday night which blew part of the roof off the big barn and I was needed to help pull a tarpaulin over the gap. Our neighbour, Jed Winstanley, and his son Graham came to help us, driving over from their holding on an old tractor, towing the small animal transporter in which they'd loaded the tarpaulin.

'Ee! That's a right bloody bugger,' mumbled Jed, gazing up at the remains of the barn roof.

'Yes, it is,' Mother replied angrily. 'It never rains but it pours.'

It took hours to get the tarpaulin fixed. Jed and Mother did the bulk of the work while Graham and I hauled on the ropes, trailing from one side of the barn to the other, silently obeying the orders shouted down from our respective parents. Graham barely spoke to me. He'd already left school and was working with his father and the fact that I went to St Elizabeth's had put me on a different plane from most of the children with whom I'd gone to primary school.

I caught sight of Dada watching us from the kitchen window and I waved to him.

'Stop messing about, Eleanor. Concentrate on what you're doing,' Mother barked from her vantage point on top of the barn. I saw her glance over briefly to the house and when I looked again Dada had disappeared.

That evening, after Jed and Graham had gone home, I made egg, chips and bread and butter for supper. Mother looked all in and although she didn't say anything I think she was grateful for my doing the meal.

'That roof should have been sorted out years ago, but it'll have to do as it is for now.' She poured a cup of tea for Dada and stirred two large teaspoons of sugar into it. 'Here. Drink that before it gets cold,' she ordered, putting it down in front of him before collapsing back in her chair to drink her own.

Dada got up and left the table. I thought he'd gone for the night, even though it was only half past six, but within minutes he reappeared carrying one of his tins. Dada had several tins, old cigarette tins in which he kept various possessions, coins or nails and little rolls of twine which he'd picked up from the yard. A larger tin which he often carried around with him held pieces of paper folded into four, the back and front of them covered in his tiny writing. He dropped it once and it flew open by my feet. I'd picked up the tin and all the pieces of paper and quickly put them on the table. I didn't say anything and tried to behave as though it was an everyday occurrence. Poor Dada. His hand was shaking when he reached out to gather in the papers and I shot a quick glance at him. Tears had gathered in the corners of his eyes and he looked so frightened that I quickly left the room. I couldn't bear to upset him more.

But tonight he put the tin he'd brought downstairs on the table and with a movement more deliberate than I'd ever seen him manage he pushed it towards me. I stared at it. It was one I'd never seen before, a Player's cigarette tin with a picture of a bearded sailor on the front. I didn't know what to do and looked round to Mother.

She was examining a cut on her finger which was going septic. I'd seen her soaking it in hot water yesterday but it obviously wasn't better. I turned back to my father.

'Is the lid stuck, Dada?' I asked. 'Do you want me to open it?'

He said nothing. His eyes were fixed on the tin and his hand lingered on the table beside it.

'For goodness' sake, Eleanor, open it for him,' said Mother impatiently. 'Then you can clear the pots while I go out to check on the ewes.' She yawned and reached behind her chair to grab her boots which stood warming beside the range.

I was still uncertain, hating to interfere with something that mattered so much to him. But as I hesitated, he tapped his index finger on the oiled cloth beside the tin, indicating without words that I was to open it.

The room was still and quiet as I grasped the tin and pulled off the lid.

'Oh!' I said. A spool of tightly rolled banknotes jumped out of the tin and lay on the table in front of me.

'Good God almighty!' said Mother. 'Where the hell did all that come from?'

One of Dada's little notes had jumped out of the tin

with the money and cautiously I picked it up and unfolded it. *For the girl,* his tiny writing read. *For the trip to France.*

'What does it say?' demanded Mother.

'The money is for me. For the French exchange.' I was breathless.

'What?' Mother's face went red and she stood up so quickly that her chair crashed over behind her and the cups and saucers on the table rattled dangerously. 'He's giving you money for that ridiculous trip when this bloody farm is falling to pieces? Don't think for one minute that you're keeping that. Any spare money in this house goes straight back into the stock.' Snorting with anger she reached over the table but before her calloused hand could touch the roll of banknotes Dada's hand closed over them.

'Eddy!' she shouted, flecks of spittle flying from her lips. 'Let go.'

Then the most astonishing thing I'd ever seen happened. Dada lifted his head and stared at Mother full in the face. She too must have been shocked because her hand came to an abrupt halt in mid-air and the colour drained from her cheeks. For a moment she stared back at him, her eyes wild, her frizzy orange hair standing up on end and her lips moving as words formed.

I waited, sick at heart, for the furious tirade that would burst from her, but, to my amazement, nothing happened. Instead, biting her lips, she abruptly turned away from the table and grabbed hold of her boots. I was still motionless in my seat when the back door slammed.

The silence which followed was palpable. Even the normal sound of the wind in the chimney seemed to have died down and the muffled tick of the grandfather clock in the passageway was no louder than the usual creaks that were part of our old house.

Dada was the first to move. He pushed the roll of money towards me again and watched as I closed my fist over it.

Chapter Two

'Eleanor Gill; you, Janet Blaine and Margaret Hibbotson come with me.' Miss Baxter's voice was easily audible above the bustle of trains and passengers at the Gare du Nord in Paris. In the classroom she spoke softly, even diffidently, but the excitement and responsibilities of her present situation added a frenetic element to her orders. 'We must get our connection now. Hurry!'

As we trailed along after her I noticed several French passengers pause on the platform to turn and stare. We must have looked strange in our gingham school dresses and navy blazers. We'd been told that, for once, we wouldn't need our hats – straw boaters – which was a relief, but for travelling to and from France our uniform was a must. It didn't make much difference to me, I didn't have many clothes anyway, but Suzy was fed up.

'This is a holiday, after all,' she wailed when the dress code was announced. 'And I've bought so many lovely outfits.'

Several of the girls had already been picked up. Two at Calais and one at a station between Calais and Paris. Now, French families were arriving and announcing who they were.

'These are mine,' said Suzy, grinning as an elegantly dressed woman and a smiling teenage girl came up to them, the girl holding out a card which read *Susan Franklin*. 'Don't they look just perfect?'

'Yes,' I said. 'I'm sure you're going to have a wonderful time.' But my words were lost as Suzy fell into the perfumed grip of the woman, who was kissing her on both cheeks. Suzy's exchange family was situated in Paris itself and even though I was grateful about being on the exchange, I was deeply envious of her. Why couldn't I have been exchanged with a city girl? What wouldn't I have given to experience a few weeks of shops and streets and wonderful sightseeing? It wasn't fair, really. My exchange family lived on a farm in a village in the Loire valley. A village so tiny that I couldn't find it on the map.

'Where you are placed doesn't matter,' Miss Baxter had said, kindly, during the French lesson when we were being instructed about how to behave on the school exchange. 'The whole object of the exchange is to improve your French language and for you to get a feel of the local culture.'

'Onions and cattle feed, that's what you'll be feeling,' giggled Suzy beneath her breath as she smoothed out the long letter she had received from her host family. It was written in exquisite English on thick creamy note-paper and described an exciting itinerary the host family had planned. I bit my lip and wondered if Mr Franklin had indeed 'had a word'.

The letter which I'd received from Madame Martin, my hostess to be, was written on a piece of paper which looked as if it had been torn from an exercise book. Faint blue squares covered the sheet and the blue ink writing was old-fashioned and quite difficult to read. Compared to Suzy's letter, mine was brief almost to the point of rudeness. It was in French and merely said that I would be met at the station in the nearest town and that Jean Paul was looking forward to greeting me.

'Jean Paul, eh?' said Suzy. 'Lucky you. I bet he's absolutely gorgeous.'

I nodded and grinned as one or two other girls remarked on my having a boy as an exchange host but every time I thought about it, my stomach churned. Since leaving primary school I'd rarely had occasion to meet any boys and I couldn't imagine having anything in common with one. English boys were a mystery to me so a French counterpart would be even more complicated.

When I told Mother that my exchange partner would be a boy and showed her the letter, she'd snorted with exasperation. 'Huh! I might have known it. He'll want feeding more than a girl.'

Ever since Dada had given me the money, she had avoided the subject of the exchange. The roll of notes amounted to forty-seven pounds and I gave Miss Baxter five pounds for the deposit the very next school day. The remaining forty-two pound notes went into my Post Office account. I kept the savings book under my pillow, taking it out every morning when I woke up, to examine it. It became my most pleasurable exercise and I felt stupidly bereft when I had to remove the money to pay for the balance of the holiday. It left me with seventeen pounds, but I did have the other four, so I had plenty of spending money. I planned to buy a present for Dada first when I was in France. A fancy tin, maybe. Getting something for Mother would be more difficult.

I went to the shops with Suzy and bought a dress.

She'd already been with her mother to Manchester and chosen several outfits which she showed me when I went round to her house.

'I've got to have more than one thing to wear,' she said, hanging the smart navy blue dress back in her wardrobe amongst her other clothes. 'After all, according to Madame de Fourcies, I'll be going on lots of outings.'

I'd bought a pale pink linen dress with a round neck and a full skirt. I forgot that it would need ironing and when I took it home Mother was scathing.

'What a waste of money,' she said. 'By the time you get it out of your case it'll look like a rag.'

She was right, of course. But the Martins had an iron and I did wear it.

'Bye,' called Suzy as she followed her elegant hostess and the cheerful girl to the station exit. 'Give my love to the cattle.'

I pretended to laugh and waved my hand but I had no time to brood. Orders were being shouted again and the girls who hadn't been met at Paris were lined up to be taken by a teacher to a bus which would take them to another station. I followed Miss Baxter across the Gare du Nord to the platform where our southern-bound train was waiting. The last of my travelling companions, Janet and Margaret, were best friends and had luckily found themselves placed with families in the same town. They had never stopped talking since we'd got on the train at home and although Miss Baxter told them to be quiet more than once, excitement overruled her orders and they were soon at it again.

In the compartment, we three girls sat on one bench seat and Miss Baxter sat opposite. A French man sat beside her and stared at us. He was smoking and the scent of his cigarettes was like nothing I'd smelt before. I watched as he stubbed one out and took another from the blue and white cardboard packet. *Gitanes* was the name on the packet and excitement welled up in me again. The strange smell and the name and the outskirts of Paris, which I could see flashing by my window, meant that I was actually abroad.

I leant close to the window and scanned the horizon hoping I might see the Eiffel Tower in the distance but it wasn't in sight. Other buildings caught my eye though, particularly the tall grey houses with steeply pitched roofs and shutters on the windows. They were apartment blocks, I supposed, and as the train slowed to go through a small station I saw a woman brushing the pavement outside one of them. *La concierge*, my mind told me, loving the sound of the word.

Soon the houses were left behind and we were travelling through industrial areas and they looked different too, older somehow and less harsh than the new buildings which had gone up on the outskirts of our town. Even the factories had architectural embellishments, some with different coloured brickwork around the windows and others with stone balustrades between the walls and roofs. I was fascinated and couldn't take my eyes off the scene.

'Eleanor. You'll be first to get off.' Miss Baxter broke into my sightseeing. She was studying her schedule again, knowing it by heart but nervous of the responsibility she had taken on.

'Yes, Miss Baxter.'

'I will have to leave you there so I can remain on the

train to accompany Janet and Margaret to La Rochelle. You will be all right, won't you?'

'Yes.' I nodded and turned back to look out of the window. The city had gone now and the suburbs petered out into flat countryside. I could see roads and villages and miles and miles of flat fields as our train thundered southwest.

My host family lived in the Loire valley in a village twenty miles south of Angers. I'd looked up the region in the school library and after my initial disappointment of not going to Paris I was relieved to discover that there was plenty to see in the area.

'Angers, home of the Plantagenets,' said Miss Baxter dreamily when I'd shown her the address of my hosts. 'Oh, what a lucky girl you are, Eleanor. The churches, the châteaux . . . wonderful. You couldn't be in a better place.'

'Boring!' giggled Suzy later. 'No smart shops.'

I thought about that as we headed south. Would my hosts take me to these châteaux? Would they even take me as far as the small town which was only about two miles away from where they lived? The letter I'd received had said nothing about their plans. Was I imagining that they had somehow been very grudging about my visit? Sitting on that French train as it sped towards the Loire, the excitement I'd been feeling started to dissipate and I closed my eyes, hoping that sleep would wipe away my unease. As I drifted off Dada's face swam before me, while Mother's snort of derision filled my ears. I felt torn between two poles.

By the time we pulled into Angers three hours later, I felt a bit sick. I'd never been anywhere before and now I was consumed with nerves.

'Are you ready, Eleanor?' Miss Baxter stood up and opened the compartment door.

I swallowed. 'Yes,' I said, trying to keep my voice steady. My pigskin case was on the netted shelf above my head and I reached up to get it but by now the train was rocking into the station and as it went over the points it lurched and I staggered, almost falling over.

'*Pardon, mademoiselle.*' It was the Gitanes man who stood up and carefully took the case down and set it on the floor beside me.

'Thank you,' I said and then, flustered, added, 'I mean, *merci, monsieur.*'

'Bye. Have a good time, said Margaret, remembering her manners sufficiently to pause in her ongoing conversation.

Janet grinned. 'See you in three weeks.'

It was busy at Angers station that late afternoon. I could see adventurous children being held away from the platform's edge and hear their little squeals of joy or terror as they were enveloped in steam. Their mothers were struggling with raffia baskets full of produce and one even had a couple of live chickens stuffed into a shopping basket.

But as I stood waiting, the platform rapidly emptied. A few stragglers were heading towards the exit and the only people now left were those bidding goodbye to the passengers who had just got on board.

'Oh dear, oh dear.' Miss Baxter stood beside me, her small head bobbing this way and that as she searched for a person or persons making their way towards us. 'Where can they be?'

The whistle sounded and the guard at the rear of the

train waved his flag and leapt athletically on board. Porters were hurrying down the platform, slamming the doors, and one lone passenger raced through the barrier and wrestled open a door in the coach close to the engine.

'Oh!' Miss Baxter moaned desperately and pulled anxiously on my arm. Nearly five minutes had passed since the train had pulled in, ample time for my hosts to arrive, and it was obvious that they weren't coming.

This was it. I turned back towards the open door of the train knowing that I would have to go home, somehow. The exchange was the disaster Mother, if not in words, but in her own inimical way, had predicted.

Suddenly Miss Baxter gave a little scream and pointed dramatically down the platform.

'It's them, I'm sure,' she said. Without further thought or question, she called out, 'Goodbye, Eleanor. Have a lovely holiday,' before jumping eagerly back on to the train. I watched, dumbfounded, as her excited face disappeared in a cloud of steam.

Despairing, I turned away from the departing train to look back up the platform. A man and a woman were approaching, the man eagerly, striding along with easy confident steps. The woman who followed was almost dragging her feet and, to my dismay, I realised that she wore an expression of what could only be described as profound boredom.

They stopped in front of me.

'Perhaps it is Miss Eleanor?' asked the man.

He was of more than middle height and strongly built with broad shoulders which so strained the seams of his blue cotton jacket that the stitching could be seen. His dark brown hair was partially covered by a faded cap which he wore pushed to the back of his head.

'Yes.'

The concerned face broke into a smile. 'Good,' he said and shot out a large tanned hand to shake mine. 'Welcome, Miss Eleanor. Welcome to Angers.' He flung out his arms in an expressive gesture that I soon learned was his normal way. 'To France. I am Étienne Martin. This,' he looked down at the silent woman beside him, 'is my wife, Mathilde, Madame Martin.'

'Hello.' I reached out to shake her hand. Somehow I didn't think I was going to get a kiss on both cheeks like the one Suzy had received from her hostess.

Madame Martin parted her thin lips in a tiny smile. She was small, smaller than me, and had a slight, girlish body and a pale heart-shaped face. Her eyebrows had been plucked out completely and two black pencilled crescents drawn in their place. She had dark brown eyes which bulged slightly, making the whites seem contrastingly prominent, like cow's eyes. They gave her a strange look, not unattractive but almost audacious as though she might at any time do anything.

She wore a purple felt hat shaped like a small trilby which was perched at an angle on top of her head. It must have been held in place with elastic under her hair which was the blackest I'd ever seen. It hung smoothly down to her shoulders from a side parting so that one of her unusual eyes was partially covered.

If I'd expected a warm welcome my feelings would have been dashed, but I think I'd always known that I wouldn't get one. 'Good afternoon,' she said evenly and, transferring the cigarette which she'd been holding between her fingers to her lips, limply took my hand.

We stood there, the three of us staring at each other, Étienne grinning and me gawky and shy. Mathilde gave up her smile and waited.

The train carrying Miss Baxter and her two charges to La Rochelle was now out of sight and the platform was empty. Overhead the sky had darkened and raindrops the size of pennies started to fall, splashing dark circles on to my school blazer. In the distance there was a rumble of thunder and looking over the tracks to the gold and green fields which stretched away beyond the town, I could see a bright rainbow arcing across the purple sky.

'Come on, now,' Étienne ordered, picking up my case, 'before the storm arrives,' and he led the way out of the station, past the taxi cab rank and into the street.

We drove the twenty miles to our destination in a small silvery-blue metal van, the three of us squeezed together on a wooden bench seat. My precious suitcase had been stowed in the back, wedged between an oil canister and a wooden box of groceries; I was concerned for its safety. Once, I looked over my shoulder at it and saw, with horror, that the box of groceries swayed every time Étienne dragged the van round a corner or applied one of his last minute brakings. He drove with verve, never slowing until absolutely necessary and exchanging insults out of his open window with other less adventurous drivers.

I found myself praying not only for safety but that the oil wouldn't spill out of the rusting canister or the melons which perched unsteadily on top of the wooden box burst and spread their golden flesh over the lustrous pigskin.

'You have a good journey, yes?' asked Étienne after we'd left the outskirts of Angers and were tearing along a country road.

'Yes,' I said, faintly, too panicky to speak up or to venture into a longer reply.

Étienne didn't appear to notice my nervousness. 'I have been to England, once,' he said. 'But I didn't learn to speak the language very well. So you must speak to us in French. That is all right, nnn, yes?'

I swallowed, now speechless, and was only able to nod. When I looked at him out of the corner of my eye he was grinning.

We were now driving along a broad, tree-lined road and looking ahead I was entranced. This was exactly the picture of France that I'd imagined. A Napoleonic road where the stormy light was splintered by dark tree trunks. The photograph in my French grammar could have been taken at this very spot. But even as I marvelled, Étienne swerved the steering wheel to the right and we left that road to drive down a small winding lane, where the verges overflowed with tall vegetation and a smell of hay fields and vineyards wafted in through the open windows.

Mathilde gave a little tut of annoyance, the only sign of animation she had shown during the entire journey. The ash from her cigarette fell on to her black and white dress and she brushed it away with small irritated movements. I watched as she threw the stub out of the window and then opened her shiny black handbag to take out another loose cigarette. She lit it from a paper match-book that she had been holding in her hand.

It had stopped raining now and the black rain clouds had moved majestically away to the north exposing a dazzling sun, which reflected fascinating shimmers of light on the road ahead. My blazer itched around my neck and I could feel my face getting redder as the heat intensified.

I was wondering how much longer this journey would take when suddenly Étienne took his hand from the wheel and pointed through his window. 'That is my farm, there,' he said and I leant forward and looked over the fields to where a low stone building could just be glimpsed between the profusion of pale pink musk mallow and hedge parsley.

Oh, it was beautiful! I remembered reading a book when I was a little child which had a coloured picture of a farm. Then I couldn't believe it, because I lived on a farm and our place was nothing like the drawing, and I had thrown the book aside in dismay. Now I realised what the artist had been imagining. Étienne's farm could have been the one in the picture that I'd seen, long ago.

His house was pillowed in the midst of rising lush green fields and huge shade trees. I could see fat, pinky beige cattle grazing contentedly, their tails giving the occasional swish to drive away insects. Beyond them was another, higher field planted with rows of little trees, and, with a rush of excitement, I realised that they were grape vines.

I thought of home. I thought of how hard it was and how even the smallest job involved a struggle. Compared to our bleak stony hillside where the scrubby grass only just provided enough food for the sheep, Étienne's farmland was bursting with life.

We drove on for a few more minutes, winding round the narrow lanes until we rattled through an imposing arched stone gateway and came to an abrupt halt in a cobbled courtyard.

'It is here,' Étienne announced. 'Riverain. My home.'

It was a pretty house, built of the same pale beige stone as the gateway and covered with a white flowering creeper. A higgledy-piggledy array of small, blue-shuttered windows faced the courtyard, their bizarre distribution giving no indication of where the floors of the house could possibly be. Eventually, when I was taken inside, the oddness of internal steps and landings and rooms off rooms confused me for days. It was a house which had been added to over the centuries without any apparent thought other than to provide extra space. But it was utterly entrancing and I adored it from the first. It's not only people you fall in love with, and stones and brick shouldn't be able to love you back. But I was enchanted by the place and it comforted me. Foolishly, I thought I would fall in love too with the group of people who waited in front of the arched doorway.

The teenage boy would be Jean Paul, I supposed. I'd wondered why he hadn't come to meet me at the station, but when I thought about it afterwards, his absence was quite reasonable. That bench seat in the van only held three people and it would have been awkward for me to ride with Jean Paul and Étienne. Later, I re-thought this when I realised that Mathilde drove perfectly well, but by then I also understood that she wouldn't have done it for me.

Jean Paul was dark like his mother and at sixteen had heavy eyebrows and the shadow of a pubescent moustache. He leant against the stone porch, one hand in his pocket, watching as Étienne braked in front of the group.

I noticed, with dismay, that far from giving my arrival a welcoming grin, his face was set and unsmiling. A mirror image of Mathilde's.

The other two in the group were an older woman and a little girl. The woman was in her sixties I guessed and was short and heavyset, with iron grey hair scraped off her face into a tight knot on the top of her head. That face was strong and tanned and almost like a man's face, an older version of Étienne's. She was dressed entirely in black from the long-sleeved blouse held at the neck by a gold bar brooch to the calf-length cotton skirt. I almost expected her feet to be shod in boots, like the women in the Impressionist posters Miss Baxter stuck up in the French room. Instead she wore a pair of comfortable-looking black gym shoes. She wasn't smiling either and as my heart sank even further I took a deep breath and reluctantly slid out of the van to stand on the cobbled courtyard in front of my hosts. Mathilde, who had been sitting between me and the door, had got out as soon as the van came to a halt and gone straight into the house. I envied her. What wouldn't I have given at that moment to disappear from sight?

'I can present *ma mère*, Madame Martin,' said Étienne, coming to join her. 'Grandmère,' he added unnecessarily.

'Good evening, mademoiselle,' said Grandmère, taking my hand and examining my face carefully. 'Welcome.'

'Thank you,' I said and smiled.

'Now,' said Étienne. 'Here is my son, Jean Paul.'

Jean Paul nodded silently and stood upright and stuck out his hand. *'Bonjour,'* he muttered, and obviously feeling he'd done his duty he started to turn away. A small growl from his father stopped him in mid-step.

You wanted this, my mind was screaming at me. You wanted so much to come to France. And it was going to be wonderful, wasn't it?

I felt weary. I'd been travelling since midnight and all my hopes were being dashed. I could see Mother's sarcastic face swimming before my eyes and hear her dismissive chuckle. And it was that thought which forced me to look him in the eye and speak.

'Hello,' I said, searching for a correct thing to say. 'I have been so looking forward to meeting you.'

Immediately I could have bitten out my tongue. How foolish, how forward that made me sound and I could feel a flush surging into my face. In embarrassment I dropped my eyes and stared at the little puddles in the yard which were glittering and steaming in the sun.

But maybe my French hadn't been very clear or maybe Jean Paul was too stupid to appreciate a possible faux pas; I learned over the following weeks that it was the latter, because all he did was to mumble a further greeting in execrable English and then look hopelessly at his father.

We could have stood there for ever but the third member of the group came forward and grabbed my hand.

'This is Lisette,' said Étienne. 'Jean Paul's sister.'

Lisette was about six or seven years old.

'Allo,' she said. 'You are tall, like Papa. Have you other clothes? Those aren't very pretty.'

I laughed. It was impossible to take offence at the child's remarks. She was small and willowy with pale brown hair and hazel eyes. She was wearing a washed out blue smocked dress with short sleeves and over it a little white pinafore. As I gently shook her hand, my eyes travelled down to her thin legs which disappeared into white ankle socks and, incongruously, a pair of women's red high-heeled shoes.

'I like your shoes,' I said. '*They* are very pretty.'

'They belong to Maman. But she lets me wear them.' The child poked out one foot and then another before twirling round to show off her whole outfit.

Grandmère grabbed her by the hand. 'That's enough, Lisette,' she warned her. 'Go and wash before supper.'

Unmoved, the little girl pulled her hand away, but obediently tripped unsteadily towards the house and I had to turn back to Jean Paul.

He was about my height, shorter than Étienne and darker. His eyes were a little like Mathilde's, round and slightly prominent, but where her look was unconsciously bold his was even more bovine, as though nothing that other humans did was entirely clear to him. Presently he looked bored and, to my added dismay, angry. He didn't want to talk to me.

Étienne came to the rescue. 'Maman,' he said, addressing Grandmère who had followed the various exchanges closely, 'will you show Miss Eleanor to her room while I feed the calves?' He turned to his son and when he spoke he didn't bother to hide the exasperation in his voice. 'Put the van away, and get out the tractor. I have work to do after supper.'

My arm was grasped gently and I turned to see Grandmère. 'Come, Miss Eleanor. I will show you your room and then it will be time for supper.'

Chapter Three

My first supper at Riverain was an experience which in the long years since I have never forgotten. Seventeen-year-old children, and I was a child then, are impressionable and although I didn't understand what was happening, the beginnings of a jigsaw puzzle were laid before me.

We sat on large exquisitely carved chairs around a polished wooden table in the cool dining room. This and the salon, a room I rarely entered, had the best furniture in the house but it was formal and uncomfortable and I soon learned to stay in my bedroom or lie on the grassy bank beside the river for relaxation. Later, when we became friends, I would sit with Grandmère in the little parlour where the chairs were old but soft and the oil lamps smoked a dim light. But during the first few days, I trailed about the house, wondering where I was supposed to be, for Jean Paul was no help and would disappear off and leave me for hours. It was Grandmère who saved me.

The room to which she showed me on arrival was up the first flight of stairs and then along a corridor and up another three steps. Grandmère had opened the door into a pretty little room which, when I pulled back the shutters, had a view of the countryside at the back of the house. I could see the river, moving sluggishly and gleaming in the evening sun. Its stench drifted up to me, hot and sour like compost, and I wrinkled my nose in distaste wondering how I would live with it day and night. Strangely, after the first few days, I didn't notice it. Maybe the whole ambience of Étienne's farm had entered me and I smelt of the river and the fields too. Whatever it was, it no longer mattered.

But that first evening my view of the river and the drooping shade trees which dipped their arrow leaves into the water seemed entirely foreign to my northern eyes. There, rising up beyond the river, was the field of vines, neat rows of green and brown, a place I knew I would have to explore. At the top of the vine field I could see a building, a cottage perhaps or a barn but built from beige stone like all the buildings on the farm.

Grandmère had come to stand beside me. 'Ah,' she said. 'My son goes to check on his vines. It is necessary. The mildew can be a problem at this time of the year.'

I looked down. Étienne was walking across a narrow wooden bridge which spanned the river. The wood looked old and some of the planks were broken. I wondered if it was safe and if I would dare to try it but even as I wondered I saw Étienne striding across, obviously not seeing any danger.

'We must close the shutters,' said Grandmère. 'The sun is strong at this time of the day and you will be too warm. Yes?'

'Yes,' I replied and stepping back into the centre of the whitewashed room I gazed around. I loved my room immediately. I loved the big iron bed and the fat soft duvet which covered it. Miss Baxter had warned us to expect duvets and told us to remember to air them by throwing them across the window ledge of our room in the morning.

'That is correct in the country, girls,' she instructed. 'Those of you with city placements must take advice from your hostess.'

I smoothed my hand across it and studied the other pieces of furniture. Grandmère had put my case beside a big wardrobe which when I opened it I saw would hold the contents of ten cases. My few clothes looked forlorn hanging from the metal rail. But the wardrobe smelt of cedar and in years to come whenever I happened across that aroma I was immediately back at Riverain.

'Here,' said Grandmère, taking my arm and showing me to a door which opened off my room. When she pushed it open I saw a shower and washbasin and, to my confusion, a lavatory and bidet. Miss Baxter had been too modest to explain the function of that particular piece of bathroom equipment.

'Very nice,' I mumbled, pleased and surprised that I would have my own bathroom.

Grandmère straightened one of the embroidered towels which hung over a wooden stand. 'It was put here when the . . . lodgers . . . visitors were in the house. During the war.'

I struggled over the word 'lodgers', as Grandmère had too. Then I realised that she probably meant evacuees. We'd had them too during the war. A woman and her little boy who had been bombed out of Liverpool and sent to the country. They hated our house and only stayed for a few weeks. I was glad when they went.

'And here,' she opened another door, 'is a staircase. It

goes directly to the kitchen. Be careful if you use it. Some of the steps are loose and it has no light.'

I was careful and on that first evening walked along the corridor on the first floor until I found the main staircase. The doors to the rooms I passed were open and looking in I saw fat bedding on iron beds and bare floorboards. The room closest to mine had a man's suit on a hanger hooked over the wardrobe door. Was it Jean Paul's?

One room had pretty blue and white toile de Jouy wallpaper and a dark blue rug. The red shoes that Lisette had been wearing were lying on the rug and I guessed that this must be Étienne and Mathilde's bedroom. The one next to it was much smaller and had a single bed pushed against the wall. On the floor beside the bed was a miniature iron bedstead with a similar white cover but this one had occupants . . . dolls. They were sitting up, half covered in bedding but dressed elegantly in velvet and silk, six of them propped against the head and foot boards looking as though their presence was the most natural thing in the world. It had to be Lisette's room. Another corridor led off to the side where I could see more doors. More bedrooms.

I descended slowly to the little square hall. It was dark, the shutters half closed against the evening sun and only fingers of brilliant light pointing on to the stone flags.

A well polished hall stand leant against one wall, bare of coats or hats on the wooden hooks and only a single black umbrella in the iron well. I stood in front of the rectangular mirror set in the middle of the stand and examined myself. My hair was tidy, brushed off my face and held in a ponytail, and my dress, my blue gingham school dress which I'd worn all day, would do. It would have to.

I looked taller in that mirror and thinner and for the first time saw how like Dada I looked. I had his finely chiselled face and pale skin.

'That girl has the map of Ireland on her face,' Jed Winstanley used to joke, 'like him indoors.'

Mother hated him saying that; she would turn her mouth even further down and quickly change the subject but now I could see that Jed was right. There was nothing of Mother to see in me. No ginger hair, no rough red cheeks. Nothing to show that I was her daughter. Staring at me was a girl from the west of Ireland with Atlantic blood in her veins.

I turned away and swallowed the small lump in my throat. Dada would be missing me; I knew it even if no one else did.

'Ah! Miss Eleanor.' It was Grandmère, her shoes making a soft slapping sound on the stone flags in the hall. 'Come to the dining room.'

The family were gathered. Étienne was at the head of the table, wearing a clean blue shirt and water-slicked hair. My seat, which remained my seat for the entire visit, was between him and Mathilde. Grandmère sat opposite Étienne and Jean Paul and Lisette were seated along the other side.

Only Étienne greeted me with a grin. 'You are hungry, Miss Eleanor, ready to eat?'

I nodded and sat down. No one else spoke, not even to each other, but awkwardly fingered their cutlery and draped their napkins as though this was the first time they'd used this room and they felt uneasy.

Étienne poured wine into our glasses, even a little into Lisette's, and while I watched amazed she put it to her lips and drank.

'Wait,' said Grandmère sharply, and poured water from a big earthenware jug into Lisette's wine. Étienne stood up, and reaching for the baton of bread and the knife carved a piece off and gave it to the little girl.

'Thank you,' she said in her small, bell-like voice, and pulled the bread to pieces on the table. I watched as the pieces were dipped into her glass before being popped into her mouth. Drips from her bread made tiny puddles on the polished table and I glanced at Mathilde out of the side of my eye wondering if she would say something to Lisette, but there was silence. Mathilde wasn't looking at her daughter. Her strange eyes were fixed on Jean Paul and when I followed her gaze I saw that Jean Paul was staring back at her. They didn't speak out loud at all but his lips moved slightly in what might have been a word and then relaxed into what could have been a smile but appeared to me more of a smirk. I think that even then I must have loathed him.

The glass of wine in front of me was a problem. I'd never drunk wine or alcohol of any description and I was nervous about making a fool of myself in front of my hosts. Cautiously, I lifted the glass and took a sip. To me it tasted sour but not unpleasant and, thirsty, I took a larger mouthful.

Étienne watched me and nodded his head approvingly. 'It is good to try everything. Yes?'

'Yes,' I said slowly. 'This is the first wine I've ever had.'

That caused Jean Paul to move his stare from Mathilde to me. I thought he might say something, anything, to make the conversation flow, but nothing came out of his mouth and after a moment he looked away.

In front of Grandmère was a white china soup tureen and when she lifted the lid steam rose and filtered into the room, carrying a herby smell which I couldn't recognise. The pale green soup when I tried it was like nothing I'd ever tasted, sharp with the flavour of the vegetable garden and loaded with tiny scraps of ham. I loved it, scooping it into my mouth greedily but with one eye on the way my hosts tore up their bread and used chunks to wipe round their bowls. I eagerly followed suit.

The soup was followed by a plate of little pink pieces of meat which were impossible to identify but I still felt incredibly hungry and ate the meat without questioning.

I thought of home and remembered that it was Saturday and Mother would have made a pan of mince. I could almost smell it, but that memory was diluted by a waft of rosemary. I looked at my plate and saw a sprig of herbs lying beneath the meat. What would Mother think, I wondered, and felt a smile beginning. Would she like this food? The pink meat, the sliced sautéed potatoes which oozed with butter and the green beans, whole and shiny with odd flecks of red between them. I thought not. Fuss and nonsense, she would say. And a ridiculous waste of butter.

I didn't care. Anything was better than grey mince and heaps of boiled potatoes and cabbage.

'Do you like your supper?' Étienne leant forward and offered me some vegetables. 'Is it to your taste?'

'It's very nice,' I muttered. 'Delicious.'

Later I learned that Grandmère liked to add pimentos to the beans and tiny silvery onions and shredded lettuce to the peas. In the weeks that followed I came to love those tastes and many a night after, when back in the gloomy farm kitchen at home, I craved a wooden bowl of pungently dressed salad, or a dish of tiny shrimps served simply with a baton of crusty bread. But on this first night, despite my hunger and the delicious tastes, I watched with alarmed fascination as Étienne tucked the baguette under his arm and sawed off roughly cut pieces which he tossed across to each diner. All I wanted was for the meal to end and to escape to my bedroom.

The conversation when it started was muted. Lisette chattered, but of such inconsequential matters that no one listened. Jean Paul ate steadily, all the while staring at his food and looking up only on the rare occasions when I spoke. Then he would watch my mouth as I formed unfamiliar words and struggled to remember French grammar.

It was so difficult. I, who had been the best French speaker in my class, the one who was always top, was now struck almost dumb with embarrassment. I wondered briefly how the other girls in my group were getting on. Suzy was hopeless at languages and could barely speak more than a few words. She was so poor at French translation that she would get me to do her homework. But Suzy would be all right, I was sure. She always came out on top and hadn't she gone to a family who appeared to speak perfect English? I bet she's in some fancy restaurant now on the Champs Élysées, I thought, miserably. She's having a really wonderful time. While I'm stuck with this family of . . . peasants.

But as soon as the word 'peasants' came into my head

I was ashamed of myself. I was being pathetic, exactly as Mother had suspected I would be, and heading for a disastrous holiday. It was up to me to make an effort and I turned to Mathilde, who was sitting next to me, planning to make some remark about the weather. To my astonishment, I saw that my hostess had finished her meal, lit a cigarette and was leaning on her elbow, reading a paperback book which she had put on the table beside her plate.

I turned round, amazed, to look at Étienne, wondering if he too would be reading. Perhaps this was usual behaviour in French families and I would be expected to bring my own book to dinner tomorrow evening. One glance at Étienne's face, however, assured me that I wouldn't be. The look of rage and despair which clouded his previously cheerful expression was too obvious to ignore. He was furious.

'Your mother and father, they are well?' Grandmère's cool voice from the foot of the table broke the uncomfortable silence.

I let out the breath I'd been unconsciously holding and nodded. 'My mother is very well, thank you. Dada is . . .' How could I put it? I started again. 'My father came home from the war in a bad way. He is mentally damaged.'

'Oh,' said Grandmère sympathetically. 'It was the Nazis?'

'No. The Japs. He was a prisoner of war and they tortured him. He doesn't speak now.'

Grandmère shook her head and Étienne, his face clearing and his normal good humour returning, said, 'The war was terrible. For us all. The Germans were bastards.'

There was a rustle of sound beside me and from the

corner of my eye I caught the quick movement of Mathilde's hand as it curled around the corner of the page she was holding and angrily crumpled the paper between her thin fingers. In the silence which followed she suddenly stood up, scraping her chair on the wooden floor, and book in hand left the room.

I thought that the meal was over and started to lift my napkin from my knee, but Grandmère put her hand up.

'We have dessert and cheese. You must try them.'

I looked at Jean Paul. He was expressionless and merely picked up his spoon and waited for Grandmère to pass round the bowls of *les crémets* and wild strawberries.

Lisette hummed a little tune and Étienne poured himself more wine and nobody remarked on Mathilde's abrupt departure. I was not that surprised. Dada often made sudden exits from the room, especially when something out of the ordinary had happened, and I had grown used to it. Maybe Mathilde had found my presence too difficult to cope with.

'I think, Miss Eleanor, you must be tired,' said Grandmère, rising from the table. 'We will see you in the morning.'

I went up to my room then, happy to escape from the strained atmosphere and ready for bed. However, despite my weariness, sleep wouldn't come. I lay for hours, my mind whirling, examining all the new experiences and mentally tracing the faces of the Martin family until they were lined up in an uncomfortable row. My picture had them like the dolls in the little bed.

Restless, I got up and opened the shutters and leant out of the open window. The rain had returned, pattering gently on the tiled roofs and on to my outstretched hand. It was warm and soft, like bath water. I heard an owl screech in the trees and an answering call from across the river and then, finally exhausted, I pulled the shutter closed and turned away to get back into bed. That's when another sound cut into the night. It was footsteps on the bridge. Short tapping female footsteps going away from the house and over the river.

As I drifted off into a troubled sleep I briefly wondered where Mathilde might be going during the middle of the night.

Chapter Four

The rain had gone by the time I woke up and through the cracks in the closed shutters I could see that it was a brilliantly sunny day. It was hot, too, and throwing off the duvet I lay half awake, drowsily staring at the white-washed ceiling, going over in my mind all the events of yesterday.

Had I landed up in a particularly strange family? Or was this how every French family behaved? I didn't know. I had no parameters except my own experience.

In a way, apart from the feeling that I would never be able to get on with him, I cautiously felt better about taking Jean Paul home with me. Dada's silences were no worse than Mathilde's and if Mother wasn't such a good cook it couldn't matter that much. Jean Paul appeared prepared to eat anything without comment. Mother's carelessly cooked food would probably be shovelled in with the same lack of interest he'd shown at last night's extraordinary dinner.

As for the social side of things, well, I thought I could manage that. The school and the local council had arranged a series of outings and entertainments for the visiting French students and we would be occupied most days. Maybe it wouldn't be too bad.

I got up then and dressed in my white Aertex shirt and navy shorts. These were my normal holiday clothes, albeit at home with an added jumper because on our hillside the weather was rarely warm enough for bare arms.

It wasn't that early, I thought, not for a farming family to be up, and when I opened the shutters I could hear voices coming from the yard below my bedroom. Looking down I saw Étienne talking to a man and a boy, not Jean Paul but a taller, thinner boy who was dressed in blue cotton workman's trousers like Étienne and the other man. The man was holding a cow by a halter and I could hear them all laughing. I drew away then, not wanting to seem as though I was spying, and sat on the bed. I had to go downstairs, but to where?

The kitchen would be the place, I thought, and I looked at the door which would open on to the little staircase. What if I walked in on them in the middle of a conversation, or, worse, a row? It would be embarrassing, and deciding not to try it I went out of my room and down the three steps to the long corridor which separated my room from the rest of the house.

This morning, all the doors in the hall were open, even the front door which led to the porch and the courtyard. Brilliant shafts of early sunlight pierced the dark wood room, lighting up the panelled corners and the rough whitewashed ceiling. Under my sandal-shod feet the stone flags had taken on a warmer, rosier glow so that the whole atmosphere of Riverain seemed calmer and more cheerful.

The open door to the dining room where we'd eaten supper last night showed evidence of cleaning and a view of a little garden through the tall many-paned windows. The table which last night had presented me with exciting new tastes was now covered by a lace runner which stretched its full length.

The closest open door to where I was standing revealed a room with polished floorboards and fancy gold-painted wooden furniture. A chaise longue covered in shiny gold and red striped fabric dominated the space and the two little carved tables at either end of it carried matching glass ashtrays and china figures. That was the salon, I learned later.

Another door opened on to a study or perhaps an office. I could see a large wooden roll-top desk, the top open and all the little compartments inside stuffed with papers. Above the desk was a photograph in a frame showing a man in uniform. I couldn't see the man clearly from where I was standing but I thought it must be Étienne. He, like my father, would have gone to war. I wondered who had managed the farm while he was away but then I supposed it would have been Mathilde. That's what women did.

My mother ran our farm all through the war. It had been her parents' holding and she and I had gone there to be safe from the bombing in the city. Dada wasn't a farmer. He'd been a reporter on the local paper who had come over from Ireland during the thirties. I often wondered how he and Mother had met and why they'd been attracted to each other. They seemed almost like creatures from a different planet, but I barely remembered how he'd been before he went away. When he came home he was an entirely different person, at least that's what everyone said. Maybe Mother was too.

To the rear of the hall running away under the stairs was a passageway that I guessed would lead to the back of the house and the kitchen. I half turned towards it. It was where I should go, but lingering and now anxious again I looked out of the front door to where the brilliant sunlight was calling me and changed my mind.

The air outside was warm, balmy even, and the tang of the river felt sharp in my nostrils. I looked up. The sky was clear, a bright blue with occasional slow-moving little clouds. I took a deep breath, expanding my lungs with the morning air, hoping it would settle me and sweep away the nervousness I'd felt since coming here. And to a certain extent, it worked.

Everything seemed different to me. This French day was hot, foreign and somehow moved more slowly than at home. I smiled, thinking about our farm. There was nothing relaxing there so why had I been wishing for it? Even in summer the wind on the hill behind our house had a bite and the smell from the early heather had a clean cold perfume. And if the weather wasn't cruel then Mother would sour the atmosphere by bossing me around and complaining about her hard life. Had she ever been happy?

The sound of a child's voice interrupted my thoughts and looking down I saw Lisette sitting on the cobbles to the side of the arched porch, playing with a couple of dolls. She had put them in a box and covered them with a piece of cloth, as though they were in bed.

'Stay there, Jacques. And you too, Angélique. You can't play because you've been bad.'

'Hello.' I wandered over to her. 'Are these your dollies?'

Lisette looked up. 'Yes,' she said carefully in her small

precise voice. 'These are two of my dollies. I have lots of dollies. But Jacques and Angélique have been naughty and must go to bed.'

'Oh dear,' I said. 'What did they do?'

Lisette stood up and laughed. 'I can't tell you. But they have been very naughty.' She was still giggling when she put her cool little hand in mine. 'Grandmère said I was to wake you and bring you for breakfast. I forgot. Now we'll go.'

She picked up her box of dolls and we went back into the house and followed the narrow passageway. As I'd guessed, it opened on to the kitchen.

It was a wonderful room, large and airy with a huge range and a selection of heavy wooden cupboards and sideboards which shone cleanly in the sunlight. It had a blue and red tiled floor and on the wall around the range were more tiles, blue and red also but interspersed with tiled flower pictures. A pair of broad, shallow sinks sat beneath the large window, and to the side a dresser which reached to the ceiling was loaded with pretty plates and casseroles. A large wooden table took up the middle of the room, its boards scrubbed almost white so it looked fresh and inviting.

Grandmère was there, her black dress covered by a white apron, busy by the cooking range and looking up she waved me to a chair by the table.

'Good morning, Eleanor. Did you sleep well?'

I nodded.

Grandmère gave me a searching look and then her stern face softened. 'It is difficult when you are staying in a strange place. Yes?'

'Yes,' I said.

'Well, you'll get used to it, I'm sure. Now, are you hungry?'

She didn't wait for me to reply but lifted the white tea towel draped in the middle of the table to reveal a crisp baguette on a thick board. 'After today, you must help yourself as we all do,' she said. 'Here is bread, and the butter and *confiture* are in the larder.' Another wave of the hand, this time in the direction of a door next to the window.

She bustled around, getting a plate from the dresser, and disappeared into the larder. I waited, fingering the bread until she returned with a dish of butter and a glass jar of apricot jam.

'The coffee is on the range or if you prefer you may have hot chocolate. It's in that jug.' She looked at me anxiously. 'I haven't tea although I know that English people like it.'

'Coffee will be lovely,' I said hastily, not wanting to make a fuss but also because I was eager to try it. We didn't have coffee at home. Mother had pronounced it nasty, and when I returned home and bought coffee in town it was nasty. It took years for the cafés at home to reproduce proper French coffee.

Grandmère's coffee, served in a white bowl, was delicious and I sipped at it in between putting butter and jam on a piece of baguette. Shyly I tore the bread in pieces as I'd seen the rest of the family do last night and that was obviously the right thing to do because neither Grandmère nor Lisette seemed affronted.

'I like chocolate best,' said Lisette, pulling out a chair and getting ready to sit down. 'I want some more.'

'No,' said Grandmère. 'You've had enough breakfast. Go upstairs and change ready for church.'

With an uncomfortable jolt I realised that it was Sunday and I was in a Catholic country. In all my preparations for the exchange, religion was something I'd never considered. I suppose Miss Baxter imagined we were all regular churchgoers like her and she didn't need to mention it. I wished she had. We never went at home. Dada didn't leave the farm and Mother said she'd ceased believing years ago and was now convinced that religion was mumbo jumbo.

Everything of which she didn't approve was declared mumbo jumbo. She had a list of things she 'didn't hold with' and thought a waste of time, and as far as I remember nothing was ever removed from her list but lots were added. Prominent on her register of scorn were Charles Dickens, philosophy, the shipping forecast but not the weather forecast, the royal family and, most derided of all, religion. I never debated any of this with her; it would have been pointless. She had long since made up her mind and any argument I could possibly venture would be dismissed almost before the words were uttered.

Now I was confronted with a problem and I would have to face it by myself. I bit into my bread slowly and waited.

'Will you accompany us? To church?' Grandmère was clearing the table around me.

'I'm not a Catholic.'

She shrugged. 'It doesn't matter. Think about it.'

I thought about it for less than twenty seconds. Of

course I would go with them; I wanted to experience everything I possibly could whilst I was on this holiday. Who knew when I would ever get another one?

'Yes,' I said. 'I'd like to.'

'Good. Finish your breakfast then go and change into your dress. You have half an hour.'

Lisette was still sitting at the table and she grinned at me. 'You can't go to church in those funny clothes,' she said. 'Boys wear shorts. Girls wear pretty dresses.'

'Enough!' Grandmère's face darkened and she held up her finger. 'That is rude, Lisette. Say you're sorry to Eleanor.'

Suddenly the cheerful atmosphere had changed. A shadow fell over Lisette's wan little face and tears came into her pale hazel eyes. 'Sorry,' she whispered.

I smiled. 'It doesn't matter. Don't worry.'

Grandmère nodded and took Lisette's arm. 'Go upstairs and change and don't go out in the yard again and get your dress dirty.'

Her head drooping, the little girl picked up her dolls and slowly left the room.

'I didn't mind,' I said, hoping to avoid another embarrassment.

'She needs to be taught her manners. If I don't say something, nobody else will.' Grandmère smoothed her hands down her white apron. 'Even though she's . . .'

The sentence petered out while I sat waiting for her to continue. Though she's a child . . . Though she's a girl . . . What?

But the subject was changed. 'Come back down here when you're ready,' Grandmère ordered and went out of the kitchen and along the passageway. I watched her.

There were two doors opening off the corridor and she opened one of them and went in.

The anxious feeling had returned to the pit of my stomach and the coffee and bread no longer appealed. I got up and took my dishes to the sink where I quickly rinsed them under the tap and left them to dry as I'd seen Grandmère do. Mother's last words to me at the station before she'd given me a brief peck on the cheek and hurried away were 'don't be a nuisance'.

I looked at the door beside the big fireplace. That must be the one leading to my room, I decided, and opened it. I was right. Before me was a narrow staircase with steep steps and walls so close that only one person could be on it at a time. It was dark and some of the wooden steps were loose, but I made my way up, and when I opened the door at the top a flood of light welcomed me into my room. Next time I would leave my door open. Then I would be able to see. I didn't know then that I would be using it at night.

Back down in the kitchen, dressed in my gingham school frock, I waited for Grandmère.

'Ah, Eleanor,' she said, coming in from the yard outside. 'You are ready?'

'Yes.'

'Mm . . .' She looked at me critically for a moment and I nervously smoothed down some of the creases in my skirt. 'Come with me.'

I followed her down the corridor to the two doors.

'This is my sitting room; next door I have my bedroom,' she said and then added with a hint of resignation or perhaps regret, 'In the old days our housekeeper lived here but . . . times have changed. Now I live down here.'

She ushered me into the room. It was a little parlour, with two soft chairs covered in red velvet and a round table with a plush cloth. The only light in the room came from a tiny window and after the brightness of the kitchen it took a moment for my eyes to adjust. I thought that it would be cosy in here on a winter evening with a fire in the little tiled grate and the lamps lit. Much more so than the formal salon which I'd seen opening off the hall.

'You need something to cover your hair,' said Grandmère. 'It's what women must do in church.' She was wearing a flat black straw hat which was held on her head by a large pin. The end of the pin had a black stone which matched the black beads round her neck. My heart sank. Surely she wasn't going to find me a hat like that?

'Look in that drawer,' she commanded, pointing to a wooden cabinet pushed against the wall. 'The top one. I think I have a piece of lace in there and that will be perfect for you.' She turned away and looked around the room. 'Now, where have I put my prayer book?'

While she bent down to look through the books and newspapers on the table I cautiously opened the drawer and peered inside. It was full of documents and photographs and, surprisingly, an old-fashioned baby's white leather boot, but I couldn't see any lace.

'I can't see a piece of lace,' I said.

'It must be underneath the other things. Push them aside.'

I grabbed a handful of papers and holding them in one hand rooted about with the other. The little boot fell on the floor.

'That was Étienne's,' said Grandmère, coming over and picking it up. 'Oh, he was a lovely baby. So plump, so healthy. My only child . . . that lived.'

I didn't know what to say but continued to search. Suddenly my hand touched a piece of fabric.

'I've got it,' I said and withdrew a prettily worked piece of black lace.

'Good,' said Grandmère. 'You can put that over your hair when you go into church.' She handed me the little kid boot. 'Now, put all those things away and let's go. Étienne is waiting in the yard. Mathilde and Jean Paul have already walked on.'

She picked up her prayer book and started for the door, and eager to hurry I started to stuff the documents and the boot back in the drawer. In my haste, some papers slipped out of my hand and scattered on the floor.

'Oh dear,' I said and bent to pick them up.

'Quick!' said Grandmère from the corridor.

'Yes. Sorry.' I dropped to my knees and started to gather the papers, but my eye was caught by one yellowing sheet and despite my determination to hurry I stopped to stare at it.

It was a newspaper cutting with a photograph showing a semicircle of people gathered together in what looked like a town square. Peering closer I saw the semicircle was made up of men, some of whom were laughing and one or two looking at the camera and pointing to other people in the centre of the group.

The light in Grandmère's parlour was dim so I couldn't see properly what the picture showed and I held it up to examine it more closely. How strange, I thought, looking at the semicircle of men. Their laughter seemed forced and their faces mocking not joyful. I turned my attention to the central figures. Suddenly, the paper was snatched out of my hand.

Grandmère was standing above me. 'Put everything back, Eleanor,' she said quietly, and when I looked up her eyes were steely and frightening.

We walked to church. The village was only about half a mile down the dusty lane and we strolled along, Étienne and Grandmère on either side of me and Lisette, her earlier tears forgotten, skipping along behind us.

Ahead I could see Mathilde and Jean Paul. They walked close together, their shoulders almost touching, and every now and then Jean Paul would bend down and say something into Mathilde's ear. After one remark he looked back at our group and I knew he'd said something about me. I stole a look at Étienne, wondering if he'd caught the look, but he was gazing at the fields across the hedge.

He was wearing a suit this morning, the one I'd seen hanging from the wardrobe in the room closest to mine. It was grey with thin pale stripes through it and like his jacket yesterday appeared to be strained at the seams. I guessed that this suit came out only for formal occasions and he was more comfortable in his working clothes. My father wore the same clothes every day. Grey slacks and a tweed jacket. I didn't know if he had anything else. But Dada always wore a shirt and tie, the shirt collar loose round his neck as though it had been bought for a larger man and the neat brown woollen tie tucked in between the third and fourth buttons of his shirt.

Étienne wasn't wearing a tie with his shirt this morning and his top button was open showing his strong tanned neck. He turned round from his contemplation of the fields where the fat blonde cows were grazing and caught me staring.

'Well, Miss Eleanor, are you settling in?'

'Yes,' I mumbled, embarrassed to have been caught. 'Thank you.'

'I was looking to see if there are any breaks in the fence. One of the cows got out this morning. My neighbour brought her back. And then I must think about cutting the grass over there.' He waved his arm towards the pasture. 'For hay, for the cattle. Do you understand?'

'Oh yes.' I knew about winter feed although we didn't do much of it. Mother usually bought in turnips which were cheaper than hay. It was only when the winter had been especially hard that she resorted to hay. Most of the time our flock had to fend for themselves.

'Your father cuts hay, yes?'

'No. We have a hill farm. Mother has sheep. There is no pasture, just hillside. Sometimes we give the sheep . . .' I searched my brain for the French for turnips but I couldn't find it. 'Er . . . a vegetable . . . I'm sorry, I don't know the word.'

He smiled. 'Your French is very good, Miss Eleanor. Perhaps you mean *les navets*?'

'I think so.'

'You said your mother has sheep? Is she the farmer?' Grandmère asked, as we walked along.

'Yes. She inherited it from her parents. Dada doesn't . . .' I wondered how to put it. 'My father was a newspaper reporter before the war and since then he has been . . . ill. Mother has to do it all.'

We had reached the village square, a large cobbled space surrounded by houses and one or two shops. Arched arcades fronted the buildings and I could see a few people lingering beneath them in the shade, waiting for the last moment before going in to church. Some of them called greetings to Étienne and Grandmère and greetings were called back. I noticed that I was being stared at but not unpleasantly and no doubt, after church, the family would be questioned.

Mathilde and Jean Paul had gone on ahead towards the church, which dominated one whole side of the square. It was huge, much bigger than the church in the village nearest to our house, and was built of the same pale stone as the other buildings in the area. A statue of the Madonna and child stood on a stone plinth to the left of the first entrance step, the plinth decorated by little vases of wax flowers. The statue was painted in dazzlingly bright colours, red cheeks on chalk white skin and blue and gold on the Madonna's robes. The gold crowns that the Madonna and child both wore glittered in the morning sun. One or two people crossed themselves as they passed the statue and I bit my lip. I had no idea what I was supposed to do.

A bell was pealing, calling the worshippers, and as we approached the steps that led up to the great wooden doors several people hurried up behind us.

I paused on the top step to look back over the square and realised with an uneasy jolt that this was the place pictured in that newspaper clipping. Were any of the men who had called out to Étienne this morning the same as the laughing people in the photograph? Suddenly, I felt uncomfortable and homesick. Our cold little hillside might have been bleak but it was familiar and at that moment I wanted to be there.

Chapter Five

It was cool and echoing inside the large pale stone church. The sound of footsteps on the tiled floor struck sharply over the quiet murmured responses of the worshippers but it didn't matter. It sounded right.

I sat next to Grandmère at the end of the row beside the central aisle. Lisette sat between Étienne and Mathilde, whilst at the far end Jean Paul shuffled noisily in his seat. Once, when he'd been particularly noisy, Grandmère leant over and smacked his hand with her little black prayer book.

'Ow!' His smooth cheeks coloured fiercely and snarling stupidly he gave her an insolent look. I sneaked a look at him along the pew and to my alarm the look was transferred to me.

So far this morning this was the first time he'd acknowledged my presence. Neither he nor Mathilde had spoken to me as we came into the church. Jean Paul had leant against the huge entrance door, kicking at a tuft of dry grass which poked up between the stone flags, while beside him Mathilde ground out her cigarette beneath her neat high-heeled shoe.

'Good morning,' I'd said when I reached them. I was determined to take the initiative today and forget about being shy. After all, I had been seventeen for several days now and consequently nearly an adult. If my English reserve was the reason for their coolness then from now on I would start to alter their opinion of me. 'It's a lovely day,' I added and smiled at them both, hoping that they would see that I wanted to be friendly.

It made no difference. My effort came to nothing and I might as well not have bothered because neither mother nor son deigned to reply. Jean Paul didn't even look up from his feet and Mathilde merely turned her head and gave me a long cool look. I felt my cheeks burning and my palms, already hot from the walk to the village, were suddenly slippery with sweat. I couldn't think how I had offended them.

Out of the corner of my eye I saw Grandmère's strong fingers clutch at Étienne's jacket sleeve as though to prevent him from raising his hand. The tension in the family was palpable and with a sinking heart I realised that I was causing it. Tears pricked at the corners of my eyes. I wanted to go home.

'Put the lace on your head, Eleanor.' I was startled by Grandmère's firm voice as she came to stand beside me. Then she added, 'We'll go in now.'

At school, we went en masse to the cathedral every year for our dedication service and for various Christian festivals. Added to that, we had assembly each morning with prayers and a hymn so I was quite familiar with the Book of Common Prayer and Hymns Ancient and Modern, but nothing I saw or heard that first Sunday in France bore any resemblance to any service I'd experienced before.

We sat halfway down the aisle on a polished pew. Grandmère had curtsied to the altar when we went in but Étienne ushered me forward, understanding, I think, that this form of worship was foreign to me. Mathilde made a brief nod with her head but nothing more and Jean Paul didn't bother at all. Grandmère was holding Lisette's arm and pushing her towards the pew and I guessed that she was preventing the child from making some sort of show.

Two priests led the service, assisted by altar boys, and I watched, fascinated, as they swung the incense and read out the prayers. I couldn't understand what they were saying at first and then I realised that they were chanting in Latin and began to pick out the odd word. We did Latin at school and I was quite good at it.

The wall behind the altar was painted a brilliant blue dotted with yellow stars in a sort of arch with a huge silver star at its apex. I gazed at it and then allowed my eyes to wander, picking out statues and plaques placed in the walls and stands of candles and so much else to see that it seemed more like a religious department store than a church. I loved it.

Jean Paul obviously didn't. He squirmed and shuffled in his seat, the most animated I'd seen him since my arrival. I stole another look at him and saw that he was fiddling with the feather that drooped from Mathilde's green hat. Mathilde pretended to ignore him but I could see a little twist of her lips that meant she was amused. He saw it too and suddenly let out a high-pitched giggle.

That was too much for Étienne. He raised his head from his rosary and glowered at his son. 'Shut up!' he growled. 'In the name of Christ, behave yourself.'

It made a small difference. Scowling but now quiet, Jean Paul leant back against the pew and gazed up to the ceiling, deliberately ignoring the rest of the service and rudely pursing his lips in a silent whistle.

The pews filled up, people coming and going all the time, their shoes clipping sharply upon the stone flags. The priests ignored them and carried on saying Mass, and my fascination with the proceedings started to fade.

A young family occupied the seats immediately in front of me, mother, father and a little boy who sat on his father's knee. At one point he struggled to his feet and stood staring over his father's shoulder directly at me. A quick glance down the pew assured me that my family were all looking directly ahead so I wiggled my fingers at the baby and made a little face. The child stared at me for a moment and then his face creased. For a horrified moment I thought I had made him cry and waited in trepidation for the wail that would surely ensue. But to my relief the creased face was followed by a delighted smile and he let out a noisy crow of pleasure and banged his little fists on his father's serge-covered shoulder. His papa, shushing him indulgently, gently pulled him down back on his knee and I returned to examining the architecture and decoration of the church. After a bit the baby peeped at me round his father's arm and I hid my eyes behind Grandmère's piece of lace and poked out my tongue. This time the baby's laugh caused his father to look round and, embarrassed, I hastily took to studying the ceiling, not unlike Jean Paul. When I dared to look along the pew again I caught Étienne's eye. He was grinning at me.

The furnace blast which met us as we came out of the church caused me to step back under the arched entrance for a moment. I could smell the heat from the buildings and the stifling air which wafted up from the river.

'It is very hot today,' said Grandmère sympathetically. 'You're not used to it, Eleanor?'

'No. Sorry,' I apologised foolishly, and taking off my lace head scarf I followed her into the square. It was busy with people mingling and chatting to each other as they left the church and I could see Étienne in conversation with a couple and a boy. I recognised him as the boy who had been in the yard that morning with Étienne and the older man.

'Come,' said Grandmère. 'I will introduce you to our friends.'

They were Monsieur and Madame d'Amboise, he a farmer like Étienne and Madame d'Amboise a teacher at the village school. They shook hands with me enthusiastically and welcomed me to the community.

'Are you enjoying your visit?' asked Madame d'Amboise.

'Yes, thank you,' I said. 'Although I am finding things very strange.'

Was it my imagination or did the couple give each other a quick glance?

'I mean,' I said quickly, anxious that I shouldn't be giving the wrong impression, 'I mean that I'm not used to the food, nor the hot weather. And my French isn't very good.'

'Monsieur Martin tells me that your French is excellent,' said Madame d'Amboise kindly, 'and would put even teachers like me to shame.' She looked fondly at the boy standing beside her. 'My Luc has practically no English. He should study more.'

I smiled at Luc and he shook my hand. 'How are you,'

he said formally and I gave him a formal reply. He was a few inches taller than me and had brown hair and a narrow clever face like his mother. When he smiled his face softened and he looked younger.

'Luc is in school with Jean Paul,' said Monsieur d'Amboise. 'He is studying to be a doctor.' This last was said with great pride and he beamed with obvious pleasure.

I looked around, wondering if Jean Paul would finally join in the conversation now that we were with one of his contemporaries, but he was nowhere to be seen. Turning in the other direction I caught sight of him walking quickly with Mathilde towards the road which led to Riverain. Lisette was trailing behind them, not really keeping up but wandering along in her own private world. When I looked back again, Luc was still smiling and I smiled too.

'You must come round one evening, all of you, and Eleanor can tell you how she's getting on,' said Grandmère. 'She can tell you about her parents' farm. It is on a hill.'

'A hill!' Monsieur d'Amboise pursed his lips. 'Not dairy then.'

'Sheep,' I said.

'Difficult creatures, I believe. They need a lot of care.'

I nodded. Mother certainly grumbled enough about them and always looked exhausted. The thought struck me then that perhaps I didn't help her enough, and there in that pretty French square, with the July heat burning the tiny hairs off my bare arms and the backs of my legs, I felt mean. Mother never had a holiday.

Grandmère took my arm. 'We must go and prepare lunch.'

'Me, also,' said Madame d'Amboise. 'Marie is coming from Angers with the children.'

We walked home, just the two of us. Étienne and Monsieur d'Amboise had gone to the bar in the square and Luc had gone home with his mother.

'Marie is the d'Amboises' daughter. She is about ten years older than Luc and sadly her husband was killed in a road accident three years ago, just before her little boy was born. She has a daughter too, the same age as Lisette.' Grandmère sighed and fanned her face with her prayer book. 'It has been hard for her, bringing up the children on her own, and Édith d'Amboise is hoping she'll come back to live in the village. But then,' Grandmère shrugged, a gesture I came to know well, 'is it not a comfort to know that there is always someone with worse troubles than us?'

'Yes,' I said, not giving a thought to what her troubles might be but only wondering who I knew at home who had a harder life than me.

There was no sign of Mathilde or Jean Paul when we got back to the farm but Lisette was sitting on the bridge over the river with her dollies. 'Naughty Jacques,' her little voice sang. 'Naughty Angélique.'

'Lisette! Go and change out of that dress. This minute!' Grandmère called, and turning to me she said, 'And you'd better do the same, Eleanor.' Her stern face relaxed for a moment. 'You did well this morning. Keep the lace for your next visit to church.'

I have it still.

Our lunch was roast chicken smothered in herbs and so aromatic that my mouth watered as Grandmère put it on the table. To start our meal she had served soup, which I came to learn they had every day before their main meal, but today tiny pink things floated in the liquid and I stared at them, not entirely sure what they were.

'Do you like shrimps?' asked Étienne. He had taken off his suit jacket and rolled up his shirt sleeves before sitting at his place. I could smell the alcohol on him and beads of sweat had gathered on his forehead, which he wiped away with the back of his hand.

'I don't know,' I said. 'I've never had a shrimp.'

The family paused, their spoons halfway to their mouths, but only Lisette spoke. 'Shrimps are little fish,' she announced importantly. 'Very little.'

I tried one, taking a gulp of the pale orangey soup with it in case, but to my relief it was delicious. 'Really nice,' I said. I hoped that the relief didn't sound in my voice. Étienne grinned and Grandmère gave her careful smile.

'Good,' she said. 'I thought you'd like it. My secret is that I put tarragon and lemon thyme with it.'

I had no idea then what she was talking about. I'd never heard of tarragon or lemon thyme and I mentally searched my French vocabulary for a match. Later, I picked both for Grandmère and many other herbs too and learned to rub them through my fingers as she did whilst imagining how they would flavour the meals we planned.

Neither Mathilde nor Jean Paul joined in the conversation, although they had looked at each other with raised eyebrows before continuing with their meal. Mathilde never spoke at meal times and Jean Paul only when made to by his father or grandmother. These were difficult conversations, generally descending into embarrassing shouting matches which, strangely, like Lisette, I hated but learned to accept. But that was later. On this hot Sunday he was silent.

'I like shrimps,' said Lisette, nodding at me across the table.

'So do I,' I said. 'They are a delicious discovery.' My French was stretched with this sentence but I was glad I tried for Lisette gleefully repeated 'delicious discovery' and laughed.

'What sort of food do you have at home?' Grandmère asked. 'Jean Paul will have to know what to expect.'

I looked at him. We had finished the soup and now he was shovelling chicken and tiny buttered potatoes into his mouth, barely stopping for breath. 'Meat and potatoes,' I offered, 'sometimes sausages and chips and bacon. That sort of stuff.' It sounded pathetic compared to the couple of exquisite meals I'd enjoyed so far and my excuse was worse. 'Mother doesn't have much time to cook.'

How could I explain that she also slapped the food on the table having taken as little interest in its preparation as possible. That she had grubby hands and that our plates were chipped and we served ourselves from the saucepans on the stove. My heart sank.

'I had bacon and eggs in England.' Étienne poured wine into all our glasses. 'It was good. I liked it.' He drained his glass and poured himself another. 'And fish and chips. That's what they eat in England. D'you have that?'

I nodded. 'Yes, we do.'

That afternoon I walked across the rickety bridge and through the trees to the vineyard. Each vine shrub was held by wire to a post and more guiding wires led along the rows. Several small bunches of dark green grapes hung from every plant, each individual grape no larger than a pearl, and I wondered when they would be ready for harvest. I touched the nearest bunch, curious to know what it felt like, and as I'd guessed the grapes were hard and didn't give between my finger and thumb. Now I needed to taste one and guiltily glanced back towards the house for a quick look before slyly pulling a few of the immature grapes from the nearest bunch.

'They'll be very sour.'

The voice from beside me gave me such a fright that the tiny grapes I'd popped into my mouth got stuck in my throat and I choked and coughed while I worked desperately to locate and swallow them.

'Oh, sorry.' The voice was now apologetic and I turned to see a faintly amused Luc d'Amboise standing in the row of vines.

'Sorry,' he repeated, walking towards me. 'I didn't mean to startle you.' The grin on his narrow face belied the concern in his voice.

'I just wondered what they tasted like,' I muttered. I knew that my cheeks were flooding scarlet and I could feel the hard little grapes lodged halfway down my gullet. The ways in which I showed myself to be an idiot seemed to be endless. 'I've never seen them growing before. I don't think they grow in England.'

I didn't add that we didn't eat them either, or at least not at home. I'd only ever had grapes at Suzy's house where a succulent-looking bunch was always draped on top of the fruit bowl. When I'd mentioned that fruit bowl to mother she'd done one of her usual dismissive snorts. Foreign and a waste of money, had been her verdict. What was wrong with apples?

Luc seemed to consider what I'd said. 'I think the Romans grew them in England once but it isn't warm enough there now. You must come back in September. They'll be ready then. Although Monsieur Martin grows for wine so they won't be as tasty as ours. Papa grows for the table. You would love them.'

I sighed. 'I'll be in England then.'

He must have caught something in my words, a bitterness, a lack of hope maybe, I don't know. But he suddenly put his hand out and touched my arm and I felt like crying.

'Where's your house?' I asked quickly, swallowing the lump of homesickness, or whatever it was that had overwhelmed me.

Luc lifted his arm and waved it towards the hill. I noticed for the first time that he had a book in his hand and felt an immediate kinship. 'You can't see it from here,' he said, 'but it's over there, the other side of Monsieur Martin's vineyard. I was walking on the hill when I saw you.' He smiled. 'Come and see, and have a cup of coffee with Maman. She would like that. And you can meet my sister and her children.'

'I don't think I can,' I said. 'The Martins might think I was being rude. You know, er . . . going off without telling them.'

Luc nodded. 'That's all right. You can come over another time.'

I was relieved. 'What's your book?'

He laughed and held it out so I could read the title.

Le Comte de Monte-Cristo was inscribed on the spine. 'Have you read it?'

I shook my head.

'I've read it many times,' he said. 'It's one of my favourites and I know almost every line by heart. But still I go back to it.'

'I have books like that,' I said, and we grinned at each other.

As we talked we were strolling through the vines towards the top of the hill. Ahead was the barn that I had noticed from my bedroom window. The afternoon sun shimmered on its red tiled roof and I saw that although the shutters were closed the wooden door swung slightly in the wind.

'Is that a house?' I asked.

'No, it's Monsieur Martin's grape barn. It's for storage and I think there's an old press inside. He doesn't use it though, now. His grapes go to the co-operative. We have one just like it.'

A grape barn and a grape press. I was thrilled. This would be something I could write about in the essay that, no doubt, Miss Baxter would expect when the new term started.

'Oh,' I said, excitement bubbling into my voice, 'I would love to see that.'

Luc stopped and bent to tie the lace on his brown shoe. 'I don't think you should go in there,' he said carefully. 'The machinery might be in a bad way and dangerous.'

'But you could come inside with me.' As soon as I said it I realised how forward I was being and that dreadful blush which I could never control flooded my face again.

'I mean, couldn't I just look through the door . . . it's open.'

He straightened up. 'Sorry,' he said, 'I have to go now. My father will need me to help him and I want to see my sister before she leaves.'

It was a rebuff and I didn't know why. Was it my wanting him to go to the barn with me, or to pay me back for refusing to visit his mother? A girl might have done that – some of them were like that at school – but I was confused. I didn't know about boys and how they behaved. He raised a hand and strode off up the hill and I stood like a foolish child and watched him.

The sun blazed down and sweat or perhaps tears beaded on my face as I turned and slowly made my way back through the vines. The trees which stood between me and the river made a welcome area of shade and I sat down on a stump to wipe my face before crossing the bridge. I hated the thought that Étienne or, worse, Mathilde would see I'd been crying. I hadn't really.

My sandals were sticking to the soles of my feet because after lunch I'd taken off my socks in an effort to get cool, but now I was sorry. The leather insoles were rough and I was sure that when I removed my sandals my feet would be stained brown. I wished that I had other shoes, plimsolls perhaps, like the ones Grandmère wore. They would definitely be more comfortable.

A distant sound caught my ear. It was a door slamming and I looked across the river to the house, expecting to see Lisette or Étienne coming over the bridge, but no one appeared. Puzzled, I stood up. I turned to look back and to my astonishment I recognised the figure of Mathilde in her olive green dress walking downhill through the vines. The door to the grape barn was now shut and on the top of the hill I could see Luc. He was standing there watching her.

I shrank into the trees, appalled at the prospect of her seeing me and thinking that I had been spying. Quietly I slipped away from the bridge and crept a few yards down the river bank until I was in a sheltered little grove of grey-leaved alders. After a few minutes I heard her footsteps on the bridge and even then I waited while my thoughts tumbled over each other as possibilities raced around my mind. What on earth could Mathilde have been doing in the barn? And had Luc known she was in there and not wanted me to see her?

The footsteps stopped and cautiously I looked through the trees and saw that she had paused on the bridge. She had turned her head and was looking back at the vineyard. I followed her eyes. There was someone else on the hill now, not Luc, but a man I didn't recognise. He was too far away to see clearly but I knew from the way he walked that it wasn't Étienne or even Jean Paul.

I looked back to Mathilde. She had put her hand up and was smoothing her hair but as I watched her fingers left her head and moved in a little wave towards the hill. Like a tennis match watcher my eyes swivelled back to the hill. The man had gone.

Half an hour later, when I walked across the bridge back to the house seeking the relative security of my room, my head was still whirling. I needed time to think and I was lucky. The house was quiet and I met no one as I went through the rear door into the empty kitchen. I took a glass from the cupboard and filled it with water.

I'll drink this, I thought, and go upstairs. My room will be cool and I will be able to think properly.

'Ah, Eleanor.' I jumped and nearly dropped the glass. Grandmère appeared from the door to the back corridor. She stared hard at me. 'Are you not well?'

'I'm fine,' I said quickly. 'Just hot. I'm not used to temperatures like this. It's much cooler at home.'

'The weather is hot,' she conceded, 'more so than usual. Étienne is concerned about the grapes.'

'I went to the vineyard just now,' I said, draining the glass. 'I was surprised at how very dusty the ground seemed. At home we have a lot of rain. The fields are wet all the time.'

She watched me as I rinsed the glass under the tap and put it to dry on the board. 'Did you see anybody on your little walk?'

I nodded.

Her face didn't change, but was there a hint of annoyance in the way she picked up the poker and riddled the ashes in the range? 'Who?' she asked. 'Who did you meet?'

'Oh, it was Luc,' I said. 'Luc d'Amboise. He was in the vineyard. I think he'd been on the hill reading his book and saw me. We talked for a while but then he had to go and help his father.'

'He's a nice boy . . . a good scholar. A boy that any parent would be proud of.'

Then, I didn't connect her kind words about Luc with her disappointment in Jean Paul. But now it is so obvious. Jean Paul had nothing praiseworthy about him.

Grandmère stopped her vigorous riddling and turned back to me. 'I'm sure your parents are proud of you too.'

Proud? I didn't think so. Mother thought I was pretty useless and turning into a snob and who knew what Dada thought. Although he had given me the money to come on the exchange. So he must love me in his own way, mustn't he?

I smiled. 'I don't know,' I said shyly. 'We don't talk like that at home. Besides, Mother wouldn't want me to get a swelled head.'

'No,' said Grandmère. 'Pride is a foolish emotion. It leads a person along a dangerous path.'

Chapter Six

Grandmère's words came back to me as I lay on my bed miserably turning the pages of my book. She used extravagant expressions, I decided, and perhaps this was old French. Country French, maybe.

It was the following day and I had spent the morning with Jean Paul and his friends in the little town and had returned at lunch time in despair. Now, in my lovely white room, I went over all the events of my brief stay. It was an uncomfortable exercise. No one had really welcomed me, except perhaps Étienne. Grandmère and Lisette accepted my presence but Mathilde and Jean Paul were openly unfriendly. As far as they were concerned I was an interloper, an unwanted stranger in the house.

Had I noticed that they all loathed each other, then? That there was a poisonous atmosphere in the house? No. I don't think so. I was wrapped in my own misery and could only think that it was me who had caused the difficulty.

The morning had started well. I was down earlier for breakfast than I had been the day before, having slept deeply and awoken fresh and ready for an adventure. In the calm of a new day the events in the vineyard of the afternoon before seemed petty. I'd misunderstood, I decided, and as I brushed my hair in front of the mirror on the carved wardrobe I smiled impatiently at myself.

Fancy hiding in the trees in case Mathilde saw me. Whatever could I have been thinking?

'Good morning, Eleanor,' said Grandmère and as I nodded back I saw that Jean Paul was sitting at the table. I had entered the kitchen from the back stairs and, feeling more confident than the night before, walked straight to the larder to get the butter and apricot preserve.

'Hello,' I greeted them and took bread from the board and poured coffee into the white bowl that had been put out for me. 'It's another lovely day.'

'You look well today,' said Grandmère, 'and we have a little treat for you. Jean Paul is going to take you to meet his friends.'

I should have known. If I'd looked more carefully at his sullen face and the way he wouldn't meet my eyes I'd have guessed that this was a forced expedition. The hint of steel in Grandmère's voice should also have alerted me but it didn't.

Foolishly I was pleased. At last, I thought, I'll get to meet people of my own age. Jean Paul and I will become friends. 'Thank you,' I said. 'It sounds like fun.'

He said nothing and continued to crumble a crust of bread into little balls on the table. It was hot in the kitchen and a film of sweat beaded his upper lip, darkening the burgeoning moustache. I glanced at him out of the corner of my eye while I drank my bowl of coffee. 'Will Luc d'Amboise be there? I already know him.'

For the first time he looked up. 'No, of course not.' It was said in a pitying way as though I should have known and I immediately felt embarrassed again.

'Can you ride a bicycle, Eleanor?' Grandmère came to sit beside me at the table, interposing her solid body between me and Jean Paul. Her black blouse was open at the neck and her sleeves rolled up ready for the day's work and I remembered Mother's instructions about not being a nuisance.

'Yes, I can. Do you want me to go on a message for you?'

'No. Nothing like that. You'll need the cycle to get into town with Jean Paul. He has his *vélo* cycle and you can borrow Mathilde's ordinary one.'

Lisette came into the kitchen with an armful of dolls. 'Can I go with them? I want to. I can sit on the crossbar.'

'No,' said Grandmère and Jean Paul at the same time, and the little girl pouted. Clutching the dolls, she turned and went back into the hall the way she had come in. I found myself wishing that she could have accompanied us.

At the café where Jean Paul's friends gathered, I was greeted with curiosity at first and a small effort at politeness.

'Cigarette?' Guy, a scrawny seventeen-year-old, pushed one across the small metal table towards me.

'No thank you.' I smiled, keen to be friendly. 'I don't smoke.'

The group laughed. There were five of them, three boys and two girls, and Jean Paul settled easily amongst them. For the first time I saw him laugh, responding to something one of the other boys said. The remark was repeated behind a cupped hand to the others and they looked at me and laughed too.

'D'you want a beer?' A waiter who had shuffled out from behind the bar stood beside me. He had a dirty green apron wrapped around his black trousers and wore a white shirt which was grubby at the collar. A thin cigarette drooped from between his lips.

'I don't know,' I said. 'I've never had a beer.'

This drew more laughter from the group and too embarrassed to ask for a soft drink I nodded a yes to the waiter. I should try, I told myself. Everyone else was drinking it and they'll think me stuck up or babyish if I don't. When the beer came, golden and fizzing in a tall glass, I took a tentative sip. I didn't like it. It remained untouched on the round white table until we left.

The two girls had short dark hair, clipped close in a *gamin* style which I found very attractive. They looked cool and modern and I wondered if I dared to cut mine. Because of the heat in this little bar my hairline was already damp with sweat and my ponytail felt heavy and uncomfortable where it touched the back of my neck.

Under the pixie-styled hair, Gabrielle and Danni had almost identical faces, little pointed chins and sculpted cheekbones.

'Are you two sisters?' I asked when one of them stopped talking and turned to face me.

'Sisters?' Danni snorted. 'Of course not.' Her feigned anger was cause for more sniggers and I looked at Jean Paul, hoping he would say something. But he was giggling too and I squirmed on the metal seat, already wanting to run out of the café and cycle away.

The other girl, Gabrielle, stared at me. 'Is that the fashion in England?' she asked, nodding towards my blue and white gingham dress. She and Danni wore tight sleeveless black jumpers and narrow skirts with slits up the side.

'No.' I shook my head. I was going to add that this was my school uniform dress but thought better of it and avoiding their sneering gaze dropped my head. That made things worse. I caught sight of my feet, bare in buckled sandals. They looked impossibly childish.

'Well,' Gabrielle demanded. 'What is the fashion?'

What could I say? I had no idea. The girls talked about clothes in school and discussed the latest styles all the time but somehow it had passed over my head. Mother wore almost the same clothes every day and I lived in my books where the heroines were dressed in a variety of costumes from the empire style of Jane Austen through Victorian crinolines to the thirties and forties of the modern writers. Desperately I dragged an image of Phyllis Franklin into my mind. 'Longer skirts and tight waists,' I said hopelessly. Then, remembering something Suzy had said, I added, 'I think it's called the New Look.' Suzy had been talking about that for ages although I wasn't really sure what she meant.

The girls nodded. They'd heard of that too and I was relieved but not for long. 'Your dress isn't New Look,' said Gabrielle with a sneer. 'It's like a kid's frock.'

'So, how old are you?' Danni asked, barely restraining a smirking grin.

'Seventeen.'

They all laughed again. One of the boys sniggered and not bothering to whisper spoke to Jean Paul in rapid French. I caught a few words. '. . . old enough, *mon brave* . . . and pink meat . . .'

The laughter became hysterical and the ones who had been holding bottles of Stella to their mouths choked and spluttered beer down their shirts and over the table.

I thought I must have missed something, and still trying to be polite looked for help to Jean Paul, hoping he would explain the joke, but now he wasn't sniggering. He was blushing fiercely and had turned his head away.

Nobody bothered with me after that and for the remaining hour I sat listening to their conversation and smiling inanely as I tried to be part of their youthful group. Jean Paul turned his back to me and spoke mainly to the boy called Guy. At one point they rolled up their shirt sleeves to the shoulder and compared muscles, each squeezing the other's biceps. Jean Paul's arms were twice the size of Guy's.

'It's hard work on the farm,' said Jean Paul proudly. 'You grow strong.'

Guy grinned. 'You? Work? Not what I hear.'

Suddenly the mood changed. I learned over the coming days and had probably guessed already that Jean Paul couldn't bear to be criticised. His face darkened. 'Well at least I don't mess about with my little sister,' he snarled.

There was an intake of breath from the group as though something of importance had been said. I looked from one boy to another and then at the girls. They were grinning excitedly and Danni put her mouth to Gabrielle's ear and whispered something that made her companion explode into laughter.

'What did you say?' bellowed Jean Paul, his cheeks burning. 'What?'

'Nothing.' Danni struggled to disguise her grin but Gabrielle wasn't so contained. Her laughter continued and in between gasps repeated what Danni had said to the boys. I was bewildered. She had said that it was better than messing around with one's mother.

Jean Paul stood up, throwing the metal chair in which he'd been lounging to one side. He shot a furious glance at me and shouted, 'Come on, we're going.'

He cycled home on his motorised bike at full speed, leaving me pedalling like a maniac trying to keep up with him.

'Wait,' I called. 'Wait.' He ignored me and eventually I gave up and left him to cycle away and rode slowly through the pretty lanes where the green smell of wild herbs and flowers filled the air. It gave me time to go over the scenes in the café. There was much I didn't understand and I was sure it wasn't only my lack of French. If these were Jean Paul's friends it was no wonder he seemed permanently angry: they had teased him almost as much as they had me. And at home the only person he got on with was his mother so it wasn't surprising that he spent so much time with her.

One thing I was absolutely sure of. I was just as bad at connecting with people in France as I had been at home. It was me, not them, and it was turning into another disastrous day. No friendship with Jean Paul, and the rest of the family too busy with their own lives to pay me any attention. The three weeks of my proposed stay stretched endlessly ahead and I would have nothing to tell Suzy. I shuddered at the prospect of Mother meeting Jean Paul. And poor Dada. He would be so frightened.

Grandmère was waiting for me in the kitchen when I walked in. 'Did you have a good time?' she asked, her back to me as she chopped vegetables for the soup.

'Yes, thank you,' I answered but there must have been something in my voice because she turned round and gave me a long cool look.

She started to say something but checked herself and returned to the onions and carrots on her chopping board. 'We'll have lunch in half an hour,' she murmured. 'Perhaps you would like to have a rest until then.'

I left the kitchen and went up the back stairs to my room. I was angry with her too. I don't want a rest, I raged to myself. I'm not an invalid or something. At that moment I hated them all, and when Grandmère called me for lunch I excused myself. 'I have a headache,' I called down the kitchen stairs. 'Do you mind if I stay in my room?'

Now, lying on my bed after another fruitless afternoon of reading and daydreaming, I was restless. I got up and went to the window and leaning on the sill gazed out. The heat of the day was dropping into the cornfields and shadows were lengthening. Birds twittered in the willows and somewhere over the fields a dog was barking, but out there beside the river all was still and lovely. The sight calmed me.

Étienne was standing on the bridge, fishing. The sweet strange perfume of his cigarette added to the odour of hay and cattle that wafted through the window and I stood half hidden by the slatted shutter and watched him.

During the day, he was always working. He went from one job to another the way Mother did, only stopping for mealtimes and then straight out again as long as it was light. I didn't find that unusual. It was how it should be on a farm. But now he looked relaxed and contented and I envied him. Here was a person who didn't seem to be troubled at all.

He threw the line again into the river, moving along the bridge to get into place, and I leant forward against the sill to follow his movements. Clumsily, I caught my arm on the old iron window latch causing it to clatter off its hook and scratch a thin bleeding line across my wrist.

'Oh!' I gasped and quickly put my arm to my mouth as I'd been taught as a child. Mother insisted that spit was the best thing for cuts.

My cry must have been louder than I thought for looking out again I saw that Étienne had turned round and was looking up at the house.

'Hello! Miss Eleanor, come and join me,' he called, and, embarrassed that he had caught me watching him, I hastily retreated behind the shutter. But he called again. 'Come on, help me catch the dinner.'

I had no choice.

'At last,' he said when I'd trailed through the house and garden to join him on the bridge. 'Do you like to fish?'

'I don't know,' I said. I felt shy. 'I've never tried it. The boys in the village fish in the reservoir.' I paused for a moment and then continued, 'People say it's dangerous.'

'Well,' he laughed, 'it is not dangerous here. Not if you can swim. Can you swim?'

I nodded. We had learned in school during our weekly visits to the town baths.

'Then you must swim in this river. I have always swum here. Since I was a boy.' He concentrated on the fishing line for a moment before giving a little grunt of satisfaction and starting to turn the reel.

'We have a bite,' he said, turning the reel faster and faster until, suddenly, a bright, leaping fish was jerked out of the water and slammed down beside my sandals on the wooden boards.

'Goodbye, my beauty,' he said, and hit the fish swiftly on the head with a wooden mallet. I was too surprised to be shocked and merely watched as Étienne rebaited the hook and cast the line back into the water.

Fascinated, I leant beside him on the bridge, inches away from his strong brown arms, and watched the float bobbing in the water. 'You do make it look so easy.'

Étienne grinned, his teeth startlingly white in his tanned face. 'Everything is,' he said. 'When you know how.'

The six trout that I later carried in triumphantly to Grandmère had been caught in less than an hour. 'Take these to *ma mère*,' Étienne said, gently placing the fish into a wooden box. 'She is in the kitchen waiting. I must do more work before my meal. I will see you at dinner.'

I took the box and started to walk back across the bridge. When I reached the end I paused and looked back. Étienne was gathering up his fishing gear and mallet and whistling a little tune. He looked healthy and strong and I found myself comparing him to Dada. Then I was cross with myself. Dada can't help how he is, part of my mind told me, but then the other part put the memory of Étienne's hands efficiently dispatching the hooked fish into my head and the comparison was shocking.

He looked up and caught me staring and I turned and stepped on to the grass bank.

'Miss Eleanor.'

I stopped again and looked over my shoulder. He was standing where I'd left him, unsmiling now as though he was thinking about something difficult. Oh God, I thought. How have I shown myself up now?

'Yes?' I whispered.

'I'll teach you to fish one day,' he said, and walked away towards the fields beyond the river.

My stay in France really began that evening when I took the trout into the kitchen.

'Ah, the fish, good,' said Grandmère, fastening her black apron around her skirt. 'Did you help to catch these?'

'No.' I shook my head. 'I just watched.'

'Well, they've got to be cleaned.' She got her big knife out of the drawer and then paused. 'Will you do that for me?'

I shuffled my feet uncomfortably. 'I don't know how to.'

'Mon Dieu!' Grandmère put the knife down on the scrubbed chopping block and stared at me. 'You don't know how? And you are seventeen years old?'

'Yes,' I agreed miserably. 'But we don't have fish . . . well, fish like this . . . ever.' I thought of the horrible fillets of greyish white coley that Mother bought from the travelling fish man every Friday. She steamed them between two enamel plates on top of the stove and like everything else she cooked it was done without any real effort. Even the fish we had at school was better than hers and I didn't like that. At home I could never finish my portion of coley and would cut some bread and fill up on that instead.

'A waste of good food,' Mother would grumble angrily. 'Anyone would think we were made of money.'

And now, watching as Grandmère tipped the trout out of the box into the shallow porcelain sink and turned on the tap, I groaned inwardly. The prospect of the meal ahead didn't fill me with any pleasure. I began to walk towards the door to the back stairs. I could read a few more pages of my book before supper time.

'Wait, Eleanor. I have made a decision. You must learn how to cook,' Grandmère said sternly. 'Then, at least, your stay with us will not have been a complete waste of time.'

Was it because I'd cleaned some of the fish, sliced the lemon and watched as Grandmère dropped chunks of butter into a huge black pan? I don't know. But that trout was glorious. From the smooth white flesh packed with herbs and flavoured with lemon to the ends of the tails, crisp and black where they had burnt in the butter, every mouthful was wonderful.

'It's good, isn't it?' said Étienne from the head of the table, watching me dissect out little bones and place choice pieces of fish into my mouth.

'Mm,' I mumbled and wiped a piece of bread around my plate to collect the last dregs of butter and herb sauce. 'Lovely.'

'Miss Eleanor helped me catch it.' Étienne grinned.

'She helped me cook it.' Grandmère's cool voice came from the other end and I smiled happily. It didn't matter that Mathilde and Jean Paul smirked at each other across the table and that Lisette wasn't listening but singing a little song; the two people who really mattered in the house had taken notice of me. 'Tomorrow you will learn to make soup and after that I'm going to show you the vegetable garden. You must understand herbs, it is most important.'

I finished mopping up my buttery fish sauce with a last piece of bread and wiped my mouth. 'Perhaps you will let me help with the chickens too. I'd love that.' I leant across Mathilde to address my remarks to Grandmère.

Was I too enthusiastic? Did the excitement in my voice upset Mathilde? Or maybe my leaning across invaded her closely guarded space. I don't know even now but I do remember the dismissive cackled laugh she gave and the deliberate way she pulled away from the nearness of my shoulder as though it was something dirty or unpleasant. Her even making a sound at mealtime was unusual but this obvious insult was sickening. When I looked across at Jean Paul I saw that his lip was curled in a horrible smirk.

I think my face turned scarlet and I remember flinching as though I'd been struck.

'What is it, Mathilde?' asked Étienne, his voice unnaturally quiet from beside me. 'What's so funny?'

The sunny evening light in the dining room seemed to have disappeared and the fish that I'd been enjoying so keenly started to curdle in my stomach. I waited, confused and embarrassed. Thoughts raced through my head. Perhaps it was nothing and she would laugh again and make a joke about my ignorance and all the family would join in and tease me. I wouldn't mind that. That would make me part of them which is what I wanted to be. But her sudden laugh hadn't sounded like a joke and I knew really that it wasn't.

Mathilde sat for a moment studying her plate. She had barely touched her fish. 'Nothing,' she said, 'it's nothing,' and scraping her chair back she stood up.

'There is dessert,' said Grandmère.

'No, thank you.' Mathilde's small voice was coldly polite and gathering up her packet of cigarettes and the paper book of matches which always sat on the table beside her she left the room.

Jean Paul put his napkin down and shuffled in his chair as though he was getting ready to follow her but Étienne growled, 'Sit, for Christ's sake!' and with a sulky face Jean Paul resumed his place.

We ate the *îles flottantes* which Grandmère had made in silence. Even Lisette had stopped her singing and my appetite, which had been stimulated by the wonderful trout, now disappeared. Getting the meringue pudding down was proving difficult and I longed for the meal to end. Étienne twitched with anger beside me and I could feel the heat emanating from his body. It was when he was pouring more wine into his glass that he turned to me.

'Did you enjoy your trip with Jean Paul?'

No, I hated every moment, I longed to say. His friends made fun of me and he ignored me. I pray that I never have to go anywhere with him again. But of course I didn't say that, instead I just nodded.

Étienne turned to Jean Paul. 'Where did you take her?'

Jean Paul shrugged. 'We met friends,' he muttered.

'What friends?'

'Guy and Henri and their friends.'

'Guy Daudet whose father sells stolen cars?'

Jean Paul shrugged again. 'That's only a rumour,' he said.

Étienne looked at Grandmère and spread his arms out wide. 'How is it that my stupid son will only mix with the dregs of the neighbourhood?'

She said nothing and when he looked at me I was careful not to meet his eyes. I didn't want to be part of the row. In truth, I was scared.

He transferred his eyes to Jean Paul. 'Listen to me and listen well. You will not take Eleanor to meet those "friends" again. She is supposed to be discovering the best of France, not the worst.'

Jean Paul wouldn't meet his father's eye either. 'All right,' he muttered.

'So.' Étienne drained his glass. 'Where will you take her?'

'I don't know.'

'Don't know? Don't know? Idiot.' Étienne slammed his hand on the table. 'Haven't you planned something? You've known about this for months.'

Suddenly Jean Paul leapt to his feet. His chair teetered on its back legs before crashing back down again and I watched appalled as he ran to the door.

'Shut up, Papa. Shut up. I'm not taking her anywhere,' he shouted as he went through into the hall. 'This was your idea, not mine. I don't care if I never see her ugly face again!'

'Bastard!' Étienne threw his chair back and bounded round the table.

God knows what might have happened had Grandmère not grabbed Étienne's arm as he drew level with her chair.

'Leave it, son,' she said, her voice firm. 'Leave it.'

It was later when I helped Grandmère clear the dishes that I noticed that Lisette was sitting under the table. She was clutching a doll close to her chest and her hazel eyes glistened with tears.

Chapter Seven

Lisette told me, a long time after, when we were both adults, that when she was little she'd been scared of Étienne but could never understand why. He was always pleasant to her and never once struck her although she'd seen him hit Jean Paul many times.

'Jean Paul deserved it,' I said sticking up as always for Étienne. 'He was a dreadful person.'

'Yes,' she said simply. 'I know.'

It was after that evening that I knew for certain that Jean Paul wouldn't come to England with me and I felt as though a huge boulder had been lifted from my shoulders. All the worries that had kept me awake at night in my lovely white room were wiped away and I slept easily.

He and Mathilde caused all the problems, I happily told myself, and it was nothing to do with me. Later, I realised that I should have been more concerned, that I was an interloper in this troubled household and probably the catalyst for what happened after. At the time, though, my freedom from Jean Paul was all that mattered. That and my friendship with Grandmère. Nothing was said but from that meal onwards I barely spoke to Jean Paul and life in the Martin household carried on as normal. I spent my time with Grandmère in the kitchen or garden and I was happy.

Jean Paul did speak to me once, properly. I was in

the garden one brilliant afternoon during the second week, picking beans. They grew low and were round and smooth and smelt green and earthy. I was bending down, tugging carefully at each individual bean so as not to pull up the whole plant, when suddenly he was behind me.

'Listen,' he said. His voice was unnaturally loud and harsh and it gave me a fright. I was so startled that I jumped up quickly up and a few of the beans dropped out of my hand on to the dusty ground.

'What?'

'I won't go to England with you, no matter what my father says.' The words burst out of his mouth without any preliminary greeting and as he spoke he kept looking over his shoulder. I looked too, wondering who was with him, but no one was about.

'Oh!' I collected my thoughts, which were as scattered as the beans. 'Well, all right,' I said slowly. 'If that's what you want, I don't mind.'

I tried a smile to reassure him. I didn't mind, not one little bit, and anyway I knew what his real feelings were. I still found him utterly loathsome but I thought a smile might ease the situation. For a moment it seemed that it had. He stopped looking over his shoulder and instead stared at me. His face was hot and sweaty as though he had been running and his blue shirt had damp circles at the armpits. He wiped his arm over his forehead and muttered, 'You're very English. Unfeeling and cold.' Then, after a while, 'I was told you would be.'

I supposed it was one of those girls at the café who'd said that. I knew they hadn't thought much of me.

'I'm not,' I protested. 'I mean, I am English, but I'm

only trying to make things easy for you. I know you don't want to come home with me. You've made that obvious.' I took a step towards him and held out my hand. 'We could be friends though.'

I thought he might take my hand because his face softened and he looked more relaxed. Then I heard sharp clicking footsteps on the flagged path that led around the house from the courtyard. Jean Paul jerked back and looked over his shoulder. I waited. Mathilde would appear any moment and maybe I could make friends with her too. But before she came into view Jean Paul turned and went towards the sound.

I went back to picking beans, my mind whirling. It must have been Mathilde who'd told Jean Paul I was cold. Why did she hate me so much?

Grandmère, her arms full of sweet-smelling sheets, came into the vegetable garden. Earlier I'd helped her peg them on to the line. I used to peg out the washing at home but it took ages to dry and more often than not would be blown off the line and end up wrapped around the side of the stone barn. Am I imagining it or did we always go to bed in slightly damp and grubby sheets? I think we did.

'Eleanor,' Grandmère demanded. 'Go and get the eggs now and then come back inside.'

'Yes,' I said, happy to be useful, and taking my basket of beans with me I made my way over to the chicken coops. I had learned to love the hens, fat grey-speckled birds who clucked and scratched contentedly in their pens and didn't seem to mind being prisoners. Grandmère wouldn't let them roam free because of her vegetable garden.

'Hello, hens,' I called, undoing the catch on the wire door and entering the pen. I had taken over the duty of feeding them night and morning and now they gathered around my feet clucking eagerly, expecting handfuls of grain. I'm going to get hens at home, I told myself. Omelettes would be better than mince any day. Perhaps even Mother will like them. I thought Dada would. Yes, I decided. Hens will be the start of a change in the way we live at home.

With a dozen brown eggs nestling on top of the beans in my basket I wandered out of the garden and into the yard. In front of me was the big barn, which was filled with hay, brought in from the far meadow probably six weeks before I'd arrived at the farm.

I strolled towards it and paused at the open double doors. It smelled sweet and hot inside and there was Étienne, stripped to the waist, forking the hay over and over while he hummed a little tune.

'Hello, Miss Eleanor,' he greeted me, looking up as my shadow darkened the doorway. 'Come to watch me work?'

'I'll help you, if you like,' I said shyly, but he laughed.

'No. This work is too heavy for you. Besides, I hear that you are becoming a chef *par excellence*. Maman will be waiting for you in the kitchen.'

'She is teaching me to make soufflés today. Asparagus soufflé.' I looked down at the small raffia basket hooked over my arm. 'I've been collecting the eggs.'

'Good. I like soufflés, especially asparagus. Do you have them at home?'

I shook my head slowly. 'I never ate asparagus till I came here. Nor trout, nor green peppers, nor whole beans.

Oh, so many things. You couldn't imagine how different it is.'

Étienne stopped work and leant against the fork. His skin was tanned and glistening and the rivulets of sweat which ran from his hair dropped unheeded on to his muscled shoulders. Specks of hay dust danced around him on a shaft of sunlight which pierced the loose tiles on the roof, brightening the otherwise dark barn. It was almost as if he was behind a veil of gauze and I found myself peering at him intently. I'd never seen anyone who looked so . . . so *foreign*.

'Are you homesick?' He grinned as he wiped his hands down the sides of his dusty blue trousers.

'No. No, not at all.' The words came out slowly and surprised me, for I hadn't realised it. 'Not now.'

'You like my farm?'

'I am enchanted by it.' It was an odd description but I can hear myself saying it now and I know that that was how I truly felt. I had gone through a door into a different world, and in that sense I was enchanted.

The sun was beating down on my head and unconsciously I moved further into the barn to find some shade. The sweet smell of the hay mingled with the earthier smell which emanated from Étienne and I found myself breathing in deeply. I wanted to remember all of this when I went home. The heavy moist air, the scents of a hot summer and this man, so strong and healthy and so unbelievably different.

'Enchanted?' Étienne started to smile but then his face grew still and I felt mine flushing as he stared at me. What could he see, I wondered. A silly girl dressed in navy shorts and a white Aertex shirt with hot bare legs stuffed into buckled sandals. He must think I'm impossibly childish. I bit my lip and turned to go.

'Perhaps you are not the only one to feel the enchantment,' he said softly and I lifted my head to see a puzzled look in his brown eyes.

'Eleanor!' Grandmère's imperious voice calling from the kitchen door interrupted the mood.

'I have to go,' I whispered.

'Yes, for sure.' The odd mood was broken and he grinned as he picked up his hay fork. 'Maman can be very insistent.'

As I hurried back to the house I considered my lack of homesickness. It was strange. At first I'd wondered how I could ever survive the three weeks exchange visit. More worrying was the thought that I would have to take Jean Paul back to our bleak house on the high moorland, where, with no opportunity for him to escape to his friends, we would be stuck together every day. It would be hell for both of us. But now he'd said he wasn't coming and I was free.

I hurried into the kitchen. The blinds had been pulled down against the afternoon sun and it was blessedly cool.

'I'm here,' I said. 'I have the eggs.'

'*Bien*. Put them down and come here. You must help with the preparations.'

Grandmère was washing vegetables in the square sink and lifting the colander out of the water to put it down beside the wooden board and knife which lay on the table. 'You must chop these.'

'Yes,' I said, and grabbed eagerly at the knife.

'*Non! Non!*' Grandmère said sharply a few minutes

later, her strong face hardening as I clumsily chopped the onions and cut carrot batons into inedibly large chunks. '*Comme ça*. Like this. Pay attention.' The criticism was said with authority and I didn't take offence. I was used to Mother's sharp tongue and the reproofs rolled off my back like water.

'Sorry,' I muttered, holding the large knife tightly and cutting the vegetables with more care. It was difficult but I knew that it wasn't beyond my ability. My renewed efforts lay on the board in front of me.

'Good!' Grandmère's praise was wonderful, and when I looked up with a grin of relief I was delighted to see my mentor's face break into an awkward smile and her dark eyes dance in amusement. 'Much better, Eleanor. Come here to the stove and bring that bottle of oil with you.'

And, keen to watch the next part of the preparations, I stood happily next to Grandmère. I can see now the two of us, gawky in young and old age, leaning over a large blackened pan whilst onions and garlic sautéed slowly in aromatic oil.

'Now watch,' ordered Grandmère as she threw in the neatly cut pieces of carrot and celery and a handful of freshly picked herbs to join the simmering base of a chicken casserole. 'This is for tomorrow. We'll make the stock now and leave it to settle. The flavour will improve.'

'Yes,' I said, storing the information in that section of my mind which had opened to all things French.

Jean Paul came into the kitchen.

'Hello,' he grunted, a flush coming to his fleshy cheek, and he gave me a brief glance. I guessed he was wondering if I'd told Grandmère what he'd said in the garden. To reassure him I shook my head but I think that was too subtle for him because he continued to stand there shuffling his feet and pushing out his lower lip like a large cross baby.

That's how I saw him then and afterwards, even when I learned more about him. A teenage baby, despicably childish and utterly worthless. Even the faint moustache, which was showing darker every day and he fingered constantly in a sort of dull amazement at its presence, failed to impress. Everything about him repelled me.

Why he had taken part in the school exchange scheme remained a mystery. I knew it wasn't his idea. It was more likely that Étienne or Grandmère had wanted it. They had wanted a visitor in the house and perhaps hoped my presence would make Jean Paul less reliant on his mother. It hadn't. Both of them resented me.

Whatever it was, it didn't matter. Not to me and certainly not to him. He had made his stand about not coming to England, and whatever his father might say he wouldn't be moved. He was prepared for the row and had ceased to care. His life was back to normal. I was now simply an adjunct to Grandmère, an extra presence in the kitchen but otherwise someone to ignore.

'I'm hungry.'

He addressed his remark to Grandmère and she, sighing but without looking up from her cooking, said, 'Take some bread. And a slice of sausage.'

He turned and sulkily went to the larder. I watched anxiously as he lifted the latch on the wooden door. I loved the larder and after only a few days as Grandmère's kitchen helper felt stupidly proprietorial towards it.

My first exploration into that long cool room and the sights which confronted me had nearly taken my breath away.

Thin purply brown sausages dangled on white string from old hooks and behind them on larger hooks cloth-wrapped hams gave off a faint meaty odour. On the stone floor I saw hessian sacks of creamy coloured dried beans and smaller bags of peas and lentils. Beside them were wooden boxes of waxy potatoes still covered in reddish soil, and a wicker basket of onions.

Running along the wall opposite the wire-covered window was a broad marble shelf where pale blocks of butter covered in muslin sat on earthenware dishes. A trickle of liquid surrounded each block which, when I surreptitiously dabbed a finger in, tasted at once salty and fresh. Bowls of eggs, jugs of milk and cream and circles of soft cheese lay beside the butter, and downy berries picked from the garden nestled in wicker baskets. Above all these fresh riches, white wooden shelves groaned with jars. Peaches preserved in brandy and cherries and prunes and apricots, all similarly conserved, all glistening and all promising intoxicating delights.

What a difference from the pantry at home. A picture of it came into my mind. It was a grimy place of cobwebs, empty jam jars and unpleasant-smelling sacks of potatoes. The small window let in the rain, making it impossible for Mother's meagre supplies of flour and sugar to be kept in there. They resided in their blue bags on the shelf above the stove and jostled for space beside matches and candles and any other odd bits and pieces Mother carelessly threw up to join them. Apparently no one had considered the usefulness of repairing the pantry window or even the necessity of cleaning the room. I'll do it when I get home, I thought. A coat of whitewash would help too. I could see it in a few months' time, cleaned and fresh with vegetables on trays and covered tins of flour and sugar and a bowl of eggs collected from my hens. It would be wonderful.

Jean Paul emerged with a chunk of bread in his hand and a cheek bulging with the large slice of sausage he had cut off with his penknife.

'When's supper?' he grunted.

'The usual time.' Grandmère was short with him. 'Go and find your father. There's work to be done outside.'

But I watched as he left the kitchen and I saw him turn towards the salon. Mathilde would be there, lying on the red velvet-covered couch, a cigarette drooping from her mouth and a book in her hand. Jean Paul would join her in that cool dark room and they would spend the hour before supper casually smoking and listening to the wireless.

Lisette would appear later. The little girl spent most of her time alone, playing in her mother's bedroom. There she would dress up in Mathilde's clothes and paint garish lipstick on to her pale thin mouth, all the time singing and chattering to the collection of dolls which she had arranged on the bed. Nobody played with her, nobody asked what she'd been doing or how she was. Even Grandmère, who ran the house, paid her scant attention.

The weather broke that evening and after supper I sat with Grandmère in her parlour listening to the rain. She sat at the table laying cards on the plush table cover in intricate patterns.

'What are you doing?' I asked.

'I'm searching.'

'Searching?' I was intrigued. 'Searching for what?'

'Guidance.'

She was telling her fortune, I knew that. The girls in school talked about it sometimes and Suzy said that her mother regularly consulted a woman who lived in one of the streets behind the cinema.

'Madame Rose told Mummy that she would have two husbands,' whispered Suzy one afternoon when we were in her bedroom looking at her latest new dress.

'Does your mother believe her?' I was, well, scandalised, I suppose.

'Oh, yes.'

This was said matter-of-factly and I wondered if poor Mr Franklin knew.

'Have you been to see her?'

'Yes. She's very good. She said I'll lead a lovely life.'

I didn't doubt that. You didn't have to be a Madame Rose to see that Suzy would always be lucky.

I got up and went to sit at the table opposite Grandmère. This part of the house had oil lamps, and even though it was summer and only eight o'clock in the evening the room was dark. The lamp smoked slightly but the pool of light gave a gentle mystic air to the room.

Grandmère gathered up the cards and pushed the pack towards me. 'Here,' she said. 'Lay the cards down in the way that I tell you.'

In the back of my mind I could hear Mother's scornful voice exclaiming, 'Mumbo jumbo, absolute mumbo jumbo. How can you be so foolish?' but I was excited. I had never had my fortune told.

The cards were old and battered, with the shiny facing coming away from the cardboard in some places. They had a picture of Marianne on the back and under Grandmère's instructions I shuffled them clumsily and smoothed them out face down in a crescent on the pink plush table cover.

'Pick the nine that call to you,' ordered Grandmère, and with my hand hovering over the fan of cards I forgot my mother and chose my fate.

The lamp threw a dull light into the room and on to the cards as I picked them out. It was strange sitting in this room with its heavy furniture and low ceiling. Even in daytime it was dark and now in the evening the intricate carving on the dresser and mantelpiece was quite lost in shadows. The small window which looked on to the yard was closed against the west wind, but as I followed Grandmère's instructions and laid the cards out in a rectangular pattern I could hear a faint sound of footsteps outside, walking across the cobbles. I supposed it was Étienne. He would be heading for the river with his fishing rod even though it was raining and getting dark.

'Is it good?' I was impatient, and watched eagerly as Grandmère slowly turned over and examined the nine cards.

She was frowning. Each card seemed to tell her something different and she tapped her finger slowly on the ten of hearts, which covered the king of clubs. Then, with an irritated tut, she gathered the chosen cards together. She shuffled them and then laid them out into a wider and different pattern.

'Is that good?' I repeated.

She looked up, unsmiling. Her face showed surprise, she was almost slightly afraid, I thought, but as I continued to stare, questioning, the surprise cleared and she smiled.

'It is good, I think. Exciting. Change. We'll have to work on it.'

'What do you mean?' I asked, totally confused.

'I mean that sometimes, if you try very hard, you can affect the future. The cards have told me what must be done.' That was all she would say and after a moment she cleared the cards away and stood up. 'Come. We are having visitors this evening. Monsieur and Madame d'Amboise. You remember them?'

'Yes,' I said. 'Will Luc be coming too?'

'I don't know.'

He didn't. I think now he couldn't bear to be in the company of Jean Paul, or maybe Mathilde. When I spoke to him later, I asked about Jean Paul and why they weren't friends.

'We're different.' It was enough. He was a charming boy and grew into a charming man, respected amongst all his peers. Jean Paul, despite his rather heroic early death, in the army in Indochina, has been almost forgotten in the village and only the family ever think of him now.

'Hello, hello,' Madame d'Amboise exclaimed, warmly shaking my hand when she came in. We were standing in the hall, Grandmère and I, as a welcoming committee.

Monsieur d'Amboise shook my hand too and said rapidly to his wife, 'The girl is very pretty, don't you think?'

'Oh, indeed,' she replied and gave me a little wink. She knew I'd understood and that that was why I was blushing so fiercely.

Étienne came into the hall. He had been outside and he smelt of the river and the hay barn but he had washed his hands and slicked back his hair ready to meet his guests. Looking up I saw Mathilde standing on the turn of the staircase, and behind her, in the gloom, Jean Paul leant against the wall.

'Come in, come into the dining room,' said Étienne, leading the way. 'I have some wine that you must try. I want your opinion.'

An open bottle of wine waited on the table, centred on a flowered tin tray and surrounded by an array of unmatched glasses. Without a word of enquiry, Étienne poured wine into a glass and offered it to Henri d'Amboise. Then he sat back to watch his friend's reaction.

Henri sniffed, then held the glass up to the light. The light was a low voltage glass-shaded pendant but as I looked through the open door to the two men, I could see the wine glowing, almost as blue as damsons, but then red when the light caught it.

'Good,' said Henri, taking a sip, and then another. 'Very . . . profound.'

Étienne nodded his head slowly and poured some into a glass for himself. 'From the market last week. Not local, but . . .' He shrugged his shoulders. 'It is right to try everything.'

Grandmère took Madame d'Amboise by the arm and urged her into the dining room. 'Come, sit and have a little wine. You as well, Eleanor.'

I looked over my shoulder as I was ushered into the room. Mathilde and Jean Paul were following us, Mathilde expressionless and Jean Paul wearing his usual bored face. Lisette could have been anywhere; I hadn't seen her since supper time.

'Are you enjoying your holiday?' Madame d'Amboise asked, settling her well padded behind into a chair next to me.

'Yes.' I nodded. Then, with an effort to join in the conversation, I added, 'Madame Martin is teaching me to cook.'

'Indeed!' Madame d'Amboise raised her eyebrows and looked round to Mathilde who sat at the far end of the table beside Jean Paul, leaving empty chairs between them and the rest of the company. The low light cast shadows into the corners of the room but I could see the glowing tip of Mathilde's cigarette and smell the acrid smoke. Jean Paul was smoking too, tipping his chair back so that it rocked uneasily on its back legs. He had balanced it by hooking his feet under the solid oak trestle which ran the length of the long table.

'Jean Paul!' Étienne growled, and with everybody looking at him the boy reluctantly put down his feet and scraped the chair into an upright position. He flushed a violent red which spread quickly from his cheeks to his hairline and from this darkened face he raised his eyes and shot a look in his father's direction that was utterly malevolent.

The room fell silent. The d'Amboises glanced at each other while Étienne continued to glare at his son. I was embarrassed. I felt that again I'd caused a horrible moment by allowing Mathilde to be confused with Grandmère. I remember how shrill my voice sounded when I broke the silence.

'No,' I gulped. 'I meant Madame Martin senior. Grandmère.'

'Ah.' Madame d'Amboise smiled and took a sip of her wine. 'Madame is a renowned cook in this area. You have an excellent professor.'

It sounded odd, Grandmère being described as a 'professor', and for a moment I wondered if I was being teased or patronised in some way, but looking at her kindly face and feeling Étienne relax beside me I realised that nothing was untoward and I grinned and looked at Grandmère. Her normally stern face had softened and I saw for the first time, but not the last, an affectionate twinkle in her eye.

'Good, good,' said Étienne and jumped up. 'Another bottle, eh, Henri?'

'Eleanor.' Grandmère looked across to me. 'Go to the larder and bring the tray I've laid in there, if you please. We'll need a biscuit or two to go with the wine.'

I went gladly, happy to do something for her, and when I returned with the platter of canapés, the conversation in the dining room was no longer stilted but jolly and noisy as Étienne and Monsieur d'Amboise railed against the government and Madame d'Amboise told Grandmère that Marie was recovering and that the baby boy was walking well.

'Oh,' Madame d'Amboise was saying as I put the platter on the table, 'it is so funny to watch him. He toddles all over the place, even trying the stairs. And he never cries. I swear, that child has the sunniest disposition.'

Only Mathilde and Jean Paul remained outside the friendly atmosphere that now pervaded the room. They sat in the shadows, affecting or perhaps actually feeling boredom, their faces closed against an invasion of communality. Resuming my seat, I glanced quickly in their direction and was chilled by the poisonous look I received from Mathilde.

'Where is Luc this evening?' asked Grandmère. 'We thought he might come with you.'

'Ah, no.' Monsieur d'Amboise broke off his complaints about the government. 'The boy is studying again. He is determined to pass his exams. He has a goal and will not be swayed from it.'

'He still wants to be a doctor?'

'Yes.' Monsieur d'Amboise nodded proudly and looked at his wife with affection. 'The brains come from Édith's side of the family, not mine, eh?' He gave her a little punch on the shoulder and received an embarrassed 'tut tut' in return.

'And Eleanor?' Madame d'Amboise patted me on the arm. 'What will you do when you leave school?'

'I want to go to university,' I said, surprised at myself. I'd never before spoken about my plans, knowing that there was no chance of their being fulfilled. I knew I would have to work on the farm and, for money, because Mother would never give me any, to have a part time job as a shop assistant in Woolworth's. But here, where the cheerful people sitting around the polished oak table would never know my dismal future, I spoke my dreams. 'To read French and German,' I continued breathlessly. 'Then, perhaps, to be a teacher.'

'Very commendable,' said Madame d'Amboise and Étienne nodded his head vigorously.

'This girl also has brains,' he said, 'and is prepared to use them. She's not lazy.'

It was a direct dig at Jean Paul and I looked into the shadows to see his response but he gave no indication that he'd even heard what Étienne said. He had two cigarettes between his lips and was lighting them. He pulled one out and, while I watched, placed it carefully between Mathilde's thin scarlet-painted lips.

I looked away. The action seemed altogether too intimate.

I glanced instead towards Grandmère, sure that her approval would be indicated too, but her strong face was still and when she looked back at me I saw a calculating look in her eye very similar to the one she'd had when reading my cards.

Madame d'Amboise wanted to know more about me. 'Have you brothers and sisters?' she asked.

'No.' I shook my head. 'There's just my mother and father and me at home.'

'And your father is a farmer like Monsieur Martin and my husband?'

I shook my head again, my heart sinking as I wondered how to explain Dada to people who would never meet him. 'He . . .' I started, but Grandmère interrupted.

'Eleanor has told us that her papa was injured during the war. He is not able to work.'

'Oh!' Madame d'Amboise smoothed her hand over my arm. 'How sad. The war was dreadful for so many of us. The Germans were here, you know. In the village.' She shuddered. 'How I hated them.'

'Come, come,' Monsieur d'Amboise said stoutly. 'They weren't all bad. Some were no more than boys. Scared boys too.' He drank his wine quickly. 'It was the officers mostly. The Nazis.'

'They were scum. All of them.' Étienne's harsh voice broke into the conversation. 'Officers and men.'

I looked at him from the corner of my eye. His face was flushed and his hand, when he reached out to grab the bottle of wine, shook. Sweat had gathered at his temples and his shoulders moved angrily, straining the seams of his blue shirt. The atmosphere in the room darkened and I waited anxiously for someone, Grandmère maybe, to say something calming, but she was silent. She obviously felt the same contempt for the invaders. It was Madame d'Amboise who came to the rescue.

'You had it harder than most, Étienne,' she said kindly. 'So we must accept your opinion.' She didn't add 'whether we agree with it or not', but I thought, then and after, that it was implied.

Étienne wiped a hand over his forehead and, seeing it damp, searched in his pocket for a handkerchief. 'Let's forget it, shall we?' he said, mopping his hands and stuffing the red-dotted handkerchief back in his pocket. 'Now. More wine.'

'Not for us, Étienne, thank you.' Madame d'Amboise pushed back her chair. 'We must go.'

'Yes,' her husband agreed. 'Early milking, you know. But I'll be over in the morning to look at that young bull of yours. Maybe we can do a deal, eh?'

I helped Grandmère clear the table and wash the glasses. Étienne had gone outside again and Mathilde and Jean Paul had disappeared upstairs.

'Has Étienne taught you to fish yet?' Grandmère asked as I stacked the glasses on the draining board.

'No. Not yet.'

'Well, he will, but not tomorrow. We are going to

Angers for the day.' She put her head on one side as she looked at me. 'You'll like that?'

'Oh, yes,' I cried, overjoyed at the prospect of a trip outside the area. 'I'm dying to see the city. Thank you.'

'Good,' she said, and untied her apron. It would go outside into the washroom before she went to bed. I thought of Mother's filthy apron, washed only occasionally and stiff with grease and splatters of gravy. I wondered why I hadn't noticed it before, but then I hadn't noticed many things.

'Off you go, Eleanor,' said Grandmère before she went out. 'Get some rest. We'll have a busy day tomorrow.'

Chapter Eight

I was excited. Too excited to sleep and I lay awake for an hour thinking about Angers. I'd looked it up in the school encyclopaedia and taken note of the various sights. I hoped that we would be able to visit at least some of them, the château maybe and the cathedral.

My pocket money, changed at the bank at home into French francs, was in my purse, still unused after ten days at Riverain, and, restless, I got out of bed to open the drawer in the wardrobe. I hadn't even thought about it once since coming here but now I had plans for presents to take home.

My gift to the family here had been a small whole Lancashire cheese bought at the open market in town and carefully wrapped in muslin and greaseproof paper. Suzy had laughed when I said what I was bringing.

'They'll have masses of cheese, idiot,' she'd said. 'The French are renowned for their cheese.'

She and her mother had bought a little framed picture of a snowy scene in the Lake District. 'It's lovely, isn't it,' Suzy said, unwrapping the brown paper cover to show me.

'Yes,' I agreed, 'but it's not exactly local.'

'Goodness, Eleanor, it's only about forty miles away and we're going to take my exchange there for a day out. Anyway, Mummy says good artwork, properly placed, enhances any home and she's sure my hostess will love it.'

Miss Baxter told me that my cheese was exactly the sort of gift that the organisers had in mind. 'Gifts of food are always welcome.'

When I presented it to Grandmère and Étienne, I wondered if Miss Baxter had been right. This house had food in abundance; the larder shelves seemed to squeak a protest at the weight of it all. But Grandmère, carefully unwrapping the muslin cloth and holding my cheese up to her nose for a calculating sniff, announced that it had a '*bouquet par excellence*' and that she was eager to try it.

Étienne had grinned at me and winked. '*Ma mère* is an expert on cheeses. If she says it is good, then it is. Thank you, Miss Eleanor.'

We'd had some of it on little biscuits when the d'Amboises came and it was pronounced 'different but most enjoyable'. I was satisfied and looked around the dining room contentedly, knowing that for once my choice had been correct. A painting of a snowy scene would disappear against the whitewashed walls in this house.

My French money was where I'd left it and I sat on the edge of the bed fingering the crackly notes and putting them in order of value. I wondered what I'd be able to buy with it.

That's when I heard the noise from outside. It was shouting, two voices in an angry exchange, and as I listened a third joined in. I recognised Étienne's voice straight away, I'd frequently heard him yell at Jean Paul, but who else was there?

I switched off my light and waited for a few moments

before going to the window. The shutter was slightly open and, standing to one side, I peered out.

The rain had stopped and the heavy clouds had blown away on a light southerly breeze. A pale moon gleamed in a star-sprinkled sky and the wooden bridge over the river was illuminated as if it was a scene from a picture show. In another context it would have been exquisite.

I could see everything quite clearly, Étienne on the house side of the river and Mathilde standing on the bridge with her back to the balustrade and her small hands resting on the old wood. On the far bank another man waited, a small man in a suit, wearing a dark trilby hat. Apart from his obvious nervousness, his whole demeanour showed him to be someone totally out of place. He was a city man, not a local.

'Putain!' Étienne yelled, his arm thrust out towards Mathilde, and in the moonlight I could see spittle flying from his mouth and the muscles in his shoulders quivering and bunching in rage.

'Putain' was not a word I recognised and when I learned later that it meant 'whore' I knew that Miss Baxter could never have brought herself to mention it in our vocabulary classes. But that night, watching a drama being played out before me, I could understand that it was an insult.

Mathilde remained frozen against the wooden railing but the man on the opposite bank shuffled his feet anxiously. I wondered if he would leap to Mathilde's defence.

As I understood it then, Mathilde and the stranger had done something to upset Étienne. Surely the man would be able to explain and the situation would be resolved.

Handshakes would follow, and the inevitable invitation to a glass of wine. But when, seconds later, Étienne put a boot on to the bridge the man turned and fled into the woodland. I could hear small branches cracking as he sped through and then, clearly in the moonlight, I saw him break cover and run towards the vineyard.

'You can't give it up, can you?' Étienne snarled but Mathilde was silent and motionless, her head cocked to one side the way it often was and the inevitable cigarette burning between her fingers. Étienne hadn't stepped further on to the bridge. It was as if he couldn't bear to get close to her no matter how angry he was. 'You can't give it up,' he said again.

The repeated words had lost their fire and Étienne sounded weary and almost defeated. Watching his shoulders droop, I felt a spear of pity drive through me. Poor Étienne, normally so cheerful, so healthy and brimming over with life. Even when he shouted at Jean Paul he did it with energy and meaning and never in this despairing way.

This time Mathilde turned her head. 'Why should I?' Her small voice carried clearly in the night air. 'It is more pleasurable than anything this place has to offer me.'

I didn't properly understand. Remember, I was barely seventeen and had lived a sheltered life, a life where even at school we didn't really talk about the goings-on of adults. Was she having an affair, I wondered. Like Anna Karenina or Madame Bovary? I had borrowed both of those novels from the library and devoured them eagerly in the privacy of my bedroom. Did Mathilde perhaps find rural life so dull that she had fallen for the charms of an impossibly handsome lover?

I looked up towards the vineyard, hoping to study again the man in the suit, but he was long gone. From the brief sight I'd had of him, he wasn't impossibly handsome. I looked back at the bridge. Mathilde had straightened up and turned towards the opposite bank. She started to walk away, her high heels clicking on the wooden boards and the end of her cigarette now glowing red between her lips.

'*Mon Dieu!*' Étienne called after her. 'You truly are a monster.'

I went back to bed then and slept immediately. No dreams, no lying awake going over the recent events, and in the morning I was drowsy and hardly able to wake up.

Sitting at the table in the kitchen with my coffee bowl cradled in my hands I was still warm and slow with sleep and could only stare at the steam from the coffee spiralling slowly upwards. I noticed how tanned my hands were and how white my fingernails looked in contrast. I liked these new hands and imagined how well red nail polish, the kind Mrs Franklin wore, would set them off.

'You are quiet this morning. Did you sleep badly? Were you disturbed in the night?'

Grandmère's sharp voice pervaded the clouds in my head and dragged my attention away from my elegant hands. 'What? What . . . oh, no. I slept very well.' I wasn't going to tell her about the row on the bridge. Étienne wouldn't like her to know and I couldn't bear to shame him by telling his mother. I smiled. 'It must be all the fresh air. I sleep so well here.'

She frowned and stirred the liquid in the pan on the

range. It would be stock or soup; something was always on the go. 'You must get plenty of fresh air at home.'

'I do.' I nodded. 'But it isn't the same.' That was true. The air at home was fresh all right, so fresh that even in summer it cut at your cheeks and dragged your hair out of the firmest of hair slides. The contrast between that and the sunshiny breeze which bathed my skin in a southern glow and only slightly lifted the small curls on my hairline couldn't have been greater. 'No,' I repeated. 'It isn't the same.'

'Hello.' Lisette wandered into the kitchen, her thin bare arms clutching a bundle of dolls. She sat beside me and selecting two of the dolls put them down, side by side, on the table.

'Is that one Angélique?' I asked, remembering her telling me the names of a couple of her toys.

'Yes,' she said, smoothing down the folds of Angélique's red taffeta dress. 'And this is Christian.' She pointed to the battered creature lying beside pretty Angélique. The doll's pot head was damaged with chips and scratches and its knitted jacket was beginning to unravel at the edges.

'Oh,' I said. 'Where is Jacques?'

She giggled. 'He's gone away. He was very, very naughty.'

Grandmère made a little noise, like 'tch', and I looked over to her. She was pouring the pan of stock into a large earthenware jug. It would be allowed to cool and then go into the pantry to wait until tomorrow.

'Grandmère?' I asked. 'Did you say something?'

'Nothing.' Her back was to me but I could see that her shoulders were twitching and I knew that if she turned she would be scowling. I decided to ignore her and turned back to Lisette.

'What about these dollies on your knee?' I said.

'This is Pierre, this is Frédéric and this one,' she held up a baby doll on which she or someone else had crayoned in a moustache and thick eyebrows, 'is Georges.'

'But they're all boys. No girl dolls,' I said, 'for Angélique to be friends with.'

'Don't be silly, Eleanor.' Lisette shook her head reprovingly. 'Angélique only likes boys.'

Grandmère turned away from the range. 'Get something to eat, Lisette,' she ordered. 'I want to get finished early this morning before we set off to Angers.'

'Oh!' The little girl clapped her hands and a delighted grin lit up her wan face. 'How wonderful. I'll go now and put on my prettiest dress.'

'No. You can't come with us, Lisette. There won't be room for you in the van.'

'But . . .' The child's lower lip wobbled and tears came into her slanted hazel eyes. 'I would so like to go to Angers.'

'She could sit on my knee,' I ventured, unwilling to further upset Grandmère but sorry for the little girl. 'I wouldn't mind.'

'Oh, Eleanor!' Lisette flung her skinny arms round my neck and planted tiny kisses on my cheek. 'Thank you, thank you.'

There were four of us in the van. Étienne was driving, of course, looking uncomfortable in his Sunday suit. He was very quiet and despite driving with his elbow resting on the open window he didn't indulge in his usual shouting matches with other road users.

Grandmère sat looking straight ahead, her black straw hat pinned in place and her face stony. I knew she was cross with me for including Lisette in the outing but I didn't care. In ten short days I'd grown close to Grandmère but her treatment of Lisette seemed to me monstrously unfair. It wasn't as if the child was naughty or even rudely bad-mannered like Jean Paul. She was surprisingly intelligent but even so ignored by the adults in this strange household. Now she was wriggling on my knee, chattering like a little starling, unaware or even unconcerned that no one was listening to her.

'Be quiet, Lisette,' snapped Grandmère, eventually breaking her glowering silence, 'you're giving me a headache.'

'Sorry.' The child leant her head on my shoulder and snuggled closer. I wondered when had been the last time she'd sat on anyone's knee.

'You have decided what you want to see in Angers, Miss Eleanor?' Étienne turned his head away from the road to speak to me.

'Yes,' I said hesitantly. 'I know that there is a fine cathedral and a château. I'd love to see both of those. If it's not difficult for you.'

'No, there'll be no problem. The cathedral is very beautiful and we can go there, but I don't think we can go inside the château. It was damaged in the war and is being repaired. I think it's still too dangerous for people to enter. You can see the outside, though.'

I was puzzled. Why would the Allies have attacked a château in the middle of a mediaeval town? As far as I knew the only targets we attacked in France were those occupied by the Germans, troop emplacements or munitions factories.

'Was it bombed?' I asked.

'Well, yes.' Étienne grinned. 'The RAF did have a go in 1944. But it blew up a little before then.'

I leant forward to look beyond Grandmère to Étienne. He was whistling a little tune and tapping his hands in time on the steering wheel. His good humour had returned.

'Blew up?'

'Yes.' He nodded. 'Part of it, anyway. The Nazis stored arms in it. We had to get rid of them.'

I sat heavily back on my metal seat. Lisette had dropped off to sleep with her head pushed against my neck and her arm draped over my shoulder. For once colour had come into her cheeks.

I considered Étienne's words. *We* had to get rid of them? That's what he'd said, and sneaking another look at his tanned face, so open and friendly, I could hardly believe what I was now suspecting. But deep down I knew. I knew what he'd done in the war.

No wonder, I thought, that he hated the Germans. He had been in the Résistance and fought a most dangerous and dirty war. He must have had total belief in the evil of the occupation and put aside all compassion for the enemy. That's why he was so angry when Monsieur d'Amboise said that some of the ordinary German soldiers hadn't been so bad.

I wanted to ask more. About his exploits, his compatriots, had he killed anyone? And had he been captured? Madame d'Amboise had said he'd 'had it harder than most'. What did she mean?

I was intrigued and impressed at the same time and excitedly opened my mouth to ask him, but I could feel Grandmère twitching beside me and glancing round her I saw Étienne's face set and closed again and thought better of it. Settling in my seat with my arm around Lisette, I let the questions tumble around unasked in my head. Maybe another opportunity would come, but really, and here I gave myself a little shake, it was none of my business.

We were on the outskirts of the city. I could see the twin spires of the cathedral in the distance and we were soon driving alongside the castle. Now I gave myself over to looking outside and forgot about Étienne. Strange how young people always live for the moment.

It was a lovely day and by mid-afternoon I was exhausted. We'd visited all the sights, and eaten Grandmère's packed lunch in the park beside the river. Afterwards I played chase with Lisette between the beds of petunias and lilies until both she and I had pink faces.

'Enough,' said Grandmère sharply after a while. 'You're giving me a headache.'

We weren't but she always said it and I learned like Lisette to ignore the reproof. Étienne, who'd wandered off to watch the fishermen on the bridge, came back. 'Didn't you tell me you want to do some shopping?' he asked.

We went back uphill to the centre of the city and while Grandmère and Étienne settled themselves at a pavement café, Lisette, who would not let go of my hand, and I went to see what we could find.

When we came back Étienne ordered *citrons pressés* for us. He was drinking beer and Grandmère sipped at a small coffee.

'Eleanor bought presents for her *maman* and papa,' said Lisette. 'Lovely presents.'

I thought I had too. I'd found a green silk scarf for Mother with pictures of the cathedral and the castle and for Dada a lovely tin box with a map of the Loire valley on the lid. The box contained chocolate liqueurs which I thought he'd enjoy.

'This is for you, Grandmère,' I said, handing over a small package. I felt very shy about giving her something but she had been kind to me and what else was I to spend my money on?

'A gift?' Grandmère looked surprised. 'No, no, Eleanor, I don't need a present from you.'

'But I want to give you something,' I said.

'Take it, take it.' Lisette hopped from one foot to the other. 'I helped to choose.'

With a frown Grandmère carefully opened the tissue paper and drew out the pair of black lace gloves I'd seen in the shop where I bought Mother's scarf.

'For Sunday. To wear to church.' I had been as excited as Lisette but in the ensuing silence I began to worry. Maybe I'd been too familiar in giving this woman, whom I'd only known for ten days, a gift and I bit my lip anxiously. Lisette's little hand crept back into mine and I could feel the slight tremor fleeting through her.

It seemed like hours but of course was only moments before Grandmère looked up and I saw with relief her rare smile.

'Thank you, Eleanor,' she said, and leaning over she kissed me on each cheek.

'Oh!' If I'd felt shy before it was nothing to how I felt now. I was rarely kissed. Mother had given me a peck at the station before this journey but I couldn't remember when she'd kissed me before. And Dada, well, he didn't touch anyone.

Lisette laughed. 'I knew you'd like them,' she warbled in her little bird voice and Grandmère smiled at her too, grabbing hold of her and retying the green ribbon in her wispy brown hair and pulling up her socks. It was the first time I'd seen her pay real attention to the little girl and I could see that Lisette enjoyed the rather rough handling.

'Eleanor bought me *bon-bons*, look.' The child held up a paper bag and offered it to Grandmère and to Étienne.

'Ah.' Étienne put one of the icing sugar sweets in his mouth. 'So my present is a *bon-bon*?'

I flushed. 'I didn't know what to buy you.'

He grinned. 'I'm joking. I don't need a gift. You are a gift. You make us laugh.'

I thought about that remark on the way home and decided that it was meant kindly. They didn't think I was just a silly girl. They liked me and that was good. I liked them.

We sat as before in the front of the van rattling along the dusty lanes with Lisette tiredly quiet on my knee and Grandmère thoughtful beside me. Étienne whistled softly as he dragged the steering wheel left and right, cheerful now and shouting abuse at other drivers in his old way. Mathilde and Jean Paul hadn't been mentioned once all day. It was almost as if they didn't exist, that I had dreamt them up and that we four in the car were the only family at Riverain. But the closer we got to the farm the less buoyant my mood became.

I think it was the same for all of us. Étienne had stopped

whistling and when I looked at Grandmère she looked back at me with a an odd, uncomfortable expression.

'Are you tired?' she asked.

'A bit.'

'Étienne will take you fishing after supper, if you like. He promised, didn't he?'

I nodded and looked beyond her to her son. He was grinning again. 'Yes, Miss Eleanor. *Ma mère* teaches cooking, I teach fishing.'

Chapter Nine

They were there at supper, in their usual places, smirking at each other. Neither Mathilde nor Jean Paul asked about the day out but in a way I was glad. Their voices would have spoilt what was for me the best day I had ever spent.

The pea soup and ham omelettes were eaten in near silence and even Lisette's chattering was sporadic, the little girl's eyelids drooping with tiredness. I hugged the experience of the day close and found myself smiling as I ate my omelette and helped myself to salad. I looked up to see Jean Paul staring at me and I left the smile on my face, hoping to encourage him to be more friendly, but he quickly looked back at his food as he shovelled the rest of it into his mouth.

'Did you feed the calves?' Étienne's voice sounded unnaturally sharp and I slid my eyes sideways to get a quick look at him. He had the jug of wine in his hand and was pouring himself another glass.

Jean Paul nodded. 'Yes.'

'What else?'

There was an awkward silence before Jean Paul shrugged his heavy shoulders. 'Nothing.'

'Nothing?' Étienne dropped his fork on his plate with a clatter. 'Nothing?' The calm of the dining room was deteriorating and from the corner of my eye I could see

Étienne's fist bunching. I knew that any minute he would explode with rage.

'Has everyone finished?' Grandmère's cool voice cut through the darkening atmosphere and eager to be out of the room I stood up and started to clear the plates. Mathilde stood up too and after the slightest pause picked up her plate and pushed it into my hand. It was so quickly and so meanly done that I had to juggle with the two I was already holding. For a moment I thought I would drop them all but Étienne with an exclamation of annoyance reached out his large hand and covered mine, holding the pretty pink and white dinner plates securely.

'Thank you,' I said, and waited while he slowly released my fingers. His hand was warm and slightly damp and left mine the same. 'Sorry.' I was upset that I'd annoyed him and knew that my cheeks were red when I lifted my eyes to his.

'It was not your fault,' he muttered. 'It was . . .' The rest of the sentence was left unsaid and I was grateful; it allowed me to calm down. Mathilde had already left the room, but when I turned with the plates in my hand ready to take them to the kitchen I met Grandmère's calculating eye.

Later, when Lisette had drifted off to bed and Jean Paul had disappeared to wherever he went in the evenings, I lingered in the kitchen with Grandmère. She was doing her usual preparation for tomorrow's meal while I washed the dishes, in the way she had taught me, soapy water in one sink and clean rinse in the other. I was waiting for her to go into the little parlour. Surprisingly, I wasn't tired at all; rather I felt exhilarated as though my relationship with her and Étienne and even Lisette had moved on to a more intimate plane. I hoped she would tell my fortune again.

'Étienne will be waiting for you on the bridge.' Grandmère spoke over her shoulder. 'He's taken a spare rod for you.'

'Oh, I forgot.' I hadn't really, but now I felt nervous. At dinner Étienne had been angry and maybe a little drunk and somehow his casual remarks about teaching me to fish had taken on importance. 'It's very hot this evening. Will it still be all right for fishing?'

'Of course.' Grandmère turned round to face me and gesturing with a wooden spoon pointed towards the door. 'Off you go.'

The pastel moon was rising in a lilac-coloured sky. The sun had disappeared behind the vineyard hill but it wasn't properly dark yet and I wondered how one could fish at night. I supposed one did it by moonlight, and judging by the clear unclouded sky it would be a very bright night.

Étienne was standing in the middle of the bridge, his rod and line cast over the river. He was quiet this evening, no whistling or humming, and the only sound was the occasional last twitter from the finches in the alders as they settled for the night. In the distance a dog was barking but here on the river it was still and utterly peaceful.

'Hello,' I said, setting a foot on the bridge.

'Come here, Eleanor,' he ordered. 'I have your fishing rod ready.'

I noticed that he no longer addressed me as 'Miss' Eleanor. Could I call him Étienne instead of Monsieur Martin? I didn't dare.

'Come on,' he urged me as I lingered. 'This is for you.'

That night I learned to cast a line and caught my first fish, but that was not all. I learned how to kiss a man and more important how to let him kiss me.

'I'll be no good,' I said, taking the fishing rod in my hand and watching as Étienne baited the hook. 'It's really a waste of time.'

'No it isn't.' He looked down into my face, his eyes serious. 'You have to try everything.'

At first I couldn't get the hang of casting the line. The hook landed on the bank, caught in the overhanging branches and even, embarrassingly, clattered stupidly beside me on the bridge. 'I'm hopeless,' I wailed.

'No. You are learning.' Étienne reeled in the line, checked the fly and putting a hand on my shoulder urged me to move further along the bridge. 'I must check the railing there,' he said, looking back to where we'd been standing. 'It's loose. Might be dangerous. Now, Eleanor, try again.'

We were close to the far bank in the shadow of the overhanging willows and it was almost too dark to see. I heard a bird squawking quietly upriver and small animals rustled purposefully in the undergrowth. I began to lose my sense of space. It was as if we were part of the landscape, as natural as the trees and the water, and we were fading into it. We had become river creatures and so it was no real surprise when suddenly I got the hang of casting a line. I swished the rod and the line flew gently away, snaking in a low quivering arc until it landed softly on the river and was taken into the flow.

'Good.' Étienne's hand squeezed my shoulder. 'Very good.'

It was luck, of course, when immediately a small tug on the line indicated a catch. 'Oh,' I gasped, and my hand holding the rod shook with excitement. 'I've caught something. It's pulling.'

'Careful.' Étienne put his hand over mine to hold the rod steady. 'Now. Slowly reel in.'

My fish – it was a trout – was landed and curled and struggled on the bridge, silvery in the moonlight, while I stood with the wooden mallet in my hand. 'Hit it,' said Étienne. 'It's suffering.'

So that night I killed a fish and after the first faltering revulsion at the act of murder thought no more about it.

'I caught a fish!' I looked up into Étienne's amused brown eyes. 'I actually caught a fish.'

'You did. Well done.'

He put out a hand, maybe I thought to shake mine in congratulation, and I moved closer to him. I was grinning and felt utterly elated with my success. I had had a wonderful day and it had culminated in this achievement. Why had I been so worried about coming out this evening?

'Eleanor.' Étienne's voice sounded throaty and unsure and as my grin faded his proffered hand moved away from mine and touched me on the neck. 'You are so young,' he muttered. 'So . . . unused.'

I could feel myself trembling. Something was happening, something different. I should turn and go back across the bridge to the kitchen and to Grandmère where I would be safe.

But I didn't. Instead I turned my face up to Étienne's and welcomed his mouth pressing on to my lips and his arms crushing me into his body. Unlike my little silvery fish I didn't struggle. Why would I when his very touch sent thrills of undreamt of pleasure through me? I wasn't even merely unresisting; rather I melted my body into his and put my own arms around his shoulders. I wanted this so much.

He broke away. 'I am sorry,' he muttered. 'That was wrong.'

I nodded. My lips felt swollen but when I licked them I could taste him and my whole body quivered from his touch. When I got to my room I would look in the mirror and see if I could find the imprint of his hands. I hoped I would.

'You are so young and so very lovely, Eleanor. I could not resist.'

He should have resisted, I suppose. He was an adult, much older than me and married. These days we would say that he had a duty of care towards me, in loco parentis, but then he was far removed from any idea I had of a parent. In my eyes he was simply Étienne and I was spellbound.

'It doesn't matter,' I said, still tasting him. 'I am not . . .' I searched for the word, 'I am not offended.' I wasn't offended. From what I'd seen he didn't get much comfort in life. Mathilde wasn't a loving wife and Jean Paul and even little Lisette seemed to exist only to irritate him. I knew what it felt like to be unloved and if he needed to kiss me then he could. 'I liked you kissing me,' I added, blushing with sudden shyness. 'It's the first time anyone has ever kissed me.'

He stared at me then, frowning and nervously biting his lip. 'You have not a boyfriend in England?'

'No.' I shook my head.

'I have a wife. It is wrong of me to kiss you.'

I said nothing. I knew it was wrong. My literary heroines had known it was wrong but they had done it anyway, hadn't they? Anna and Emma and certainly Becky Sharp. The girls in school talked about boyfriends all the time. Was this what they meant? Did they experience what I had just experienced? Had they been overwhelmed? A small triumphant thought shot into my head. Would I tell Suzy?

Étienne turned and looked back at the house. A light shone in the kitchen and from one of the upstairs rooms but otherwise all was quiet and still. A streak of cloud had slowly covered the moon and now we were in darkness. I felt that we were alone in the world, so that when Étienne took me in his arms again I knew that it was the perfect thing to do.

We kissed, pressing our lips together at first slowly and then with more urgency, and I let him force my mouth open and explore it with his tongue. His arms pulled me closer so that I could feel the length of his body while I lifted my hand to his hair. My fingers threaded through his black curls and I found myself pulling his head harder on to my lips until I felt bruised and eaten up. How long we would have stayed there I don't know. Grandmère's voice called from the kitchen door and broke the spell.

'Étienne, Eleanor. It is late. Come inside now.'

Did she notice my bruised lips? I don't know, but to me they stung and throbbed and I couldn't resist putting a finger up to feel them.

'It's late. You must go to bed now.' She didn't look at me but bustled into the larder with a *clafoutis* which she'd just taken from the oven.

'Yes,' I said, and taking a glass of water I walked up the little back stairs to my room. She hasn't asked me about the fish, I thought, and I wondered what had become of my catch. Would Étienne throw it back in the river? After all, one little trout would barely make a meal.

I undressed slowly and looked at my body in the oval mirror that fronted the carved wardrobe. My face, arms and legs were tanned but the rest was white; the small girlish breasts, the flat, almost hollow belly and, turning slowly, the equally flat boyish backside. I let my eyes travel up to my back and there they were. Slight red marks where Étienne had grasped me so tightly.

Marks of shame? I didn't think so, and as I took my cotton nightdress from the hook behind the door I smiled. This had been a wonderful day.

I didn't see Étienne next day until supper time. At breakfast Grandmère said he'd gone to the cattle market with Monsieur d'Amboise and that she and I would be visiting Madame d'Amboise for lunch.

'I'd like that,' I said, thinking that it would fill in the time until Étienne and I could go fishing again. That we wouldn't continue the kissing never occurred to me. 'Will Luc be there?'

'I don't know.' Grandmère sat down at the kitchen table and buttered a scrap of bread. My bowl of coffee steamed gently between my fingers and while I sipped I thought about the evening before. Had I been too bold? I remembered saying that I liked him kissing me and holding his head hard down on my mouth. That memory brought back almost the same squirming thrill in my belly and I shifted in my chair and drained my bowl so that my face was hidden from Grandmère's penetrating gaze.

'Do you like Luc?'

I put down my bowl and wiped a hand over my mouth. 'Yes, very much,' I said. 'He likes the same things as I do.'

'What things?'

'Oh, I don't know. Learning, reading, those sorts of things. New ideas.'

Grandmère got up. 'I see,' she said, her voice cool and rather dismissive. 'You and he both want to be away from the farming life. You want to be city people.'

'No, no.' I hadn't meant to offend her. 'You asked me if I liked him and I do.' I looked around the kitchen and through the open window to the vegetable garden beyond. Bright red geraniums on the sill swayed in the slight breeze and the green musky smell from the herb patch beyond pervaded the room. I couldn't imagine anyone wanting to live away from this farm. 'I love it here,' I said slowly. 'It's like heaven.'

She nodded, satisfied I think.

Lisette was in the garden when I went there later to get eggs. 'I saw you and Papa on the bridge last night,' she warbled. 'Did you catch a fish?'

'Were you still awake?' My breath caught in my throat and I had to force myself to speak.

'Oh, yes.' She was making a little bouquet of chive flowers. 'I woke up and it was too hot in my room. I went to the river bank to make a sleeping nest for my dollies. They were too hot as well.'

God! What had she seen? For the first time I started to worry. What if she told Mathilde or worse still Grandmère? Or, and my heart sank, she could easily say something at supper. One throwaway remark amongst all her non-stop chattering. Then I wondered if her telling them might not be necessary. Perhaps others had seen us too. A stone settled in the pit of my stomach.

I didn't know what to say, how to warn her to be quiet or even whether to try to get her to believe she'd been mistaken, and I unlatched the chicken coop door with a trembling hand. The hens gathered around me clucking and scratching at my feet as I threw handfuls of corn and shredded greens to them and I was grateful for the distraction. They at least wouldn't question me.

'Well, did you?' Lisette's pale little face pressed against the wire mesh.

'Did I what?' I was searching in a nesting box for an egg and dreaded the answer.

'Did you catch a fish, silly?'

Relief swept over me. 'Yes.' I nodded. 'One little trout.'

'Are we going to eat it?'

I backed out of the coop and put my basket of eggs on the grass beside Lisette. 'I don't know. Your papa left after I did. I think he might have thrown it back in the river.'

'Oh.' She sat down on the grass and bound the chive flowers with a long blade of grass. I waited for another question but none came so I sat down beside her and made her a daisy chain. We were still there when Grandmère came to find us.

'Hurry up,' she demanded. 'Lisette, wash your hands and face and brush your hair.'

'Why?'

'Because you're coming with Eleanor and me for lunch with Madame d'Amboise.'

'Oh!' The child was almost speechless with pleasure.

I was happy for her. Being included was what she wanted more than anything and I felt that my insisting that she came with us to Angers had changed Grandmère's mind. It was a small victory.

'You too, Eleanor. Put on your nice dress.'

The d'Amboise farmhouse was smaller than the Martins' and a newer building. We walked down the lane about half a mile to get to it and although I thought it would be quicker to go through the vineyard and over the hill Grandmère insisted on the lane.

'They built this house three years ago. The old one is there, behind it. See?'

I looked. Les Pines was a white-painted villa sitting in a pretty garden while to the rear, amongst pine trees, was a larger stone house. The roof of the old house was in poor condition and some of the windows were boarded up. I wondered why they hadn't pulled it down. Surely they didn't need two houses.

'One day,' Madame d'Amboise smiled, 'we will repair the stone house for Luc. He will have somewhere to bring his bride when the time comes.' I hadn't asked her but the subject came up while we were eating the veal stew she had prepared. It was the first time I'd ever tasted veal and I was loving it.

'I can taste the tarragon,' said Grandmère approvingly, and I nodded. I could taste it too and marvelled. Me, who had never heard of the herb ten days ago – I could identify it amongst the other delicious flavours.

'I like it,' announced Lisette. 'It is a delicious discovery.'

Madame d'Amboise laughed out loud. 'You funny little girl,' she said, and Grandmère, who had begun to frown at Lisette's interruption, relaxed and smiled. It was obviously a surprise to our hostess when Lisette arrived with Grandmère and me but she quickly recovered and welcomed the child as if her presence was completely normal.

At lunch Luc sat opposite me and we talked about school while his mother and Grandmère discussed the recipe for *daube de veau* and other veal dishes.

'I am good at maths and physics,' he said, wiping his mouth on the lace-trimmed napkin. There was a lot of lace in Les Pines. Doilies on the little tables, trimmings on the dresser shelves and surprisingly, for the villa was not overlooked, delicate lace curtains inside the heavy drapes. When I mentioned it to Grandmère later she nodded. 'Édith likes her decorations. To me they make unnecessary work.'

Madame d'Amboise liked her ornaments too. Porcelain vases, empty of flowers, were scattered around the room and a group of china shepherdesses frolicked on the mantelpiece. I wondered how long the pieces would last in Mother's hands. Not long, I suspected, and then for the first time in days I thought about home. How were they? Did they miss me? Dada would, I was sure, but Mother? The fact that I no longer missed them suddenly made me feel a little guilty.

'What about you?' Luc's question broke through my thoughts and dragged me back from our cold hillside into the d'Amboises' over-furnished dining room. 'What are you good at?'

'Well, languages, maybe,' I said, reluctantly. 'And literature and history. I love history.'

'Ah!' said Luc. 'Henry the Eighth and his six wives, eh? We too have learned about him.'

We both laughed and got further into a conversation about school and life in our different countries. Why couldn't Jean Paul have been like him, I thought, but then a private little corner of my mind whispered to me that Monsieur d'Amboise wasn't Étienne. My cheeks felt hot and I knew I was blushing. I quickly took a gulp from my water glass. Just thinking about Étienne was thrilling.

'Are you all right, Eleanor?' Grandmère's even voice broke into my thoughts. When I looked up she was staring at me, her hooded brown eyes studying my face as though trying to read my mind.

'Yes,' I said hurriedly. 'Yes, I'm fine, thank you. I was a little hot. That's all.'

'We'll go outside,' said Luc. 'Is that all right, Maman?'

'Of course, dear.' Madame d'Amboise smiled indulgently at her son.

'Lisette. You go outside too,' Grandmère instructed, and the child obediently pushed away her chair and skipped after us through the long doors into the garden.

'That little one looks better than I've seen her for ages,' I heard Madame d'Amboise say as I followed Luc outside.

'Yes, maybe. She likes having Eleanor with us.'

'I'm not surprised. The girl is quite charming.'

'Was I supposed to hear that?' I whispered to Luc, who had raised a quizzical eyebrow.

'Oh, yes. Maman never wastes words.'

We giggled together and slowly walked towards the pine trees and the old house. It was blessedly cool in the shade and I loved the feel of the tall, unmowed grass brushing my bare legs. Lisette danced into the trees and squeaked with joy at the sight of so many pine cones scattering the dusty ground.

'Can I take some, please,' she begged Luc.

He grinned. 'Of course.'

'Don't get your dress dirty,' I warned her. 'Grandmère will be cross.'

Luc and I sat on an old wooden bench which had been abandoned beside the wall of the stone house. I could see newer, smarter iron chairs on the small patio outside the living room. The seats were adorned with blue lacy cushions, which would have saved bare thighs from the iron scrollwork but looked really too precious to sit on.

'Are you enjoying your holiday?' Luc leant back on the bench and rested his head against a flat piece of stone. He looked unbelievably relaxed and free from care and I realised how different this household was from the Martins' and, for that matter, from mine. He was looking up to the tops of the pine trees, watching as the sun pierced the close trunks and sent shafts of brilliant light into the dark woodland. I looked too, entranced by the almost magical scene. If a unicorn with a silver horn had trotted out in front of us, I wouldn't have been surprised.

'Oh, yes,' I said.

'And you get on all right with the family?'

'Yes,' I said carefully. 'Well, with Grandmère and Monsieur Martin. And Lisette.' I turned my head to look for the little girl, suddenly concerned that she might have wandered off. But she was there, sitting on the ground under the trees, shaking out her skirtful of pine cones.

'But not Jean Paul and Madame Martin.'

I shook my head, still looking away. 'They don't like me.'

Did I sound pathetic? I must have for Luc put his hand on my arm and gave it a sympathetic squeeze. 'They don't like anybody,' he said. 'It's not you specifically.'

I was confused. Luc's long fingers gripping my arm felt good and rather welcome. I didn't want him to think I was complaining, or, worse, being childish, but the need to discuss the Martins with someone was becoming difficult to suppress.

'Jean Paul hates me,' I said, lowering my voice in case Lisette heard me. 'I have no idea why he agreed to be part of the exchange programme.'

'It was his father and grandmother's idea. I think they thought it might get him away from his mother.'

Now I was more confused. 'How?' I stared at him. 'Why?'

'You must have noticed,' Luc said, lowering his gaze from the pine tops to look directly at me. 'Jean Paul and Madame Martin spend a lot of time together. An awful lot.'

I nodded, thinking about their evening sessions in the salon and the giggling as they walked together to church. They even mouthed to each other at supper time. Was this how mothers and sons always behaved? Simply a normal loving relationship? I had no basis to work on, certainly nothing from home. Our neighbours on the hillside, the Winstanleys, appeared to have the same cool attachment to each other as everyone else I knew. Mrs Winstanley, on the few occasions I'd met her with Graham, was pleasant but not especially affectionate with him. She was nicer to me, if anything.

I glanced quickly at Luc. He was still looking at me, his face serious and his clever brown eyes examining my expression as though to ensure that I had understood exactly what he was saying. I wasn't certain I had.

'Maybe,' I said, 'it's because he and his father don't get on. They fight a lot.'

'I know.'

'And Monsieur Martin and his wife seem to be . . .' I held back, concerned that I was gossiping about my hosts.

'They loathe each other too.' Luc stood up and glanced over to Lisette, who was arranging the pine cones in patterns. 'Eleanor,' he said, also lowering his voice so that the child wouldn't hear. 'Watch your step. Mathilde can be dangerous. She is . . . how shall I put it . . . reckless.'

I was still taking this in when he added almost casually, 'And by the way, Jean Paul is not Étienne's child. She brought him with her when they married.' He looked again at Lisette. 'Neither is she, for that matter.'

Chapter Ten

I changed out of my best dress when we got home from the d'Amboise house and immediately Grandmère put me to work dropping tomatoes in boiling water in order to skin them.

'After you've done that, Eleanor, collect the eggs and pick some beans and courgettes. And I want a couple of lettuce too.'

'All right.' I nodded, careful not to show my reluctance. Normally I was glad to do Grandmère's bidding but this afternoon I yearned to go somewhere quiet and think about the things Luc had told me. I could hardly believe them and wondered if he had made a mistake, or was telling mean tales because he didn't like Jean Paul.

But even as I thought it I knew that it couldn't be true. Luc simply wasn't like that. Even at sixteen Luc was an honourable person and he has remained so.

There was a smear of blood on the door of the chicken house and I looked around, suddenly nervous that a fox had got in and killed my flock. I thought of them now as *my* flock, having taken over feeding them and changing the straw bedding in the nest boxes. They clucked around my feet as I scattered corn and shredded greens for them and would lie happily in my arms if I picked one up. God! Had I left the wire door open in my confusion after the events of last evening? But no. All was quiet and secure. The birds were sitting quietly under the shade of the oak tree whose enormous branches hung over half the run. One of them was muttering to herself and I saw that her comb and cheeks were bloodied. She must have caught herself on something, I thought, and when I went back into the kitchen with my basket of eggs I told Grandmère.

'No,' Grandmère said. 'She's being pecked and I know which one is doing it. I think it's time for it to go.'

I didn't like the thought that one of my hens was going to be killed, but worse was to come. 'You can dispatch it, Eleanor. I'll show you how.'

It was a horrid business, my first kill, but I reasoned with myself that if I was going to keep hens at home I would have to learn to do it. After all, Grandmère killed them regularly and I ate the delicious results with relish. So later, when I trailed outside in the wake of a very purposeful Grandmère, I had almost put my sensitive nature aside.

'This is the one,' said Grandmère, and suddenly she grabbed a large white chicken who'd been strutting importantly through the flock and brought it to me. 'Look,' she said, 'it has blood on its beak. Thinks it's in charge.'

I looked at the condemned bird. It did indeed have a bloodied beak, but it was now sitting quietly in Grandmère's grasp quite unaware of its fate. 'Can't we leave it?' I said. 'Perhaps the hot weather has upset it.'

'No,' she said. 'It has become a bully and I won't have that.'

I must have shown my distaste for the task ahead because she frowned. 'Come on, girl. Knowing how to kill is a necessity on a farm. I'm sure your mother knows that.'

I thought of Mother in the fields and could never remember her killing anything. Maybe she had and I never knew, although a sheep would be a bigger prospect than a chicken.

'I tell you, once it starts this nonsense it won't give up,' Grandmère continued, taking a firmer grip on the unsuspecting chicken. 'And the others will be put off laying. Anyway, I need a bird for tomorrow's lunch and this is a good plump one. Now,' she shifted her hand and beckoned me forward, 'I'll show you how and you must do it.'

Her instructions must have been good for I pulled the neck of the white hen cleanly in one go. It didn't struggle, and although its wings flapped for a little while afterwards it was dead immediately.

'Well done.' Étienne was standing outside the chicken run watching us and my stomach lurched. So hard was I concentrating that I hadn't noticed his arrival. He had returned home.

'Fish yesterday, chicken today. You are learning.' He was smiling indulgently at me like a father praising a clever child and I searched his face for some recognition of the fact that our relationship was not that. There was nothing to see.

'How did you get on at the market?' asked Grandmère, taking the lifeless bird out of my hands and walking towards the wire door. 'Did you get a good price for the heifers?'

'Excellent. I could have sold twice as many. Henri d'Amboise was a little jealous, I think.'

Grandmère shrugged. 'Our land is better than theirs.'

I could hear the put-put of Jean Paul's bike coming into the yard. Where he'd been I didn't know and didn't care. And it occurred to me that I hadn't seen even a glimpse of Mathilde. I usually saw her at lunch for half an hour or so, but we'd been out.

Étienne's face altered and his smile faded. He jerked his head towards the sound of the bike. 'I suppose he's been off all day. Drinking beer with that damned rubbish he calls friends. Done none of the jobs I wanted.' He was almost snarling. 'Christ! I'll kill him.' He strode towards the yard and Grandmère, shaking her head, followed, the dead white chicken dangling in her strong grasp. 'Come on, Eleanor,' she sighed. 'We have to get on with the supper.'

I lingered in the chicken run, hoping to avoid the scene. I didn't want to see Étienne in that way, being an angry father. I wanted him as he had been last evening. I wanted him young-looking, passionate. I wanted his hands on me.

But my name was being called and I carefully fastened the wire door of the coop and walked slowly round the house into the yard.

'Eleanor!' Étienne was waving a small brown envelope. 'Look. This is for you.' He didn't look angry any more and there was no sign of Jean Paul. We had been mistaken; he had not returned. The *vélo* belonged to a young postman, neat in a blue uniform, who was standing astride his bike, ready to leave but too excited or too interested to depart.

'It's a telegram,' said Grandmère. Her voice was low, concerned, and I hurried up to the group and took the envelope from Étienne's hand. 'It is from your mama?'

'No.' I read the short message. It was from the British consul in Angers, an M. J. Castres. *Your mother taken ill stop Father in hospital stop Phone this office for more information stop* A phone number followed.

'My mother is ill,' I said, holding out the telegram for Étienne and Grandmère to read. They stared at the crinkly paper with the stuck-on white tape and then lifted their eyes and gazed at me. They were unable to understand the English words so I read it out, including the telephone number, and then wondered what to do. There was no phone at Riverain.

'Come,' said Étienne. 'We will go to the post office and you can make a call from there.

On the short journey from Riverain to the little village neither Étienne nor I spoke. I was almost struck dumb by the sudden intrusion of home into the dream life I was living. Mother ill? I could hardly believe it. She was always so strong, so fit and impatient with anything that might be construed as illness. I was never allowed days off school; bad colds, stomach ache, even a badly twisted wrist made no difference. My record of attendance at St Elizabeth's must have been the best they had.

I began to get angry. She was doing it on purpose. She wanted to spoil my holiday, prevent my French visitor from coming home with me. Claiming to be ill was all part of the plan. But then I remembered that the telegram had said that Dada was in hospital. That meant that she was either too ill to look after him or that he was ill too. Oh, God!

The postmaster helped me dial because I'd never made a phone call before and from the way Étienne was nervously watching me I don't think he had either.

'Miss Gill?'

'Yes.'

The British consul spoke English with a French accent. 'We have had news that your mother has been taken ill. She is in hospital.'

'Mother? What's wrong with her?' I was confused. The telegram had said that Dada was in hospital.

'It seems she has some infection. It is quite serious but not critical. I believe your home is quite remote. Is that right?'

I nodded and then remembered to speak. 'Yes, it is. We have a farm on the Pennines.'

'Well,' the consul continued, 'her doctor preferred her to be under constant supervision.'

'Oh,' I said and then, 'but your telegram said that my father was in hospital.'

There was a short pause before he spoke. 'Your father, he is . . . not well?'

'No. He . . .' I didn't know how to say it and then, in a rush, thought of suitable words. 'He has shell shock . . . after the war.'

'Ah, that explains it. He has been sent to the asylum until your mother gets better. It seems he can't manage by himself. Now, practicalities. There is no question, of course, of your exchange visitor going to England. You will have to apologise to him and his parents. But you are a problem. Have you a relative you can stay with?'

I hadn't. Both my parents were only children and all four grandparents were dead. How would I manage the farm and get food? My savings were very depleted and if Mother had money in the bank, which I doubted, I had no way of getting hold of it. I looked through the glass telephone cubicle to Étienne. His face was asking questions.

'No, I have no family,' I said. 'I don't think I can manage the farm, either.'

'The farm is being looked after by a neighbour, Miss Gill. A Mr Winstanley, I believe. That isn't a problem.'

I looked again at Étienne and saw his encouraging smile. He had no idea what was being said but he was letting me know that he would help me. 'Monsieur Castres,' my words broke the consul's worried silence, 'perhaps Monsieur Martin will let me stay here for another few weeks. He is here. Would you like to speak to him and explain the situation? . . . He wants to talk to you,' I hissed, offering the receiver to Étienne. 'To explain.'

Now it was his turn to look worried as we awkwardly exchanged places and he bent his ear to the phone. I watched him anxiously, backing away from the cubicle and leaning against the post office counter.

'You have bad news?' the postmaster asked sympathetically.

'Yes.' I nodded. 'My mother is sick and I can't go home at the moment.' Saying it made me realise how serious my situation was. How would I manage? What about school? I looked at the glass cubicle. Étienne was speaking, his mouth close to the receiver and his free arm animatedly jabbing the air to emphasise a point as it always did.

'I have a cousin in England,' the postmaster whispered. 'He is a waiter in London. Perhaps that's near where you live?'

'No.' I shook my head.

Étienne waved to me from the phone cubicle. 'Come, speak to Monsieur Castres.'

'Miss Gill?'

'Yes.'

'Now, Monsieur Martin has said that he and his family are happy to let you stay at their home for as long as is necessary. He has added that the cost of your keep doesn't matter, so that wouldn't be a problem. Apparently you have been very useful about the farm and have helped look after their small girl. Of course, you will have to return to England when school starts but I'm sure that your parents will have recovered by then. Will that suit you?'

'Oh, yes,' I said, trying to stop myself from sounding as overjoyed as I felt. 'Will you let me know what's happening at home?'

'Of course I will.'

I don't know which of us had sounded more relieved, him or me and in the van back to Riverain I relived the conversation over and over again.

'Did Monsieur Castres say what is wrong with your mother?' Étienne asked.

'No, not really. An infection which is serious but not critical. I don't know more than that. I don't think he does, either.'

'And your papa?'

Now I felt guilty for being so happy at not going home. Poor Dada. He mustn't have been able to get food while Mother was ill or known what to do. He would have been so frightened. I ought to go home, really, and look after him. 'The consul said he needed looking after while Mother is in hospital. Maybe I should . . .' I turned my head and looked at him. We were turning into the yard and through the open window I could smell the musty odour of the river which had become so familiar to me. 'I should go home to look after my father.' The words rushed out of my mouth almost without my thinking of the sense of them. In reality there was no way I could go, but I had to assuage my guilt.

Étienne pulled on the brake. 'Do you want to?' he asked, staring straight ahead through the windscreen to the pale stone walls of the house. 'If you really must go, I will drive you to Paris or to Calais for the boat. You only have to ask.'

I shook my head. 'I want to stay here,' I muttered. 'With you . . .'

'What's happened?' Grandmère's head suddenly appeared at my window. I hadn't noticed her coming round the side of the house. She was carrying the lettuce and courgettes that I'd forgotten to pick earlier.

'Eleanor is staying with us for a few more weeks, until her mother is better.' Étienne climbed out of the van and strode away towards the barn. My stomach curdled as I followed his strong body with my eyes. What must he think of me?

Grandmère stepped away to let me out. Her face was almost unreadable but I thought I saw a glimmer of satisfaction in her dark eyes. 'Come,' she said. 'We have work to do and you can tell me all about it in the kitchen.'

We were quietly happy at supper that evening. Neither Mathilde nor Jean Paul appeared, although their places had been laid and they were obviously expected. Étienne gave no sign of what I now thought of as our relationship but Lisette kept grinning at me and didn't bother with her usual quiet singing.

'Oh!' she'd squealed when I told her that I would be staying a little longer. 'How delightfully delicious,' and she wrapped her thin little arms joyfully around my waist. She'd even lingered in the kitchen while Grandmère and I prepared supper until she was sent out to wash her face and hands. When I carried the tureen of water-cress soup into the dining room she was in her place, hair combed and wearing a clean frock.

'Good girl,' Grandmère said, her stern face briefly softening, and from the head of the table Étienne gave the child a little nod. He had also put a wet comb through his hair and changed out of his overalls.

'Where are the others?' he asked. 'Have you seen Jean Paul at all?'

'No.' Grandmère ladled soup into the blue flowered bowls. 'Not since breakfast. He went out on his bike straight after.'

'And Mathilde?'

Grandmère shook her head. 'I haven't seen her.'

'Oh well, it doesn't matter.' Étienne carved chunks of bread for us all and we dipped our spoons into the delicious pale green soup and started our supper.

It felt as though it was my first day at Riverain. The normal strained atmosphere had gone and we chatted calmly and laughed at Étienne's description of Monsieur d'Amboise's disappointment at the price his cattle got at market. 'He swore that his beasts were in better condition than mine,' Étienne said, vigorously mopping out his bowl. 'Ours did better, of course, but Henri still got a decent amount.'

'Your father built up that herd long before the war,' said Grandmère. 'He bought the best we could afford.'

'I know, and I'm grateful.'

As I got up to gather the soup plates I thought about the family. Étienne's father had never been mentioned before and I wondered how long he'd been dead. I'd vaguely presumed that he'd been killed in the first war. But if he'd built up the herd before the recent war then he must have survived.

'Grandmère,' I asked, while I was waiting for her to lift the courgettes into a serving dish. She had sautéed them in olive oil and butter and added the tomatoes I'd skinned. 'How long have you been a widow?'

It was bold of me, I think, but she didn't mind. 'My Paul, he died, oh, more than twenty years ago. He had never been really well since the war – the first war, I mean,' she answered. 'It was the gas, you know. They were gassed. He had a bad chest afterwards, and every winter he was ill. Finally, he couldn't fight it any more.' She arranged the courgettes neatly and put the dish into my hands. 'Étienne was only a youngster but he had to grow up. Now, come on.'

I thought about Étienne having to grow up quickly while we were eating the grilled rib steaks. He must have married Mathilde not many years after his father died. I didn't question the why, then. My father had married my mother and they didn't seem happy. Suzy's parents were distant too. As far as I was concerned, that was normal married life.

'Does your father have the infection too?' Lisette asked quietly as she and I washed the plates after supper. Her little voice reminded me again about the troubles at home.

'No, he's not well in another way,' I replied carefully. 'He isn't well in his head and can't manage without my mother to get his food and wash his clothes.'

'Then he should come here to be with you. You could look after him.'

It was, of course, impossible, but it did drag my mind back to the uncomfortable feeling that I'd let him down. Oh dear, I thought to myself, I should go home, no matter what.

'Lisette.' Grandmère's voice broke into my thoughts. 'It's time for bed.' She didn't sound as gruff with the child as she usually did and Lisette, responding, lifted her little face for a goodnight kiss from me and uncertainly turned to Grandmère.

'Goodnight, child.' A brief peck on both cheeks was delivered, startling, I thought, to both of them but none the less satisfactory.

'Goodnight, everyone,' the child sang and skipped away.

Grandmère took off her apron and took it out to the washroom. I looked through the open door and wondered about Étienne. Was he on the bridge waiting for me? Would we continue the kissing? Should I wander out there?

'Come through to the parlour,' said Grandmère, bustling back into the room. 'I want to look at the cards.'

I was restless that evening, not as content in Grandmère's company as usual, but I followed her into her dimly lit room and sat opposite her at the table whilst she shuffled the tattered cards. She had taken them from the top drawer of her cabinet and from where I was sitting I could see the black lace gloves I'd bought her lying on top of a collection of papers and pieces of material – scarves, I think. I wondered how long it had been since she'd had a present. Ages, I supposed, if the Martin family were anything like mine.

'Now, pay attention, Eleanor. Let's see what they tell us tonight.' She swiftly chose nine cards from the pack and laid them out in a fan shape. The queen of spades with her sly dark face was the first card and sat on the far left of the pattern. On the far right was the ace of hearts.

'Am I there?' I asked, suddenly curious about Grandmère's obsession with fate.

Grandmère's finger pointed to the ace of hearts. 'I think that's you.'

'And you?'

She shook her head. 'No. Nothing in this shows me, although . . .' she tapped her finger on a three of spades, 'I could be involved here.'

'Tell me,' I said. 'What do they all mean?'

'Another time.' Grandmère stood up and gathered together the cards. She seemed restless too. 'Put these away . . . in that drawer.' She nodded to the cabinet. 'I must check that I've enough butter and cheese for the market tomorrow.'

Alone in the dark little parlour I took the battered cards and pushing aside the papers and old photographs slid them into the drawer. I thought about the other time I'd searched in that drawer and the newspaper cutting that Grandmère had snatched out of my hand. Was it still there?

With a guilty look over my shoulder, I riffled through the pile of documents until it was in my hand. Why did I need to look at it? I didn't really know. Maybe I thought that, in some way, it would explain what was wrong in this house, but for whatever reason I slipped it out of the drawer and put it in the pocket of my shorts. I would look at it in my bedroom later and then find an opportunity to put it back.

I was already in the corridor when Grandmère called me. 'Have you shut up the hens?'

'No,' I called. 'I'm going now.'

Chapter Eleven

Outside it was still hot. The sun was going down and the trees hanging over the river had already melted into dusk. My hens had taken themselves to bed and all I needed to do was to close tight the coop door and empty the brackish water from their trough. I would rinse it out and refill it first thing, when I opened them up. I enjoyed the responsibility of them, and with my new-found skill of dispatching I thought that I would be well able to keep a dozen or so hens at home.

This thought drew me closer to the problems of Mother and Father. I couldn't imagine what had happened to Mother. An infection? Of where? I remembered the cuts she was always getting on her hands which turned septic and seemed to bother her. Maybe a dose of penicillin was all she needed, but . . . why did she need to go to hospital?

Then there was Dada. I squirmed as I walked through the vegetable garden back to the house. How could I be happy here when he was locked in an insane asylum? I must go home.

My uncomfortable thoughts were interrupted by the put-put noise of Jean Paul's bike. He'd pulled up in the yard and as I walked towards the kitchen door he was there, standing beside his machine with a vacant expression on his face.

'Hello,' I said, smiling and trying to put him at ease. He didn't answer but merely turned his large head and stared at me. After a moment he raised his hand to wipe away the greasy beads of sweat which had gathered on his forehead.

I tried again. 'Have you had a good day?'

He frowned as if trying to understand me and then swallowed several times, his fast-growing Adam's apple bobbing violently in his neck. I could see that he was swaying, and as I watched he grabbed hold of the handlebars of his bike to support him.

'Go away,' he mumbled and then said more words which I didn't understand. I know now that he was swearing at me but then I just stood in front of him, trying to be friendly.

Suddenly, he lurched forward and vomited, the sick flying across the yard, missing me but splattering horribly over the cobbled ground.

'Oh!' I leapt back, horrified, but continued to watch as, bent double and making terrible groaning noises, he vomited again and again.

Étienne rushed into the yard from the barn and, alerted by the noise, Grandmère appeared at the kitchen door, her hands wringing out a dish cloth.

'He's ill,' I called out in alarm, pointing my finger towards the pathetic figure who was now on his knees amongst the horrible debris of his stomach contents. 'Jean Paul is terribly ill. He must have eaten something bad.'

'Drunk, more like,' shouted Étienne, his face twisted and ugly in disgust and utterly devoid of sympathy. 'The little bastard has spent the day pouring beer down his neck. My God! How dare he!' And, grasping Jean Paul's shirt by the collar, he dragged the boy through the puddle of vomit across the yard and flung him bodily through the barn door.

A small hand crept into mine. Lisette was standing beside me in her white cotton nightdress, her light brown hair drooping over her little face. She must have slipped out of bed and come into the yard, through a window, maybe. She certainly wouldn't have got past Grandmère at the kitchen door.

'Oh dear,' she whispered. 'Papa will do something awful.'

My heart felt as though it had swollen in my chest and I could hear every galloping beat. That wonderful atmosphere we'd all enjoyed at supper time, when we'd laughed about Monsieur d'Amboise and his cattle and Lisette and I had been part of a happy family, had dispersed as quickly as the early evening mist. Étienne had been full of life and excitement then and I'd exulted in the sight of his strong face and the bulging muscles in his shoulders which strained the stitching of his shirt. Now, in the lowering gloom, the old mood of despair and anger prevailed and Étienne wasn't laughing. I found that I was as frightened as Lisette.

At the door to the barn Étienne was unbuckling his belt and I could guess what he was going to do. I'd never seen anyone beaten and although Mother was constantly shouting and grumbling at me she had never hit me, not even the smallest slap. Physical contact with me or Dada was not something she cared for. She wasted none of her time on hugs and the same applied to smacks. We lived at a distance in our house.

But I knew that Jean Paul was about to get a thrashing

and I was scared. Lisette's hand in mine was shaking; I could hear the tiny gulps and moans that escaped her pale lips and the shuddering breaths rocking her little body.

I straightened up and letting go of Lisette's hand took a step forward. It would have to be me who stopped him. I must have upset Jean Paul somehow, I reasoned, and the vomiting was my fault. Looking back over the years, I wonder at my naivety. How could I have possibly believed that? Why did I not see that the lives of these people were ruined long before I arrived among them? But at the time I felt I was responsible and it was up to me to try to make things right. I didn't know what I was going to say. All I knew was that a beating would be intolerable.

'Monsieur Martin!' I started but at the same moment Grandmère called 'Étienne!' and I turned my head to see that she had walked out of the kitchen door and was halfway across the yard. 'Étienne. Don't!' Her order was quite clear and Étienne, almost unrecognisable with rage, the broad leather belt dangling from his hand, stopped and looked back at us. A lifetime seemed to pass and Lisette's hand was once more in mine while we watched the frenzy slowly clear from Étienne's face, to be replaced by a look of utter desolation. Was I holding my breath? I think so. Certainly I remember that the wind had dropped and the evening twittering of the birds in the willows had died away. And in that thick silence, there came the click, click sound of Mathilde's shoes as she walked across the bridge.

'Lisette, go inside.' Grandmère had reached me and was standing, a dark solid figure, not looking at me or the little girl but frowning at the sight of Mathilde, who had stopped beside the barn. 'You too, Eleanor.'

'But . . .' I started to argue.

'Go on. It will be all right.' Her large hand touched my arm and gave me a gentle push. 'It will be all right,' she repeated. 'Go.'

I turned then and, pulling on Lisette's hand, walked reluctantly to the house, looking back once to see the tableau of Étienne, Mathilde and Grandmère standing beside the barn door. Étienne, his fists clenched, hadn't moved inside the barn and Grandmère was between him and Mathilde, her forefinger raised as if giving more orders. Mathilde was leaning against the barn door, a lit cigarette dangling from her bright red lips and her face turned up to the sky in an attitude of declared boredom. As I watched, she moved to go into the barn but was stopped by Étienne who leant forward and roughly snatched the cigarette from between her lips and ground it out on the cobbles before she disappeared from sight.

Inside the house the rooms seemed to echo as Lisette and I walked through the kitchen. 'Do you want a drink?' I asked her.

'No, thank you.'

'Then you must go back to bed,' I said. 'Come on.'

'I do love you, Eleanor,' she whispered as I tucked her under her duvet and put her chosen dolly beside her. 'You are a discovery delicious.'

I smiled and held her hand for a few minutes, until she drifted off to sleep. I'd wondered if she would make any comment about what had happened in the yard, but she didn't. Perhaps it was a common occurrence. Perhaps the ever present threat of violence in this household had washed over the little girl and she didn't notice it. But even thinking it, I knew I was wrong. She'd been very afraid.

My ears nervously strained for sounds of shouting from outside, maybe even screaming from Jean Paul if Étienne had decided to go ahead with the beating, but there was nothing. Only the rustle and swish of leaves from the trees by the river as the evening breeze got up again and the occasional lowing of the cattle in the fields where a fox or a rat had disturbed them. I did hear the kitchen door slam and then water running as though into a bucket, but nothing more.

I went to my room and switched on the lamp beside my bed. It had a milky white globe over a brass base and it lent a gentle light to the safe harbour that I now regarded as mine. The shutters were closed but I opened them and looked out. I could see nothing untoward. The river flowed and the trees swayed and dipped as usual. The moon was rising, bright in a starry sky so that the bridge and banks were almost as clear as in daylight. On the far side, above the vineyard, a figure walked uphill towards the stone barn. At this distance I couldn't work out who it was, man or woman, but in my mind it had to be Mathilde. It was her place.

It was when I was taking off my clothes, ready to get into bed, that the crackle of the newspaper cutting in my pocket reminded me that I'd stolen it from Grandmère's drawer. Alone in my room, I blushed, ashamed at what I'd done and determined to replace it as soon as possible. But . . . I had to look at it first.

The photograph had been taken from a balcony or a first floor room overlooking a square and I knew it was the square outside the church where we went for Mass on Sunday. It showed thirty or so men standing in a semicircle around a metal café chair on which a woman sat. Behind her was a man with a pair of scissors, in the process of cutting off all her hair. One side had already been done; you could see the little tufts sticking up where his inexpert attention had left her head bald in places and with bits of hair in others. Dark hair lay on the ground beside her and one of her hands was on her lap, caught in the action of brushing the strands away from her skirt.

She was staring straight ahead, not crying nor looking frightened and even from the distance that the photographer had been standing, I knew who it was. Those large cow-like eyes and the sneering expression told me immediately. Mathilde.

Confused, I put the cutting down on the bed and stood up. The evening breeze had strengthened and the shutter, which I hadn't properly fastened, was banging. Hooking it on to the latch, I looked out. Étienne was leaning against the rail on the bridge, not fishing, but just standing there. He looked desolate, and somehow almost lost. I yearned to run downstairs and go out to comfort him but I didn't. I couldn't. He was an adult and I thought of myself as still a child. So I sat on my bed and looked again at the newspaper cutting.

I could tell that the photograph had been taken a while ago. Mathilde looked younger and the clothes that the men were wearing seemed slightly old-fashioned. Looking closer, I noticed that on the edge of the semicircle and slightly apart from the other men was an American soldier. He wasn't laughing like the others but fingering the strap of his rifle as though concerned that things might turn nasty. As far as I was concerned, things, in that picture, had already turned nasty.

Surprisingly, after all that had happened, when I got into bed I slept straight away and didn't dream. It was early morning when I suddenly woke, so early that the light filtering through the shutters was dim and grey, and I guessed that it must be about five o'clock. Guessing was what I had to do. I didn't have a wristwatch. Most of my friends at school had them, bought by their parents as presents or rewards for passing exams. Mother patently hadn't thought that a justifiable expense and I'd never questioned it. I knew money was tight.

I lay for a moment trying to work out what it was that had disturbed me. A noise? A splash in the river? It was impossible to know so I got out of bed and slowly opened the shutters. Outside, clouds covered the sky and it was cooler than it had been. So far, during my holiday at Riverain, the days had been terribly hot with cloudless, bleached blue skies broken only by occasional sharp evening rainstorms. But this morning it was gloomy and grey and almost English.

There was a sound of steps on the bridge and looking down I saw Étienne striding across. He walked purposefully, as though he had been doing something in the vineyard and was now returning to the yard. I was surprised that, whatever it was, he'd been doing it so early. The other thing that surprised me was that he was cradling his shotgun in his arms.

I got up then. Even if I was in the kitchen before Grandmère, it wouldn't matter. She had taught me how to make coffee, or better still I could cycle to the village to fetch the bread. The bakery would be open and I'd been before, so I knew what to get.

Dragging on my shorts, I remembered the newspaper

cutting which had crackled in the pocket. It was there on the table beside my bed and I quickly stuffed it away, ready to return it to Grandmère's cabinet at the very first opportunity.

'*Bonjour*,' said the baker when I walked through the open door into his shop. He looked tired and was cradling a steaming cup of coffee in one floury hand.

I smiled back and picking out two baguettes from the wire holder passed them over the counter to be wrapped in the piece of greaseproof paper.

'You're an early riser, Miss Eleanor,' he said as he wrapped them and handed them back. 'I thought you were on holiday. My children lie in bed for hours when they don't have to go to school.'

I was surprised that he knew my name, but I shouldn't have been. This was a very small place. I shrugged, demonstrating the local response to difficult questions.

'Any news of your *maman*?'

Again, he knew all about Mother's illness and that I was staying on at Riverain.

'No.' I shook my head. 'Nothing new. She's in hospital. I can't go home yet.'

'So I heard,' he said, then reached over and patted my hand. 'You are a most welcome addition to our village.'

Stupidly, I felt tears coming to my eyes. I wasn't used to such kindness. 'Thank you,' I mumbled and hurried out, eager to get on the bike and pedal home.

'You are up very early, Eleanor,' said Grandmère, echoing the baker's remark. She was bustling around the kitchen with a couple of leeks in her hand. The stock pot was already bubbling on the range, giving off fresh aromas of onions and garlic. I could smell meat too. Beef. She was making a meaty soup for lunch. I was about to ask her about it when she continued, 'Did you have trouble sleeping?'

'No, not at all.' I shook my head. 'It's just that something woke me and I couldn't get back to sleep.'

'What?' She frowned. 'What woke you?'

'I don't know,' I said, reaching for the coffee and tearing a chunk off the fresh-baked baton. 'A noise or something.'

Neither of us mentioned the scene of last night but its occurrence lay heavily in the air. I'd noticed as I rode through the yard that the cobbles had been washed clean, with no sign of Jean Paul's vomit. I supposed that it had been done last evening after I'd gone upstairs.

'Monsieur Martin was up early too,' I said. 'I saw him coming from the vineyard.'

'Yes.' Grandmère nodded. 'He needs to prune away the vine leaves so that the sun gets to the grapes. It makes them sweeter.'

'But he . . .' I was going to say he was carrying his shotgun, not pruning shears.

'But what?'

'Oh, nothing. It doesn't matter.' Étienne's reasons for carrying a gun were nothing to do with me, but Grandmère wasn't going to let it go. She pulled out a chair and sat at the table opposite me, her eyes drilling into my head.

'He had his shotgun.' My voice had dropped as though I was telling some sort of dreadful secret, and I think I felt that I was.

'Oh, is that all?' Grandmère shrugged and I could see that she had relaxed. Her shoulders dropped and the

V-shaped crease in her forehead disappeared. 'I expect he's been after rabbits. Maybe we'll have a casserole tonight.'

I got on with my breakfast then and she went into the pantry, but I wondered what she had been expecting me to say.

Chapter Twelve

I decided to go for a walk before lunch. Lisette was playing with her dolls in the vegetable garden and Grandmère had been at the roll-top desk for the last hour working, I think, on the account books. I'd seen Jean Paul briefly, in the kitchen, while I was still drinking my breakfast coffee. He'd come through the door from the yard and without a word put his head under the tap and drunk noisy gulps of water.

When he straightened up I could see that his face and the front of his black hair were wet. Dribbles of water ran down his chin and on to the vomit-stained white shirt. He must have slept in the barn, I thought, sorry for him in a way, and now I could see the little bits of straw and dust from the barn floor on his trousers. He bent and took more gulps of water and then wiped his hand over his mouth. More water dripped from his hair and he shook himself slowly, his face grimacing in pain. Water sprayed across the room, hitting the window above the sink and dropping on to the table.

Lisette, who was sitting beside me, gave one of her high little laughs. 'Jean Paul looks like a dog who's been in the river,' she giggled.

'Shush,' I warned, thinking that Jean Paul might turn on her, but he ignored us and grabbed the last piece of bread before going through the kitchen door into the corridor.

'Was that Jean Paul?' asked Grandmère, coming in from the vegetable garden.

I nodded. 'Yes.'

'Did he get something to eat?'

'A piece of bread.'

'Good. Now I want to clear the table and get on.'

'What about Papa?' asked Lisette. 'He hasn't had any breakfast.'

'He'll get something in town,' said Grandmère. 'He's gone in on business.'

Why did Lisette and I look at each other, then? Was it so unusual? Didn't Étienne go to the town on business regularly? I thought back. In the time I'd been with them, he hadn't, but that was only three weeks. Surely a busy farmer would have to go to the bank or to the solicitor on regular occasions. That brought up another thought. Did Mother go into town to talk to the bank? I couldn't remember. Then I wondered how she was. How was she managing? Who was visiting her in hospital? Who was getting her clean nightdresses . . . did she have any clean nightdresses? Oh, God . . . I must go home.

I walked up the hill through the vineyard, my mind whirling with difficult thoughts. I loved this place where, despite the unwelcoming attitude of Jean Paul and Mathilde, I felt happier, more at home and more useful than I'd ever felt on our bleak Pennine farm. I'd give anything to stay . . . but did that include ignoring my duty to my parents?

Shafts of sunlight pierced the heavy clouds which lay over the farm and lent a strange, uncomfortable atmosphere to the vine-covered hillside. I could see the grape barn near the top of the hill, the pale stone intermittently bleached by sudden beams of light then dull again when the grey and purple clouds rolled together and dimmed the scene. I'd never been in it, and since that first time when I'd suggested to Luc that we explore it together and I'd been rebuffed I'd stayed well clear. But now, this morning, I was in an awkward mood, feeling fretful and unsure of myself and ready to be rebellious. Why shouldn't I go and have a look, I thought. After all, neither Grandmère nor Étienne had said that it was off limits. I headed towards it.

The newspaper cutting crackled in my shorts pocket. I still hadn't found an opportunity to replace it and I felt miserable about what I'd done. Grandmère had kept me busy for much of the morning gathering eggs and vegetables, and later on took me into the dairy to explain the mysteries of cheese making.

'I'll start you off with it tomorrow, Eleanor,' she said, lining the small moulds with clean muslin squares. 'This is something you must learn. All farmer's wives should know how to make cheese and butter.'

I nodded, happy to go along with her plans but knowing in my heart that I'd never make cheese at home. As for being a 'farmer's wife', well, that was never going to happen either. I'd be a shop assistant at best and Mother's unpaid helper in all my spare time. My future was bleak. That's why I was grasping every moment of my stay at Riverain. It was the best that was going to be.

Now as I walked through the vineyard towards the barn I thought about my future. Could I possibly escape home and come back to France? Could I live here? Be Grandmère's unpaid helper? And Étienne's . . . Étienne's what? Even as I thought it I felt my face flushing, alone here, surrounded by green and brown vines and the ripening bunches of grapes. Stupid, I admonished myself. That was never going to happen either.

By the time I reached the barn the sunlight was totally obscured and it had started to rain, heavy drops spaced apart so that when they fell on to a stone they made a tiny splash. I looked up at the sky, at the full grey clouds which seemed closer to the ground than before, and heard a rumble of thunder. A flash of lightning suddenly brightened the hillside and then, almost before it had gone, another, louder rumble shook the earth.

The grape barn was only yards away and I hurried towards it. I could see that the door was swinging slightly in the breeze and was glad. At least I would be able to get in out of the rain.

Suddenly the door swung completely open and Jean Paul stood in the entrance, a cigarette hanging from his lips and a bottle of beer clutched in his fist. He had changed his shirt and looked clean and fresh, his black hair slicked back from his forehead and the nascent moustache very prominent.

'Hello!' I called.

'What d'you want?' he answered, scowling and stepping forward a little, barring my way into the barn.

'I want to come in. There's a thunderstorm,' I said, rain falling heavily on my head and shirt. 'Can't you see? Can't you hear it?'

He didn't move but looked back over his shoulder into the dark interior of the stone building. I leant forward and looked too. It was hard to see inside but I could make out what looked like a rug covering the floor. How strange, I thought.

'Go away.' Jean Paul turned abruptly and went back through the door.

I was angry. I couldn't understand why he was refusing me permission to shelter from the rain and, emboldened by the soaking I was getting, recklessly hurried after him.

'No, don't,' he breathed, coming to a halt and blocking my way. I thought he sounded panicky and I had paused for a moment, wondering what was wrong, when suddenly I was barged into by a man who pushed past Jean Paul and straight into me.

'*Pardon, mademoiselle,*' he said, then stopped and gave me a long stare. He was old, older than Étienne and older than my father. He wore a dark striped jacket which didn't match his trousers and had a smooth, plump face and a fleshy neck which bulged over his collar. He turned to Jean Paul, who was standing behind him with an inexplicably horrified look on his face. 'Is she available? This pretty girl?'

'No.' Jean Paul's voice came out in an agonised choke. 'No!'

The man shrugged. 'Oh well . . . a pity, though.'

I watched him, puzzled, as he turned up the collar of his jacket against the rain and pulled his trilby hat further down his head. He gave me one last appraising stare before striding away from the barn and starting to walk up the hill. I turned back to Jean Paul.

'What did he mean?' I asked. 'Who is that man?'

He said nothing. His cheeks were fiery red and I saw him close his eyes in what must have been despair.

'Has he gone?' Mathilde appeared in the darkness behind Jean Paul and, bending her head, kissed his shoulder. She seemed to be hardly dressed; I could see the broad shoulder straps of a slip but no dress and as my eyes trailed down I saw that her usual high-heeled shoes were absent. She wasn't looking out; her head was lowered, frowning at something in her hands.

'Yes,' he muttered, 'but . . .'

At that moment she looked up and saw me and the flash of pure poison that swept her white face chilled me to the bone. 'What the hell are you doing here, you stupid little cow?' she spat. 'Sent to spy, by that evil old woman, eh?' Her thin red-painted lips curled in a sneer and she flicked back her head, sending the black curtain of hair away from her face like a wave leaving a pale stone jetty. 'Get out of here, now. Or I'll kill you!'

My shock was profound. Nobody had ever spoken to me like that. I'd been reprimanded often for daydreaming in school, but gently by polite, educated teachers, and Mother constantly grumbled about everything I did. But nobody had ever frightened me as much as Mathilde Martin did on that dark, wet day, when huge purple clouds crashed in the heavens and only the zigzag lightning illuminated the hillside. I stood, gaping at her like a rabbit caught in the headlights, quite unable to move. This witch-like creature in her flesh-coloured slip and bare feet terrified me. Then I turned and ran.

By the time I stopped running I found I was on the lane which led to the d'Amboises' house. I'd clattered across the bridge but run past the house and on to the lane behind. Out of the corner of my eye, I'd seen Grandmère by the chicken run and felt her eyes on me as I flew by. Sometime I would have to explain to her but not now. Not now. I needed time to think.

The storm had passed over and for the first time that

day the sun shone brightly, causing steam to rise from the soggy grass beneath the trees which lined the road. I could hear birds twittering carelessly in the branches above me and others making rustling noises as they hopped in and out of the scrubby bushes below, searching for insects and seeds.

It was all as it should be. A bright sunny day in August and I was walking along a quiet country lane which led to a friend's house. I might be in France and the heat on that tree-enclosed path overwhelming, but I was used to that now and I loved being here. So why had I been so frightened? Surely my encounter with Mathilde was just an extension of her usual unpleasantness and nothing out of the ordinary? I knew that she didn't like me. She'd made that obvious on more than one occasion, but even as I thought it and tried to convince myself, I knew that this was different. The events I'd witnessed at the grape barn couldn't possibly be normal life, even here, in this corner of rural France, where everything was so foreign to me.

In my naivety I'd accepted the tense family life of the Martins. Put their arguments and silences down to normal behaviour, not really so different from that of my own family. Yet now I was beginning to realise that I'd been wrong. There was a strange, dangerous atmosphere around this place where holding your breath in anticipation of what might happen next was the norm. I had been sent to a house of secrets where there was no recognisable warmth and even simple civility seemed to be balanced on a cliff edge.

I thought of Suzy and her stay in Paris with the sophisticated English-speaking family. Nothing like this would be happening to her, I knew it. She'd have been all over the city, in and out of wonderful buildings and eating at fashionable restaurants. She would be going home in a couple of days having had a memorable holiday and taking a charming French companion with her. They would have a lovely time in England, with all sorts of treats and outings organised by Suzy's parents. Suzy and the French girl would probably remain friends for the rest of their lives, visiting each other, holidaying in each other's homes, having children who would grow up to be friends also. While I was unable to go home yet and, when I did go home, I'd have nobody to take with me. People at school would gossip about my failure, not only the girls but the teachers, and Miss Baxter would shake her head sadly and whisper to the headmistress that 'Eleanor Gill has an unhappy home life, so I'm not surprised that the French exchange hasn't worked out'. I'd be a laughing stock.

I stopped walking and sat down on the damp grass verge amongst the willowherb and cow parsley. The hot smell of vegetation made me feel slightly sick and I had to swallow rising bile which burnt my throat and brought tears to my eyes. It was so unfair, I told myself, but what else did I expect? Mother had said it would be a disaster and she was right. Then I thought again about Mother and poor Dada and before I knew it I was sobbing, hot, convulsive, uncontrollable sobbing, and that's how Luc d'Amboise found me.

'Eleanor? What is it?' He squatted down and put a hand on my shoulder. 'What's the matter?'

I couldn't speak. Not only because of the shuddering sobs that took all my breath away but because of the sheer embarrassment of his finding me here, sitting on the side of the road.

I shook my head. 'It doesn't matter,' I managed to whisper between sobs, hoping he'd get up and carry on walking along the lane towards his house, but instead he sat down beside me and put his arm round me.

I cried on his shoulder for what seemed like hours but in reality was probably only minutes. He didn't say anything but squeezed my shoulders comfortingly and waited until the last heaving of my chest had subsided and I could drag a hand across my face to wipe away the streaky tears.

'Now,' he said, and his voice carried the authority of someone twice his age. 'Tell me. Are you ill?'

'No.' I shook my head.

'Is it about your mother and father?'

'No. Not really.'

'Well, what?'

'It's . . .' I didn't know how to put it. 'It was Mathilde. She frightened me.' The explanation came out in a rush and I blushed as I said it. How childish I sounded.

Strangely, Luc didn't seem to think it was childish. When I turned to look at him he was frowning. 'What did she do?' He sounded serious.

'I went to the grape barn and wanted to get out of the thunderstorm but Jean Paul wouldn't let me in. And then a man came out and asked if I was available and then Mathilde came out and . . .' I went over the scene in my head, remembering things that had flashed by me at the time. 'Luc,' I gabbled, 'she wasn't wearing her dress and had no shoes on. She was holding money.'

'Oh, God,' Luc groaned. 'You shouldn't have seen that.'

I felt all the emotions rising again. 'What?' I grasped his arm. 'What did I see? I don't understand.' But the thing was I did understand. My friends in school whispered about women who worked on the streets and some even knew which streets in town those women went to. But here? On this idyllic farm? I couldn't bear to think about it. Then I thought, does Étienne know? Grandmère? But of course they did. That's why they hated her so much.

'Did she see you?' Luc took my hand.

I nodded. 'She was furious. She accused me of spying on her . . . I wasn't, honestly, but then she said . . .' I swallowed, the burning bile again in my throat making my voice croaky and hesitant. 'She said she would kill me.'

At first he said nothing but stared at my tear-stained face, his boyishly handsome features twisted into a frown. 'She didn't mean it,' he said eventually. 'Not really. But . . . stay away from her as much as you can. I don't think she's to be trusted.'

Why, I longed to say. What do you know about her that you aren't telling me? Is she really a . . . I didn't know the word and wouldn't have said it out loud even if I did. Instead I got up. 'I have to go. It's lunch time.'

'Yes, me too.' Luc got up and shook hands with me in that polite French way.

We started walking in opposite directions; then I turned and called, 'Luc, thank you.'

He waved his hand and grinned. 'It's all right.'

When I got back to Riverain I went straight to my room. I needed to wash my face and hands and change my clothes but really I wasn't ready to face Grandmère yet. Those dark eyes of hers would penetrate my mind and I would be unable to avoid her questions.

She was in the kitchen piling tiny pink shrimps on to an earthenware dish and didn't look up when I finally came down the back stairs. A lettuce was on the draining board ready to be washed and I went straight to it, tearing off the root and separating the leaves carefully. It was when I was drying it on a clean tea towel that she spoke.

'I know something has happened, Eleanor. If you want to tell me, this is a good time. We are on our own.'

Should I keep quiet, shrugging the incident away as they all seemed to, or lie, pretending not to have witnessed anything? The last thing I wanted was for her to disbelieve me or, worse, to think that I was a meddling interloper, so perhaps it would be better to say nothing. But when I looked round she was staring at me, her face strangely softened and full of compassion. It was the expression I'd longed to see on my mother's face.

I told her then, everything, from start to finish, including Luc finding me in the lane and comforting me. 'And Grandmère,' I added, my face scarlet, 'there is another thing.' I put the lettuce leaves in the wire draining basket and pulled the crumpled newspaper cutting from my pocket. 'This was in your drawer when I put the cards away last night. I was curious. I'm sorry.' I put it on the table beside the dish of shrimps.

Lisette wandered into the room and Grandmère snatched up the newspaper cutting and put it into the pocket of her apron.

'Is it time to eat? Papa has come home.'

'Yes it is. Wash your hands, Lisette, and then go and sit in your place. Eleanor and I will bring in the food.'

As I carried the salad into the dining room Grandmère murmured, 'We'll talk later,' and gave me a little pat on the arm. I felt calmer.

There was no sign of Mathilde at the table but Jean Paul was sitting in his place, his head lowered, not looking at anyone. Étienne was uncharacteristically silent too. I supposed that his business dealings in town hadn't gone well that morning. Maybe it was to do with money. My mother was obsessed with money, how she hadn't any, and it made her furious. Étienne hadn't changed out of his striped suit and looked hot and uncomfortable, but as I watched him out of the corner of my eye he shrugged out of his jacket and placed it on the back of his chair. His white shirt looked damp and crumpled. It had a tiny pink wine stain on the front and the sleeves were rolled up over his muscular arms. He must have been drinking in town, I thought, watching him as he carved the bread into thick diagonal slices and tossed them across the table.

Even Lisette picked up on the sombre mood, not chattering as usual but eating her shrimps quietly, dipping them neatly into the delicious mayonnaise that Grandmère had prepared to go with them.

It was Grandmère who broke the silence. 'Lisette,' she said, 'Madame d'Amboise's daughter is coming this afternoon with her children. She has asked if you would like to go and play.'

'Me?' Lisette breathed, her face pink with excitement.

'Yes. After lunch you can walk down the lane to their house. Make sure you behave yourself and don't be rough with the little boy.'

I couldn't imagine Lisette being rough with anyone

and raised an eyebrow in amusement. Grandmère caught it and gave me one of her rare smiles.

'Lisette is always a good girl,' Étienne grunted from the head of the table and we all turned to look at him. He was pouring wine, his hand rather unsteady so that the earthenware carafe clinked against his glass. He had opened the top two buttons of his shirt, exposing the sheen of sweat on his neck and some of the black hair on his chest.

'Thank you, Papa,' squeaked Lisette, her cheeks pink with excitement. 'I will be good.'

'I'm sure you will.' He drained his glass and reached for the jug again, then stopped his hand in mid-air. 'Oh! I've remembered. I have to go to the *cave*, the *tuffeau*, this afternoon. Perhaps Eleanor would like to come with me.' He turned to me and to my delight I saw that his grin had returned. 'You'll find it interesting, I think. Something different.'

The *tuffeau*? The *cave*? I smiled back at him, uncomprehending. Why would he need to go to a cave? I mentally searched my French vocabulary for a translation of the words. Did he mean the cellar, or maybe some sort of a cavern? A tourist spot, maybe. I turned to Grandmère for help.

'Étienne has to go to the place where he buys wine,' she said. 'The *cave* is like a shop for wine. A cellar.'

'Oh,' I said, slightly disappointed that he was only going shopping but thrilled that he wanted me to go with him. 'Yes, I'd like to see it. That is,' I added, turning back to Grandmère, 'if you don't need me.'

Grandmère started gathering the plates. 'Go and enjoy yourself,' she said, not looking me in the eye. 'I'll see you later.'

I looked around the table, happy for the first time today. Lisette was singing quietly, excited about her trip to the d'Amboises', and when I caught her eye she showed her little mouse teeth in a sweet smile. Étienne had stopped drinking and was writing a list on the back of an envelope. Perhaps it was a list of wines he wanted to buy.

It was only later, when I sat beside Étienne in the van on the way to the *cave,* that I thought about Jean Paul and remembered the look on his face. It was one of bewildered fury. He must have been so angry, so jealous, even frustrated that no one wanted to include him in any activity. I felt almost sorry for him, but only almost.

Chapter Thirteen

We drove away from the village on to the main road to the city, then, after a few miles, took a side road which led through acres of vineyards until we reached a road which ran alongside a river. Big puddles, the remains of the morning's thunderstorm, spread across the unmade road but now it was hot and steam was rising from them. There was a haze about the area which made the verdant scenery look as though one was viewing it through a piece of gauze.

'This,' said Étienne, 'is the Loire.' He waved his arm, pointing to the broad expanse of water, which shone a metalled blue in the hazy sunlight. It flowed more swiftly than the river which ran through the farm, although the current was broken up by an island, a long wooded strip of land which seemed to be midway between the nearer bank and the far side. I wondered if anyone lived on the island and looked for tiled roofs between the trees but could see none.

We arrived at a riverside village. On the bank beside us fishing punts and larger craft were tied up to posts dug into the sandy mud beach whilst out in the river it was all activity, with boats of various sizes making their way up- and downstream. As well as fishing smacks I saw barges – one close by had a cargo of coal – and pushing through the river traffic was a smart white police motor launch. On shore several men worked on their boats, caps pushed to the backs of their heads and oily rags in their hands. Others relaxed with wine glasses in front of them in a café close to where Étienne parked the van. Further along the road I could see houses and shops and more people, mostly women and children, and a bridge across to the far bank. This was a lively place, quite different from the sleepy village near to Riverain.

'The *cave* is just beyond that café,' said Étienne, as I scrambled out of the van. 'My old friend Robert Brissac owns it and there's nothing he doesn't know about viniculture. His family have been trading wine since before the Revolution.'

I nodded and followed him along the road. He stopped to exchange a few joking words with the drinkers at the café and I marvelled at how different he seemed away from home, freer somehow, almost like a different person.

'Robert and I grew up together and were compatriots during the war. He was my leader.' This last was said with what sounded like respect and admiration.

Leader in what, I wondered, and then smiled to myself. Leader in blowing up castles.

The shops and cafés were built on and in some cases directly into the white limestone rock face which bordered the road. I even saw a few two-storey houses, with the windows at the front decorated by iron trellis baskets which held pots of red geraniums. I could only imagine how dark it would be inside at the back, cosy perhaps but claustrophobic. I thought of home, my house on the hill, uncomfortably open to the elements where the raw wind blew in through the badly fitting windows and under the doors, so that the outside was always part of our lives. Standing on that sandy river road in the steam-laden heat of a summer afternoon in France, I felt homesick for a moment.

'Ah, Robert!'

A man was waiting by the wooden arched door of his *cave*. A painted sign swung above the door, announcing that these were the premises of Brissac and son, wine merchants, established in 1782. As if to prove it, a picture of a small round man with his head happily thrown back as he downed a glass of wine was painted on the old wood beneath the legend.

Robert Brissac couldn't have looked more different from the little painted man. He was tall and reed thin, with collar-length dark hair which was liberally sprinkled with grey. He was old, I thought, older than my father. But when he greeted Étienne his lined face relaxed into a broad smile and I saw that they must have been about the same age. That stern exterior was not due to the simple passage of time.

'This young lady is Eleanor, our visitor,' said Étienne, and he put a hand between my shoulder blades and gently pushed me forward. The heat from his hand on my back added to my confusion and I must have looked like a silly little girl as I blushed through my reply to Robert's polite remarks.

'*Ah, trés jolie*,' he said, his dark eyes probing my face. As he shook my hand he looked over my head to Étienne. 'Something different at Riverain, eh?'

'Yes.' I could hear the small choke in Étienne's voice and looked round curiously, but he seemed no different from seconds before.

'And Madame Martin, she is well?'

'She is, thank you. She is teaching Eleanor to cook. They are great friends.'

It was very strange. Madame Martin. He meant Grandmère. Mathilde and Jean Paul weren't mentioned or referred to. It was as if they never existed.

Robert fixed his gaze on me. He had dark, deeply set eyes which seemed as though they would permit no dissembling.'Now, where in England do you live?'

'In the Pennines.'

He frowned and then shook his head slowly. 'I don't know that area. What is your nearest big city?'

'Manchester. We live about twenty-five miles away, up in the hills.'

'Ah.' He nodded. 'Now I know. The north of England, yes? I was never there. Étienne and I spent time in Scotland, then went down to the south of England before . . .'

He stopped at that point and looked at his friend. I was surprised to see Étienne gently punch Robert's shoulder before winking at me.

'Robert and I learned to do many things in Scotland.' He laughed softly. 'Things that we needed later. Isn't that so, Robert?'

'Yes, my friend.' Robert heaved a sigh. 'But we must forget all that now. We have to talk business. Yes?'

He led the way through the shop and we walked a narrow path between racks of wine and stacked up crates into a well lit back room where a desk was pushed against the limestone wall with two chairs beside it. I noticed that Robert walked with a slight limp, and when he pulled chairs up to the desk I saw that his hands were bent and the fingers terribly out of shape. I wondered what had happened to them.

'Papa?' A girl had come through the shop into the office. She was my age, I thought, tall and thin like her father with dark hair cut short in a straight bob.

'Jeanne, how timely. You know Monsieur Martin, of course.' The girl went up to Étienne and shook his hand warmly. 'And this,' her father continued, 'is Miss Eleanor, his visitor from England.'

We shook hands and I was glad that I'd changed into my pink frock. She looked quite smart in a grey knee-length dress with a white Peter Pan collar and a row of tiny mother of pearl buttons down the front. I wondered if she was wearing school uniform.

'Étienne and I have business to discuss. Perhaps you'll take Miss Eleanor for a little walk?'

We went out of the shop and on to the lane beside the river. It was very hot again and I could feel the hairs on my arms prickle under a sheen of sweat as we strolled up the road towards the bridge. A few curious glances came my way as people nodded to Jeanne or stopped briefly to shake her hand. She seemed to know everybody.

We sat on a bench beside the bridge and I watched men with fishing rods leaning against the metal railing casting their lines into the water. I thought about the other night, when Étienne had put his arms round me, and knew I was blushing.

'Are you too hot?' asked Jeanne.

'No, I'm fine,' I said quickly. 'I found it difficult here at first because this area is so much warmer than where I live, but I think I'm used to it now.'

'Are you still at school?'

'Oh, yes. Are you?'

'Of course.' She made a disdainful face. 'I'm not going

to end up mending nets or serving in cafés like the stupid girls around here. After university I shall be a lawyer. In Paris, perhaps.' She looked back over her shoulder down the road to the *cave* where her father and Étienne were discussing business before continuing, 'Then I shall come home and take over. Papa will be ready to retire.'

'Oh.' I didn't know what to say and I hoped that she wouldn't ask me about my plans. I'd have to lie, if she did. I changed the subject. 'You seem to know everyone round here.'

'I do, or rather everybody knows me. We are an established family. My father is famous, you see. He's a hero. A war hero.' She smoothed a hand down her glossy hair and then straightened her collar. I wondered how she remained so neat and cool on this baking afternoon. My linen dress was wilting badly and I knew that tiny curls were already twining damply around my hairline.

'What does your father do?' Her questions were rapped out as though she was already a lawyer. I thought she would have no problems in a court room and worried that she would see through my vague answer.

'We have a farm, a hill farm. We run sheep.'

'Oh,' she said. 'And do your brothers help on the farm or are they going to continue their education?'

She sounded so adult, so like my teachers in school, that I began to wonder if she was older than she looked.

'No,' I said. 'I have no brothers or sisters. My mother helps with the sheep.' I didn't say anything about my father's illness. I didn't want to think about it.

Jeanne nodded. 'I too am an only child,' she said, her face very solemn, 'but my mother was killed in the war by the Germans. My father relies on my constant companionship. Sometimes he is ill and his wounds still hurt dreadfully, but he never complains. Oh, he is a truly remarkable man.'

I turned my head away from the anglers on the bridge to stare at her. To my unsophisticated ears what she said sounded extraordinary. In my experience children didn't talk about their parents that way. Clearly, she worshipped Robert Brissac.

Two boys on bicycles sped along the lane shouting and laughing to each other. They came to a dusty screeching halt beside us. Jeanne Brissac frowned and flicked the raised specks of sand from her skirt. 'Did you have to do that?' she grumbled.

They laughed and then looked at me. 'Who's this?' one boy asked. He was small with a foxy narrow face and big ears. 'Your cousin, perhaps?'

'No, certainly not.' The very thought seemed to horrify her and I suppose I should have been offended, but the insult, if indeed it was one, passed over me. I accepted her attitude as I accepted everything in France. Simply a cultural difference. It was easier for me.

'This is Miss Eleanor. From England. She is staying with Monsieur and Madame Martin.'

'Étienne Martin who worked with your father during the war?'

Jeanne nodded and I smiled, hoping for a friendly conversation.

'And Mathilde,' spat the other boy, taller and more heavyset. 'The collaborator.'

My gasp was audible and Jeanne stood up and pulled on my arm. 'We must get back,' she said. 'My father will be waiting.'

I looked back at the boys once, as we walked away. They were watching us with their heads together and suddenly one boy made his hand into the shape of a pistol and pretended to shoot me. I was bewildered. 'What did he mean?' I asked. 'About Mathilde?'

'She was friendly with the Germans when we were occupied. That was a very bad thing.'

'But they don't despise Étienne – I mean Monsieur Martin?'

'No,' she answered. 'He was very brave and fought in the Résistance with my father. He saved my life when I was a child.'

He saved her life? How? I was frustrated by the snippets of information that kept being revealed and longed to ask more questions about Mathilde and Étienne, but we had arrived back at her father's *cave* and Jeanne was leading the way through the shop. Suddenly she stopped and held her hand up.

'Wait.'

From the office at the back I could hear raised voices. 'I can't.' That was Étienne. 'I have planned it so many times and God knows I want to so much.'

'You must.' Robert Brissac's voice had the unmistakable quality of leadership. 'Those were the orders given. As far as I know, they've never been rescinded.'

'Come on.' Jeanne went further into the shop, knocking her arm noisily against an empty rack, and when we got to the office the two men were sitting by the desk, holding up glasses of wine to the light.

Étienne and I left soon after. I had shaken hands with Jeanne and Robert Brissac at the door and he had complimented me once again. 'You're a pretty girl with excellent

French. We could have done with someone like you during the war.' When he said goodbye to Étienne, he gave him a meaningful stare. 'Remember what I said,' he muttered.

I was still going over what Jeanne Brissac and those two boys had said when I got into the van beside Étienne. He was quiet too, although his fingers drummed constantly on the window frame.

We drove the first few miles in silence and then Étienne cleared his throat and turned his head to me. 'I'm thinking of extending my vineyard,' he said, his voice loud in the rattling van. 'Robert believes that my grapes are too good to go to the co-op and that I should go back to producing my own wine. We used to, you know, in my father's time, but when I took over I wasn't keen. I thought cattle and the dairy would be better.'

'It will be hard work, I think,' I murmured absently, trying to push away thoughts of Mathilde, the collaborator.

'It will. I'll have to buy hundreds of plants, take on workers and get new machinery. He shrugged and swung the van violently in his usual way on to the side road that led to Riverain. 'But Robert thinks I need a new beginning. That things must change. He will help me make that change.'

He carried on, noisy now, cheerfully telling me his plans for the farm while I sat beside him in that rattling, swerving van staring silently ahead at the shimmer on the road, my mind a furious muddle of conflicting thoughts.

We drove into the yard and came to one of Étienne's shuddering stops. 'What is it, Eleanor? Why are you so quiet?' he asked, not moving from the van but sitting with his hands on the steering wheel and his eyes fixed on the open door of the barn in front of us. 'You are thinking of your parents, maybe?'

'No.' I shook my head.

'Then what? Have I upset you?'

'Jeanne Brissac said that Mathilde was a collaborator.' The words fell out of my mouth almost without my forming them and I was immediately horrified at what I'd said. I waited, my stomach churning, for him to shout at me, to get into a rage as he did with Jean Paul and throw me out of the van or even ban me from the house. I could see myself packing my few clothes into the pigskin suitcase and walking down the road to the village. I was sure that the British consul would help me if only I could remember his number.

There was a long silence while I chewed my lip nervously, drawing a speck of salty blood, before Étienne heaved a sigh. 'Yes,' he muttered. 'She was. She went with the German officer who was billeted here and perhaps with others.' He shrugged, his voice cold and bitter. 'Oh yes, Mathilde would certainly go with others.'

I swallowed. What had I done, bringing this into the open? How could I have been so cruel? 'I'm sorry, Étienne,' I whispered, not noticing that I had used his first name. 'I know it's none of my business . . . it was just . . .' What? What was it? Surprising? No, not really. I thought of the newspaper cutting and what was happening in the picture. It was clear that the village had been taking revenge, but then why was she still here?

'I'm so sorry,' I repeated, hating to see his previously

cheerful face still and drawn. 'I shouldn't have mentioned . . .'

'Hello!' Lisette poked her little head through the van window. She had danced home from her afternoon at the d'Amboises' and was pink with excitement. 'Oh, Eleanor,' she squeaked. 'I've had such a lovely time.'

I tore my head to the side and put on a smile. 'Have you? Well, you must tell me all about it.'

As I walked to the kitchen door with Lisette's hand tucked in mine I heard the van door slam, and glancing back saw Étienne standing uncertainly by it. He was watching me, his face creased into a frown, and a shiver ran down my back. Our friendship must be over.

I hoped that Mathilde would give supper a miss that evening. Surely, after my finding her entertaining a man in the grape barn, she wouldn't have the face to sit beside me throughout a meal. Maybe she would go into town, have something to eat there, in a bar or wherever she usually went. With her friends. With men.

I told Grandmère what Jeanne Brissac had said while I was drying the lettuce.

'Huh!' she snorted, waving floury hands in the air. 'That girl should keep her big mouth shut.'

'It wasn't her fault, really. She introduced me to some boys and they spat when Mathilde's name was mentioned. Anyway, Monsieur Martin said it was true.'

'You told him?'

I found myself squeezing the lettuce so tightly in the tea cloth that my hands hurt. 'Yes,' I muttered, knowing that my cheeks were scarlet. 'I didn't mean to, but . . . it just came out.'

'Never mind,' Grandmère growled. She was standing beside the stove where the large black frying pan spat and crackled with hot olive oil. Her fingers were busy dusting different types of small fish fillets in flour and as I watched she threw a cube of bread into the frying pan to test the temperature. 'It is no secret, not around here,' she added, scooping out the frizzled bread and carefully lowering the first two fillets into the pan. 'But we had hoped that you would be spared our shame.'

I let my breath out, feeling calmer, and stopped squeezing the lettuce. It was very dry and I shook out the leaves carefully before putting them into the salad bowl. Automatically I smashed up a clove of garlic in some butter and, after smearing it on a piece of bread, buried it in the lettuce. 'Shall I do the dressing?'

'Yes, but be careful with the vinegar. Not too much. And quarter some lemons.'

We hadn't mentioned the morning's events yet and I knew that Grandmère would winkle the whole story out of me before the day was over, but Jeanne Brissac's 'big mouth' was enough for her for now.

'Drain the beans,' was her next order, and she continued to fry the fish whilst I drained the tender little beans, put them swiftly back in the pan and swirled them in flecks of butter and black pepper.

'Good. We're ready now.' She picked up the platter of fish and went to the dining room, leaving me to follow with the dish of beans and another of fried potatoes. The panicky feeling I'd had after telling Étienne what Jeanne Brissac had said came back and my stomach was churning with the prospect of facing him at the table. Would he want to talk to me? Would he even look at me? For a moment I considered leaving the vegetables on the kitchen table and rushing upstairs to my room. I could plead illness. Nobody would believe me, of course, but it would be easier for everyone.

I lowered the dishes on to the table and wiping my hands on a cloth edged towards the door which led to the back stairway. Once through it I would be on my own, away from these strange people, most of whom had reasons to hate me now. A tear began to squeeze itself from my eye.

'Come on, Eleanor. We're waiting.' Grandmère had appeared at the kitchen door and as I looked up she nodded to me. 'It will be all right,' she said.

When I passed her, going through the door, carrying the dishes, she touched my shoulder and somehow those bony fingers gave me the courage to enter the dining room. I thought I could face Étienne now.

I could and it was all right. But what I hadn't bargained for was the presence of Mathilde, who was sitting audaciously in her place and flicked me a vicious sneer as I sat down beside her.

Chapter Fourteen

I couldn't believe that she was there. Behaving as though this was a normal evening, peering unconcernedly through her curtain of black hair and doing her usual silent mouthing across the table to Jean Paul. Had she forgotten what had happened this morning? What she'd said to me?

Of course she hadn't. She was probably revelling in it and loving the fact that she was making me uncomfortable. I was utterly dismayed, lonelier than I had ever felt at Riverain, and it was at that moment that my feelings for her crystallised. She'd been rude to me, ignored me, forced Jean Paul's attitude towards me and then this morning had absolutely terrified me. I hated her.

I looked across to Jean Paul. He sat waiting for his meal, his eyes flicking this way and that, his cheeks scarlet. It was obvious that he was in an agony of embarrassment. Even if she was prepared to brazen it out, he was finding it almost impossible and was longing to escape as I'd been only minutes before. Did I feel sorry for him? No, I don't think I did.

'Did you enjoy your afternoon with the d'Amboise children?' Grandmère asked Lisette, putting small portions of potatoes and beans on her plate. The fish had been handed round and I held the platter tightly when it came my turn to pass it to Mathilde. I guessed she would spitefully endeavour to drop it and I was determined not to give her the opportunity. She did try, her hands dipping the moment I turned to her, and I felt a moment of triumph when instead of putting it into them, I placed it on the table in front of her. The small, irritated 'tch' sound was victory indeed.

'Oh yes. So much. We played in the garden and then Claudine showed me the doll's house that her grandmère has. It's in one of the upstairs rooms and very precious. It has lace covers on the tiny beds and curtains and rugs. Oh, I loved it. We couldn't touch it, of course, but we looked at it. It was lovely. Then her little brother came in so we pushed him out and shut the door. He would break it, Claudine said, and her grandmère would cry. I didn't think she would. Grown-ups don't cry.'

'And what about you, Eleanor? What did you think of the *cave*?' Grandmère was making conversation, for Étienne was silent, eating his dinner without enthusiasm but topping up his glass constantly. At one point he took the carafe into the kitchen to refill it. Grandmère frowned and when he came back shook her head at him.

'It was interesting,' I said. 'I've never seen anything like it before. But I don't think I would like to live in one of those houses built into the rock. I think they would be too dark and airless.'

'They are warm in the winter and cool in summer, my friends tell me,' she said, 'but like you, I prefer a house that is open.'

'I'm going to extend the vineyard.' Étienne suddenly burst into the halting conversation and everyone, even Mathilde, turned to look at him. 'I've been to the bank and seen my lawyer. More vines will be laid down and new machinery will be bought. The grape barn will have to be demolished and a larger one built to house the new press.'

I heard the gasp from Mathilde. It was under her breath but I saw her chest move and just caught the hissed intake of breath. Étienne's fist crashed unsteadily on the table and Lisette sank lower in her chair. 'Yes,' Étienne continued loudly, almost shouting. 'Things will be different from now on. I'm getting rid of the rubbish.'

I flinched as Mathilde jumped to her feet, deliberately scraping her chair backwards on the stone tiles. She was still holding her knife and she pointed it at Étienne. 'You leave that barn alone.' Her voice had risen above the normal cold sneering tone she usually adopted.

'No.' He raised his glass to his mouth and, with a swagger, took a long swig of wine. Some of it dribbled down his chin and dripped on to his shirt. 'It goes. It all goes.'

I was sure that there was another conversation going on, something that I didn't properly understand, but after my experience with Mathilde only this morning the hidden meaning was beginning to trickle through my naive brain.

'Bastard!' The word shot out of Mathilde's thin mouth and I could see that she was shaking with rage. 'You'll be sorry,' she shrieked. 'Just wait.'

'I've been sorry for years,' Étienne replied. He didn't even seem angry but instead almost buoyed by her rage, and as I watched, one hand to my mouth, he started to grin. He was drunk, drunker than I'd ever seen him. 'For years,' he repeated and laughed wildly, out loud.

The laughing was more upsetting than his shouting

and I heard a tiny moan escape from Lisette's mouth. The evening sunlight coming in through the long window glistened on the tears filling her hazel eyes and her little body was shaking. I began to get up from my seat but surprisingly it was Grandmère who pulled her from her chair and wrapped her close in her arms.

Mathilde's chair was flung aside as she stalked out of the room. We all watched her, even Jean Paul, who had continued to eat mechanically throughout, and Lisette lifted her head from Grandmère's ample bosom and followed her mother's exit from the room with what appeared to be relief.

In the silence which followed Grandmère cleared her throat. 'I think we've all finished now. Eleanor, take away the plates and bring in some cheese from the pantry. And Lisette,' the child was held away from the older woman and her tear-stained face gently wiped with Grandmère's napkin, 'can you carefully carry in the basket of peaches from the kitchen table?'

Our supper continued, the conversation hesitant at first, but then Étienne talked more about his plans and smiled drunkenly at me on more than one occasion so I felt I'd been forgiven. Jean Paul stayed in his place throughout the meal, keeping his eyes on his plate except once when he looked up and caught me staring at him. He immediately coloured up, but feeling more cheerful I gave him a little smile. Lisette fell into her habit of aimless singing and had got over her tears. But when I put her to bed later she held my hand very tightly and wouldn't let me go, so I knew that she was still upset. Gradually, though, her grasp slackened and she drifted into sleep and I was able to leave. Looking back at her from her bedroom door I wondered yet again at how quickly my need to care for her had grown.

'Come to my room and tell me about this morning,' said Grandmère when I came downstairs.

'Yes,' I said, surprising myself by actually wanting to talk about it.

'Do you understand what Mathilde is doing?' Grandmère asked after I'd related the whole story. She looked old and weighed down with worry, quite unlike her usual self. She had brought a tray with glasses and a bottle of brandy into her parlour and poured us both a small drink. I sipped it, not really liking the taste but loving the closeness between us. Grandmère sipped at hers too, almost as though it was medicine.

I nodded. 'I think I understand.' The truth was that I still wasn't really sure what Mathilde did but I knew I couldn't ask Grandmère to explain further. I thought of the d'Amboise family. They must know, and Robert Brissac and his strange daughter. Everybody in the village, even the baker, the postmaster and the priest in the church where we went on Sunday. I thought about what Luc had said about Jean Paul and Lisette not being Étienne's children.

'The truth is,' muttered Grandmère, resting her head against the soft back of her chair, as though she was reading my mind, 'Mathilde has shamed us and made us a family without respect in the district.'

Yes, I thought, she has, and why does Étienne put up with it? Why doesn't he stop her? That was what I really didn't understand.

Grandmère sighed. Strands of iron grey hair had escaped from the tight bun which generally kept it neatly in place. She looked so tired I would have done anything to make her happy again.

I leant forward. 'You're wrong,' I said urgently. 'People do respect you. Everyone has been nice to me and they wouldn't if they didn't like you and Monsieur Martin. And . . .' I was embarrassed to say this after only knowing the family for three weeks. 'I feel no differently towards you, now that I know. I love you and Monsieur Martin and Lisette.'

Grandmère took my hand and squeezed it. 'Thank you, Eleanor, for saying that.'

We sat on in companionable silence, listening to the wind in the trees by the river and the sharp patter of a brief rainfall.

'No cards tonight, I think.' Grandmère heaved herself up from her chair and headed off to the kitchen. 'You must go to bed, Eleanor, and tomorrow you had better phone the consulate for news of your parents. Yes?'

'Yes,' I agreed, immediately ashamed of myself for only intermittently thinking about them all day. 'Yes, I must.'

I went up the main staircase to my room, looking in on Lisette on the way. She was deeply asleep, on her back with her hands clasped on her chest, looking for all the world like an effigy on a tomb. Miss Baxter had shown us pictures of the Plantagenet tombs at Fontevraud Abbey, which was quite near here. King Henry the second and his wife Eleanor of Aquitaine, and King Richard the Lionheart and his wife Berengaria. 'Their bodies probably aren't there any more,' said Miss Baxter, 'and there is a question over the identity of the second woman. The graves were desecrated during the Huguenot wars in the sixteenth century and then again during the Napoleonic era. The bones are thought to have been mostly scattered, but the carvings on the tombs are thought to be genuine likenesses. They were great kings and Queen Eleanor, your namesake, was the most important lady of her age. She was the wife of two kings and the mother of two.' Miss Baxter had pushed her hand through her wispy hair and shaken her head admiringly. 'A wonderful lady,' she added.

Later, when I knew that I was being placed in the Loire valley, she got quite excited, her cheeks glowing pink and her watery blue eyes focusing on one of the map posters which adorned the walls of the French room. 'Fontevraud is very close to where you'll be, Eleanor. Try to get to see it.'

I shrugged as I backed out of Lisette's bedroom. There was little chance of another trip now, but it didn't matter. Étienne, Grandmère and I were all friends again and I could enjoy . . .

'You told them, *salope*!'

Mathilde was in the corridor outside Lisette's room, her poison green dress fading into the gloom of the poorly lit landing and her hand grabbing my arm.

'What?' I gabbled, not understanding the insult.

'You told them about the barn.'

Her fingers were curled cruelly around my arm and her painted red nails dug into my flesh, raising weals that would linger for days.

'I didn't.' I choked the words out. 'I didn't have to because they knew. Everyone knows.' I was struggling to breathe calmly because she terrified me, but I was determined not to show it. I shook off her hand and looked down to her pale, spiteful face. 'Everyone despises you.'

'Oh!' she gasped, the whites of her strange eyes growing larger and seeming to fill the air between us. 'How dare you!' and she repeated the insult '*salope*', which I later knew to mean 'bitch', as well as other words that even now I can't say out loud. 'Watch out,' she hissed. 'I'll get you. If you don't get out of this house, I'll make you suffer.'

I walked away from her then along the corridor and up the steps to my bedroom, my heart thumping and unbidden frightened tears spilling down my face. She was watching me; I could feel it, and almost expected her to run after me. Was she capable of physically hurting me? Would she dare? Could she hit me, or worse . . . I imagined a knife being plunged into my back and blood running down my legs on to the bare floorboards. By the time I got into my room with the door shut behind me, I was shaking.

Washing my face in my little bathroom helped calm me and I undressed and put on my cotton nightdress. The room felt stifling and I opened the shutters so that air from the river would cool me, and leant against the sill. The faint breeze that blew against my face was warm too, coming up from the south, presaging another hot day in this foreign country. I have to go home, I thought. Apart from the fact that my parents needed me, the reasons for going were obvious. I was causing trouble here and it was bound to get worse because Mathilde, the witch, wanted me out of the house.

Outside it was quiet, no clip-clip of Mathilde's shoes nor sight of Étienne on the bridge. Only the cry of an owl and small rustling noises among the saplings on the bank disturbed the night.

I lay on the bed, still too hot to get under the duvet, and closed my eyes. Sleep came quickly, perhaps a subconscious desire to escape from reality, but it wasn't restful. I dreamt, confused, violent dreams where I could hear people whispering and see ghostly faces appearing from behind doors. There was no sense to be made, no story or purpose, just episodes which seemed like threats and danger. Then the dream became worse. I could feel pressure as though all the breath was being squeezed from my chest and, desperate, I tossed my body this way and that to try to relieve it.

'Lie still,' the voice in my ear demanded. 'You know you want it.'

For a split second I did lie still, and listened. Was this still a dream, or . . .? My eyes shot open, and blind at first in the darkness of my room I grappled frantically with the heavy body on top of me.

'Get off,' I screamed. 'Get off me.'

I grabbed the sleeve of his shirt and pushed as hard as I could, removing one of his hands from my shoulder only for it to fasten round my face and push my head into the pillow. My legs were held down by his; I could feel trousers and an open belt buckle pressing against my knees. His other hand was pushing up my nightdress and in a horror of confused recognition I knew which part of his body was rubbing against me.

'No,' I wailed, twisting my head so that my mouth was free. 'Stop!'

'Shut up!' he panted. A hand was on my breast and then on my belly and . . . oh, God . . . Using all my strength, I heaved myself up, pushing him to the side and dislodging his hand from my face. 'Get away from me,' I screamed and at that moment, my eyes now accustomed to the dark, I caught a fleeting glimpse of Mathilde, peering out from behind the door that led down to the kitchen. Her terrible smirk told me all I needed to know.

But I was being grabbed again, my nightdress ripping and his hands once more pressing me down. He was strong, stronger than I'd imagined, and now one of his hands was clutched around my throat. I tore my nails down his face, hating the feel of his skin, and desperately brought up my knee ready to jam it into his genitals, but suddenly it wasn't necessary. He had gone.

'You little bastard,' roared Étienne, throwing Jean Paul across the room with such force that he crashed against the wardrobe and landed in a heap on the floor. 'Now I will kill you!'

'No, Papa,' howled Jean Paul. 'She wanted me to do it. I was told.'

I curled myself into a ball and dragged the duvet over my nakedness. My nightdress was torn and hanging off me. 'I didn't,' I sobbed, trying not to look at him although the sight of his trousers around his knees leaving his lower body exposed had a dreadful fascination. 'I loathe him.'

'But Mathilde said . . .' Jean Paul whimpered.

Through my tears I looked quickly to the door, but Mathilde had gone and now I wasn't even sure that I'd seen her. Did I dream that?

Étienne turned to me. 'Are you all right? Did he . . .?'

'No.' I shook my head, my voice a tremulous whisper.

'Thank Christ.'

A light came on through the open door to the landing. 'Eleanor?' Lisette was standing in the doorway. 'What is wrong?'

My screams must have woken her up as they had Étienne. She looked very frightened and was already beginning to cry. 'Don't worry.' I forced a smile on my face. 'It's nothing. I had a bad dream.'

'Lisette.' Étienne walked round my bed to the little girl and touched her shoulder. 'Will you go downstairs to Grandmère and tell her that Eleanor needs her? Can you do that?'

'Yes, Papa,' the child whispered and disappeared from the doorway.

'Now, you little bastard.' Étienne turned and looked back to where Jean Paul had been lying but in vain. He was gone. Slipped down the back stairs and disappeared. I never saw him again.

'Damn him,' Étienne shouted, 'damn him to hell.' Then he looked at me and heaved a sigh. 'I'm sorry,' he said. 'So, so sorry,' and came over and sat on the bed. He put his arms round me and held me tight while I sobbed on his shoulder. To my shame, it was almost worth what had happened before to be in his arms with his face next to mine. If he'd wanted to kiss me, I'd have let him.

We both heard Grandmère climbing the kitchen stairs and soon she appeared in my bedroom, pushing Étienne out of the way and taking me in her arms.

'What happened?' she asked. Her hair was hanging in a plait and she wore a black shawl over her voluminous white nightdress.

'Jean Paul tried to . . .' Étienne stopped, his eyes on Lisette who had followed Grandmère into the room.

Grandmère understood straight away. 'Now,' she said, 'as we're all awake, I think we'll go downstairs and have something to drink and perhaps a little snack. Is that all right, Eleanor?'

I nodded.

'Good. Hot chocolate, I think.'

'Me too, Grandmère?' Lisette pleaded.

'Yes. Put your shoes on first.'

'I'm going to look for Jean Paul,' said Étienne. 'I'll teach him a lesson he'll never forget.'

Grandmère said nothing. This time . . . she agreed with him.

Chapter Fifteen

I felt strange the next day, almost like an invalid, and Grandmère, Étienne and even Lisette hovered around me, their eyes not quite meeting mine but all trying to stick to their normal routine.

There was no sign of Jean Paul or Mathilde and before lunch I watched, from my bedroom window, Étienne attacking the grape barn with what looked, from a distance, like a sledgehammer. He was wasting no time.

'Papa is breaking the barn,' said Lisette, who was leaning against the window beside me. 'He's knocked the door down. And now he's starting a bonfire.'

'Good,' Grandmère grunted. She was stripping my bed and putting clean, sweet-smelling sheets and pillowcases on it. The duvet had been stripped too, taken downstairs and hung on the washing line.

'Let me help you,' I said, but Grandmère shook her head.

'No,' she said. 'This is a job I must do.' It was another way, I thought, of saying how sorry she was.

Lisette and I went downstairs then and wandered into the vegetable garden. A new row of beans had ripened and I wondered about picking some for lunch. Maybe Grandmère had already done so, but I did pick courgettes and courgette flowers. These Grandmère dipped in a thin batter and fried. I loved them.

'I saw a man on the bridge last night,' said Lisette.

'Did you? When?' I was bending over the courgette patch and wasn't really listening. I had too much on my mind.

'After the chocolate, when we'd all gone back to bed. He was with Papa.'

I straightened up with the courgette flowers in my hand and looked down at the little girl. 'Are you sure?' I said. I hated the thought that she might have seen one of Mathilde's . . . visitors.

Lisette put a finger to her chin in an exaggerated gesture of thinking. 'No.' She giggled. 'I think I might have had a dream.'

'Silly girl,' I said.

She picked up a flower that I'd dropped. 'What did you dream about last night?' she asked. 'Was it very frightening?'

Nobody else had mentioned it. Even at breakfast Grandmère had chatted about going to the market tomorrow and perhaps inviting Édith d'Amboise for lunch. Étienne was dipping bread in his coffee when I came into the kitchen and apart from a 'good morning' didn't speak. That was fine. I was grateful to drink my coffee in silence and when I came back from the pantry with the butter and apricot jam he had gone.

'Do you know,' I said gently, 'I can't remember. But it must have been something awful to make me scream like that. I'm sorry I woke you.'

'I don't mind. And I was the one who went for Grandmère,' she added importantly.

'Yes, you did.'

'I liked the hot chocolate and the almond biscuits. It was exciting to have food in the night.'

I took her hand and we walked back to the house. Just before we went through the kitchen door she stopped and looked up at me. 'I always remember my dreams,' she whispered. 'They make me cry too.'

We were a quiet group at lunch. Étienne looked hot and sweaty. Flecks of ash from the bonfire were scattered through his hair and his arms above the wrist were streaked with soot. He had washed only cursorily before coming to the table.

'You can go on the bike to the village after lunch, Eleanor,' said Grandmère, while she was ladling green pea soup into our bowls. 'There you can telephone the consul and find out about your parents.'

'Yes,' I said. Her insistence that I should phone for news suddenly seemed slightly sinister. Was she keen now for me to leave?

'And Lisette, you must have a lie down this afternoon. Even if you can't sleep, I want you to go to your room and rest.'

The child nodded. She did look tired, and far from begging to come with me she seemed glad to be told what to do. The fact that Grandmère was thinking of her was apparently enough.

I glanced at Étienne. He wasn't drinking but still looked angry and frustrated and ate the mushroom omelette which followed the soup with the same sort of mechanical disinterest that Jean Paul usually showed. 'Have you seen either of them?' he asked suddenly.

'No.' Grandmère shook her head. 'Not a sign.'

'Jean Paul has taken his *vélo*,' Lisette piped up. 'I saw him wheeling it out of the shed very early this morning. He had a bag with him too.'

'Very early?' Grandmère tutted. 'No wonder you look tired, Lisette,' but her eyes were on Étienne and they were both frowning.

I cycled to the village when the lunch dishes were cleared away. It was very hot and I borrowed the white canvas hat that Grandmère wore when she worked in the garden to save my head from getting burnt. My arms and legs, though, prickled with sweat and the short downy hairs on them felt again as though they were being scalded off.

'Good afternoon, Miss Eleanor,' the postmaster greeted me. 'Another phone call, or a letter home?'

'Phone please, Monsieur le Brun.' I had learned his name and was pleased to use it. 'Can you get the number for me?'

'But of course.' I handed him the coins and the piece of paper with Monsieur Castres' number and waited outside the glass box while he made the call. 'Here you are, Miss Eleanor,' he called, and stepped out, leaving the receiver dangling. I squeezed past.

'Monsieur Castres.' I heard myself shouting, then, blushing and knowing that Monsieur le Brun would be listening, repeated the consul's name more quietly. 'It's Eleanor Gill. Have you any news for me?'

'Ah, Miss Gill. How strange that you should telephone this afternoon. I was just composing a short letter to you. No . . . no . . . nothing urgent. We've heard from England that your mother is still in hospital. I'm sorry to tell you that apparently she is no better, but she is having every care possible.'

'Oh,' I said. 'And my father?'

There was a brief silence, and then Monsieur Castres gave a short cough. 'That's a little more difficult to assess, Miss Gill. It seems that Captain Gill walked out of the . . . er . . . hospital and was missing for several days. Please don't worry. He's been caught . . . I mean he's been found now and is back in care. In a more secure part of the hospital, as I understand.'

Poor Dada. Caught? I felt desperately sorry for him. He must have thought he was back in the prisoner of war camp. He'd be so frightened.

'Are you still happy to stay with Monsieur and Madame Martin?' Monsieur Castres interrupted my thoughts.

'Well, I don't know,' I said. 'Maybe I've been with them for too long. They haven't said anything but I do think I should go home.'

'But where will you stay? I've been told that your home is remote and you'll need to be able to get to the hospitals to see your parents.'

'I know,' I said miserably. 'I just can't think of . . .' Suddenly it struck me. Suzy. I was sure her parents would let me stay with them for a week or two until Mother and Dada could come home. They had plenty of room and Phyllis wouldn't care. I didn't think Mr Franklin would mind either.

'Monsieur Castres. I have a friend who might put me up. In the town. If I give you their address maybe you can get in touch with them and explain the situation. They do have a telephone but I'm afraid I don't know the number.'

'Well, Miss Gill,' he sounded relieved, 'give me the name and address of your friends and I'll see what I can do. That might be a very good solution. And as for your homeward travel . . . we can lend you the money for it and your parents can repay it when they are better. Now, the address, please.'

It was only when I was cycling back to Riverain that I realised it was past the date when I should have returned to England and Suzy would already be home, accompanied by her French exchange girl. The visitor would be sleeping in their spare bedroom, so would Suzy want me there too? Oh, God. It was a mess.

The yard was empty and quiet when I cycled in and Grandmère wasn't in the kitchen, so I had no one to tell what Monsieur Castres and I had decided. It would have to wait until supper, and that would be difficult too. Would Étienne and Grandmère feel that I was rejecting their kindness? Or would they think that Jean Paul's attack on me was the cause of my decision to leave? Of course they didn't know that Mathilde had threatened me and that I was very scared of her, or that I thought that my presence in this lovely place was making things difficult for everyone.

I wandered across the bridge and up into the vineyard. The bonfire beside the grape barn was still burning, sending a spire of acrid blue smoke into the clear sky, and as I walked between the vines I saw Étienne come out of the wrecked door of the barn with a pile of what looked like clothes.

'Hello,' I said, reaching him. I recognised one of Mathilde's dresses, the black and purple one she wore for church, and also the little green hat with the drooping feather. Flames from the bonfire were already licking around a shiny cream sheet and the remains of a heavily patterned rug, and with a gesture of distaste Étienne dumped Mathilde's clothes on top of them.

'What are you doing?' I asked, astonished. 'Those are Mathilde's.'

'She won't need them any more,' Étienne grunted. Picking up a long stick he stirred the bonfire so that sparks cracked and danced into the air and the fire burnt more fiercely.

I was dumbfounded. 'Why?' I asked.

'Because she's gone. These were left and I'm getting rid of them.'

I stood, bewildered, and watched the fire crackle. Étienne went back into the barn, and almost in a dream I followed him. I had longed to see inside but now, with the door sledgehammered off its hinges and the stone surrounding it broken and knocked aside, it had taken on a menacing air. So it was with very cautious steps that I turned my back on the brilliant afternoon and entered the barn.

At first it was difficult to see anything, but gradually the light coming in from the enlarged doorway and from a small window in one of the walls revealed a stone interior with a dusty floor. Wooden beams, painted black, criss-crossed the high roof, which was peppered with pin-prick holes. Larger holes appeared where the roof met the walls and I could see clay and twig nests at intervals and even some small birds flying around. It was blessedly cool in the barn after the baking heat outside, so much so that my bare arms felt suddenly cold and I shivered. Thinking back, I wonder if that was cold or the realisation that I was in the witch's lair.

I looked round, taking in the old machinery: presses

and large round tanks and other iron and wood equipment, none of which I understood. To my surprise, a mattress lay on the floor next to one of the old basket presses and I had to step aside quickly because Étienne was dragging it out.

'Does Mathilde sleep here?' I asked, too surprised for tact and forgetting that she had gone. I had thought the bedroom next to Lisette's was hers.

'She . . . entertained . . . her friends here,' Étienne grunted. He was struggling with the mattress and I grabbed the other end and helped to lift it through the door. It too went on the bonfire and Étienne had to add more wood from the smashed door to keep it going.

I went back inside the barn. Apart from the detritus of Mathilde's occupation – cigarette ends, pieces of clothing and empty beer bottles – the space was filled with original machinery which had been left unused for years. Several wooden barrels on stands were lined up against one wall and three basket presses stood in the middle of the floor. At the far end of the barn was a large desk with drawers and next to it a rack whose diamond-shaped holes contained many empty bottles.

'Were those bottles once full?' I asked Étienne, who was now standing beside me.

'No.' He smiled. 'The wine went into the cellar beneath the house. My father bottled it in here. This was where he did all his experiments: testing, tasting, even blending. I used to come in and he would make me describe what flavours I could make out and choose my favourite.' He chuckled at the memory. 'I never wanted to stay, too impatient to be out with my friends, and for me the vineyard wasn't important. I wanted to be a farmer. But now . . .' he shrugged, 'I'm getting old. Turning into my father.'

'I don't think you're old,' I said shyly.

He shook his head and rubbed his boot into the dusty floor. 'Have you forgiven us for last night?'

'It wasn't your fault,' I said. 'It was Jean Paul, and . . .' I paused. 'I think I saw Mathilde watching from the door.' I wasn't looking at him when I said, 'Perhaps she was going to stop him.'

'Christ no,' he sighed. 'That bitch was encouraging him. She was sick, you know. Sick in the head. She has made him the same.'

'It wasn't your fault,' I repeated. My phone call to Monsieur Castres was playing in my head and I knew I would have to say something about going home. He and Grandmère would think it was because of Jean Paul and Mathilde and part of me knew that it was. Another part felt that Étienne's initial interest in me had gone. I'd had a silly crush on him and it wasn't being reciprocated.

I went outside into the bright blue afternoon and looked at the feathers from the mattress curling then shrinking to nothing on the bonfire. It would take a long time to burn, I thought, and as I watched Étienne came out behind me with an old wooden chair which he smashed against the tumbled stones and threw on top of the mattress. The smashing and breaking seemed to be giving him some relief and I was glad. Now perhaps I could tell him about leaving. 'Monsieur Castres said . . .' I started, but he held up a hand.

'I have to go down to the yard. It's time to get the cattle in,' he said, giving the bonfire one last stir, 'and Grandmère will be looking for you. You can tell us at supper.'

'Yes, all right,' I said, and trailed after him down through the rows of ripening grapes whose scent was heavy on the air, sweet and sharp at the same time. I felt drowsy and slow this afternoon, the horrible events of last night finally catching up with me. For the first time I stopped and thought about what had really happened and what Jean Paul had tried to do. He had tried to . . . what? I didn't know the word 'rape' then. Nobody had ever said it to me and it wasn't in any of the books I'd read. But I did know 'ravish' and 'violate' and that was what it was, wasn't it?

I'd reached the bridge and leant on the railing. The planks were more rickety than ever and I noticed that part of the railing was splintered as though a rock had been thrown at it. But that was by the way; my thoughts were on Jean Paul. Had I encouraged him? Did that little smile I'd given him at supper mean more than I'd intended? Even as I thought about it I blushed. Oh, God, the whole thing must have been my fault. Then I remembered his anger and cruelty and how he'd brutally forced my head into the pillow and torn my nightdress. He hadn't been doing it out of desire. Foremost in my memory was the fleeting glimpse of Mathilde smirking at me from the doorway. And then I knew. Jean Paul had been obeying orders.

Étienne was in the yard with one of the farm workers when I walked across it. They were looking at the engine of the old tractor and Étienne was hitting something inside with a hammer and swearing.

'This tractor is a load of shit,' he shouted, throwing the hammer against the folded up engine cover where it clanged and bounced back at him. 'Shit!' he repeated, then stopped and looked at me. '*Ma mère* has been looking for you,' he called out, still sounding angry, but the other man grinned and touched his cap to me. I shuddered. Had he been told about what had happened? Had Étienne told the farm workers and they'd all had a good laugh and punched each other on the shoulder? I was sure there was nothing working men liked better than dirty gossip about sex. But as soon as I thought it I knew it was entirely my imagination. Étienne would never do that.

'All right,' I called, and went in through the kitchen door.

'Wherever have you been?' asked Grandmère. 'Did you speak to Monsieur Castres? What did he say?'

Her questions were rapped out while I picked up a glass from the shelf above the sink and took a long drink from the tap. For once Grandmère wasn't at the stove and it seemed unnatural. She was sitting at the kitchen table, fanning herself with the raffia fan that usually hung on the hook behind the kitchen door. Her cheeks were very pink and the collar of her black blouse was undone.

'Are you feeling ill, Grandmère?' I asked. 'Shall I get Étienne?'

'No. No, child. It's nothing. A little fever, that's all. I'll be all right. Just tell me about Monsieur Castres.'

I sat beside her then and repeated what the consul had said. About Mother being no better and about Dada running away from the asylum. That made me think again about Dada. Where had he gone? And how had he fed himself? 'He must be so frightened in there,' I said aloud.

'And your mother is no better?'

'No. She isn't. And I don't really know what's the matter with her.'

'Mm.' Grandmère's fanning slowed down. 'But you can stay on with us?'

'Well,' I started, intending to tell her the whole conversation, but a knock on the door and a called *'Bonjour'* announced Monsieur d'Amboise and Luc.

'Madame Martin!' boomed Monsieur d'Amboise. 'I bring greetings from Édith and this basket of late cherries. They're the last from our trees and should be very sweet.'

'Thank you, indeed,' said Grandmère, 'and thank Édith. We'll have them this evening. Now, can I offer you a drink?'

'No. Very kind of you, but I must have a word with Étienne and then I'm on my way into town. Luc might, though. He's brought a gift for Miss Eleanor.'

Out of the corner of my eye I saw Grandmère start fanning herself again but I was turning to Luc, wondering what gift he'd brought for me.

'Here,' he said, holding out a book towards me. 'I thought you'd like to read it.'

It was a French copy of *The Count of Monte Cristo*. 'Oh, I couldn't take it,' I said. 'You said you loved it. I wouldn't want to deprive you of it.'

He laughed. 'I've got mine. I bought this for you when I went into town.'

I was thrilled. It was almost the best present I'd ever had. 'Thank you, Luc. Thank you.'

Walking in the garden with him a little later I told him that we thought Jean Paul had gone. I said nothing about the events of last night nor about Étienne burning Mathilde's clothes. 'I'm going to have to leave soon too,' I added. 'My parents are no better and need me.'

'Will someone help you in England?'

'I think my friend Suzy's parents will. The consul is going to ask them.'

'What do the Martins think of that?'

I sighed. 'Oh, Luc, I haven't told them yet. I know they'll think it's because of Mathilde and Jean Paul and maybe it is. She scares me, and last night Jean Paul . . .' I left the rest of the sentence unsaid.

'What? What did he do?'

'Nothing.' I said it quickly. 'It doesn't matter.'

I think he would have pressed me for more but I could hear Grandmère calling me from the kitchen and he left then and I went inside.

Again it was just the four of us at supper, which I had prepared because Grandmère was still hot and flustered and happy to let me heat up the soup and make a mayonnaise to go with the shrimps.

'Where's Lisette?' I asked when I was ready to take in the soup.

'She went out a few minutes ago,' said Grandmère. 'Call her.'

I heard the child shout 'Coming' and took in the soup. Étienne was in his place, clean now with wet hair which had recently been in the shower and a white shirt. He seemed quiet but more cheerful and gave me a big grin when I ladled out a helping for him.

'So, you are the cook tonight?' he asked.

I nodded, smiling. 'Only under supervision.'

'She's getting very good,' grunted Grandmère, and

then to Lisette who had wandered in, 'Where on earth have you been?'

'On the bridge,' said the little girl, settling in her chair and taking the piece of bread from Étienne. 'I saw Maman.'

Étienne and Grandmère looked up sharply. 'Where?' said Étienne. Was I mistaken or was there a choke in his voice?

'In the river,' said Lisette. 'She is floating.'

Chapter Sixteen

It was as if a bomb had gone off somewhere outside, the shrapnel not touching but the explosion stunning us all into silence. We sat, mouths slightly open and eyes fixed on the child in disbelief. All appetite had flown away and only Lisette continued with her meal, spooning soup into her little mouth and humming a tuneless song.

'What did you say?' Étienne asked carefully, his voice unnaturally quiet. 'About your mother?'

'She's in the river. I saw her.'

Before she'd finished speaking he jumped up, his chair crashing down behind him, and ran from the room. I followed, and Grandmère, grunting with the effort, wasn't far behind me.

'Wait, Eleanor,' Grandmère panted. 'This is not for you.' But I took no notice. I wanted to see. Could it be true?

It was. I stood beside Étienne on the bridge and we looked down on Mathilde's body, floating on the surface of the river, her poison green dress caught on a tree branch which had dipped into the water. Her black hair streamed out behind her, melting into the dusk like all the weeds close to the bank, and her sightless cow eyes gazed at the violet evening sky. She was patently dead.

'Oh, Christ,' murmured Étienne, and turned to me. 'You shouldn't have seen this.'

I couldn't tear my eyes away from Mathilde's corpse. This was my first sight of a dead body but strangely I felt no alarm; for me, she was infinitely less frightening in death than she had been in life. I remember feeling no horror, no emotion and not really any surprise. Certainly I felt no sympathy, and looking at Étienne and Grandmère it was obvious that they felt none either. She was so hated that death seemed to be the best outcome.

But she had stunned us, and although in the distance I could hear a car engine and birds in the willows tweeting as they searched for insects, it felt as though we humans had been frozen into silence. I shook myself. 'She must have fallen,' I ventured. 'The railing is splintered there.' I pointed to the place I'd noticed earlier, and then a thought struck me. Why hadn't I seen her, then?

'Get her out of the river.' Grandmère had found her voice and was issuing instructions to Étienne. 'It isn't decent.'

He nodded but didn't move, seemingly unable to drag his eyes away from the sight of his dead wife bobbing gently amongst the weeds and willow branches. 'Yes, I must,' he said. But he still didn't move and neither did Grandmère, nor I. I suppose we would have stood there longer, immobilised by shock, but with a rustle of the undergrowth Lisette appeared on the near bank leading Monsieur d'Amboise by the hand.

'My papa is there on the bridge.' Her little voice carried on the evening air and we turned in unison to look at the newcomers.

'Look, Étienne. I have the tractor part. François at the

garage had just the piece you wanted. The child told me where to find you.' Henri d'Amboise's cheerful voice faded away as he looked at our faces one by one. Puzzlement etched lines across his brow and then, as if drawn by an invisible string, he turned towards the river.

'Mon Dieu!' he shouted, crossing himself quickly. 'What has happened?' He leant over the railing and pointed to the body in the slow-moving river. 'That surely can't be Mathilde?'

'It is.' Étienne's voice was bleak. 'She is dead.'

'We're just going to get her out,' said Grandmère, gathering her senses. 'I'm glad you're here, Henri. You can help my son.'

'Of course, of course. Then I'll drive to the town and get the doctor and the police. They'll have to be informed. Shall I call on the priest too?'

'Tomorrow will be soon enough for him.'

I realised as I walked back to the house with Lisette that Monsieur d'Amboise hadn't offered condolences. He, like everyone else who subsequently came to the house, knew that expressions of sympathy were not necessary.

'I'll never see my mother again,' said Lisette. Her hand was clutched in mine and I stopped walking to kneel down and wrap my arms around her.

'I'm so sorry,' I said, suddenly realising that the girl was now an orphan. 'This has been a terrible day for you.'

She snuggled into my chest like a little cat, her thin fingers kneading my shoulders, almost purring in her pleasure at being held. 'It's all right, Eleanor,' she said, her voice muffled in my shirt. 'I don't mind.'

'But . . .' I started to say, then stopped. Mathilde had shown little affection for her daughter and clearly the lack was reciprocated. Lisette wasn't at all upset, quite the reverse.

'Come on,' I said. 'Let's get some food into you.'

An hour later two local policemen came to the farm, and the doctor from the town. I went out to watch them even though it was nearly dark and it was difficult to see what they were doing. They had torches which they shone down on Mathilde's body, which had now been dragged on to the far bank, while the doctor did a quick examination.

'I can confirm that she is dead,' he said unnecessarily, 'but she'll have to be moved to the mortuary for further examination. Can you radio that in for me?'

'No, doctor,' said one. 'We don't have radios with us, but I'll drive into town and organise it. Jacques here,' he jerked his head towards the other policeman, 'will stay with the body so you can get back.'

'Good man,' said the doctor, pulling the blanket that Grandmère had brought from the house back over Mathilde. He stood up, pushing his trilby hat to the back of his head, and looked up to the bridge where Étienne and I were standing together. He was young, almost too young to be a doctor, I thought, and because it was a hot evening he'd left his jacket in the car and was in his shirt sleeves. 'Monsieur Martin,' he called. 'Does anyone in the house need my attention? A sedative perhaps?'

'No, thank you, sir. We are fine.'

The doctor paused for a moment, and although I couldn't see his face clearly his look to the policemen was telling. Even he knew that Mathilde wouldn't be missed.

'Grandmère has a little fever,' I said as Étienne and I left the bridge after the doctor had gone. 'Maybe the doctor could have given her something?'

'She'll be all right,' Étienne grunted. 'Once this is all over she'll be back to normal.'

I wanted to say that she was ill before we found Mathilde but he'd made up his mind and it wasn't for me to interfere. 'I'll look in on her before I go to bed,' was all I said.

'Thanks.' He heaved a sigh, and, getting out a handkerchief, blew his nose. 'Thank you, Eleanor,' he repeated, not looking at me although we had stopped in the yard. 'I didn't mean to be unpleasant. I'm surprised you can be so kind after the awful time you've had with us.'

He turned to go and so did I, heading for the kitchen door, but suddenly he gently took my arm. His hand was rough on my bare skin but it was nice.'I'd almost forgotten how normal people behave,' he muttered. 'You've reminded me.'

He went off to the calving pen while I was still thinking about what he'd said when I went into the kitchen. It had been cleared after our interrupted meal but I could see that Grandmère hadn't made her usual preparations for the morning. Her apron was hanging over the back of a chair and I took it out to the wash house. I looked in the pantry, wondering what she had thought of for tomorrow's meals, and saw a piece of frying beef wrapped in greaseproof paper lying on the stone slab and stock for soup in a large jug. If Grandmère wasn't well tomorrow, I thought I could manage lunch and supper.

I tapped on the parlour door and went in. It was dark in there – the lamp hadn't been lit – but I could see Grandmère in her chair. She had wrapped a shawl around her shoulders and despite the hot night she was shivering.

'Oh, Grandmère,' I said. 'You're really not well. What can I do?'

'Get me the cover from my bed,' she said quietly. 'I'm cold,' and she leant back and closed her eyes.

I did as she asked and tucked the cover around her. After lighting the oil lamp I went back to the kitchen and fetched her a glass of water and a small round cardboard box which contained aspirin. 'Take two of these,' I said, but she was reluctant.

'I don't need them. Get me brandy instead.'

'No,' I said firmly, amazed at my own boldness. 'You must take some medicine.' And I took two tablets out of the box and held them out. 'They'll make you feel better.'

Too weary to argue with me she swallowed the pills and drank deeply from the water glass.

'Shall I help you into bed?' I asked. 'You'll be more comfortable.'

'No. People die in bed.' We looked at each other. Not all people, I thought, and knew that she was thinking that too. 'I'll be all right here. Just leave me. I'll be better in the morning.'

'Well,' I said, 'if you're sure. I'll refill your glass before I go.'

'Where's Lisette?' Grandmère suddenly sounded like her old self. In charge.

'I've put her to bed,' I said. 'She's all right. Not really upset.'

'She wouldn't be,' said Grandmère. 'Still . . .'

'Don't worry. I'll look after her, and I'll see to the cooking tomorrow. You rest.' Of course I'd forgotten that I'd asked Monsieur Castres to help me leave. My conversation with him seemed to have happened years ago, not merely hours.

I left her then and went to my room and thought that I would lie awake for ages thinking about the extraordinary happenings of the day, but I didn't. As soon as my head hit the pillow I was asleep, and I woke up only when the early light was filtering through my shutters.

The baker was glad, I think, to see me. He knew, of course, about Mathilde but was careful in his questioning. 'She drowned, I hear,' he said. 'Please convey my good wishes to Monsieur Martin and Madame Martin senior.'

'I will, thank you,' I said, taking two baguettes this morning because I thought maybe we could have a sort of sandwich for lunch and we might be required to feed more people throughout the day. 'Have you cake?'

'I have *galette*.' He pointed to an open fruit tart, the pastry base filled with peaches and what looked to me like custard.

'Good,' I said. 'I'll take one of those.'

He paused, his hand hovering over the tart. 'Madame Martin usually makes her own desserts.'

'She isn't well,' I said. 'She has a fever.'

'Well, in that case,' he said, carefully wrapping the *galette* in shiny paper, 'please give this to her with my compliments. No charge.'

'Thank you.' I had turned to leave the shop when the postmaster came in.

'Ah, Miss Eleanor. Terrible events at Riverain, I hear.'

I nodded, anxious to leave, but he continued. 'How did it happen? Did she fall? Or was it . . . ?'

The baker was leaning eagerly over his counter. 'Was it an accident?'

'Yes, of course,' I said, surprised that they would think it was anything else, but when I was cycling home I thought about Mathilde in the river and wondered.

I made coffee and took some in to Grandmère. She was still in her chair and looked pale but she wasn't shivering as she had been last night.

'How are you this morning?' I asked, putting the coffee bowl on the little table beside her and shaking two aspirin out of the box.

'Better, I think.' Her voice was firmer and there was a suggestion of the old glint in her eye. 'I'll come into the kitchen in a while.'

'No you won't.' I smiled. 'Stay here a bit longer and rest. I'll bring you some breakfast and see to the food today. It won't be up to your standard, but I'll do my best.'

'I know you will.' She took a long drink while I opened the little window in her room and let some air in. The room was stifling and smelt muggy and I thought of my mother saying 'Fresh air blows illness away' when I tried not to go to school, pleading a cold or sickness.

Grandmère wasn't so keen, though. 'Close it, Eleanor. All the flies will come in.'

Étienne was in the pantry when I went back. He was using his penknife to carve off a chunk of sausage. He looked tired, as though he hadn't slept well, and I supposed he hadn't. No matter how much he loathed her, the circumstances of Mathilde's death were bound to have an effect. I squeezed past him to get at the butter and jam and he smelt of the farmyard and cattle.

'I've got fresh bread,' I said, backing out and putting them on the table.

'Good.' He came then and sat opposite me and we drank coffee and tore at the baguette together.

'The police will be here again today,' he mumbled, his mouth full. 'I don't think they'll want to speak to you, but,' he shrugged, 'who knows?'

'I don't mind,' I said. 'There's nothing much for me to say.'

'That's right,' he said firmly. 'The less we tell the police, the better.'

It was a coded message which I understood at once and it suited me. I had no wish to tell anybody about what Jean Paul had done to me, and if it was related to Mathilde's death, well, so be it. That brought a new thought. Where was Jean Paul?

'Étienne,' I said, tentatively, my face buried in my coffee bowl. 'Do you think Mathilde had an accident or did she do it deliberately? There was talk at the baker's. People are wondering.'

He ran his fingers through his hair. 'I don't know,' he sighed, 'although I can't imagine Mathilde killing herself. She wasn't . . .' He pushed his coffee bowl away and stood up, ready to go back into the yard. 'Mathilde wasn't afraid of anything or anyone. Certainly not me.'

'But you said she'd gone.' I looked up at him. 'You were burning her clothes.'

He was heading for the door and had his back to me. 'I thought she'd left with her son,' he said bleakly. 'Hadn't you noticed? They couldn't bear to be apart. They were . . .' He stopped and turned his head so that I could see the revulsion in his eyes. 'They were evil.'

Chapter Seventeen

It was a strange day. People came to and went from the house constantly. First Édith d'Amboise and Luc, who came to see if they could help. When Madame d'Amboise discovered that Grandmère was ill she immediately went home and returned with a beef and red wine stew which I think she had planned for their own dinner.

'We have meat in the pantry,' I said, embarrassed for Grandmère. I knew she would hate to be thought of as an invalid. 'I can't take your food.'

Madame d'Amboise behaved like the schoolmistress she was and would have no argument. She even wagged her finger at me. 'Listen, Eleanor. People will be here, the police, the priest even. There won't be time for cooking. That stew can go in the oven and look after itself. You might have other things to do.'

I nodded. She was right.

'And,' Madame d'Amboise said, 'where's Lisette? I'll take her back with me. Get her out of the way for a while. It's not good for her to be listening to all the . . . well, all the unpleasant words that might be spoken.'

But I couldn't find her. She'd had breakfast and seemed to be her normal self, not sad about her mother but very concerned when I told her that Grandmère was ill.

'Oh no,' she'd whispered, her hazel eyes filling with tears. 'I don't want her to die too.' A ring of chocolate drink surrounded her mouth and I leant over and wiped it away with her napkin.

'She won't,' I said. 'Now eat up your breakfast and don't wander off today. There might be a lot of people coming here and I don't want you talking to them. Stay close by me or your papa.'

'Is he still angry?'

'No.' I looked at her, wondering what she'd seen or heard. 'He isn't angry.'

She carefully put apricot jam on her bread. 'But he isn't sad. He didn't like Maman.'

What she said sounded very cold coming from her little mouth and was an awful thing to hear from a child about her parents. But it was true. Neither Étienne nor Mathilde had hidden their feelings about each other and there was no point in my trying to deny it.

'He's worried,' I said, 'and there'll be lots of arrangements to be made and people to speak to, so you be a good girl and not get in the way.'

'I will,' she promised. 'Shall I pick some flowers for Grandmère?'

Then Édith d'Amboise and Luc arrived and Lisette disappeared.

Luc sat at the kitchen table while his mother went to fetch the stew. I washed up the breakfast dishes and started on the ingredients for a vegetable soup. He didn't waste any time and came straight out with it.

'What d'you think happened?'

'I don't know,' I said, chopping the leeks into neat roundels. 'I suppose she tripped.'

'In daylight?'

I shrugged. 'What else could it be?'

'Think,' said Luc. 'You had a big row with her in the morning. You found out what she was up to in the grape barn and she would know that you'd tell Grandmère. How long would it be before they turned her out? Jean Paul has left. Come to think of it,' he stared at me, 'why has Jean Paul run off?'

'No idea.'

He wouldn't let it go. 'Something happened yesterday. You nearly told me. Tell me now.'

Had I nearly told him? So much had happened in the last two days that events and conversations were muddling in my head and I was struggling to remember what I'd said to whom. 'It was in the night,' I started and he leant forward in his chair, urging me to continue.

Then Étienne came in through the kitchen door and I remembered what we'd discussed and said no more.

'The police are down by the river,' Étienne muttered. 'The two local men and another one not in uniform. I don't know him.'

I poured him some coffee and he drank it gratefully. 'What are they looking for?' I asked.

He shrugged. 'They didn't tell me.' I could see his leg jerking up and down under the table and I knew he was nervous. When I looked up I saw Luc had noticed it too and he caught my eye and frowned.

'I've come to see if I can help, Monsieur Martin. My father said I must make myself useful.'

Étienne shook his head. 'There's nothing, boy. The men are in the yard and I'll go up to the vines when the police go. They've told me to hang around the house for now. Thank you, though, and thank your father.'

The atmosphere in the kitchen was strained and Luc

got up. 'I'll go then,' he said, and left Étienne and me alone in the kitchen.

'You should leave, Eleanor.' The blurted-out words came as an unwelcome surprise. 'This . . .' he waved his hand in a gesture of disgust, 'is not for you.'

'It was an accident, surely,' I said, 'and I'm not really upset except . . .' I wondered how to say it, because it wasn't for me to interfere, but I was sorry for him. 'I feel embarrassed for you. None of this is your fault.'

'You should go home,' he repeated, not looking at me. 'It will get worse.'

I longed to ask 'What will get worse?' but he got up then and went out and I went to Grandmère to see if I could get some sense from her.

She looked better, not so pale, and had dressed. I told her about Édith d'Amboise's stew, expecting her to make a fuss, but she was quite calm about it. 'It will be edible,' was her verdict, 'and I'm late getting to the kitchen today. We'll probably need a good meal this evening.'

'I've started the soup,' I said. 'I thought omelettes for lunch. I can do those.'

'Good girl.' She sat back in her chair. 'How's Étienne?'

'He's . . . very nervous, I think. The police are here. He says I must go home.'

'Do you want to?'

For a moment I was going to say yes. I thought of my conversation with Monsieur Castres yesterday, and saying that I wanted him to arrange my departure. There could be no doubt that my parents needed me and that I was indulging myself by staying on in this lovely place. But if I was honest, despite the police hanging around the farm, now that Mathilde and Jean Paul had gone I was happier here in France than I'd ever been in my life.

'No.' The word sounded loud in Grandmère's parlour but I repeated it. 'No. I want to stay.'

'And you shall.' Grandmère reached out and took my hand. 'For ever, if I have my way.'

I found Lisette on the bridge. She was leaning over the rail watching the water drift underneath her and as I approached I saw her throw something into the river and heard her call, 'Goodbye'. I thought, hurrying towards her, that she was saying farewell to her mother. That it was the flowers she said she was going to pick for Grandmère that she was throwing in the river. How could I have imagined she didn't care? She cared too deeply to say anything. I wanted desperately to comfort her.

'Hello, darling,' I said, reaching her and putting my arm round her little waist. 'What are you doing?'

'Look,' she piped. I followed her gaze to the river, expecting to see the flowers, but all I saw were her six dolls floating slowly downstream towards the place where Mathilde had been caught in the undergrowth.

'Oh, Lisette.' I was shocked. 'Your dollies. You've thrown them in the water.'

'I don't want them any more. They were naughty.' We watched as they swirled around the little isthmus where we'd seen Mathilde and then followed them as they travelled further down the river.

'Have you kept any of them?'

'No.' Her face was set and I could feel through my arm the rigidity of her slight body.

The two local policemen were on the opposite bank

watching the dolls float by. A man in a city suit whom I hadn't seen before was grinding his cigarette out on a tree stump beside them while keeping his eyes on Lisette and me. I felt quite uneasy about him.

'Come on,' I said to Lisette. 'We'd better go inside and leave these men to do what they have to do.'

'You are Miss Gill?' The city suit man came into the kitchen while I was beating eggs in Grandmère's white bowl.

'Yes.'

'I am Monsieur Hubert, a police detective. I need to ask you some questions.'

Lisette, who was sitting at the table, stared at him. 'The button on your shirt is undone,' she said. 'I can see your belly. I can see your *nombril*.'

I hadn't known the word for belly button before but I guessed that was what she'd said because Monsieur Hubert reddened and hastily buttoned his shirt over his navel. All the buttons on his shirt were under strain and it wouldn't be long before they gave way again. I was about to reprove Lisette for her rudeness but she caught my eye and parted her lips in a little grin and I had to grin with her. My earlier unease about him vanished.

I think my grin rather disconcerted Monsieur Hubert because he hesitated before speaking again. 'Miss Gill,' he started. 'I believe you are a guest in this house.'

'Yes,' I said, putting down the bowl of eggs and sitting at the table next to Lisette.

Monsieur Hubert sat too, opposite us, and studied our faces. He took out a notebook and pencil. 'You are a relative of the family here, perhaps?'

'No. I'm on a school exchange holiday. I'll be going home to England soon.'

'And this little girl?'

'I'm Lisette Martin.' She didn't appear to be at all concerned about talking to this stranger. 'My mother is dead but I'm not an orphan for I have my papa and Grandmère.'

'And do you know how your mother died?' Monsieur Hubert's pencil hovered over his notebook.

I was angry and scowled. This fat buffoon was asking an impossible thing for a child to answer and I was about to protest when Lisette said, 'She fell in the river. I saw her.'

'You saw her fall?' Monsieur Hubert sounded quite excited.

There was a slight pause while Lisette fiddled with the eggshells I'd left on the table. 'No,' she said eventually. 'Maman was in the river.'

'Was anyone else . . .'

I'd had enough. 'Lisette,' I said. 'Go and ask Grandmère if she wants a drink. But first,' I grabbed her hand, 'did you pick the flowers for her?'

'No. I forgot.'

'Well, I think she would like some, so off you go.'

Monsieur Hubert was not pleased and tapped deep pencil marks into his notebook. 'I need to ask the child what she knows, Miss Gill. It's important that we get to the bottom of Madame Martin's accident. After all, she was the one who found the body, so I'm told.'

'She did, but' – I was surprised at my own boldness – 'I think you should remember that she's only a little girl. Madame Martin was her mother, you know.'

'But no love is lost in this family, they tell me.' He flipped over a page in his notebook and wrote my surname then underlined it several times. It was as if he wasn't certain about what he had to write. I relaxed in my seat. I knew that I'd have very little to tell him and my thoughts drifted away to the omelettes and whether I should get some herbs from the garden to flavour them. Would thyme and oregano grow at home? What if I made a little herb bed in the shelter of the big barn?

'When did you last see Madame Martin?' The question, rapped out, invaded my musings on horticulture.

'What?' I mentally shook myself and gazed at Monsieur Hubert's face, ready to form the answer. Suddenly, I couldn't remember. The events were all running together and I was scared that I might say the wrong thing. When did I see her? In the night, peeping round my door? At the grape barn? Later?

'At lunch, yesterday.' I gabbled the words out. 'That's when I last saw her.'

Monsieur Hubert pursed his lips and flipped back several pages of his notebook. I noticed that his button had come undone again and a triangle of hairy belly was protruding over his grey trousers. 'Be aware, Miss Gill. I have been talking to other people.'

I shrugged. 'Of course.'

'Would you say that you and Madame Martin were friends?'

I stared at him. What sort of question was that? How could it possibly matter whether Mathilde and I were friends? His eyes, dark and hooded in his plump cheeks, were drilling into mine and I realised that I'd misjudged him. He wasn't simply a fat man who happened also to be a detective. He was a lot cleverer than that. I dragged my eyes from him and looked at the table, at the scars in the wood and the chips missing from the edges, and wondered what would happen if I told the truth.

'Er . . . no. Not particularly.'

'Why?'

'I don't know,' I said. 'She just didn't like me.'

'And so you didn't like her.'

I could see Lisette by the kitchen door, a few wild flowers in her hand, and wondered how long she'd been standing there. She was singing a little song when she came in and skipped past Monsieur Hubert's chair into the corridor to where Grandmère's rooms were. I followed her with my eyes, wishing I too could leave the kitchen and go to the safety of Grandmère's parlour. At the doorway Lisette turned and gave me a reassuring little nod. And that brought a new thought. Why did I feel unsafe?

'You wanted to get back at her for not liking you.'

Monsieur Hubert's words immediately confirmed my anxieties. Was he suggesting that I'd pushed Mathilde into the river? Suddenly I was very frightened. I was a foreigner and it would be convenient to put the blame, if there were any blame to be put, on me.

'No,' I said, louder than I'd intended. 'Not at all. She was the one who said she'd kill me.' As soon as the words were out of my mouth I knew I'd made a mistake. The detective's reptilian eyes gleamed with pleasure and he stood up.

'Miss Gill,' he started, but the noise of Grandmère's door opening and the sight of her bustling in her old style down the corridor stopped him in mid-voice.

'Eleanor.' Grandmère went to the stove and stirred the soup. 'Lettuce, please, from the garden, and take Lisette with you.' She turned from the stove and fixed the detective with a thunderous glare. As Lisette and I went out I heard her say, 'A child and a young visitor? How dare you question them without Monsieur Martin or myself present?'

On our way back from the vegetable garden I saw Monsieur Hubert marching out of the yard and getting into his Citroën. Good, I thought, we've seen the last of him. Of course, I was wrong.

He came back at supper time.

The four of us were eating Madame d'Amboise's stew, all enjoying it, I think, because it had been quite a fraught afternoon. The priest had arrived after lunch, apologising that he hadn't come earlier but he had been in Angers overnight and only just heard. His condolences were perfunctory. He blessed us all, particularly Lisette, who thoroughly enjoyed the experience and genuflected extravagantly until Grandmère grabbed hold of her in mid-gesture and told her to behave herself. He told Étienne that he would visit Mathilde in the mortuary and say the necessary prayers. I went outside because it was really none of my business and besides, I needed time to think.

After a while, Lisette came out to sit on the river bank with me and we chewed stalks of grass and basked in the healing sun. I looked up to the vineyard and noticed that the fire outside the grape barn had gone out. I wondered if Étienne was still talking to the priest and what they were saying. Maybe the priest was offering comfort but I didn't really think so; he would know as well as anyone that Étienne didn't need comforting. Not in a priestly way.

I remembered the night we were fishing and he kissed me. That seemed to give him comfort, and just thinking about it I felt a flush rising through my body.

'Do you like my papa?' asked Lisette, rolling on her back and flinging her arms up so that she could touch the bottommost leaves of the willow tree above us.

'Yes, I do,' I answered, wondering how she knew I was thinking about him.

'The policeman said he was a good man.'

I was surprised. 'Do you mean Monsieur Hubert?'

'No, silly, not him. The other one. The one who lives in the village. I heard him say that Étienne Martin was a good man and a hero.' She thought for a moment and then asked, 'What's a hero?'

'It's someone who does something brave. Maybe a man who does something that other people wouldn't do. I think your father did very brave things during the war. When you were a baby.'

'Is your father a hero?'

Dada. I hadn't thought about him all day, nor my mother. Oh, God, what sort of daughter was I? 'Yes, he is,' I said, hoping she didn't hear the choke in my voice. 'In a different way.'

We were still lying there when Grandmère came to find us. She looked so much better than she had earlier that it seemed she'd been right about her fever's only lasting a day. She handed me a brown envelope. It was another telegram.

'Oh,' I said, looking at her worried face and turning the envelope round and round in my hands.

'Open it,' piped Lisette, and Grandmère nodded.

It was from Monsieur Castres. *Unable to contact Mr Franklin stop Will try again tomorrow stop No word from hospital stop Best wishes Castres*

Two pairs of eyes studied me anxiously. 'It's from Monsieur Castres. He says there is no more news about my parents and he's been trying to contact my friend's family.'

'Why?' asked Grandmère.

'Because . . . well, they might be able to let me stay if my mother and father are still in hospital when I go home.'

'Didn't you tell him you could stay here?'

I couldn't meet her eye, remembering how I'd instigated Monsieur Castres's efforts to contact the Franklins. 'Yes,' I muttered, 'but I'll have to go back sometime. There's school, and . . .'

Lisette leant against me. 'I don't want you to leave. You make me happy.'

I put an arm round her and dropped a kiss on her head. 'You make me happy too, but now I think you should be tickled.'

Her squeals of delight echoed joyfully along the river, causing small birds to fly startled out of the trees and the water rats to scurry into their nests. As I rolled her over and wriggled my fingers about her thin little shape I wondered if she'd ever been tickled before. I remember being tickled by a friend in junior school and being shocked. It was something that my parents had never done to me.

'Enough,' said Grandmère after a while. 'Laughter isn't seemly today.'

So that evening we sat at the table eating our supper, quiet but contented, with no malevolent presence to make conversation uncomfortable. We talked about the farm and the continuing hot weather and how it was becoming necessary to water the vines more frequently. Neither Mathilde nor Jean Paul was mentioned so it came as a terrible shock when Monsieur Hubert walked, unannounced, into the dining room.

'Mathilde Martin did not drown,' he said, looking at our stunned faces one by one. 'She was already dead when she went into the water. Someone murdered her.'

Chapter Eighteen

'What's murdered?' Lisette's little voice pierced the silence which followed Monsieur Hubert's terrible statement.

'Shush,' Grandmère demanded and Lisette dropped her eyes from the detective's flushed face and popped a spoonful of stew in her mouth. The rest of us ignored our meal. Étienne reached out his hand for the carafe and poured a large glassful of his favourite red wine. He looked at me and offered the carafe but I shook my head. I was feeling a bit sick.

I glanced back at Monsieur Hubert. He was excited, anyone could see that; he had enjoyed announcing the shocking news and was looking forward to the next part.

'You'll all have to be questioned again, but this time at the station. So,' he took out a handkerchief and wiped the sweat from his fleshy jowls, 'so, Monsieur Martin, you must come with me and you as well, Miss . . . er . . .' He'd forgotten my name but was unmistakably pointing at me.

'Miss Gill has nothing to do with this business,' snapped Étienne. He swigged down the wine and stood up. I held my breath as he walked round the table until he was in front of Monsieur Hubert. He was taller than the detective and although he wasn't as fat – indeed, Étienne never had an ounce of extra fat on him – he was broader and looked a formidable opponent. Monsieur Hubert took an involuntary step backwards.

'Leave the girl alone.' Étienne's voice was quiet but full of menace and he seemed dangerously close to grabbing the policeman by the jacket and doing something awful which would get him into more trouble. I was shocked, because this was an Étienne I'd never seen. Gone was the angry, frustrated man who seemed always on the point of exploding into impotent rage or despairing of the way his life had turned out. I couldn't see the other Étienne I knew either. The laughing, relaxed, happy-go-lucky man who'd held me in his arms and kissed me so hard that my whole body had melted.

Now I was seeing someone entirely different. This was a man totally in control of himself, a man, I supposed, who had fought a dirty underground war and killed with impunity. And even as I thought those words another thread of understanding was trailing through my brain. He had killed with impunity in the past; was it possible that . . .'

'I don't mind going with you.' I heard my voice, girlish in the heavy atmosphere that pervaded the dining room. 'I can answer any questions.'

Étienne looked at me over his shoulder. 'Keep out of this, Eleanor. You don't understand how things work here.'

It was true, I didn't understand how things worked there, or anywhere, really, but I was terrified for Étienne. If I thought that he could be a cold-blooded killer then Monsieur Hubert would too. The local police would know all about Étienne's exploits with the Résistance; I imagined them speaking admiringly about him and

Monsieur Hubert listening and coming to his conclusion. Why I thought it was up to me to help him I had no idea, but I do remember how desperate I felt. Was it because I was in love? In love with a man more than twice my age, whom I'd known for only a month? No, not then, I don't think, because I barely knew the meaning of the word. In my mind love was something noble, dramatic, conducted between romantic characters like the ones in the books I read. My feeling for Étienne was something I couldn't put into words. It was as if I'd found the person I'd been longing for all my life and I had to keep him safe.

I cast my mind about for something to say which would soften Monsieur Hubert's attack, endorsements of the kindness of all the members of this household, how I loved being here, and that what had happened to Mathilde must have been to do with the men she entertained. In the end I said none of those things. I simply repeated my statement.

'Ask me anything you like, Monsieur Hubert.'

'Good,' said Monsieur Hubert. He nodded his head, then looking up at Étienne added meanly, 'I can arrange for you to be arrested now, if you prefer.'

Grandmère, who had sat quietly throughout the exchange, now stood up. 'I can answer questions too,' she growled, staring at Monsieur Hubert as though he was something deeply unpleasant. 'What do you want to know?'

'And me.' Lisette joined the clamour and suddenly Étienne burst out laughing and relaxed.

We did go to the police station; Étienne and I were driven away in the police car and were put in separate rooms to wait. I thought about my parents while I sat on a wooden chair next to an old varnished table. Mother had been in hospital for two weeks now, not getting any better it would appear, and I wondered, yet again, what was the matter with her. Had she been ill when I left? I thought back to that brief peck on the cheek she'd given me at the station and tried to picture her face, hollow-cheeked in the cold, unforgiving station lights. Was it different? Oh, God. Maybe it was but I'd been too excited to notice. How could I have been so blind?

Then Dada. Here I almost cried. He'd endured four unspeakable years in a prisoner of war camp, torture, starvation, the most utter privation, and now, as far as he was concerned, he was imprisoned again. I could imagine him leaning against a wall in the asylum, watching nurses, doctors and other patients walking about and all the time never uttering a word.

I'd heard our doctor once telling Mother that the reason Dada didn't speak was that he'd trained himself not to when he was being tortured by the Japanese guards and now it had somehow become imprinted on his brain. 'Or at least,' our GP had said, helplessly, 'something like that. The psychiatrists aren't entirely sure and there is no treatment.'

Well, I thought, pulling myself together, if he could resist his captors, so can I.

Monsieur Hubert got very little out of me. I gave him a brief outline of my holiday and how my parents were ill and Étienne had let me stay longer. 'He has been very kind,' I added. 'So have all the family.'

'Except Mathilde Martin, eh?'

I let that pass.

'The boy, Jean Paul, where is he?'

I shook my head. 'I don't know.'

Monsieur Hubert took out a packet of cigarettes, Gitanes, the same as the man on the train, and I thought about Miss Baxter and Janet and Margaret. They'd all be back in England now and people would be talking about me and wondering why I wasn't back.

'Surely, Miss Gill, he must have said something to you. The boy. Same age as you, you got close, maybe?' The detective lit one of the cigarettes and took a long pull at it before breathing smoke out into the small room. I shook my head and made a great play of heavy coughing, wafting my hand in front of my face and appearing generally disconcerted. He flushed and dropped the cigarette on the floor, grinding it out with his shoe.

'So you don't know where he went?'

I cleared my throat extravagantly before choking out an answer. 'No. No idea.'

He flicked through the notebook where he'd written my answers to his previous questions but he didn't seem to know what to ask next. He had never asked if I needed a translator, and I thought that if he started trying to winkle out details that I wanted to keep to myself that would be my escape. I could pretend that I didn't understand. While I waited, I looked at the little square window, out of which I could see nothing because night had fallen, and drummed my fingers on the table. I felt that I had the measure of this man and that nothing he could do or say would bother me.

I was still drumming when Monsieur Hubert spoke again. 'Do you know how Madame Martin died?'

'No.' I frowned and gazed beyond him to the shiny green-painted walls of the small room while I thought about it. She'd been murdered, he'd said. Did that mean someone had deliberately pushed her into the river? The wooden railing on the bridge was cracked. Was she pushed against it?

When I looked back he was staring at me. 'You've thought of something?' he said, eagerly. 'Something you want to tell me?'

'No.' I shrugged, trying to sound girlish and ignorant. 'Nothing. What could there possibly be?' Maybe I was too flippant, because the eagerness was wiped off his face in an instant.

'Well, I'll tell you, girl.' He angrily slammed his hand on to the table, making me jump, and leant forward so that his face was only inches away from mine. 'Madame Martin's neck was broken, not in an accident but deliberately, and almost certainly by someone you know!' My shock must have been evident because Monsieur Hubert's eyes glittered and he smiled, showing small yellowy teeth. 'She was murdered, Miss Gill.' The next thing he said filled me with horror. 'It will be the guillotine for the murderer, Miss Gill. The guillotine.'

We were taken back to the farm in the back of a police car. It seemed that Monsieur Hubert had no proof that either Étienne or I had any involvement in Mathilde's death and he had to let us go. 'But I'm not finished with you,' he'd shouted as we walked out of the police station. 'I'll find something. Just you see.'

Étienne ignored him and turned to me. 'Are you all right?' he asked, taking my arm. He looked exhausted, and I noticed that the collar of his shirt was torn and the top two buttons missing. There was a red mark on his face just below his left eye.

'You've been hit,' I said anxiously, and forgetting that we were still in full view of Monsieur Hubert I reached up my hand and touched his cheek.

'It's nothing,' said Étienne, and helped me into the back of the police car. I turned round as we swung away and saw through the narrow back window the detective watching us with a calculating frown on his face.

We hardly spoke on the drive home but sat, shoulders touching, facing away from each other, watching the trees on the sides of the road looming out of the shadows. I thought about Mathilde being murdered and I knew Étienne was thinking about it too. Monsieur Hubert had said that she'd been killed by someone I knew and that could only be a member of the family, couldn't it? A shiver ran through me, and Étienne must have felt it because he took my hand and held it gently in his. That calmed me, but even so I refused to think about the guillotine. The police driver asked directions once and was given them, but that was all. I think we were too shocked or too exhausted to speak. That would come later.

Grandmère was waiting for us in the yard. She'd heard the car turning through the gateway and had come out. Holding on to her hand was Lisette.

'The child wouldn't go to bed,' she said gruffly after kissing me on both cheeks and putting a hand on Étienne's shoulder. 'I've soup and bread in the kitchen. Come along now.'

So the four of us sat round the kitchen table, smiling at each other in relief and enjoying the hot soup. Lisette sat beside me, her little hand on my arm, her eyelids drooping sleepily. She'd wrapped her arms about my waist when I got out of the police car and wouldn't let me go until I made her sit in a chair and take a piece of bread.

'Oh, Eleanor,' she'd breathed. 'I thought you'd never come back.'

'Silly girl.' I smiled and kissed her cool cheek. 'I'm here now.'

Grandmère got up and went into the pantry. I looked across to Étienne. He was clutching a glass of wine in front of him but he wasn't drinking it. He had put his head under the tap in the sink when we went into the kitchen, letting the cold water soothe his swelling cheek. Now he sat with his damp hair black and curling on his collar and his half-open shirt sticking to his chest.

'Did Hubert touch you?' he muttered, one eye on Lisette.

'No,' I said. 'I hated him interrogating me but he kept his distance.'

'Good.' He nodded and swirled the wine around in his glass, but he still didn't drink it.

'Look.' Grandmère came back with a plate of sweet pastries. 'I made these while I was waiting. Gave me something to do.'

'Lovely,' I said, but I hesitated. 'I'm sorry, Grandmère. I can't eat any more tonight.'

She looked at Étienne but he shook his head and when she turned to Lisette she smiled and shook her head. 'The child's asleep. I'll take her up to bed.'

'Sit, Maman. I'll take her.' Étienne got up, and gathering Lisette gently into his arms he carried her out of the kitchen.

'Well,' said Grandmère. 'That's the first time he's . . .' She started clearing the table and I got up to help her.

'No, Eleanor. Let me do it. You must go to bed.'

I nodded and turned towards the door leading up to my room. 'Was it too terrible?' she asked, not properly looking at me.

'No,' I replied, softly. 'Don't worry.'

'Sweet child,' she said, more to herself than to me, as I climbed the back stairs to the blessed comfort of my room.

Chapter Nineteen

In the days that followed we were mostly left on our own. The farm workers came and went, of course, and the jobs that we all did, me included for I felt now that I was truly a part of the life at Riverain, were done as usual.

Grandmère was called into the police station once to give a statement but wasn't there very long. 'Do you want me to come with you?' asked Étienne when the police car came for her.

'No. I'm all right by myself,' she said. 'Carry on with your work, and you, Eleanor, can dig up a few potatoes and carrots. I'll call in at the butcher's while I'm in town; I'm sure Albert Charpentier won't mind waiting for me.' She fixed the young local policeman with her stern gaze.

'No, madame,' he said hastily and she nodded and got into the back of the car.

We were in the vineyard when she came back, Étienne, Lisette and me, on a hot morning when the sky was as blue as can be and there wasn't a breath of air. Even the birds in the trees down by the river were quiet, almost exhausted, I imagined, by the long days of baking weather. In the week since Mathilde and Jean Paul had gone the heat had been relentless and Étienne had spent hours pumping water through the rows of vines so as to make sure that the grapes plumped up and the harvest would be good.

'After the harvest, we'll start new planting,' he said, 'over there.' He pointed to a sloping pasture adjacent to the vineyard where beef cattle flicked their tails at buzzing insects and grazed on tinder dry grass. 'I'll keep the dairy cows on the water meadows but all of this is going back to the grape.' He waved his hand over the hillside and smiled. He looked happier than I'd ever seen him.

That morning, while Grandmère was at the police station, Étienne and I had been pruning away some of the leaves shading the ripening bunches of grapes and tying straggling tendrils back on to the wires. He'd shown me what to do, and although it was fiddly work I enjoyed it. 'Cut back some of the lower growth as well,' he'd said, guiding my hand to where I was to cut. 'We have to keep the insects away.' His hand was hot on mine and his fingers rough where they closed over my fist holding the little knife he'd given me and forced me to slice through a small green branch. 'There, that's how. Can you do that?'

'Yes.' I nodded, a little breathlessly, and cut through another branch.

'Very good. We'll make a grower of you yet.' Then he'd grinned while my cheeks glowed and I wiped away the sheen of sweat that had gathered on my face. I wore a big straw hat that Grandmère had found in one of the unused bedrooms. 'Oh, I'd forgotten this,' she'd said. 'This was my garden hat before the war. You have it now.'

Étienne stood beside me and clipped away excess leaves at the top of the vine. 'The canopy of each bush must be thinned to allow air to circulate,' he grunted as leaves fell down, some on my head. 'In five or six weeks we'll be harvesting, so I want as much sunlight on the grapes as possible. It makes them sweeter.'

'Mm,' I grunted, tossing my head so the fallen leaves dropped from my hat. Étienne was so close that I could smell him. Sweaty, yes, but more than that. It wasn't the sour, small-room stench that Monsieur Hubert gave off nor the dry, cold, almost ghostly odour that surrounded Dada. To me, it was earthy, outdoors, exciting. He smelt like a man.

'There's a car coming.' Lisette, who'd been sitting on the dusty ground beneath the vines, stood up and looked down the slope towards the bridge. 'Perhaps it's Grandmère coming home. I do hope so.'

She had been shuffling on her bottom along the rows as Étienne and I worked, gathering the cuttings into piles so they would be easier for us to collect and burn. In the last week she'd hardly let me out of her sight but she had been a good girl and Grandmère had given her little chores to do, putting out scraps for the cats who lived in the barn and tying herbs into bunches so that they could be hung up to dry. Now she was more a part of the family than she'd ever been before.

I'd started to teach her to read. Madame d'Amboise had given her a brightly coloured story book with pictures of fairies and goblins, which she loved. I read the story to her every evening and then started picking out the letters and making her say them after me. Étienne watched us as we sat at the kitchen table repeating the ABC and laughed.

'I think I learned to read exactly like that,' he said. 'But not from a book. I'm pretty sure it was the newspaper that Maman used as instruction. My first readings were all about politics and wars, not to mention births, marriages and deaths.'

I smiled because his story sounded so familiar. Feed invoices and vet's bills were what I started with, on my own, when we went to the farm. Suddenly an image came into my mind of a pop-up alphabet book and how overjoyed I'd been when Mother put it into my hands. How could I have forgotten that? Her getting something especially for me. It would have been at the beginning of the war and Dada had just been posted to the Far East. We lived in a little house in the town and although Mother was sad that Dada had gone away she was happy with me. Then we went to the farm and she changed.

I was still thinking about it when Étienne spoke again. He was leaning back in his chair staring out of the kitchen door to where the pots of geraniums wilted in the late afternoon heat. I mentally noted that I would water them when the sun had gone down. 'D'you know,' he said slowly, 'I don't think my father could read. At least, not well.' He shook his head. 'How odd. I never thought of that before.'

The book that Luc had given me was on the table beside Lisette's fairy book and I wondered if those two volumes had started him thinking. 'Well,' I said, 'that won't be a problem with this little one. She's picking it up quickly.'

'Very good.' He got up and patted the child on her shiny ash brown hair. 'School for you next month, young lady.'

But now she was skipping down between the vines to greet Grandmère on her return from the police station.

Étienne and I followed more slowly, strolling between the green leaves and letting the heady scent of ripening grapes bathe us. Walking through the undergrowth on the way to the bridge, Étienne stopped and took my arm, pulling me round to face him.

'Are you happy again, Eleanor? Like you were before?' He took off his cap and used it to wipe the sweat from his brow. 'I know you wanted to leave after what Jean Paul did to you and that was completely understandable. But now, even with' – he shrugged – 'this business with Mathilde, have you forgiven us? Forgiven me?'

Of course I had. I would have forgiven Étienne anything. Maybe I was enchanted, under a spell cast by this exquisite place, because it seemed that after a few hours each unpleasant event stealthily passed me by and dissolved in the morning mist. Attempted rape? It wasn't really all that bad, was it? After all, Jean Paul didn't hurt me, much. The few bruises I had were fading and my memory of the events had become confused and overlaid with Mathilde's death. And even that. Murder? After the first shock, the fact that Mathilde had been deliberately killed was only another difference, cultural or perhaps even inevitable, and the gravity of it seemed to float away as she had nearly done. It was something that didn't really matter.

No, I was content, loving every day and revelling in being part of what had become a happy family. The only cloud on the horizon was the fact that I would soon have to go home and I mentally winced as I remembered that I had suggested to Monsieur Castres how it could be organised. But as the days passed and I had no word from him, even thoughts of ever going back were pushed to the furthest reaches of my mind.

I put my hand on Étienne's. 'There's nothing to forgive,' I breathed. 'And yes, I am happy, happier than I have ever been. This place is heaven.'

'Then stay with us.' His voice had dropped to a murmur. He bent his head down closer to mine so I could see the tracery of white lines around his eyes where he had crinkled up his face against the sun. His eyes were a deep liquid brown and looking into them I felt as though I was drowning. I barely heard what he whispered next. 'Stay with me.'

I think he would have kissed me then but Lisette came running through the undergrowth. 'Papa! Eleanor! Grandmère is back and she's brought the bad man with her.'

Grandmère was in the yard, standing beside the police car. She looked hot and a little flustered and a strand of hair had come away from her tight bun, but otherwise she wasn't too bad. I went straight to her and took the bag of groceries from her. 'Are you all right?' I asked.

'Yes, perfectly,' she answered. 'Did you bring in carrots and potatoes?'

I nodded, but now I had one eye on Monsieur Hubert. Who was he going to question next?

'What now?' Étienne came to stand in front of the detective. 'Haven't I answered enough of your stupid questions?'

'No,' he answered carefully. 'I don't think you have.' He looked at the four of us. 'Every one of you is lying about something. Even the child.'

Lisette giggled and Grandmère took her by the arm and gave her a little shake.

Monsieur Hubert scowled. 'You country people. You think you're above the law. Well, you're not, I tell you. You are not!'

I glanced to Albert Charpentier, the local policeman, wondering what he thought of that insult. After all, he was a country person too. I raised my eyebrows at him and received a grin and a wink in reply. Monsieur Hubert turned quickly and caught the wink and his scowl deepened.

'Go and wait in the car, Charpentier.'

I watched Albert wander off to the black Citroën and wondered which of us would be accompanying Hubert back to town. I thought it might be me, for the detective turned his baleful face back in my direction.

'How old are you, miss?'

'Seventeen,' I said, astonished at his question. 'You know that; you have my passport.'

'Mm,' he grunted, then, 'We've been in touch with the British consul in Angers, a Monsieur Castres.'

My heart sank. They were going to throw me out of the country. I glanced despairingly at Étienne and then at Grandmère. They looked just as shocked as I felt.

'Monsieur Castres says that as you are a child he should decide what happens to you and that he has wheels in motion to get you back to England.'

'Oh,' I muttered. Tears were welling up, stinging my eyes, and I quickly dragged a hand across them.

Monsieur Hubert completely misread my response. 'Not so quick, young lady,' he said, and there was a gleeful glint in his eye. 'You don't get out of trouble that easily. At seventeen, you are considered of an age to accept criminal responsibility. So Monsieur Castres cannot remove you from this country without my say-so. And as of now I don't say so.' He was actually smirking. 'You must stay here until I'm satisfied that you had nothing to do with the murder of Mathilde Martin.'

I can't describe the relief I felt and I heard Grandmère breathe out a long sigh which I knew was relief too, but mindful that he was watching my reaction I said, trying to put a piteous note into my voice, 'But my parents are very ill. They need me.'

He shrugged. 'That's of no interest to me. I have to track down a killer.' He turned to go and then stopped, putting a hand to his head as though he'd just remembered something. 'The boy, Jean Paul, has been sighted in Angers. He'll soon be picked up and we'll see what he has to say about this . . . affair.' Monsieur Hubert smirked again. 'I think he'll tell me what I want to know.'

We watched as the police car drove out of the yard and then turned to each other. 'Jean Paul won't be any use to him,' Étienne said. 'Even if they catch up with him. What could he say?'

'Nothing,' said Grandmère, and smiled at me. 'So, you will stay with us a bit longer.'

'Yes,' I said and then added shyly, 'if you'll have me.'

'But of course. You belong here.'

I didn't look at Étienne but I knew he was grinning and Lisette was laughing out loud. 'The bad man has gone,' she squealed. 'Now we can be happy.'

And we were, throughout the rest of that day and the days after while the sun beat down on the farm, turning the meadow grass brown and the river even more sluggish. I, free from the worry of Monsieur Castres, worked in the kitchen and dairy with Grandmère in the morning and in the vineyard with Étienne in the afternoon. 'How ever did we manage before you came?' asked Grandmère early one day, when I came into the kitchen with the morning bread. Mathilde's bicycle had now become mine and I happily rode to the village to collect supplies and even the five miles to the little town. People were getting to know me, and if they occasionally asked how the police investigation was getting on I didn't mind. There was nothing to tell them and they accepted that and asked kindly about my parents.

Luc came over to see me, greeting me as a friend with a kiss on both cheeks. It was quite surprising, but I loved the idea of having a friend here in France. We sat by the river and talked about books and films, although neither of us had any in common, except for *The Count of Monte Cristo* which I was enjoying. He asked about the police enquiry and I told him all I knew, including the fact that Jean Paul had been seen in Angers.

'Oh, I know,' he said. 'Everyone's heard that. He was seen at the station, apparently, trying to get on a train without a ticket.' This was news to me and I wondered if Étienne knew about it.

'I wonder where he wants to go?' I mused, lying back on the bank and looking at the washed out blue of the morning sky. A few little clouds, floating like white puffs of cotton wool, had appeared in the last hour, the first clouds I'd seen in a week. Might they signal an end to the terribly hot weather?

'As far away as possible, probably,' Luc replied. 'Now that Mathilde has gone, there's no reason for him to stay.'

'But he left before she . . . well, before she died.'

'Ah,' Luc sounded enigmatic, like someone in a Sherlock Holmes story, 'but did he?'

I sat up and stared at Luc's clever face. 'What d'you mean? He went in the early morning. Lisette saw him.'

'Yes, I know that. But how do you know Mathilde wasn't already dead?'

'But we didn't find her till supper time.' Even as I said it I remembered Monsieur Hubert saying that Mathilde was already dead when she went in the river. That brought a new thought.

'Luc,' I said. 'What you said the other day about Jean Paul not being Étienne's son. Did you mean it?'

'Mm.' He nodded. 'She brought him with her when they married. He was a baby and they told everybody that he was Étienne's son, but he was born before Étienne even met her. I heard my mother telling my sister. Grandmère' – he jerked his head towards the house – 'had told her.'

I wondered why Grandmère had told Édith d'Amboise what was essentially a family secret but there were obviously lots of things I didn't know about this family. I looked up to the vineyard where I could see Étienne moving about, carrying bundles of cuttings to put on his bonfire. I should be helping him, I thought, but I wanted to talk to Luc.

'And Lisette? You said about Lisette too.'

'Oh, well. Everyone knows about her. They had a German officer billeted here during the war, a major, I think.' He looked at the river, greeny grey and moving slowly towards the sea. It occurred to me that Étienne hadn't been fishing for days. The vineyard was taking up all his spare time.

'I remember that German,' Luc continued. 'I used to see him when I walked down the lane and he would be driven past. He'd get the driver to slow down and he'd throw out a bar of chocolate sometimes. Maman didn't like me eating it but I would take it into the fields where she couldn't see me. The thing was that he wasn't a monster like some of them. Some of them were bastards.' I flinched at that swear word. It didn't sound like Luc.

'Go on,' I said, appalled but fascinated by this story.

'Well, Étienne was away, first with the Free French army and then in the Résistance, so the major was the only man in the house. Mathilde got very close to him and it was noticed and talked about, all through the village. Lisette is his child.'

I thought of the newspaper photograph and the man cutting Mathilde's hair while the others watched. That's what it was about: they were getting back at her for collaborating. But then there was Lisette. Poor little girl. I felt sorrier for her than I had before and when a few moments later she came skipping across the bridge to join us I gave her a special hug.

'Papa says can you come and help him. He says that you are so good with the vines.' She snuggled into my chest.

I beamed. Praise indeed. Dropping a kiss on her head, I scrambled to my feet.

'Oh,' said Luc, looking very disappointed. 'D'you have to go?'

'Yes, of course. Don't you go when your father asks you for help?' I was surprised that he didn't seem to understand the necessities of a farming life.

'Étienne isn't your father,' Luc said quietly. 'And you're supposed to be on holiday.'

I thought about what he said as I walked up through the rows, Lisette running and jumping beside me. He was right, Étienne wasn't my father. He was absolutely nothing like my father nor, come to think of it, like any other father I knew. Jed Winstanley was a father and so was Mr Franklin, but I couldn't see Étienne in them. And I didn't want to.

That evening a little breeze blew up from the south, rustling through the willows by the river and bringing a welcome gust of admittedly warm but moving air in through the dining room windows.

'I think the weather will break,' said Étienne, sitting in his place and carving up the baton of bread. 'Tomorrow, maybe.'

'I hope so,' Grandmère sighed, taking the cover off the tureen and stirring the soup with her huge ladle. 'My feet don't like this heat.'

'My feet don't like this heat, my feet don't like this heat,' sang Lisette and we laughed, even Grandmère, who put a bowl of soup in front of her then wagged a pretend angry finger.

'If the weather holds I thought we might spend a day out tomorrow,' said Étienne, turning to me. 'Is there somewhere you'd like to go?'

I didn't need to think for long. 'Fontevraud. Could we go there? I'd love to see it.'

'Why d'you want to go there?' Étienne looked very puzzled and rather upset. 'Fontevraud Abbey is a prison. It's an awful place.' His voice had dropped and he put down his spoon into his half-finished bowl of soup.

'Fontevraud,' I repeated, thinking that one of us had made a mistake. 'I'm sure it has the tombs of some English kings and queens. My teacher told me about it and showed us photographs. They're in the abbey. It's . . .' I stopped, not sure that they would understand, and from the look on both Étienne's and Grandmère's faces what I was saying was making them rather uncomfortable. 'It's a connection to history. I love history.' I knew I was blushing and I was puzzled too. Did Miss Baxter forget to say that the Abbaye de Fontevraud was a prison?

'I don't know if members of the public are allowed in,' said Étienne. 'It would be a waste of time.' Obviously he didn't want to go there.

I must have looked downhearted for Grandmère said, 'What about Chinon? If I remember my schooldays,' and here she paused, 'I think we were told that Jeanne d'Arc was there. That's history. And the town is very quaint too.'

'Yes.' I nodded, not wanting to make a fuss. 'I'd like that.'

'Can I come too?' pleaded Lisette. 'We had such a lovely day out last time, I know I'll love this one.'

'If you're a good girl,' Grandmère said and Lisette bounced up and down on her seat and had to be persuaded to hurry up with her soup so that I could bring in the cold chicken in tarragon sauce.

Chapter Twenty

The weather hadn't broken the next day. We awoke to high white cloud which obscured the sun most of the time. Occasionally, though, brilliant shafts of light managed to pierce through, briefly brightening the parched fields and hillsides. It was oppressively warm and the air felt heavy and full of portent.

I think the heat had got to Grandmère, for she had decided not to come with us. 'Are you feeling ill again?' I asked, concerned.

'No. But I'll stay at home today. Tell me all about it when you get back. And make sure Lisette behaves herself.'

'I will,' I promised and we set off, the three of us in the front of the van, thrilled, I think, to be away from the farm although we all loved it as we loved life.

'It's too hot to sit on my knee,' I told Lisette. 'You can sit between Papa and me. There's plenty of room.'

'Yes, Eleanor.' She was pink with excitement, the colour in her cheeks suiting her. Lately she had been looking better, not so wan and lifeless, and more than once I'd heard her squeaking with laughter at something her new friend Claudine had said. Madame d'Amboise had brought her granddaughter to play on several occasions and Lisette seemed happier than she'd ever been. At least the d'Amboise family didn't hold Lisette's parentage against her, but I wondered vaguely what might happen when she started school.

'We'll have a storm tonight,' said Étienne, looking out of the van window as we drove along the south bank of the Loire towards Chinon. The trees lining the road were still, with not even the slightest breeze to move them; nor were they throwing shadows. I had become used to the tree-lined roads in this area with their straight shadows and the glittering water mirages showing ahead. Today was different.

The road rose and fell through the gently rolling countryside and now and then we would come across a rocky outcrop on which stood the ruins of a château or a fortress. Except for those, the land was gentle and lush with vineyards and cattle pastures backed by deep green forests. It was lovely country, a planet away from my bleak Pennine hillside.

'Look,' I said, pointing to a château rising above the large town we were passing. It had a fairy tale quality with its gleaming white stone walls and pepper pot towers.

'That's Saumur,' Étienne said, leaning over to look. 'I was there for a while, during the war.'

'What were you doing?'

'Oh.' He shrugged. 'This and that.'

I grinned, imagining what 'this and that' could have been, and when he looked back at me he grinned too.

We left the river road and went inland, halting at a crossroads. 'Fontevraud is close to here,' Étienne said, waving his hand towards a road which went to the right. He was frowning. 'If you really want to,' he said, turning to me, 'we could go and have a look. Get it out of your system, eh?'

I nodded eagerly, delighted to get my own way. And I did get it out of my system, but I was sorry afterwards; my desire to visit Fontevraud brought back terrible memories for Étienne. Of course, I didn't know anything about the place, except for the tombs, but if I'd been older and perhaps a little less naive I would have said no when he'd reluctantly offered to take me there.

The abbey and its many buildings were so vast and complex that the small village seemed a mere afterthought. Now it was surrounded by a high wall and the white stone was scuffed and damaged, so the entire place looked neglected and forbidding. The abbey church dominated the other buildings with its huge mediaeval arches and pointed towers. It should have been a place of wonder and faith, but strangely it seemed cold and remote.

Étienne spoke to a man at the gatehouse and we were let in, but only to the original abbey church and the man came with us into the vast empty space which had been for seven hundred years a place of worship. To my astonishment, it was empty of all religious artefacts, no crosses, no statues, no paintings or plaques on the walls. Only one stained glass window remained to remind visitors, if indeed there were any, that this had once been one of the most important religious houses in all France. I supposed that when it had been made into a prison it had been deconsecrated. Now it was simply a stone space topped by a vanishingly high vaulted ceiling with a dirty, littered floor underfoot, damaged stonework and to one side, almost disregarded, the tombs.

They lay in a row, in curiously secular state, Henry, Eleanor and Richard carved out of white tufa stone and the smaller fourth tomb, Isabelle or Berengaria, fashioned from wood. The early mediaeval colours still clung to the effigies in places, mostly pale reds and washed out blues, although Richard's gown was a rich dark blue edged in yellow and the cleverly carved drapery on Henry's tomb was cream with dusty green stars.

I stared at the faces, thin and regal, and wondered if that is how they had looked in life. If so they'd been a handsome family although, from what I'd read, a murderous one. But now they looked at peace, having atoned for their sins, and appeared to be facing eternity in complete composure.

'The bodies aren't under there,' said the guard, pointing to the tombs. 'Long gone and good riddance, I say.'

He spoilt the moment, as I supposed he'd intended. Republicanism still held sway amongst many Frenchmen despite their exquisite châteaux and churches. I ignored him and continued to study the tombs, looking at the clothes and crowns and wonderfully carved hair while the man watched me with a sneer on his face.

'Why is she reading when she's dead?' asked Lisette, pointing to the carving of Isabelle, who lay with a book propped up between her elegant long fingers.

'Maybe she read a lot when she was alive,' I said, looking up from my contemplation of these Plantagenet kings and queens. The guard was staring at me in a rather unpleasant way and I was suddenly anxious to leave. Taking Lisette's hand, I hurried her outside where it was grey and gloomy under the oppressive clouds and the air was thick. I felt uncomfortable because Étienne, who hadn't come in with us, was walking about restlessly, his face grim and his shoulders twitching. When we finally got into the van and drove away, leaving behind the white buildings and the quiet little town, I timidly asked him what was the matter.

At first he didn't answer and then he said, 'Some of my friends were imprisoned in Fontevraud. Robert Brissac was lucky, he survived. Others did not. It is a terrible place and it still terrifies me.'

'You didn't say.' I was appalled at what I'd done. 'I would never have asked you to take me there if I'd known.'

'I know,' he sighed, and dragged the steering wheel over so that we were on the road to Chinon once more. After a bit he spoke again. 'Maybe this trip has been good in its way. Things have to be faced, no matter how bad they are. I learned that long ago, but I think that I had forgotten it.' He was thoughtful for a moment and then said, 'I don't know how you do it, Eleanor, but somehow you make me realise what it is I want and what I ought to do.' He had the ghost of a smile on his face and I didn't understand what he meant, but at least he wasn't angry.

We were a silent trio for the few remaining miles. I think even Lisette understood that something had gone wrong for she was very quiet and sat clutching my hand in her small one and didn't speak until we stopped on the side of the river Vienne to gaze at the beautiful mediaeval town across the water.

'Chinon,' said Étienne, and at that moment a shaft of sunlight broke through the clouds and lit up the creamy stone walls of the rambling château and the higgledy roofs of the town below it. The scene could have been taken from Lisette's book of fairy tales.

'Oh, it's lovely,' I breathed, and my heart lifted and stayed that way for the rest of the day.

I bought a little guide book in a paper shop and used it to take us to the various historic sites and we walked and walked. We went up and down the narrow crooked streets, where the balconies of stone and wooden houses flourished with bright geranium and tomato plants, through open squares with their statues and fountains, until I found the place where Jeanne d'Arc had drunk from a well.

'It must have been here,' I said, really to myself, for Étienne and Lisette were no longer interested. I was studying my little guide book.

'I think it was, my child. On this very spot.'

When I looked up I found I was standing next to an elderly nun dressed in full robes with a broad starched white headdress.

'Good afternoon, *ma soeur*.' Étienne removed his cap and Lisette bobbed a little curtsey. I stood awkwardly, like the Protestant English schoolgirl that I was.

'Monsieur.' She nodded to Étienne. 'These are your daughters?'

'No.' He touched my arm. 'This young lady is a visitor from England.'

She turned her head to look at me. 'Saint Joan would not be a welcome addition to your history, perhaps.'

I was a bit taken aback and wondered how to answer her. The English had, of course, burnt Joan at the stake but I thought of Miss Baxter and our lessons and said,

'It was a long time ago. Perhaps we weren't as . . . compassionate as we are now.'

'Nicely answered.' She smiled. 'How old are you, my child?'

'I'm seventeen.' I wondered why she'd asked. It was exactly the same question Monsieur Hubert had posed.

'Ah,' the nun said, 'exactly the same age as the Maid when she came here, to Chinon, to speak to the king. So young and yet . . .' She crossed herself, then moved closer to me so that her broad headdress almost filled the space between us, and while Étienne and Lisette watched she brought up her hand and made a cross on my forehead with her thumb. 'God bless you.'

'Oh!' Lisette, who was holding my hand, jumped up and down with excitement. She loved displays of religiosity.

The nun looked down at her. 'Pretty child,' she said, and turned to Étienne. 'Another visitor?'

There was a pause and I felt my stomach tighten.

'No,' he said at last, putting a protective hand on Lisette's head. 'This little one *is* my daughter.'

I wasn't able to take in the import of that statement properly because as the nun made her blessings and farewells Lisette pulled on my hand. 'Can we stop walking now, please, Eleanor,' she begged.

'Yes, of course,' I said. 'Are you tired?'

'Mm.' She nodded. 'And thirsty.'

'Well.' Étienne indicated a café with a board outside offering snacks. 'Let's go there.'

It was while we were sitting at the café eating smoked ham baguettes that I spotted a shop selling women's clothes. I'd torn my Aertex shirt while I was working in the vineyard and although Grandmère had mended it, the repaired shoulder seam and the tear across the sleeve seemed to stand out every time I put it on. I needed something else to wear.

Leaving Étienne drinking cold beer in the café, Lisette and I walked across the road to the shop. I saw the dress I wanted in the window before we went in and to my delight it fitted me perfectly when I tried it on. It was cotton, with cap sleeves, a square neck and a gathered waistline above a pretty full skirt. But it was the pattern that I fell in love with. Small flowers, pinks, blues and lilacs, the colours of sweet peas, were scattered across a cream background. I'd never seen anything like it and certainly never imagined that I would be able to buy it. I knew Suzy would think it unsophisticated and Mother would hate it. Far too colourful for her and terribly rough cotton. 'Uh,' she would sniff. 'It looks as if it's made from old kitchen curtains.' But how would she know? We didn't have any kitchen curtains. In our house only the bedrooms had curtains.

'How much?' I asked the shop girl nervously, convinced I wouldn't have enough money, but egged on by Lisette, who pronounced it delicious, I'd bravely nerved myself to enquire.

To my astonishment it was cheap, so cheap that I had enough saved from my holiday money to buy it and have some left over. Oh, I loved that dress, loved the brightness of it, loved the fact that it had been bought in such a beautiful place and most of all loved that it made me feel French. I kept it for years after.

'Eleanor's bought a dress,' said Lisette, importantly, when we rejoined Étienne. 'I helped to choose it.'

'Now let's buy something for you,' I said to her. 'What would you like?'

'Er . . . not right now,' said Étienne. 'I've seen something I need to get. Do you mind waiting for me?'

While we waited Lisette tucked into an ice cream and I had another *citron pressé* until Étienne appeared carrying a large box. He looked hot, and sweat stood out on his forehead and trickled down his bare arms.

'Christ, it's heavy,' he said.

'What is it?' I was hopping up and down almost as eagerly as Lisette.

'Wait and see.'

We were quiet on the drive home, Étienne and I both silent, looking ahead at the road, while Lisette leant against me, fast asleep. I thought about Chinon and the pretty streets and squares and about the nun and her blessing but mostly about the dress I'd bought. I preferred not to contemplate Fontevraud too deeply.

'I've been thinking about Robert Brissac,' Étienne said, as we passed Saumur.

'What about him?' I asked reluctantly. Was he going to grumble at me for making him go to Fontevraud?

'I need to see him again. I need to ask him something.'

'What?'

He shrugged. 'This and that.'

We arrived home as the sky darkened for the night, turning into the yard quietly happy and exhausted. Lisette, still asleep, had to be gently woken.

'Oh, I've had such a nice day,' she murmured sleepily, but when Grandmère came out to welcome us home she woke up properly and chattered about everything and nothing like a little starling.

'Did you see everything you wanted?' Grandmère asked while we were in the kitchen. She had prepared a simple platter of shrimps and salad which with bread and wine made an appetising meal. We were to eat it in the kitchen, too, as she thought we'd be too tired to wash and tidy up before supper.

'Yes, oh, yes,' I said. 'Chinon is wonderful and I bought a dress. I'll show you later.' I went to the pantry for the bowl of mayonnaise and put it on the table. 'The only thing was, Monsieur Martin took us to Fontevraud. It upset him.'

We were alone. Étienne had gone to check on the cattle and Lisette had done one of her usual disappearing acts. 'Oh dear,' said Grandmère. 'That place has unhappy memories for him. I shall never forget the day that Robert Brissac was released. Étienne went to get him and had to take him immediately to the hospital in Saumur. He'd been tortured and starved and was only just clinging to life. And it was Étienne who had to tell him that his wife had been taken away and shot.'

No wonder he'd been so upset, I thought, and then I remembered what he'd said after. About facing one's terrors and how it might have been a good thing. I didn't have a chance to say that to Grandmère because he came in then and Lisette appeared from the hallway and we sat down to eat.

'I've got something for you,' Étienne said to Lisette later while we were clearing away the supper plates.

'Me, Papa?' Lisette's face was shining. 'Oh, oh!'

'Wait here.'

It was the large box he'd carried through Chinon that he put on the kitchen table, and while Lisette wriggled in excitement and Grandmère and I looked at each other in amazement he pulled away the string holding it shut and, like a magician getting a rabbit out of a hat, produced a wooden doll's house.

Lisette's mouth fell open but no words came out and maybe mine was hanging open too. Perhaps unnerved by our silence, Étienne delved further into the big box and pulled out further small boxes which contained the doll's house furniture and the inhabitant dolls themselves.

We were all stunned. It was a wonderful present, but nobody could speak. We just sat there staring at it until Étienne, throwing himself back on to his chair, muttered uneasily, 'Well, say something. Is it all right?'

Lisette broke the silence. She jumped up and rushed over to Étienne, wrapping her arms around his neck and hugging him. Then she pressed little kisses on his cheek. 'Thank you, Papa,' she said breathlessly. 'Oh, thank you, thank you. It's the best present I've ever had.'

Later, when the doll's house had been carried up to Lisette's room and she'd fallen asleep with the tiny girl occupant in her hand, I went back down to Grandmère's parlour. I wasn't ready for bed, although I'd walked for what felt like miles and seen both wonderful and disturbing sights. She was sitting at her table with the cards laid out on the plush cloth. I went to sit opposite her and rested my head in my hand.

'What can you see tonight?' I asked.

'I'm not sure.' She turned over another card and frowned. 'It's confusing, contradictory. I'll try another pattern.'

The cards were shuffled and as I watched she started

to lay them out again in a wider pattern. She was absorbed in her task, carefully placing each card after the other, her belief in their power of prophecy seemingly never wavering. I wondered for a moment if she really believed in what she was doing, but only for a moment. She never doubted the cards.

'Will they tell you about Mathilde?' The words came out of my mouth in a rush and I had no idea why I'd said them. There'd been no mention of her or Monsieur Hubert all day and it was as if that terrible event had happened long ago to someone we barely knew. It seemed that Mathilde and Jean Paul were being wiped from the consciousness of Riverain and life was going on in a hugely improved way. We were happy, all of us, and strangely unconcerned about the police investigation; we were as content as those regal figures on the tombs, having somehow atoned for our sins and facing an eternity of peace.

But I must have been thinking about her somewhere deep inside me or I would never have said what I did. 'I'm sorry,' I muttered. 'I don't know why I said that.'

Grandmère's hand hovered over the complicated arrangement of cards she was making. 'What d'you think the cards will tell us about Mathilde?' Her voice had the tiniest edge of steel, perhaps a warning.

'Nothing. I don't know,' I said hurriedly. Then, 'Sorry,' again.

She wouldn't look at me and I squirmed in my seat, feeling like a stupid child. Eventually she raised her eyes and gave me a little smile. 'I think we'll concentrate on the living,' she said, and gathering up the scattered cards she shuffled them briefly then handed the pack to me.

'You deal them out, nine cards, three by three. Let's see what will happen to you.'

On that hot night in her airless little room I watched as Grandmère turned the cards over one by one and muttered out my fate. I didn't understand her vaguely worded predictions then, but later, much later, sitting in the cheerless kitchen of my home on the hill while the February snow lapped against the window, I remembered what she'd said and gripped my book tighter, trying not to cry.

Chapter Twenty-One

I went to bed then, saying goodnight to Grandmère as she put the cards away in her cabinet, my head a whirl of confusion as I tried to understand the meaning of her words. She must have realised I was uncomfortable for she smiled and came over to kiss me on both cheeks. 'Don't worry, child. It will all work out with a bit of help.'

My room was very hot, even though the shutters had been closed all day and the windows behind them thrown wide open. I undressed and tried on again the dress I'd bought in Chinon. I still loved it, and carefully taking it off I hung it in the cedar wardrobe. My nightdress was hanging on a hook behind the bathroom door and I stared at it, reluctant to put it on. The tear had been mended and it had been washed several times since that night, but it was a reminder and I didn't like it.

I got into bed naked, stretching my arms and legs out to the corners, exulting in the feel of the cool sheet against my body. I pushed away the duvet and let what little air there was in the room touch my flesh. It was the coolest I'd felt all day and I waited tiredly for sleep to cloud over me.

Images of the day in Chinon flitted across my mind. The pretty streets and squares and the nun talking to us. Then I thought of Étienne buying a present for Lisette, the child of his wife's German lover. Why had he done that? No wonder Grandmère and I had been astonished.

Fontevraud came into my mind and I shifted uncomfortably on the bed. How could I have known, I muttered to myself. It's not as if anyone had told me. And I felt quite cross with Étienne and Grandmère for not explaining the real reason for not going there.

Finally I thought of Grandmère and the cards and tried to work out what she'd meant as she told me my fate. *A change is coming to us all, very soon. And sadness and heartbreak. You, Eleanor, will never be the same again.*

I supposed she meant that I was going to leave this beautiful place, go home to all the trouble that awaited me, with Mother recovering from her illness, scornful of my attempts to look after her and Dada, and poor Dada, totally disorientated. However would I manage? I groaned silently. The prospect was depressing.

Then another thought consumed me. Maybe her prediction had to do with Mathilde? *Sadness and heartbreak*? Oh, God! Somebody in the household will be arrested and charged with her murder. Others would be accessories to that murder . . . even me. I thought of Monsieur Hubert threatening the guillotine, his obvious pleasure at the idea and his reptilian eyes glittering as he stared at me. My stomach curdled and all thoughts of sleep were gone.

I sat up, my body now damply warm, and took a deep breath. The room was stifling, or perhaps I was being stifled by the myriad thoughts that were invading my head. It was no good. Despite my tiredness, I would never sleep, and I got out of bed and pulled the hated nightdress off the hook. If I was going downstairs I would have to wear something and this was the coolest article of clothing I possessed.

The back stairs creaked as I walked down and I paused in the kitchen, listening for sounds of somebody waking up, but there were none and I opened the door and walked out into the yard.

In the distance, towards the south, I could hear the faint rumble of thunder, and when I looked in that direction I saw the brief flashes of lightning. That was Étienne's predicted storm, not here yet but on its way and hopefully bringing relief from the hot breathless days we'd endured over the last weeks.

I walked on to the bridge and stood, leaning against the mended rail, listening to the faint slap of the river as it splashed against the posts beneath me and the occasional plop of a fish jumping out of the water. Another faint rumble of thunder; the leaves on the willow trees rustled as the beginnings of a breeze moved through them and I felt the cooler air on my face. It was bliss.

'You can't sleep, *ma chérie*?' Étienne had walked on to the bridge. He was barefoot and bare-chested and I held my breath and waited. He had called me his darling, so when he strode forward and took me in his arms, I was ready.

Now, when I think of that night, oh, so many years ago, I smile. What we did was natural, with no shame attached, just two people who wanted and, more important, needed each other. Besides, I was in an enchanted place and nothing I did there could ever be wrong.

'Come,' he said after a while and led me back across the bridge to the river bank where the grass was cool on my back when he laid me down. My lips felt bruised from his kisses and my whole body throbbed with anticipation. I knew what he was going to do and, eager as he, pulled him down on top of me.

'Oh, *mon Dieu,*' he said afterwards, his breath ragged, 'you are my heart.'

I loved that. His heart. And he was mine.

He sat up on one elbow. 'Did I hurt you?' he murmured, his voice choking with emotion. 'I didn't think, before . . .'

'No,' I said. He had, of course, but it didn't matter and the next time it didn't. 'I wanted you to do it.'

His arms were around me again and I curled my body into his. The hated nightdress had been torn off in our passion and he too was naked. I could feel his body throughout the length of mine, the muscles rippling beneath his glistening skin, his strength, his power. He was everything a man should be, the personification of all the romantic heroes of the novels I'd read alone in my cold bedroom. Experiences crashed around me: first love, the feel of a man's body and, perhaps the least regarded, loss of virginity. I was almost overwhelmed.

The thunder was closer and with every louder rumble the lightning grew more intense. I felt a drop of rain and then another and soon we were being pelted with heavy drops which soaked our hair and our glowing bodies and made us laugh out loud.

Étienne took my hand, pulling me upright, and we ran along the river bank and across the yard to the kitchen door. 'Shush,' he whispered as we crept up the back stairs, but I wanted to laugh again and when he threw me on the iron bed and made love to me once more I didn't know whether to laugh or cry.

I think I did cry a little. I felt as though a huge dam

of tension had been washed away and I was so relaxed that nothing really mattered. Étienne had moist eyes too.

'I didn't think I could be so happy,' he said quietly. 'You have given me life.'

'I'm glad,' I said, 'because I love you.'

I never stopped loving him.

In the morning when I cycled to the bread shop, I couldn't stop grinning even though the rain drove into my face and soaked my clothes. Étienne had left my bed earlier to see to the cattle, and I, my body still throbbing and flushed, had quickly washed and gone off to the village.

'Good morning, Miss Eleanor,' said the baker, putting down his bowl of coffee. 'A welcome rain has come at last.'

'Yes. Yes, it has,' I replied. And not only that, I longed to say. I was made love to last night. Can you tell?

Grandmère could tell. 'You look different today,' she said, taking the bread from me as I brought my purchases into the kitchen.

'Different?' I asked, trying to sound casual. 'I'm wet. My hair's plastered to my head. That's what makes me look different.'

She didn't answer but when Étienne came in from the yard she watched us. Watched the look that passed between us and saw our faces soften and flush as we remembered the night that had just passed.

Lisette wandered in carrying the man and woman from the doll's house. 'Hello,' she said. 'It's raining.'

'Put those dolls down and have your breakfast,' said Grandmère, putting a bowl of hot chocolate in front of her. 'Eleanor has brought *pain aux raisins* this morning.'

Étienne drained his coffee bowl and with another quick look at me went out back to the yard. I ached to follow him. To touch his arm, or his neck, or . . . I took a deep breath. I had to remain calm.

'Do you still like your doll's house?' I asked Lisette.

'Oh yes,' she said, her hazel eyes shining. 'I've played with it since I woke up.' She took a big gulp of her chocolate and tore eagerly into her *pain aux raisins*.

Grandmère nodded approvingly. 'That child has discovered an appetite,' she said. 'I swear she's grown in the last few weeks.'

I think she had both in size and emotionally. Certainly she didn't seem so strange and secretive, and having a friend in Claudine allowed her to be the child she should have been. Étienne came back in carrying a couple of letters. He looked worried and my heart lurched as he put them on the table. 'The post boy brought these. They're both for you,' he said, and I know he felt as sick as I did.

'That one is from Jean Paul,' mumbled Lisette, her mouth full of bread. She pointed to one of the envelopes. 'I've seen his writing on his school book.'

I looked at it. It was addressed simply to Elenor, wrongly spelled and with no surname, then the name of the farm and the village.

'Goodness,' I exclaimed. 'Why would he write to me?'

'I don't know,' Étienne muttered. 'Open it.'

Inside was a single piece of paper. It was thick and a mottled beige colour, and looked as if it had been torn from the back of an old book. Whose book, I wondered, because I knew that Jean Paul would never have had one in his possession.

'What does he say?' asked Grandmère, leaning over and trying to read the scrawling writing.

'He says . . .' I struggled to read the barely legible sentences. 'He says. . . *I am sorry. She made me.*'

Grandmère snorted. 'Well, we knew that, didn't we?' She put a comforting hand on my shoulder while I turned the paper over to see if there was anything written on the other side. There wasn't.

'Knew what?' asked Lisette, wiping the chocolate ring from around her mouth. 'What did we know?'

'This is nothing to do with you,' said Grandmère swiftly. 'Now, Lisette, if you've finished your breakfast, what about your chores? There's a bowl in the pantry with scraps for the cats. Take it to the barn and then go into the garden and pick some parsley and thyme. And don't pull out clumps like you did last time.'

'Yes, Grandmère.' The child left her little dolls on the table and went into the pantry.

Étienne was examining the envelope. 'The postmark is Marseille. He's got all the way down there. Huh! So much for Monsieur Hubert saying that they would catch him within the next few days.' He tapped the envelope against his chin for a moment, thinking, before handing it to Grandmère. 'I wonder . . .' he said.

'What?' She looked at him, frowning.

'Well, Marseille. He could be trying to get on a ship, or . . .' he paused again. 'Or going to Algeria.'

'Why Algeria?' I asked, surprised.

Étienne shrugged, but Grandmère took the letter and the envelope out of his hands. 'I think we should get rid of this, don't you, Étienne?' she said.

He nodded. 'No point in giving Hubert any more

information than is absolutely necessary. But it's your letter, Eleanor. You decide.'

'Burn it,' I agreed.

Lisette came out of the pantry with the bowl of scraps just as Grandmère was putting the letter into the fire-box of the cooking range, but she said nothing and went out into the yard.

I was examining the other letter. It was from Angers and I knew it was from Monsieur Castres. With Étienne and Grandmère watching me I tore open the envelope and read the typed letter.

Dear Miss Gill,

You'll be pleased to hear that I have contacted Mr Franklin and he and his family have agreed to give you a home for as long as is necessary. Mr Franklin is very concerned that the police will not let you leave the country and has asked to be kept informed.

The news from the hospital is not so good. Your mother is quite ill and the doctors say that she will have to be kept in for some time. Her diagnosis is septicaemia which is, I believe, a severe infection. I'm sure she is getting the best of care.

Your father is still in the Institute and there is no further news of him.

I have spoken to the police department and requested permission for you to travel home as soon as possible, but owing to the serious nature of the crime committed on Monsieur Martin's land they have refused to permit your departure. I will continue to act on your behalf.

Please telephone my office if I can be of any further help.

I read the letter out loud, translating as I went. I knew no translation for septicaemia but it seemed as though it was nearly the same word, for they both nodded, and then I read it again.

'Who is this Mr Franklin?' asked Étienne, frowning.

'He's my friend's father. He's a solicitor. Very respectable.' I added that last bit because he was looking concerned. Maybe he thought if I would go with one older man I would go with another.

'Am I not respectable?' he whispered almost under his breath, hoping, I think, that Grandmère wouldn't hear.

'No.' I giggled. The news that the police wouldn't let me go added to the remembrance of last night was making me feel a bit light-headed.

'*La septicémie*,' mused Grandmère. She was deliberately not looking at Étienne and me. 'Some of the men who came back from the wars had that. From the wounds, you know, when they got dirt into them, I think. Maybe your mother got dirt into a wound.'

'Well, it could be, I suppose,' I agreed. I thought back to the cuts and scratches she was always getting on her hands. They often went septic but cleared up quite quickly. Maybe she'd had something bigger than a cut this time.

'It looks like you'll be staying with us for some time yet.' Étienne turned to go back into the yard. 'Even until the grape harvest.'

'Oh,' I said, overjoyed, and all thoughts of Mother and her illness callously flew from my head. 'I do hope so.'

I wasn't alone with Étienne for the rest of that day except for five minutes in the vegetable garden, when he kissed me, fiercely, and pushed his hot hand down the back of my shorts.

'Oh.' I giggled and nearly dropped the basket of eggs I was carrying. 'You mustn't. Someone will see.'

'I don't care,' he crooned, kissing me again. 'I love you.'

'Do you?' I was breathless both from the kisses and the immensity of what he'd said. 'Do you really love me?'

He stood back from me, and pushing an unsteady hand through his thick dark hair he gazed into my eyes. 'Yes, I do,' he said, and his voice sounded as though it was breaking. 'Never doubt me in this, Eleanor Gill. I will love you until the day I die.'

For the rest of the morning Grandmère found tasks for me in the kitchen and the dairy and then after lunch, when Grandmère went for her afternoon rest, Lisette wanted me to play with her doll's house.

'You look softer,' she said.

'What?' I laughed. 'You mean I look sillier?'

'No.' Her little face was quite solemn. 'You look like your edges are melting. Just a bit. It's nice, and pretty.'

I gave her a hug then and sat the dolls at the tiny dining room table with their miniature plates set out before them. The plates even had pretend food on them and there were little china cups and saucers. Each room in this house was full of furniture. Nothing had been stinted and it must have cost Étienne a fortune.

'Eleanor!' My name was being called.

'Don't go,' grumbled Lisette. 'We're having such a nice time.'

'I must,' I said. 'You come too.'

It was Luc, waiting in the kitchen for me, and we strolled out across the bridge and wandered through the trees on the far bank. The rain had stopped but water still dripped from the branches, wetting my hair and shoulders. I didn't mind; it was such a change from the days that had gone before when the only damp feeling on my head had been sweat. The air smelt sweet and fresh and even the river had lost some of its sludgy tang and was running faster and cleaner as though it had regained enthusiasm for life.

We walked towards the vineyard where I could see Étienne working at the top by the barn. He had been prevented by Monsieur Hubert from continuing to demolish the grape barn or even going inside it, but looking up I could see that he had a box of bottles in his arms. Those must have come from inside.

'I thought he wasn't allowed in there,' said Luc.

I shrugged. 'I don't know,' I lied. 'But I don't suppose it matters.'

He frowned. 'I think it does. There will be evidence to collect. That way the detectives can get to the bottom of Mathilde's death.'

'They were in and out of that barn for days,' I said, and I couldn't help letting my irritation show. 'If there was anything to find, they'd have found it by now.'

'Have you heard any more from the police?' Luc asked as we walked through the undergrowth.

'No, nothing,' I said, and then a thought came to me. 'Luc. Why would somebody go to Algeria?'

'Algeria?' He stopped and stared at me. 'What made you say that?'

Suddenly I felt as though I was giving too much away. 'Oh, nothing,' I answered quickly. 'It's just something I read . . . in a book.'

'The headquarters of the Légion Étrangère is there,' Luc said, and his eyes narrowed as though he was working out what I meant.

'Oh. The Foreign Legion, of course. *Beau Geste*. A book I took from the library.' I grinned at him and now it was his turn to look confused.

We had reached the vineyard and I cast an eye on the grapes. They were growing well: the overnight rainstorm had plumped them up and they hung in glistening purple bunches from strong stalks. I spotted a stray tendril and moved to fasten it back on the wire.

Luc grinned. 'You're getting good at that,' he said. 'It's a pity you won't be able to use this knowledge when you go home.'

'Mm,' I murmured. Being at home was something I was beginning to forget. My life was here now . . . with Étienne. 'I'm looking forward to the grape harvest.'

'But that's not for weeks yet. Surely you'll be going back to England before then.' He took my arm. 'What about school?'

I stared at him, perplexed. School? I hadn't even thought about it. If I'd imagined my life at home it had been on the hill with Mother and Dada. I'd completely forgotten about school.

'Have you heard about your exam results?' Luc's voice broke into my thoughts and I shook my head. The results would be out by now, and if I'd done well I'd be going into the sixth form.

'What's the date, Luc? D'you know?'

'The twenty-fifth of August.'

'Oh,' I said. The letter telling me how I'd done in the exams would be at home, waiting for me, and the new term would be starting in a couple of weeks. Everyone would be back at school, talking about the holidays, and for once I would have something to say. Suzy would be showing off her tan, her new watch, her new hairstyle, and telling everybody who would listen how marvellous her time in Paris had been. 'Chantal and I will be friends for ever,' she would say, 'and Mummy and Daddy have been invited there for the weekend to go to the races. Oh, the family is so smart.' Then she would turn to me and ask, 'What ever happened to you?'

I gazed at Luc's concerned face. The sun had lightened a streak in the front of his brown hair and he looked younger and more of a schoolboy than I remembered. He was such a nice person and such a good friend, but . . . I transferred my gaze up to the grape barn where Étienne was still carrying bottles out and stacking them up beside the dark patch where he had had the bonfire. 'I don't know about my exam results,' I said absently, yearning to climb up between the vines and be close to Étienne. 'But I can't go home yet, I had a letter from the British consul. He said the police insist I stay here.'

'What?' Luc shook his head. 'That's just silly.' He thought for a moment and then said, 'I'm surprised the consul hasn't got you a lawyer. After all, no one could possibly suspect you, whereas . . .' he glanced up to the grape barn, 'Monsieur Martin must . . .'

He was interrupted. 'My papa bought me a doll's house.' Lisette had crept up behind us and was now hanging on to my hand. 'When we were in Chinon yesterday.'

'So you'll be the same as Claudine now,' Luc said, smiling down at her.

'Yes, I will. And my doll's house has little people in it. A papa and a *maman* and a little boy and a little girl. I will give them names.' She looked up to where Étienne was dragging an old basket press out of the barn. 'I'm going to see my papa now. Bye.'

I watched her go, skipping through the row of vines, and wondered how much of the conversation she'd heard. I often wondered how much of all our conversations she heard, and for the first time I realised that she might know more about Mathilde's death than she had said.

'She's happy,' Luc said, watching her too.

I nodded, then thought of what he'd said about her father, the German officer. 'Luc,' I said slowly. 'Can I ask you something?'

'Of course.'

'And will you tell me the truth?'

He shrugged. 'If I can.'

'Then . . . what happened to Lisette's father?'

He was quiet for a moment, then he said, 'The story is that he deserted. A few days before the Americans liberated us in 1944, he simply disappeared, leaving all his belongings, his car and apparently, a photograph of his wife and son.' He sighed. 'The thing was that nobody believed it. They knew Étienne was in the area – he and Robert Brissac were preparing the way for the Allied advance – and everybody was certain that Étienne had killed him and hidden his body. My father says that the whole village was terrified of reprisals because the Germans would shoot anyone who attacked their soldiers. Two days later the American army swept into the village and the Germans were on the run. But Major Bergmann had gone and Mathilde was left alone, entirely despised and unprotected.'

I felt suddenly cold. Poor Lisette, I thought. How long would it be before someone told her that the man she thought was her father had killed her real one. I looked up to the barn and saw her sitting on the ground beside the growing pile of boxes that Étienne was dragging out. I knew she'd be chattering and he wouldn't be listening, but I also knew that they were all right with each other.

'I don't believe Étienne killed the German officer,' I said.

'I do,' Luc replied.

Chapter Twenty-Two

Those were golden days that followed. The warm weather had returned, every day sunny but not oppressively hot as it had been before, and we were all happy.

Grandmère went about her tasks with a secret smile on her face, cooking delicious meals and teaching me how to make wonderfully aromatic tomato sauces, which we bottled up ready for the winter. We also dried tomatoes and mushrooms and bottled peaches and plums so that the pantry shelves groaned with a multitude of produce.

I made my first butter, hard work at the churn but the results were worth it, and when I proudly brought it in from the dairy and laid it on the cold marble shelf in the pantry, Grandmère was the first to taste it.

'A little too wet, perhaps, and not enough salty,' she pronounced. 'But good for a first effort. You're a quick learner, Eleanor.' And we grinned at each other, as companionable as a mother and daughter should be. She knew about Étienne and me and I know she approved. She never commented on the hours we spent together, lying on the river bank, and if she saw anything on my bed sheets nothing was said. More than once she stopped Lisette from following me when I wandered out to the hay barn to find Étienne.

I loved lying on the sweet smelling hay with him

beside me. I would watch the birds flying in and out through the little holes in the roof, cheeping, fluttering and so alive. I would gaze at the pinpricks of sunlight which beamed through the holes, slim pencils of light, illuminating the dusty yellow hay.

This was the place where I'd first been utterly entranced by Étienne. I'd thought how foreign he looked, how different from the pale English men whom I met at home, our neighbours, the shopkeepers or the man who sold Mother the coley. I couldn't imagine Jed Winstanley stripping to the waist to fork over the hay, and the very idea of his crabby gaunt body made me giggle as I lay in the crook of Étienne's arm.

'What?' he asked, pulling his arm from under my neck and propping himself up on his elbow. 'What's so funny?'

'Oh, nothing, really. I was just thinking of someone at home.'

'Who?' he demanded in faux alarm. 'A boyfriend?'

That made me laugh even more. Jed Winstanley. A boyfriend?

'No,' I gasped. 'It's the farmer next to us. The one who's looking after our sheep. I was thinking of how he would look without his shirt.'

Étienne shook his head, not understanding what was making me laugh, but he leant over and kissed me anyway. 'Silly child,' he said.

I sat up then. 'Do you think of me as a child?'

'No. Of course not. But you are young and fresh and so, so beautiful.'

I was astonished. I'd never thought of myself as beautiful.

'Anyway,' he continued, 'I feel younger than I have

for years. I've made decisions, acted upon them and put my life in order. I have found again my strength and purpose.' He rolled on to his back and stared up at the high roof. 'Oh, Christ,' he sighed. 'I lost my way after the war.'

'Étienne.' I spoke carefully. 'What *did* you do during the war?'

'Well,' he began, quite casually, 'when France fell I went to England.' He grinned. 'Robert Brissac and I and some others got on a fishing boat going out of La Rochelle. Robert was sick all the way. He hated the sea – still does, probably. Then we were trained to fight. It was good at first, exciting. I went to North Africa with my troop and we fought alongside the British and the South Africans.'

'But after that,' I insisted. 'You came back. Here, to Anjou.'

Now he spoke more reluctantly, as though this secret that he'd kept through necessity was still difficult to tell. 'I did,' he muttered. 'I was asked to become a member of the resistance movement. Robert asked for me. He was the commander in this area and he needed someone he knew and trusted. His group was being betrayed by people who liked money and their own safety more than they did their country. My training was useful, I knew about explosives and had been in battle. Robert did the planning; he directed operations and' – he shook his head at the memory – ' he was ruthless. And now . . . what is he? A respectable wine seller with a devoted daughter. How times have changed.'

'But what sort of operations?' I needed to know more so that I could get closer to him. I needed to know this man with whom I was hopelessly in love.

'You ask so many questions,' Étienne said, trailing his fingers down my body and sending such eddies of delight through me that I almost forgot what we were talking about. 'What does it matter now?'

'Tell me,' I begged. 'Then I'll know you the way everyone else around here does.'

He sighed. 'We put explosives on railway lines when we knew that German troops would be on the train, or they were transporting munitions. We gathered information and passed it back to London. We saved people from the concentration camps, Jews and others.' Étienne's face hardened still further. 'That wasn't just the Nazis.' The disgust in his voice was palpable. 'Our own people, the Vichy regime, just east of here, sent just as many.'

'Did you kill anyone?'

'But of course.' He seemed to think that question redundant and answered me without any show of discomfort.

'Did you kill Lisette's father?'

The birds above us carried on cheeping and flying from rafter to rafter, disturbing the hay dust so that the thin streams of light shining through the holes sparkled with dancing particles. But between Étienne and me an uncomfortable silence descended.

He lay, not moving, his eyes fixed on the roof, and I, sitting up, my clothes disarrayed and my hair falling out of its clips, wished I'd never spoken. I had pushed the new-found closeness between us too far and with too many stupid questions had ruined things for ever.

'Who have you been speaking to?' he said, at last. He sounded weary.

'Luc d'Amboise,' I answered, miserably. 'I'm sorry, Étienne. I shouldn't have asked you but he said everyone knew and I wanted to know too.'

Étienne sat up and started to button his shirt. 'And I suppose it was he who told you that Lisette's father was not me but a German major?'

I nodded, then swallowed the bile which was burning in my throat.

Étienne looked at me, seeing, I supposed, an interfering little idiot whom he should never have got involved with, and I was ready for the shouting that would come or even a cold dismissal. What had I done?

But to my relief he leant over and gently pushed a strand of hair out of my face before cupping my chin in his hand.

'Listen to me, mon amour,' he whispered. 'I didn't kill Major Bergmann, although I was ordered to. I knew that if I did there would be reprisals. The village would be wiped out, and that would include my mother. So I disobeyed my orders and let him go. Where he went I don't know, and now, when I see that little child who looks so like him wandering about my farm, I am glad. How could I live with her if I'd shot her father, eh?'

I put my arms around him then, holding him to me, feeling his strong body next to mine and his heart beating steadily and truthfully. I had been right. I knew he wouldn't have killed Major Bergmann.

He spoke again, his voice muffled in my neck. 'No, my darling, it wasn't Lisette's father I killed. It was Jean Paul's.'

I gasped, gripping him tighter while my mind whirled with a million questions.

Étienne gently loosened himself from my arms and stood up. 'I have to get back to work now. The men will be here for the evening's milking and Grandmère will need you in the kitchen. We'll talk more, later.'

I watched him stride out of the barn. My lover. I rolled the word around my mouth and felt excited and daring like Becky Sharp, but then my head said 'my killer' and I couldn't find a heroine to match.

After supper that evening Grandmère grabbed me to do the cards with her. I was reluctant because I knew Étienne was waiting for me on the bridge. He'd picked up both the fishing rods and jerked his head to me as he went out of the kitchen door and I'd nodded, indicating that I'd be following very soon.

'Can I watch you with the cards tonight?' begged Lisette, who was hanging around in the kitchen after giving scraps to the barn cats. 'I've never seen you do it and it sounds such fun. Is it like a game?'

'It isn't a game,' said Grandmère, quite sternly. 'It is a way of knowing the future and how you can control it. It is not for children.'

Lisette's mouth fell and she started to trail out of the room but I stopped her. 'Let her watch,' I pleaded. 'It won't do any harm.' With Lisette in the parlour, I thought, wriggling about on her chair and asking questions, Grandmère wouldn't have the patience to make it a long session.

But I was wrong again. Lisette was quiet and attentive, kneeling upright on the chair drawn up to the plush-covered table and watching Grandmère shuffle the cards with rapt anticipation.

'I'll do you first, Lisette, then you can go to your room,'

said Grandmère and smoothed the pack into a crescent on the table. 'Now,' she said. 'Pick out nine cards.'

Slowly and almost theatrically, Lisette chose her cards and watched as they were laid out.

'This is you,' said Grandmère, pointing to the jack of hearts.

'But it's a boy,' protested Lisette.

'No, it's a young person. You are a young person. And then here and here,' she pointed to different cards, 'this tells me that your life has changed and that new things have happened.' She moved to the second row. 'You have had a gift.'

'My doll's house,' Lisette squeaked, beside herself with excitement.

'Could be,' Grandmère smiled. 'And here you found something and here you learned something.'

'I found Maman.' Lisette's voice had dropped to a whisper and she gazed at the card that Grandmère was pointing to. Then her face brightened. 'I've learned my letters, my ABC.' She looked around to me. 'I have, haven't I, Eleanor?'

'You have.'

Grandmère tapped her fingers on the final row. 'Here is disappointment and loss but finally hard work which will bring rewards.' She looked up at the little girl. 'On the whole, Lisette, it is a very good reading.'

'Oh, thank you, Grandmère. I loved that.' She turned to me, her face aglow with excitement, conveniently forgetting that she was supposed to go to bed. 'Now it's your turn.'

I quickly chose my cards, anxious to be with Étienne, and barely looked at them as they were turned over, but suddenly Grandmère gave a little gasp and I stared down at the array in front of me. Every card was black. The ace of spades was the first and then other spades and clubs filled the spaces. I could tell from Grandmère's face that it wasn't good.

'What does it mean?' I asked, now interested and even concerned. I didn't really believe in the cards – there was enough of my mother's scepticism about me to know that this was nonsense – but Grandmère believed and that made me worried.

'The ace can mean death.' Grandmère's voice had dropped and I looked quickly at Lisette, afraid that this would frighten her.

'Maman died.' Lisette's little voice rang out very calmly. 'That's what it means.'

'Yes, I suppose so,' Grandmère muttered, 'but . . .' Her hand hovered over the ten of spades and then the nine. 'These are not good cards, Eleanor. You must take care.'

'Do them again, Grandmère,' Lisette begged. 'Make them nice for Eleanor.'

'No,' she said, gathering them up. 'Not tonight. We'll do them tomorrow, it'll be better then. Now, Lisette. It's bedtime.'

When I tucked the child into her bed she put her skinny arms around my neck. 'Will you be my *maman* now, Eleanor?' she whispered. 'Because I do love you and I want you to stay here.'

'I can't,' I said, hugging her. Her face fell and little tears glistened in her sleepy hazel eyes. 'But,' I said quickly, 'I can be like your big sister. Then, wherever I am, you'll know that I love you and am thinking about you. And you'll be thinking about me.'

'Oh, yes,' she whispered, turning on her side and closing her eyes. 'I would like that very much.'

I stood on the bridge beside Étienne. The rods lay propped against the railing, unused so far this evening. He had been too restless to fish and when I finally ran on to the bridge he strode towards me and grabbing me fiercely kissed me so hard that my lips felt flattened and bruised. The rest of my body, though, throbbed with pleasure.

'Christ,' he groaned, pulling his head away. 'I can't get enough of you. You have bewitched me.'

It was the same for both of us. I felt as though I'd wandered into an enchanted kingdom and he believed I'd bewitched him. After all these years I still marvel at the extraordinary chance that of all the people in the world, we two, who were utterly right for each other, had met. It had to have been magic.

The moonlight was bright on the water and a little breeze sang through the leaves of the willows as Étienne confessed to a crime he'd committed sixteen years before, which even as he spoke could send him to the guillotine.

'I was a kid, nineteen,' he started. 'Stupid and drunk when I went into town to find a woman and, God help me, I found Mathilde. She was in a bar, flirting with the customers, and when she flirted with me I thought it meant something. Of course it didn't, or at least it only meant buy me a drink, give me money, and I think I knew that, even then.

'I couldn't stop myself, you know. I went time after time, having sex with her in a filthy room above the bar, helping her with the rent, buying her clothes. Later I discovered that I was only one of many, many men who were "helping with the rent".'

I held his hand and rested my head on his shoulder while he told his story. Much of what he said was beyond my understanding then, a few weeks into my eighteenth year. My sheltered life had kept me from the darker elements of human activity, but I understood enough. Most of all, I understood that Étienne had been young, inexperienced and ready to believe the best and not the worst of people.

'One night a man came into her room when I was there. A man I'd never seen before and he just walked in as though he owned the place, which of course he did. He picked up my wallet and emptied the money out of it, then said that I had made Mathilde pregnant and I was going to have to pay. Not just once but every month or he would send his friends to burn down the farm.'

'My God!' I said. 'Who was he? Did you pay him?'

'She said he was her brother but I didn't believe her. I thought he was another lover and I was – oh, God, I was jealous. And no, I didn't pay him. I was drunk and angry and I leapt off the bed and grabbed back the handful of notes he'd taken from my wallet.' His voice dropped to a bleak murmur. 'The man produced a knife and we fought. I killed him.'

Étienne interrupted his story and turned his face down to me. 'I've only told one person this before and I'm taking a chance, I suppose, in telling you.'

'No chance,' I said, gripping his arm. 'Nothing you could ever do will be wrong in my eyes.'

He smiled then, rather sadly. 'It was wrong, my little love. I am a flawed man.'

'But what you did was an accident. Self-defence.'

'No. It wasn't. I wrestled him to the floor and took his knife. Then I drove it into his heart.'

I could see the scene in my head, the grubby half-lit room, the tumbled bed, the two men grappling on the bare floorboards and Mathilde lying back on the bed with a horrible smirk on her face. Did the smirk vanish when it was Étienne who got up from the floor with the bloodied knife?

'I waited until the bar and the streets were empty and I carried the man to the railway line and put him on the track. The train came almost immediately.' Étienne's face was pale in the moonlight, as he remembered. 'It was the overnight express, and it thundered through, taking the body, with it. His jacket must have caught on something because the body or what was left of it, was found more than fifty miles away.'

'Oh, God,' I choked. 'That's dreadful.'

Étienne put his arm round me. 'Yes, it is, my darling, and I am tortured by it. But let me tell it all and then there'll be no secrets between us.' He took a deep breath. 'This is almost the worst part. When I went back to Mathilde she said she was going to tell the police. I'd killed her brother and got her pregnant and she wanted revenge. God, I was so terrified I almost drove the knife into her.' He shrugged. 'I should have done, there and then. Whatever happened to me would have been better than the years of misery that followed. But, at the time, she said she wouldn't tell if I married her. Gave her respectability and a home for the child she was expecting. I thought I had no choice. I believed her.'

Clouds started to drift over the moon. I stood close to

him, our arms touching, and stared through the gloom at his hands gripping the railing so hard that his knuckles stood up, white hillocks in the darkening night.

'D'you know,' he said, 'she never did tell, and she could have, easily, during the war when I was away. I don't know why – she hated me, hated the farm and wasn't frightened of anything, ever. Perhaps Riverain was a convenience. She carried on her trade both here and in town. Not for the money; she was addicted to sex. She was just evil, and taught the boy to be the same.'

'But Luc said . . .' I started and then quickly stopped.

Étienne turned his face away from the river. 'Luc told you that Jean Paul was not my son, yes?'

I nodded.

He gave a bitter laugh. 'Quite right again. After the marriage ceremony at the mayor's office Mathilde said we were to visit her friend. She took me to a stinking little house in the back streets where her friend came to the door with a child in her arms. Jean Paul. He was about six or seven months old and nothing to do with me. "This is the baby we're expecting," she told me. "You killed his father so you can bring him up."

'I never shared a bed with her again.'

We went inside then and up the back stairs to the comfort of my white room and lay quiet and thoughtful until sleep overtook us.

Chapter Twenty-Three

In the days that followed I thought about Étienne's story and several times he asked me if it had changed the way I felt about him.

'No,' I said, and meant it. My love for him was absolute.

'It should, you know,' he said one afternoon when we were working in the vineyard and he'd asked me again. 'It should tell you that I'm a violent man and perhaps not to be trusted.'

'It doesn't.' I folded my clasp knife, with which I'd carefully cut away some overhanging tendrils and exposed more bunches of grapes to the sun, and put it in my pocket. The sun was beginning to move across the hill and I would have to get down to the kitchen. Grandmère had taught me how to make meringues and I was making the dessert this evening. 'You're just looking for compliments now.'

He laughed and threw his arms around me so that we both tumbled and rolled on to the dusty ground beneath the vines. Lisette, who was a little way away, saw what we were doing and with a squeal of delight ran up and launched herself on top of us.

'Is Papa tickling you?' she giggled.

'Oh, yes, he is,' I said. 'Naughty Papa.'

Étienne grinned. 'It's your turn now, Lisette,' and I

scrambled to my feet and ran down the hill leaving them laughing and breathless until Lisette escaped and followed me into the kitchen.

'Whatever have you been doing?' Grandmère tutted. 'The pair of you have bright red cheeks and are covered in soil.'

'Papa was tickling Eleanor, on the ground,' Lisette squeaked happily. Grandmère raised an eyebrow at me but said nothing while Lisette chattered on. 'Then he tickled me. I laughed so hard.'

'Well, go and have a wash, and then you can pick some herbs for me. I want, for this chicken, um . . . tarragon and parsley. I showed you where they were.'

'Yes, I know, and I'll be careful when I pick them.'

The child danced away and I ran up the back stairs to wash my hands and brush down my shirt. When I came back into the kitchen, Grandmère had the bowls and eggs ready on the table for me and I made meringues.

'We've been invited to the d'Amboises' this evening after supper,' she said. Then she added, perhaps rather proudly, 'Our friends are sticking by us.'

It seemed a strange thing to say and then I remembered Mathilde's murder. I wondered vaguely why I never thought about it and why we were all so happy, but only briefly, and even when we were all sitting around Édith d'Amboise's table later on, the subject was hardly mentioned until we were ready to leave.

'You look very well, Eleanor,' said Madame d'Amboise when we arrived at their house. I was wearing my new dress, and with my tan and my general air of happiness the sweet pea colours of the fabric seemed to lighten any room I was in. 'Yes indeed,' Édith repeated. 'Doesn't she, Luc?'

'Yes,' he nodded, blushing and shifting the book he was carrying from hand to hand. He looked embarrassed and suddenly I realised that our friendship was deeper on his part than on mine. Madame d'Amboise realised it too, and, smiling, pushed me forward into their dining room where I was invited to sit next to Luc. I looked across the lace-covered table to Étienne and saw that he was watching me. I gave him an impudent grin, knowing that he was jealous. Was this how flirting worked? How men and women teased each other as a prelude to love? I didn't know. I'd fallen in love without experiencing that early stage, but it was fun teasing him.

Henri d'Amboise came in from the kitchen, his hands still wet from where he'd scrubbed them after working in his vineyard. 'Hello, hello!' he shouted, and took a bottle of rosé wine from the silver tray on the sideboard and put it on the table. 'I think,' he said to Étienne, 'you'll like this. It is very fine.'

Small wine glasses were produced from the cupboard and the wine poured. 'Mm.' Étienne rolled the wine over his tongue. 'Yes, it's good. Drier than usual but no acidity.' He took another sip. 'I recognise this. I tried some at Robert Brissac's place a few weeks ago. He's buying it in.'

'Ah, well.' Monsieur d'Amboise smiled. 'It seems I can't fool you. That's where this came from.'

'D'you see poor Robert often?' asked Édith, offering us small slices of almond cake. I watched as the cake was dipped into their wine by the women but not the men. I tried dipping it in mine. It was delicious.

'From time to time,' Étienne replied. 'He's not very well, these days; his injuries have left him weak and I think the terrible treatment he had has affected his heart. But he's still the determined man he used to be and still believes in justice. I respect him for it.'

'We all do, I'm sure,' Henri d'Amboise said, pouring more wine into our glasses.

'Robert is keen for me to extend my vineyard,' said Étienne. 'He remembers the wine my father produced and how well received it was.'

'Ah, yes,' said Henri. 'Monsieur Paul was an artist with the grape.'

Grandmère beamed at that and Édith offered her more cake.

'May I have some more?' asked Lisette. 'It is lovely.'

Grandmère was all for reminding her of her manners but Édith smiled and said, 'Of course you may,' then turned to Grandmère and said, 'The child looks well. She's got a lot more colour in her cheeks. And growing too, I think.'

'She's getting cheeky,' Grandmère growled, but there was a little twinkle in her eye.

'Have you heard from home?' Luc asked me while Étienne and Henri were extolling the virtues of the Chinon grape variety and Grandmère and Édith chatted about Marie, Luc's sister, and how she was coming back to the village to live.

'No, not recently,' I said. 'I had a letter from the consul who said that Mother was still in hospital and Dada is . . . where he is. The thing is that the police department won't let me leave even though the consul has arranged for me to be looked after in England. They think I know something,' here I lowered my voice so that I was speaking into Luc's ear, 'about Mathilde's death that I haven't told them.'

'And do you?'

'No.' It came out louder than I'd meant and Étienne frowned in the middle of his conversation with Henri and looked across at me. I shook my head slightly, hoping he'd understand that it was nothing, and he nodded and turned back to Henri.

'I know nothing,' I hissed. 'None of us does.'

From the look on his face, I knew that he didn't believe me. He was certain that someone at Riverain was responsible for Mathilde's death. I wondered if his parents thought the same.

'No sign of Jean Paul?' asked Monsieur d'Amboise, pouring more wine into our glasses.

'No,' said Étienne, after the slightest pause. 'Not a word. God knows where he is.'

That last was true even if the rest wasn't, and I thought again about Jean Paul. Maybe he had killed his mother. That night when he'd sat beside her at the table and couldn't look at me because he was so embarrassed meant something. She'd made him do awful things, vile acts that no mother should ask of her son, and he'd been too weak to resist. Maybe killing her was the only way he could get free.

Lisette opened her mouth to speak and I bit my lip. She'd seen the letter from Jean Paul, she'd been there when we discussed it and seen Grandmère put it on the fire. Oh, God. My stomach lurched. She was going to contradict what Étienne had said.

'I like the book you gave me, Madame d'Amboise,'

was all she said and I let out the breath I was unconsciously holding and from the corner of my eye saw that Grandmère was doing the same. 'Eleanor is teaching me to read.'

'Very good, dear.' Édith smiled at her. 'I'm sure you'll do well in school.'

Lisette's interruption had temporarily stopped Henri d'Amboise's questions and when I looked at the little girl she was wearing a rather smug expression. Did she interrupt on purpose? I think now that she did.

But Henri wasn't quite finished. When we stood up to go he said, 'When is Mathilde going to be buried? The police must have finished with her by now. I mean, it's hardly decent for her . . .' His voice trailed away as Madame d'Amboise spoke her goodbyes to us over him, her head jerking all the time towards Lisette.

As it happened, Albert Charpentier came by the next morning to say that Mathilde's body had been released and could now be buried.

'Is that it, then?' Étienne asked. 'Have they finished with us?'

The young policeman shuffled his feet. 'I don't know, monsieur. Hubert is like a tiger with this case; he's determined to find the murderer. It will increase his chances of promotion.' He looked round as though there might be someone listening but only Étienne and I were standing in the yard.

'I can tell you that he is now questioning Jean Paul's friends and has found some of Madame Martin's . . . er . . . acquaintances. That's his new line of investigation.'

Mathilde was buried a couple of days after that in the town and only Étienne went. In the morning he'd sat at the kitchen table and, pulling her close to him, spoken quite seriously to Lisette. 'Your mother is to be buried this afternoon,' he said gently. 'I shall go, of course, and I will take you with me if you would like.'

The child thought for a moment and then put her hand on Étienne's cheek. 'No thank you, Papa, I don't want to go. I don't think Maman liked me very much so she wouldn't want me there.'

So she stayed at home with Grandmère and me and had *crêpes dentelles* as a treat. These were little pancakes made with the usual mixture but Grandmère added grated orange and lemon peel and sprinkled them with lots of sugar. I could easily make these at home, I thought, although with less sugar because of rationing. It would make a change from the apple pie and custard, but then home seemed to be a long way away both in miles and, increasingly, in my consciousness.

Étienne was quiet when he came home. He took off his suit jacket and put it over the back of a kitchen chair and went to wash his hands and throw water on his face. 'Was anyone there?' asked Grandmère while he was drying himself. 'Friends? Family?'

'No.' He shook his head. 'You know she didn't have any family, and as for friends, well . . . so it was just me and the priest. Oh, and Monsieur Hubert.'

'Why would he go?' I asked.

'I don't know,' Étienne answered. 'Perhaps he wanted to see who would turn up.' He turned to Grandmère. 'He said he was surprised that you and the child weren't with me. I told him it was none of his business and that he should push off.' His expression darkened as he recalled the encounter. 'That man's a bastard.'

'Be careful,' Grandmère warned, her voice low. 'He's no fool and could be dangerous.'

August melted into September and the days began to shorten. One afternoon Étienne and I strolled in the vineyard and examined the grapes. It was a brilliant day, a little cooler than of late, and looking down to the woods by the river I could see that the leaves on the trees were losing their summer lushness and more light was showing through the branches. It's nearly autumn, I thought, and with a jolt realised that all my friends would be back at school. Would they be talking about me, I wondered. Would they want to know why I wasn't at school? Maybe Suzy would tell them that I was mixed up in a murder inquiry, that the French police were questioning me and I wasn't allowed home.

'Goodness!' Janet Blaine would say, 'Eleanor Gill? I don't believe it. Nothing ever happens to her.'

'Now, now, girls. That's enough.' I could see Miss Baxter fluttering her hands in alarm while she tried to dampen the gossip. 'Eleanor's parents are both seriously ill and she's unable to live at home for the moment. Her French hosts have kindly allowed her to stay whilst arrangements are being made for her here.'

The girls would settle down then but Suzy would whisper to Janet, 'In the break, I'll tell you what was in the letter my father had from France.'

I smiled to myself, standing beside my lover in his vineyard, and didn't have to wonder why I didn't care.

Étienne took out his knife and cut a bunch of grapes off its stalk. He held it up to the light and then pulled off a grape and tasted it. 'Here,' he said, offering the bunch to me. 'Try one.'

The grapes were blue and plump and had a downy glow. When I tasted one it was sweet and soft with a hint of perfume. 'Oh!' I gasped, taking another and another. 'They're wonderful.'

'Mm,' Étienne agreed. 'And almost ready for picking. A week at the most, then the hard work begins.'

I felt excited. Why the idea of harvesting grapes should be so entrancing I wasn't sure, but the way everyone talked about it and prepared for the days ahead seemed to presage a thrilling event. Grandmère had said that there were parties after the harvest that everyone went to and I was looking forward to them as well.

'This will be my last year of sending the crop to the co-op,' said Étienne as we walked back to the house. 'From now on I will build up the name of Riverain and in ten or fifteen years my wines will be served in the best restaurants in Europe.'

'Will it take ten years?' I asked.

'At least.' But he grinned. 'I shall enjoy the struggle, the experimenting, the tasting. Christ!' he sighed. 'I'm turning into my father.'

When we stopped on the bridge I looked at him. He had changed in the last few weeks. The man I saw now was quieter and calmer, no longer given to the frequent eruptions of rage that had previously marred his predominantly cheerful disposition. And yet he looked younger and still as handsome as ever. I put a hand on the back of his neck and pulled his face down to mine.

'What was that for,' he said when we stopped kissing and came up for air.

'Nothing. I just love you.'

'I'm so much older than you, Eleanor. Don't you mind?'

I looked at the river, flowing faster these days and less green. Étienne and I had swum in it on hot evenings, splashing in from the bank, blissfully naked and consumed with carefree joy. I could have swum the same way with a younger man, a boy even, like Luc. He could have been my French boyfriend. I know he wanted to be and had already said he would write to me when I got home, but . . . I didn't love him.

'No.'

'Even though I'm a murderer and a murder suspect?'

'No. Anyway, I'm a murder suspect too.'

He shook his head slowly. 'That's ridiculous. If anyone had cause to kill Mathilde it was me and God knows I thought about doing it all the time. Even a couple of weeks before she died I was determined to get rid of her. I went in the early morning with my shotgun up to the grape barn where I knew she'd be. Often she entertained her clients through the night, or if she didn't have one of them around, Jean Paul would be with her.' His face twisted with disgust. 'She totally corrupted that boy and I didn't know how to rescue him. All I could do was shout at him and he grew to hate me just as much as I hated her and d'you know, now I'm ashamed of myself. I should have tried harder.'

'I saw you,' I interrupted. 'Coming back with your gun.'

'Did you? Did you see the coward who hadn't the guts to shoot a sleeping woman who was curled up beside her son? Oh, if she'd woken up and poured out more of her filthy bile at me, taunted me with what she'd done and to whom, I could have shot her. I could have blown her evil head off. But she didn't wake up.'

'I'm glad,' I said. 'And you weren't a coward.'

That evening after supper I sat with Grandmère in her parlour. Étienne had gone to a meeting of the wine co-op to arrange harvesting times. 'I'll tell them mine are ready and get an early date,' he'd said as he went out. Then, 'I won't be late,' so I went to the parlour and sat with Grandmère.

Lisette had wandered in with me but within a few minutes had dropped off to sleep on one of Grandmère's soft armchairs. She had started school this week, a little bit scared on the first day but after that perfectly happy and full of excited chatter when she came home.

On that first day, I'd offered to walk her down the lane to the village school and Lisette was keen for me to do it but Grandmère had said no. 'There might be questions the schoolmaster needs to ask about date of birth and general health. Things like that. It's better for me to go.'

But surprisingly, Étienne vetoed both our plans. 'I shall take her,' he said. 'Starting school is an important occasion and Lisette's father should be the one to take her. Is that good, *mon petit lapin*?'

'Yes, Papa,' she whispered, perhaps as astonished as Grandmère and me that not only was he walking her to school but he'd called her his little rabbit.

'I wanted to,' he'd told me later. 'I have accepted her as my daughter, and the truth is she has been more in my heart these last weeks. Perhaps my taking her will help with the talk and rumours that she'll have to put up with when she gets older.'

So Lisette was taken into the classroom, her little hand held firmly in Étienne's large one, and had been given a desk next to her best friend Claudine. The head teacher had shaken hands with Étienne in front of all the other children and kindly welcomed the little girl to the school. 'It was well done,' said Étienne contentedly. 'They will look after her.'

'Are you going to read the cards tonight?' I asked, sitting opposite Grandmère at the table.

She had the pack in her hands and was absently shuffling them but looking towards the window, her mind elsewhere. I thought she looked tired and her strong face was etched with worry lines.

'Grandmère,' I said, concerned because she hadn't answered me, 'are you feeling ill?'

'What?' She turned away from the window and gazed at me. 'What? Oh, no. I'm all right. A little tired, that's all.'

She placed the pack on the table and with a sweep of her hand drew them into a half-moon. 'Take your nine.' Her voice was weary and her hand shook a little as she turned over my chosen cards. This was the first time she done them since the night when she'd told me that the cards were very bad for me. The time before that she had told me of a future that was bleak but held out a very small window of promise. 'It will be up to you, Eleanor. The cards only point the way. You have to find your own path.'

This time my cards weren't all black and I heard Grandmère give a small sigh of relief. She tapped her finger on the ten of spades, which I'd seen last time. 'This is a bad card,' she said. 'It forecasts imprisonment. Not necessarily the sort that means you are behind bars, but a loss of freedom in some way. And here, and here' – she pointed to the ace of spades and the ten of clubs – 'these are difficult to read; they mean loss and disappointment, perhaps a journey, and most of the others tell me that times ahead will not be easy. But, my dear, you do have this.' She picked up the nine of hearts and stroked her strong fingers over it. 'This is the wish card. It means that what you wish for will come true.'

'That is good, surely.' I breathed a sigh of relief. 'The bad cards won't mean anything.'

'Maybe.' Grandmère reached out and took my hand. 'Have courage, Eleanor. Whatever happens.'

Despite not believing in Grandmère's predictions I felt stupidly anxious and couldn't wait for Étienne's return. I was in the yard when he drove in and as soon as he stepped out of the van I threw myself into his arms.

'What?' he said. 'What's happened?'

'Nothing, nothing. I just wanted you to come home.'

'Has my mother been reading the cards again?' he asked as we went into the house. 'You mustn't believe what she says. She makes it all up, you know.'

'I know.'

He opened the dresser door and took out a bottle of brandy and put it on the kitchen table. 'Get some glasses,' he said, 'and we'll have a drink. It will calm your nerves.'

We talked about the co-op and Étienne's plans to buy more vines and about Lisette's school; in fact we talked like a married couple who had been together for years and would continue for many more. It was strange and it was wonderful. The uncertain girl who had come for a three-week visit had gone and an adult sat in her place.

Eventually we spoke about Mathilde. 'Grandmère has a newspaper cutting which shows Mathilde having her head shaved,' I said. 'It's a horrible picture.'

'Yes.' Étienne swirled the brandy in his glass. 'It was horrible, although I wasn't there at the time. I'd rejoined the army and was fighting with my battalion.' He was quiet for a moment. 'Four women were paraded like that in this area but only Mathilde in our village. After that she was shunned and the whole family too for a while. Robert Brissac put an end to that. He spoke up for me. He will remain my friend for the rest of my life.'

'Was she a collaborator, like Jeanne Brissac said?'

He shrugged. 'She slept with German soldiers, certainly, and Robert was convinced that she had given information that led to his arrest. She didn't give me away, though, and I came to the farm a couple of times when the German was here.'

I shook my head. 'I'd have left, gone away, changed my name, if I'd done such a shameful thing. I wonder why Mathilde didn't.'

Étienne put the cork in the brandy bottle and stood up. 'I don't know. She was bold, ruthless and maybe a little mad. Perhaps she wanted to prove that she didn't care; thumb her nose at the villagers who had always hated her. Whatever it was, my life was wrecked and I think she enjoyed that. I'm a Catholic; not a very good one, it's true, but . . . well, divorce was not an option, and as my wife she had every right to stay here.'

'You're free now.' I smiled.

He took me in his arms. 'No, I'm not,' he chuckled, his lips nuzzling my neck. 'You must know that I'm trapped in your spell, my enchantress. I don't want freedom from you. Ever.'

Chapter Twenty-Four

I felt strange the next morning. Not ill, but apprehensive, as though I knew something was going to happen. Something I wouldn't like. Nonsense, I told myself in my mother's voice, it's simply that Grandmère's cards have wormed themselves into your head. You're letting your imagination run away with you. And I resolved there and then never to let her read them to me again.

'I think I'll hear from Monsieur Castres today,' I said to Grandmère when I came back from walking Lisette to school.

'Do you?' she asked. 'Why?'

I shrugged. 'I don't know. I just feel that it's about time. Goodness, it's weeks since I last heard from him. Surely he'll have some information about my parents by now.'

She came and sat at the kitchen table opposite me. 'Do you want to hear, Eleanor?'

I was quiet, thinking about it. I knew I should be concerned about Mother and Dada, and to a certain extent I was. I didn't want them to be ill and hospitalised, but if they were better I would have to go home and that was impossible to imagine. My life was here now. Here with Étienne, Grandmère and Lisette. The house on the top of a hill in the Pennines was somewhere I used to live and I didn't want to return to it.

I shook my head. 'You know I don't want to leave. It would break my heart.'

She should have said something comforting then but she didn't and merely got up and returned to the range where a rabbit stew was already simmering.

My mood persisted and after lunch I went up the kitchen stairs to my room. My duvet was hanging over the window sill and before putting it back on to the bed I held it to my face. I could smell Étienne on the cover. I thought of the nights we'd spent on the iron bed, the passion, the laughter and the fulfilled desire. Oh, God, how I loved him and how could I possibly leave this house. I was part of it now.

I stripped off my navy shorts and Aertex shirt and opening the cedar wardrobe took out my sweet pea dress. Slipping it over my head and letting it fall over my body I immediately felt better. This dress gave me confidence; in it I was no longer the silly, uncertain girl who'd come on a school exchange. I was a woman now. More experienced than any of my school friends and far wiser in matters they had never even dreamt about.

I found Étienne in the grape barn. He was opening drawers in the old desk and tipping their contents into a wooden box. 'Ah!' He gave a whoop of delight and turned to me, brandishing a handful of labels in the air. 'Look, my darling. These were my father's,' and he pressed one of the labels into my hand. It was hard to see in the gloom of the barn and I held it up to the shaft of light which came through the small window. The label had a black and white drawing of the farm with the name *Riverain* above it. 'This will be the label I'll use on my wine. Next year I'll have hundreds of these printed.'

'It looks very elegant,' I said, studying the drawing. 'I like it.'

'Good,' he said, and then he looked closely at me. 'You are beautiful in that dress. Are we going out somewhere?'

'No.' I smiled. 'I just felt like wearing it.'

'To tempt me?'

I nodded and, grinning, waited while he let the labels flutter to the ground and took me in his arms. As kisses rained down on my face I pushed the label I was holding into my pocket and raised my arms so that they circled his shoulders. I needed him, more it seemed today than ever, and as we lay on the dusty floor of the barn I closed my eyes and let myself be carried away again into that enchanted land.

'Christ,' he said when we lay back, panting and smiling idiotically. 'I can't get enough of you.'

'I know,' I breathed. 'I feel the same.'

He rolled on to his side and put his hand on my cheek. 'I'll love you, Eleanor, until the end of my life. Believe me on this. You are the other half of me.'

'Oh, God.' I felt like crying and clutched him close to my body. Life without him was impossible to imagine.

After a while he sat up. 'Come on, you temptress.' He laughed. 'I've got work to do. We'll revisit this later.'

I stretched out, my arms above my head, and stared at the rafters and the little birds flying around. I wondered if they migrated in the winter to Africa and was about to ask Étienne about them when I heard, in the distance, my name being called.

'My God,' I said, sitting up. 'Who's that?'

Étienne went to the door and looked out. More voices were calling and amongst them I could pick out Grandmère's and it sounded strange and almost desperate. I was suddenly scared. It was as if I'd been waiting for this all day.

'There are cars in the yard, and people walking about. Oh, *mon Dieu*, Eleanor.' Étienne looked back at me and I could see real fear in his eyes. 'They have come for us.'

'Who is it? Who has come?' I was now at the door beside him, looking down through the vineyard. With a sinking heart, I saw the police car and even from this distance recognised the portly frame of Monsieur Hubert flanked by two uniformed policemen. There were two other cars beside the police car and two men in city suits whom I didn't recognise. Grandmère was standing beside them.

'Do we have to go down?' I asked and my voice was panicky. I knew the spell was breaking.

'Yes,' he said, taking my hand. 'I'm afraid we must.' He bent his head and gave me a last kiss. 'Remember, my love, I will never stop loving you. You are my heart.'

We walked hand in hand down the hill through the rows of vines, brushing past heavy bunches of ripe grapes so that the intense, sweet perfume invaded my senses and gave me comfort. I didn't notice that my dress was dusty from the barn floor or that my hair, freed from its ponytail ribbon, was flowing freely across my shoulders, but thinking back Étienne and I must have been a shocking sight to the watchers below. No one seeing us that afternoon could have been in any doubt of what we'd been doing in the barn.

In the yard, Grandmère put a protective arm about my waist while we watched the uniformed policemen take Étienne by the arms and, obeying a nod from his superior, Albert Charpentier put Étienne's wrists in handcuffs.

Monsieur Hubert was gleeful. 'Étienne Martin, you will go before the prosecutor tomorrow morning when I will present my reasons for arresting you for the murder of Mathilde Martin.'

'Oh, God,' I moaned, my eyes fixed on Étienne's. He was standing almost casually, smiling reassuringly at me. Panic was rising in my chest and I felt that at any moment I would shout or faint or show my terror to the group of men who were watching us.

'Be brave, my dear,' Grandmère whispered. 'This is not the end.'

Monsieur Hubert turned to me with a sneer on his face. 'Young lady,' he snarled. 'You have been rescued. The lawyers have had their way and although I'm certain that you know more than you're telling me, I've been forced to let you go.' He jerked his head towards Étienne who was standing beside the black Citroën police car. 'But I've got the murderer. War hero or no, it'll be the guillotine for him.'

'You can't do that,' I shouted. 'It's not true. You have no proof.'

He laughed. 'I've got proof and motive. What I've seen

here this afternoon is motive enough. The two of you in that barn?' He sniggered. 'It's so obvious. He wanted rid of his wife so he could have you.' He turned to the two strangers and spoke to them angrily. 'She was in it with him. I'm positive. It's against every tenet of the law allowing her to leave.'

One of the men stepped forward and pushing past Monsieur Hubert came to stand before me. He was tall and thin with a distinguished face topped by a luxuriant mass of grey hair. He wore a blue bow tie and an expensive-looking beige linen suit. 'Miss Gill,' he said, bending to take my hand and raise it to his lips. 'I am Jacob Castres, the English consul. I am also a lawyer, and as the police department can find nothing definite to connect you to this terrible occurrence I've insisted that you are free to return to England.' He looked over his shoulder to the other man. 'This gentleman will accompany you.'

I turned to the other man. Bile was rising in my throat and I knew that the blood had drained from my face.

'Eleanor?' The man approached. 'I hardly recognised you. What in God's name has happened to you?' He had an oddly familiar voice.

For a moment the tears stinging in my eyes blurred his face but then they cleared and I could see him. I could see the tweed suit, too hot for this time of the year, in this place, and the golf club tie.

'Mr Franklin?' I rocked on my heels and Grandmère steadied me. 'What on earth are you doing here?'

'Please.' He hesitated. 'You're speaking French. I don't understand.'

'What d'you want? Why have you come here? Go

away!' I was gabbling, frantic, desperate for everything to return to normal. I must have been still speaking in French for he lifted his arms, gesturing that he didn't comprehend.

'I've come to take you home, Eleanor,' he said slowly. 'Do you understand me?'

Now I was speechless.

There was movement beside the police car and I looked past Mr Franklin to Étienne. Albert Charpentier was holding the door open for him to get in.

'Wait!' It was Grandmère's imperious voice.

'Madame?' said Albert, uncertainly, one eye on Monsieur Hubert.

Grandmère took her arm away from me and walked over to Étienne. She lifted her head and with her hands on his arms she kissed him on both cheeks. 'Don't worry, my son,' she said, and smiled gently at him. 'It will not happen. Trust me.'

'I do, Maman.' Then he raised his eyes to me. 'Remember what I said,' he murmured, and I yearned to take him in my arms but he knew what I was thinking and gave a small shake of his head. Tears were now flowing freely down my face and I could feel my knees buckling.

'Come on,' Monsieur Hubert growled. 'Enough of this.'

Suddenly there was a rush of small footsteps from behind the cars. It was Lisette. In my own distress I'd forgotten her and she had walked home from school by herself into this scene of despair. 'Papa,' she screamed. 'Papa.' And she rushed over and wrapped her arms around his knees.

'Shush, shush, little one,' Étienne crooned. 'It will be all right.' And he looked at me to take her.

She wouldn't be held, though. Slipping out of my arms she rushed over to Monsieur Hubert and beat her little fists against his fat belly. 'Bad man, bad man!' she cried. 'You mustn't take my papa away. I won't let you.'

Monsieur Hubert's face, already dark with fury, flushed dangerously. 'I'll arrest this child if you don't get her off me,' he shouted, and as Grandmère and I rushed forward to take her he turned his head to me.

'It's you who has caused all this trouble,' he snarled. 'And I'll make sure that you'll never be allowed back in this country.'

It was Grandmère who held Lisette and shushed her wailing as the police car drew away. I, stunned at Monsieur Hubert's pronouncement, could only stand with my hand over my mouth, waiting for a last look at Étienne as the police car turned out of the yard.

'What can we do?' I cried, turning desperately to Grandmère.

'Nothing, right now. I'll go and see Robert Brissac tomorrow. He'll know what he must do. Now, take Lisette inside. Give her a drink of water and wipe her face.' She looked at me. 'And you do the same. This is a time to be brave, Eleanor.' She looked at the two men who were standing awkwardly, watching us. 'I will take these gentlemen into the house.'

Jacob Castres and Mr Franklin were sitting at the dining room table with cups of coffee before them when I went in to join them. Grandmère was in her usual place, being a careful hostess, but the conversation was muted and hesitant.

'How is the child?' she asked when I walked into the room.

'Better,' I said. 'She's stopped crying now. She's in her room.'

I'd sat with Lisette on my knee in the kitchen waiting for the sobs which racked her little body to subside.

'Where has the bad man taken my papa?' she cried.

'He's taken him to the police station in town,' I said. 'He'll be home soon. It's just for more questions.'

'But why did they put those things on his arms?'

'I don't know,' I choked and we rocked together and held each other tight for comfort. After a while she raised her tear-stained face and said, 'Who are the other men?'

'They've come to see me.'

'No,' she howled. 'They're going to take you away too.'

How could I answer no when I knew she was right? This was going to be my last day at Riverain, and now dry-eyed I gazed around this much loved kitchen storing every detail into my memory.

When Lisette had quietened I gave her a kiss and asked if she wanted something to eat.

'Bread, please. And *confiture*. Then I must go upstairs to tell the doll's house people about Papa. They like to know things.'

'That's a good idea,' I said and got her a plate of bread and jam and waited until she'd gone upstairs. I walked up the back stairs to my lovely white room and sat heavily on the bed. The late afternoon sun was streaming in and brilliant shafts of light shone on to the cedar wardrobe and the iron scrollwork at the end of my bed. Everything gleamed, everything spoke of the love I'd shared and my discovery of life. This was another room I had to store in my memory.

But that bright sun would fade the furniture and make the room hot, and mindful of Grandmère's instructions I got up and closed the shutters so that only thin fingers of light came in. It was enough, though, for me to wash my face and change into my school frock and white summer socks. My hair was brushed back into its schoolgirl ponytail and I was ready.

'Miss Gill.' Jacob Castres spoke first. 'This must have been very alarming for you . . . this dreadful event. We would have removed you immediately if we'd been able, but the police here, particularly Monsieur Hubert, were most insistent that you stay. Thankfully, your friend here,' he nodded to Mr Franklin, 'was able to contact lawyers at your Foreign Office who negotiated with the authorities here. Despite what Monsieur Hubert says, it is obvious that you have nothing to answer for and I must offer you our most profound apologies.'

'Thank you,' I said. I could barely bring myself to look up. These two men had engineered my departure from this enchanted place. I almost hated them.

'If we leave within the hour, we can get the night boat,' Mr Franklin interjected. He sounded confused and not a little angry. Maybe he'd thought of himself as a knight in shining armour coming to rescue a damsel in distress. I was a damsel in distress, but not in the way he'd expected. Had the sight of me, tousled and dusty, walking hand and hand with my lover through the vines shocked him? I knew it had.

'My parents,' I said, looking up at him. 'Can you tell me about them?'

'English please, Eleanor.' He sounded weary.

'Yes, sorry.' I repeated the question and the English words sounded strange and wrong, as though I was speaking a foreign language. 'My parents? They are better?'

His face was puzzled when he looked at me and I realised that I was getting the grammar and inflections wrong. 'Mr Franklin,' I started again. 'Is my mother getting better and have you news about my father?'

He paused before answering. 'I've seen your mother, Eleanor. I'm sorry to tell you that Mrs Gill is very seriously ill. She caught her leg on some barbed wire and made a deep wound which got terribly infected. The septicaemia was extensive, invading much of her body. Now, I believe, she has irreversible kidney damage.'

'What?' I asked, confused not only by the unfamiliar English but by the description of Mother's illness. 'What is that?'

He sighed. 'Her kidneys are failing. There is no way to make this easy for you, Eleanor, but now it's merely a question of time. She is dying.'

Mr Castres had been translating this information to Grandmère and she came over and put her arms around me. 'Courage,' she said.

I was in a daze. 'My father?'

'I haven't seen him, but I believe your doctor has. He is . . . distressed at being confined.'

I nodded. Poor Dada.

Mr Franklin cleared his throat. 'I visited your mother in hospital three days ago and took instructions from her. I have been granted power of attorney over all her affairs and that includes you and your father. It is up to me now and I am taking you back with me. You can live with us until . . . well, for as long as you want to. It is for the best, Eleanor.'

It took me only ten minutes to pack and strip the bed and I was soon back in the kitchen with my pigskin case.

Lisette clung to me, pasting little kisses on my cheeks and stroking my hair. 'Listen to me,' I said to her. 'Remember what I said about us being sisters and how we'd always be close. Well, it's true. Wherever I am I'll be thinking of you and you'll be thinking of me. I know you'll be good and help Grandmère in the kitchen and in the garden and I know that you'll work hard at school and make me proud of you. Can you do that?'

'Yes,' she sobbed. 'But why can't you stay?'

'Because I have to go and look after my mother and father. They need me now.'

'Oh, Eleanor.' She snuggled her head into my neck. 'I do love you.'

'And I love you too,' I said, pulling her gently away. 'You are my delicious discovery and always will be.'

I said goodbye to Grandmère in the yard. Mr Castres had already gone, having kissed my hand again and wished me luck. Mr Franklin was standing impatiently beside his Wolseley and watched me as I dropped my case on to the cobbles and put my arms round Grandmère.

'Did he do it?' I whispered. 'It makes no difference, but I have to know.'

'No,' she whispered back. 'He didn't.' She paused, then whispered again. 'But I found her dead that afternoon and I put her in the river. Étienne knew nothing of that.'

I gasped, holding on to her and trying to take in this new information. 'You put her in the river? How? Where was she?'

Grandmère had one eye on Mr Franklin. 'On the far bank, in the undergrowth,' she murmured. 'I dragged her as far as I could and rolled her in. I thought she would be carried downstream.' Her voice choked and I could feel the despair in her body and wanted to hug her tighter but Lisette was pulling on her apron, desperate to get her attention.

'What are you saying, Grandmère? I can't hear you. Are you telling Eleanor not to go? Please, oh, please, tell her.'

Mr Franklin's anxious voice in the background disturbed the moment. 'Eleanor,' he called. 'We must hurry.'

I drew back from them then, my dearest Grandmère and Lisette, and glancing over my shoulder to the waiting man I nodded. Through the haze of tears which brimmed my eyes I looked away to the vineyard and to the grape barn and then down to the river and the bridge. I could see Étienne and me fishing, him strong and laughing and me girlish and so unsure of myself. Then, as my eyes travelled to the bank, I remembered the delirious passion which would live with me for the rest of my life.

'Don't worry, my dear. It will be all right, and this is not the end,' Grandmère said, smiling at me through a face which was awash with tears. 'You know you have been the saving of this family, sweet girl. Remember that and know that I love you as a daughter.'

'Thank you. I love you,' was all I could say, for my own unchecked tears were rolling down my cheeks as I turned to go. The last sight I had of that enchanted place was from the back window of Mr Franklin's car. Grandmère and Lisette stood hand in hand on the cobbled yard as the sun went down behind the vineyard.

Chapter Twenty-Five

I stared at the window of the small side room. Rain was beating heavily against the glass causing rivulets of water to run down and splash into small puddles on the grimy frame. I was sitting on a wooden chair and beside me, in the hospital bed, my mother was dying. She was unconscious and had been for the last twelve hours. The ward sister had told me hours ago that she wouldn't wake up again.

'I'm sorry,' she said, carefully picking up a used kidney dish from the bed table and holding it well away from her starched apron, 'but we don't think your mother will live through the night. Quite honestly I'm amazed she's lasted this long. She must have been a very strong-willed person.' There was little compassion in the sister's voice but I didn't resent it. She was doing her job to the best of her ability. Mother was clean and, as far as I knew, kept comfortable.

'Yes,' I said. 'She was . . . is.' And had proved it because it was now eight o'clock in the morning and she was still alive.

They had let me stay at the hospital all night and now one of the nurses had put a cup of tea on the bedside locker for me. 'Would you like a piece of toast?' she asked, and smiled kindly. 'There's plenty on the trolley.'

I shook my head. 'No, thank you. I'm not hungry. But thanks for the tea.'

Mother's breathing was hoarse and becoming sporadic and I shifted my gaze from the window to her. I was mesmerised by watching her chest go up and down. Sometimes it didn't move and then suddenly, with a gulping sound, she would breathe again. How long will it go on, I wondered? How long will she keep up the fight?

It had only been a week since I'd come home and I'd been at the hospital every day watching while her illness gradually overwhelmed her. My first visit was on the day I'd come home and I could scarcely believe my eyes when the nurse pointed her out to me.

It was the evening after I'd been torn away from Riverain and I was still shaky and confused. If someone asked me something I would answer in French and then have to catch myself and repeat it in faltering English.

'Goodness,' said Suzy, when I stood, newly arrived, in the kitchen at the Franklins' house. She was giving me one of her long up and down looks. 'You have changed. Apart from the tan, you look, well . . . so grown up. The girls in school are going to be fascinated, what with the story of what happened in France and the length of time you've been there. Why, it must be nearly three months.'

'Is it?' I asked vaguely. I hadn't realised but I looked at the calendar on the lemon-painted wall of the Franklins' modern kitchen and saw that it was the last day of September. 'Yes, it must be.' I felt quite incapable of keeping the conversation going and even Suzy seemed uncomfortable. Her normal bright chatter kept faltering and she looked to her parents for help.

'We were so sorry to hear about your mother's illness,' said Phyllis Franklin. 'It must have been dreadful for you.'

'Yes.' I nodded. 'Thank you for saying that. I have to go and see her. Now.' It was four o'clock in the afternoon and despite the long journey I was anxious to get to the hospital.

'Go after tea,' said Mrs Franklin. 'They won't let you in anyway until visiting hours, half past six, I think, so you might as well have a rest until then. Settle into your room first.'

The Franklins stood in a semicircle gazing at me and suddenly I was frantic to get out of their sight. I needed to be alone, to think and to remember.

'Yes, thank you. It's very kind of you to put me up. It won't be for long but I am grateful.' I turned and hurried out, knowing that tears were welling up and anxious not to let them be seen. As I climbed the stairs I could hear Mr Franklin talking in a low voice and I knew what he would be telling them. That he'd brought home a girl who was a suspect in a murder case and added to that . . . Suzy would be told to leave the room while he told Phyllis privately what he'd learned and what he'd seen.

'Hello, Mother.' I had to say it twice on that first day before she turned her head to look at me. She was propped up against several pillows, her face yellow against the hospital white and her hair, once so fizzingly red, faded and greying.

For a moment, I didn't think she recognised me, then with an effort she gave a small difficult smile.

'Hello,' I said again, and bent to give her an awkward kiss on the cheek. 'I'm back.' I couldn't say home because my home was far away. My home was a white house nestled between rolling fields with red soil and a vineyard.

She didn't speak and I said, 'I'm sorry you're ill.'

That brought a response. 'It's nonsense,' she whispered. 'People are making too much fuss.' Then, 'Have you seen your father?'

'Not yet.' I shook my head.

'Poor Eddy.' Her eyes closed then and I sat beside her, until the bell rang for the end of the visiting hour.

I went the next day to see my father. He was in the mental hospital, which was a couple of miles out of town and required another bus journey. I found him in a large, cold day room with several other patients who were wandering about vacantly or sitting on chairs muttering and rocking. He was standing by the window, his face pressed against the reinforced glass.

'Dada?' I said, coming to stand beside him. I didn't touch him because I knew he didn't like to be touched but he did look at me properly and a small light came into his eyes. He was unshaven and in pyjamas with a thin dressing gown hanging off his shoulders. He was shivering and, looking down, I could see that his feet were bare.

I went over to the orderly who was leaning against the doorway. 'I'm Eleanor Gill,' I said. 'That man,' I pointed to the window where Dada stood, 'is my father. He has no shoes on and he's cold. Where's his room?'

The orderly jerked his head down the corridor. 'In the male ward down there. I don't know which bed is his,' he said casually. 'Just take any pair of shoes that you think might fit him.'

I was angry and nervous at the same time, wishing desperately that I had someone to help me, but just then a door opened in the corridor and a uniformed nurse came out. 'Are you in charge?' I asked and I could hear the fury in my voice. This was a different me.

It took five minutes for the nurse to locate Dada's locker and open it. She took out his shoes and socks and got him a blanket to drape over his shoulders. 'They forget,' she said, apologetically but with a whine in her voice, 'to dress themselves properly. And we can't be everywhere.'

I encouraged Dada to sit on a chair beside the window and I sat with him. When a tea trolley was pushed into the room I got up and fetched him a cup and watched while he drank it and eagerly ate the bread and butter which I'd folded into the saucer. He was hungry too.

'I've been in France,' I said, 'but now I'm home and I'll come to see you every day until . . .' I couldn't finish that sentence because I didn't know what was going to happen, but I thought he should know about Mother. 'Mother is very ill, in the hospital,' I said, making sure that he was meeting my eye and listening to me. 'We can't go home yet but I'll get us there as soon as possible.'

It was as I was leaving that awful room that my father spoke to me for the first time I could remember.

'La belle France,' he whispered and I don't know who was more surprised, him or me.

'Yes, Dada, yes.' I grinned. *'La belle France.'*

My mother died at ten o'clock in the morning, a week after I'd returned from France, having defiantly lived several hours longer than expected. Phyllis Franklin, with unexpected kindness, came to sit with me for the last hour and afterwards organised the undertaker and helped me sign the necessary forms. 'They'll have be countersigned by her legal guardian,' said the sister, speaking to Mrs Franklin. 'You know she isn't old enough.'

'My husband will be in later. He has been appointed Eleanor's legal guardian.'

'What?' I said, quite shocked.

'Your mother arranged it a couple of weeks ago.' Mrs Franklin put an arm around my shoulders. Her perfume seemed suddenly overwhelming and I sat down heavily on the chair in Sister's office. I felt sick.

Mother was buried on a raw October day in the same grave as her parents. Not many people attended the service at the village church, just Dada who was allowed out for the afternoon, me, Mr and Mrs Franklin and a few of the local farmers. Afterwards in the churchyard, Jed Winstanley shook hands with me and tipped his cap to Dada. 'Nice to see you, Eleanor, and you too, Captain Gill. Don't worry about the sheep. Graham and me are seeing to them.'

'Thank you,' I said and would have asked him who was looking after the house and the dog, but Mr Franklin interrupted. 'I need a few moments with Mr Winstanley, if you don't mind, Eleanor. Take your father to the car and wait for me.'

I was furious and beside me Dada made a curious noise, something between a cough and a growl. I don't think Mr Franklin noticed it but I did and so did Jed, who looked at my father in surprise.

After another couple of days I went back to school. My exam results had been excellent and I was now in the sixth form with most of my friends. Suzy's had been poor but she was there too, and what's more deputy head girl.

It was strange, being back in my school skirt and blouse, sitting at a desk with school books laid out in front of me. I felt out of touch and out of place, as though this was a part of my life which I should have left behind but had been dragged back into. Before class started the girls wanted to hear about what Suzy called my adventures, but I just shrugged and hurried to my desk. I didn't want to share my precious memories; they were still being hugged to my heart. Besides, what could I say that anyone would understand?

I sat idly through maths and English, automatically making notes but hardly taking anything in. The last lesson before lunch was French, and gathering up our books and cardigans we trooped into the French room.

Looking round I noticed that most of the posters which had previously adorned the walls had gone and I was glad. Reminders would be too painful.

'Good morning, girls,' said Miss Baxter. 'And a special welcome back to Eleanor Gill.' She smiled at me, her eyes twinkling behind her rimless spectacles and her hands, as usual, making their fluttery birdlike movements. 'Now, before we start, I have some new posters to put up. They will give flavour to our lessons this term.' My heart sank.

While Miss Baxter and two of the girls taped the posters to the wall I stared out of the window. Grandmère will be in the dairy now getting the cheeses ready for the market, I thought, and Lisette will be in school. Has she carried on with her reading? And Étienne? I could hardly bear to think about him. Was he still in the police cell? Or had they moved him to the gaol at Fontevraud? My heart lurched and I felt dizzy. In the distance I could hear Miss Baxter's voice and I looked round, still confused.

'I think you'll like this one, Eleanor,' she was saying and I looked the poster. *A vineyard in the Loire district* was the title and the picture showed rolling green countryside surrounding a white farmhouse and, on a rising hill beyond, neat rows of vines ripening in the sun.

For a moment I stared at it, then I got up and walked out of the classroom. That was my last day in school.

It wasn't difficult to kidnap Dada from the asylum. 'I'm taking him for a walk in the grounds,' I said to the orderly, who nodded and took a surreptitious drag on his cigarette. Since the first afternoon when I'd made a fuss about Dada's not being properly dressed the nurses had made sure that his clothes were in his open locker every day and now he looked as he'd always done: grey slacks, tweed jacket and neat brown tie.

I had a shopping bag with me and when a nurse came into the ward where Dada slept I lied. 'I've brought clean clothes for my father. I'll take the dirty ones home to wash.'

'Fine,' she said, and when she left I gathered all his belongings and put them in the bag.

'Come on,' I said to him as we walked down the main drive to the big gates. 'We're getting out of here. Let's look as if we've just been visiting.'

I thought he chuckled and he straightened up and walked with a military gait so that the porter at the entrance box almost saluted as we went past.

I'd worked out our departure from town a few days ahead, planning at night while I lay in the comfortable guest room of the Franklins' house. Most nights I revisited Riverain, going over every inch of the house and land in my head and yearning for the people I'd left behind. I knew in my heart that that phase of my life was over but I couldn't let it go. I didn't want to. But there must have been something of my mother about me because after a while I began to realise that the constant yearning was useless and I would have to learn to live with how my life was. But not here, at the Franklins' house, my head told me. Definitely not here.

Mr Franklin had told me that in Mother's will the farm had been left to me. The house, the land and the stock. 'It's not a great fortune,' he said, 'but if you sell it there'll be enough to put you through university and a bit over. Your mother was quite insistent about that.'

'Was she?' I was amazed. I had always thought she despised universities. I could hear her saying, 'Huh! A ridiculous waste of money!'

'What about Dada?'

Mr Franklin paused. 'Your father has his army pension, which is paid into the bank. He also has a small annuity, which has matured but hasn't been touched.' I gazed uncomprehendingly at him. He could have been speaking double Dutch. I didn't know what an annuity was, then. He cleared his throat and continued, 'When you reach your twenty-first birthday, all that your mother left will become yours and you will take over responsibility for your father and his monies. Until then, it's up to me. I will make the decisions for you.'

I stared at my hands, trying to understand what he was telling me. I noticed that my tan was already fading and I longed to stand on the bridge and feel the hot sun on my body. I could smell the musty odour rising from the river and hear the occasional plop as a fish jumped out of the water for an insect.

'Mr Franklin,' I asked, giving myself a little shake. 'Is there any cash? I need a few winter clothes and toiletries, toothpaste, those sorts of things. I've hardly got anything left in my Post Office account.' Without money I was trapped with this solicitor in charge of me. I could do nothing until I was twenty-one. Nearly four years.

'Mm.' He fingered his small greying moustache. 'Yes, I can see that. Well, I'll arrange to have your father's pension paid into your account; it isn't much, but it will do. And here . . .' He reached into his pocket and took out some notes. 'This will start you off. I'll invoice you for it because everything has to be accounted. Do you understand?'

'Yes,' I said, trying not to sound as overjoyed as I felt. It was enough to buy some groceries and there was plenty of wood around for fuel. We would be all right.

I'd left a thank you note on the guest room table at Suzy's house which I knew no one would find until that evening when they wondered why I hadn't come down for dinner, and once Dada and I walked away from the asylum we got on the bus and went winding up through the villages until we reached the highest point and home.

Of course there was a row when they discovered where

we'd gone. Mr Franklin came up to the farm, bringing our doctor with him.

'We're very disappointed with you, Eleanor,' he said angrily. 'Mrs Franklin, and I have endeavoured to make a home for you and this is how you repay us. By running away.'

I was very calm. 'I have a home, Mr Franklin, and my father and I would prefer to be here. I'm very grateful for all the help you've given me but I know that Mrs Franklin and Suzy will be glad to get me out from under their feet. After all, I'm not going back to school and I can't hang around your house all day, can I?'

His face reddened a little and I knew that my words struck a chord. Mrs Franklin had probably expressed exactly the same sentiments. 'But what about your father?' He went on a counter-attack. 'He isn't well enough to be out of hospital.'

'He was only there because Mother was ill and I'm perfectly able to look after him. Anyway, we're company for each other.' I looked at Dada who was sitting opposite Mr Franklin at the kitchen table. He came inside more these days and stayed up later, watching me after supper whilst I read beside the fire. One evening he picked up a library book and started turning the pages. I said nothing and continued to read but watched from the corner of my eye as he smoothed his hand over the paper. Later, I noticed the book was missing and knew he had taken it to his room. It reappeared the following week and I was able to take it back to the library. I rubbed out the tiny pencilled notes he had written on some of the pages and got him a library ticket so that I could borrow extra books which I thought might interest him.

'Doctor?' Mr Franklin turned to our GP for support. 'Surely Captain Gill should be in the hospital?'

'Actually, Mr Franklin,' the doctor said, looking closely at Dada and then at me, 'I would say the patient looks better than he has for years. I think the . . . the change of circumstances must suit him. On the other hand, I don't think Eleanor looks very well. A little pale, maybe?'

'I'm fine,' I said. 'It's just that my tan is fading.'

'Mm,' he grunted. 'How are you going to manage the sheep? Your mother had the strength and willpower of a man. I don't reckon you're cut from the same cloth.'

'She doesn't have to,' Mr Franklin cut in. 'There is an arrangement with Mr Winstanley. He'll run the sheep and take a percentage of the lamb price.'

I waited for them to go. No matter what they said, I thought, I won't go back to the town. The comfortable Franklin house with its central heating and manicured lawns no longer appealed. That lifestyle had been the dream of the old me. I'd seen better things.

In the end, they reluctantly agreed that we should stay. 'But, Eleanor,' the doctor said, 'come down to the surgery soon and let me examine you. You might need some iron pills. God knows what rubbish you've been eating in France.'

As he and Mr Franklin went out I heard him say, 'She's grieving, I think. We'll let her get on with it.' He was right. I was grieving, but not for my mother.

We lived comfortably, Dada and me, sitting beside the log fire in the winter evenings, reading and listening to the wireless I had bought with some of his money.

I cleaned out and painted the pantry and repaired the window so that it was usable again and filled it with vegetables which could be bought without coupons and made soup.

I think Dada liked my cooking: omelettes, meat stews and fresh fish, bought weekly from the fish man who would drive into our yard and try to persuade me to buy the cheap coley or whiting. 'No,' I'd say, examining the catch that he'd brought. Nothing was as fresh as it should be but sometimes there would be a nice piece of cod or haddock and once he had trout. 'My nephew gets this,' he said and tapped his nose. I presumed his nephew was a poacher but I bought the trout and made us a lovely meal.

I had a letter from Luc just before Christmas. *Good news*, he started. *Monsieur Martin was released from prison last month. The police could find no proof against him and the prosecuting judge insisted that he was freed.* The thin paper of Luc's letter shook in my hand and, aware that Dada was looking at me, I smiled at him. 'This is a letter from one of my friends in France,' I said. 'He says that the Martin family are well and . . .' I read some more, 'they are planting more vines.'

I saved the rest of the letter to read when I was on my own and despite the driving rain I put on my coat and walked out on the hill to a place where I could shout out my joy. 'Yes!' I yelled to the sky, ignoring the rain lashing my face and soaking my hair. 'He's free!' Then I burst into tears and sobbed out all the despair and frustration I'd kept to myself since I'd come back to England.

The rest of the letter I read in my room when I went to change out of my wet clothes. I was calmer then and able to take in more of what Luc had written.

There has been much talk in the village but everyone is happy that Étienne is home. Lisette is at school and my mother says she is doing well but she is missing you. She told my mother that you are her big sister and that she thinks of you every day. I do too.

Do you remember Robert Brissac? He died, having finally succumbed to all the injuries he suffered during the war. Everything has been left to Jeanne and I expect she will be more pompous than ever!

Before Monsieur Brissac died he went to the police department in Angers and spoke to the commissaire. Nobody knows what was said but Monsieur Martin was released soon after. Monsieur Brissac left his shares in the Martin vineyard back to Monsieur Martin in recognition of the part he played during the war. He mentioned particularly Monsieur Martin's bravery in rescuing Jeanne from under the noses of the Germans when her mother was killed.

I send you the best wishes of my mother and father, who hope you are well. I send you best wishes too. Please write to me. Luc.

I read the letter several times, picking apart the bits of information Luc had given, trying to understand what it all meant. Robert Brissac had been to the police and said something that had freed Étienne, and I finally realised that there was only one explanation. Sitting in my cold bedroom I cried again. Étienne had known or perhaps guessed who the murderer was, but out of respect for his friend and commander he said nothing. He would have gone to his death, still silent.

I think Grandmère knew too.

The next day I got the bus into town and bought two Christmas cards. I sent one to Luc and his family and the other, a chintzy card with robins and snow and lots of glitter, to Lisette. *To dearest Lisette,* I wrote, *wishing a happy Christmas to you from your loving sister, Eleanor.* Then I wrote, *Much love to Grandmère and to your papa. P.S. I am well. I hope you are too.*

Throughout Christmas and in the weeks after I thought I would hear from them, but nothing came and I despaired. Then, in the first week in February when the snow was heavy on the ground, a letter from France arrived. It was from Grandmère and very short. *All is well now that Étienne is back from prison. The child is growing and has learned to be good and useful. We miss you, dearest daughter and are waiting for you to come home.* That's when I started planning.

I went to see the doctor and was put on iron tablets and given a telling off. But he made all the necessary arrangements and I was grateful. At first he talked to me as though I was a child but gradually his attitude changed and we had a sensible conversation. 'I still worry about you, Eleanor,' he said. 'In that cold place.'

'I'm all right,' I assured him, 'and my father is taking on more tasks these days. He is happier, I think.'

'Yes,' the doctor sighed. 'You've done wonders for him.'

Mr Franklin visited a few times, still cross with me, and then more so when he saw my situation. 'I knew that your living up here was a mistake,' he raged. 'You need looking after.'

'I don't,' I said. 'I'm fine.' Then I changed the subject. 'How's Suzy?' I hadn't seen her since I left their house.

'She's well,' he said. 'Got some sort of boyfriend. I've met him once or twice, quite a nice young man, got a place at Oxford, I believe. Mrs Franklin likes him. He's from a county family.'

'I want to go back to France.' It wasn't subtle but I could think of no way of dropping it into a general conversation.

'Don't be ridiculous,' he said.

'I don't mean now, but in the summer. Perhaps July or August. Before the grape harvest.'

'Before the what?' He looked at me as though I was mad.

It was left in the air but as he was leaving I said, quite firmly, 'I will go, Mr Franklin. On my eighteenth birthday you won't be able to stop me. You should let me go sooner. It's the right thing to do.'

Chapter Twenty-Six

We got off the train at Angers station on a hot afternoon in early August. It was busy with people coming and going, women carrying stuffed shopping baskets and men racing down the platform to jump on the train before it resumed its journey south.

I sniffed the air and smiled. The sun shone in a clear blue sky and a gentle southern breeze blew balmy air on to my face. France was all around me, filtering into my lungs and pervading my skin. My sweet pea dress reflected the brilliant light and I felt alive and beautiful. I was home.

Dada, who was carrying the pigskin case and its larger matching companion, caught my eye and gave me one of his rare grins. He understood, and was happy for me.

We walked out of the station and I stopped at the taxi cab rank. When I told the driver where we wanted to go he frowned. 'It's twenty miles, madame, and back again for me. It won't be cheap.'

'I'll pay you now,' I said, 'if you'll take us.' And, shifting my bundle, I took out a handful of notes and offered them.

'No.' He smiled, throwing away the thin cigarette which was hanging from his mouth and opening the door of the battered Peugeot. 'Wait until we're there. Come on. Get in.'

I watched every mile of the journey to Riverain from my seat in the back of the not too clean taxi. The neat regiment of trees threw wonderful shadows on the roads, and ahead I could see the water mirages sparkling on the dusty concrete. The sight nearly brought me to tears but I controlled myself. There would be plenty of time for tears later. We turned on to the side road where the verges overflowed with vegetation, creamy cow parsley and pink mallow, and through the open window I could smell the fields.

Yesterday, we'd ridden in another taxi from our bleak hillside to the station. Jed Winstanley had taken the house keys from me and wished us luck while the taxi driver had let his engine run up the pennies. Neither Dada nor I bothered to look back as we drove away. We would never come back.

Mr Franklin had finally given in to my constant requests to be allowed to leave and had, in the end, been surprisingly helpful. He'd arranged passports and organised the sale of the house and land to Jed Winstanley. He'd even made sure that Monsieur Hubert's threat that I wouldn't be allowed to return to France was simply an idle rant. 'The money has to be kept in trust for another few years or until you marry,' he said and sighed his frustration. 'But your father's annuity has been paid into your account and you will be all right for a while.'

'We'll be all right anyway,' I'd smiled. 'I'm going home.'

'You are sure that they'll take you in?' He was still worried.

'You saw them,' I answered. 'How could you doubt it? I'm going back to people who love me and want me and to the farm where I'll stay for the rest of my life. It is enchanting. Can you imagine a more beautiful place?'

Mr Franklin stared out of his office window, at the noisy streets below and the factory tower hooting the midday break. Then, shaking his head, he turned back to me. 'No. No, I can't, Eleanor. I can't.'

So now we were on the road home, Dada and me and . . . The driver turned his head. 'We turn off around here,' he asked. 'Which way, exactly?'

'Next right,' I said dreamily, and looked over the fields to where I could see the white farmhouse nestled in its pillow of lush fields. I could smell the river, hot and sludgy, and as my eyes travelled above the white house I could see the vineyard.

'Here,' I said and the taxi drove cautiously through the pale stone arch and into the cobbled courtyard. 'Go round,' I directed, 'into the yard.'

We stood in the yard as the taxi turned and rattled off back to Angers. I looked at the kitchen door and the red geraniums on the window sill beside it. I should go in, I thought, suddenly nervous, but then I heard a small bell-like voice coming from the vegetable garden.

'I heard a car, Grandmère, I really did. I'm going to see who it is.' And within seconds a leggy brown-haired child came running round the corner of the house and skittered to halt as she saw us.

'Eleanor!' she squealed. 'Oh, Eleanor.' Her arms were wrapped around my waist and as I bent my head to kiss her the tears started.

She cried and so did I and then I saw Grandmère coming towards me with a look of so much joy that my tears overflowed.

'My dear, dear daughter,' she crooned. 'You've come home.'

We were quiet for a moment and then she stepped back. 'What have you brought us,' she breathed and I put the bundle into her arms. Lisette squeaked in excitement.

'Where is he?' I asked.

She raised her eyes to the field of neat rows above the river. 'In the vineyard, of course. He's waited so long for you.'

'And I for him.'

Dada put down the cases and, looking around the yard and up to the fields, took in a deep breath, crinkling up his nose, at the smell of the river, I think. Just as I had done, and just as I had done he would forget to notice it after the first day.

'This is my father, Edward Gill,' I said. Then I remembered. 'Don't shake hands – he doesn't like to be touched.' But I was too late. Lisette had grabbed his thin fingers and started pulling him towards the kitchen door. 'Come on, my grandpère,' she warbled. 'Let's go inside.' And he went, willingly, with a courteous bow to Grandmère and a murmured *'Bonjour, madame.'*

'I'm going to the vineyard,' I said, taking the bundle from Grandmère.

'Good.' Her voice choked. 'He'll be so . . .' Then she coughed and smoothed back her hair where a strand had come loose. 'I'll give Monsieur Édouard some coffee and then start on the vegetables for supper.'

'I'll help you when I come down.'

'Take your time, Eleanor, my dear. There'll be so much to say.'

I walked, slowly, so I could savour the bliss of being

back at Riverain. The trees swayed in a gentle southerly breeze and I fancied I could smell the grapes ripening on the hillside. The sun beat down on my head and now I could feel it on my arms and legs. Oh, it was ecstasy.

He saw me as I stepped on to the bridge, and calling my name he ran down the hill while I waited for him. The water flowed, the birds twittered in the willow trees and I was in the enchanted land once more.

Then he was by my side, breathless, glowing, his dark eyes wide with shock as I put our two-month-old child into his arms.

'This is Stephen,' I said. 'Your son. And we have come home.'

Historical Note

Fontevraud Abbey was founded in the year 1100 by wealthy patrons of the Benedictine order. It housed both monks and nuns but its ruler was always an abbess.

Many of the religious occupants came from the royal houses of Europe and the Plantagenets were amongst the abbey's early benefactors. Henry II, Eleanor of Aquitaine, Richard I and King John's wife Isabelle were buried there as well as other minor royals. Subsequently, during the religious wars, the graves were violated and the bones scattered, but the effigy tombs remain.

Napoleon declared the abbey to be national property and in 1804 turned it into a prison. It remained so for nearly two centuries before the prison was closed and restoration work begun. It is now open to the public and the effigy tombs are on display. The tomb holding Isabelle of Angoulême was originally thought to be that of Berengaria, the wife of Richard, Coeur de Lion.

Some of the captured members of the Résistance were kept in the prison at Fontevraud and some were executed there. I have taken a bit of licence and sent my characters there on a visit in 1950, but I have reasoned that Étienne might have known the guard and the guard might have known him. I hope readers will forgive me.

Mary Fitzgerald

ALSO AVAILABLE IN ARROW

The Love of a Lifetime

Mary Fitzgerald

Can love survive the worst betrayal of all?

From the moment Elizabeth Nugent arrives to live on his family's farm in Shropshire, Richard Wilde is in love with her. And as they grow up, it seems like nothing can keep them apart.

But as World War II rages, Richard goes to fight in the jungles of Burma, leaving Elizabeth to deal with a terrible secret that could destroy his family.

Despite the distance between them, though, Richard and Elizabeth's love remains constant through war, tragedy and betrayal.

But once the fighting is over, will the secrets and lies that Elizabeth has been hiding keep them apart for ever?

Available in ebook from Cornerstone Digital

Mist

Mary Fitzgerald

A beautiful romance set in the breathtaking Welsh mountains

When Matthew Williams, a young Canadian, inherits a hill farm in North Wales he leaves his college course and flies to the UK to take up his inheritance. But the farm he has inherited is run down, and with no knowledge of farming, Matthew relies on Lark, a traveller girl he meets in the village, to help him.

For Lark, Matthew's farm is the first steady home she has known for years, and enchanted by the countryside, she throws herself into getting the farm back on its feet.

But when Matthew's father arrives suddenly from Canada, none of their lives will be the same again.

Cornerstone Digital